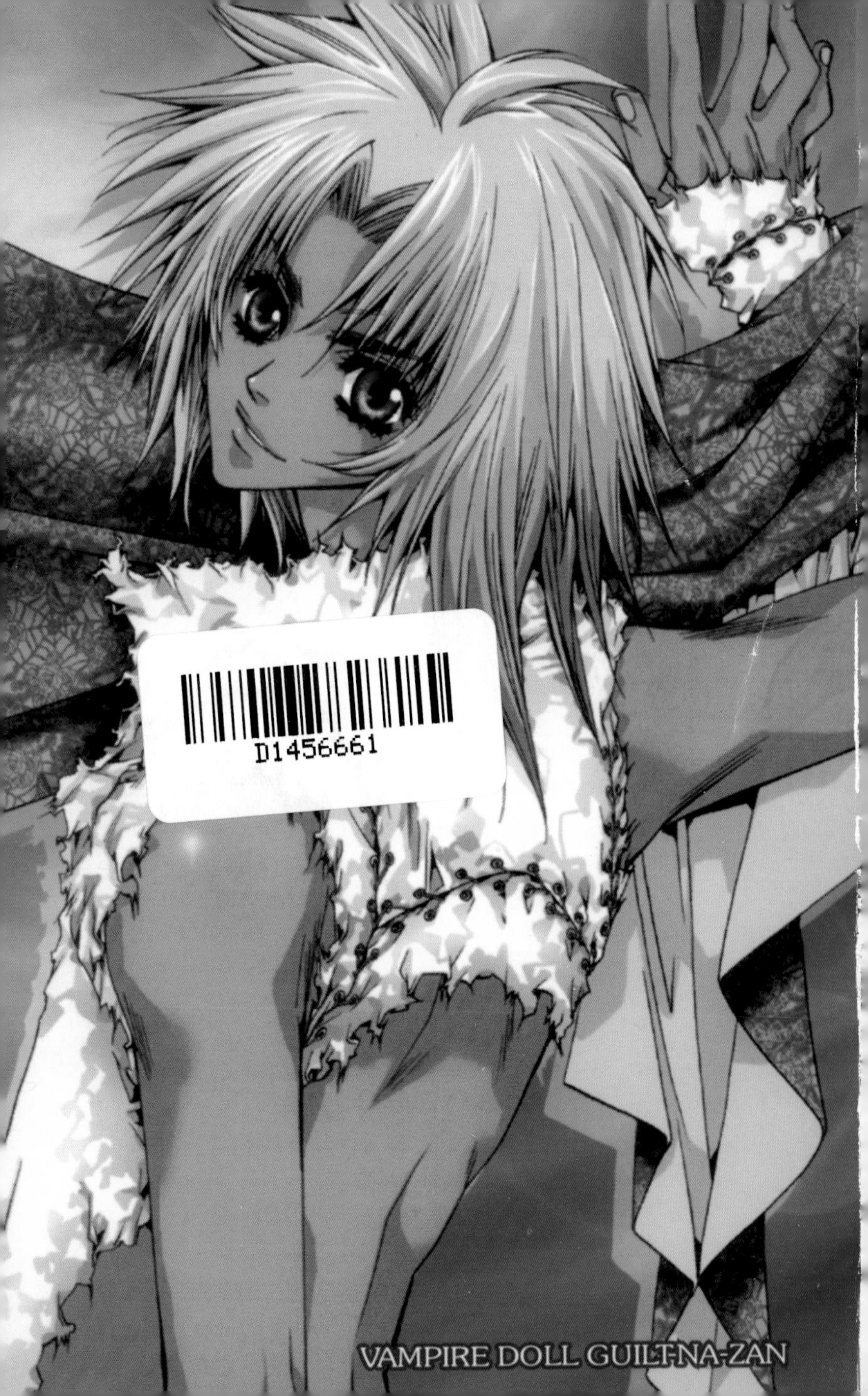
VAMPIRE DOLL GUILT-NA-ZAN

CONTENTS

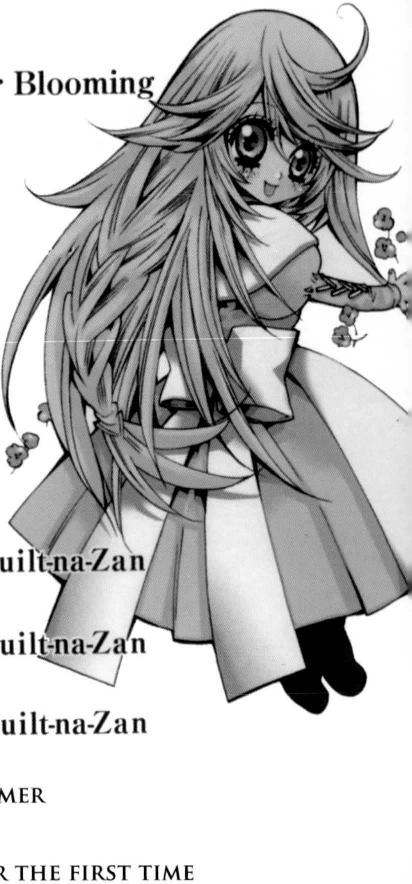

Vampire Doll

Guilt-na-Zaza

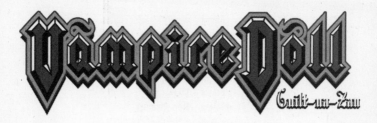

VOLUME 3

CREATED BY
ERIKA KARI

TOKYOPOP

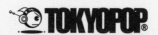

HAMBURG // LONDON // LOS ANGELES // TOKYO

Vampire Doll: Guilt-na-Zan Volume 3
Created by Erika Kari

Translation - Yoohae Yang
English Adaptation - Patricia Duffield
Retouch and Lettering - Star Print Brokers
Production Artist - Gavin Hignight
Graphic Designer - Fawn Lau

Editor - Alexis Kirsch
Digital Imaging Manager - Chris Buford
Pre-Production Supervisor - Erika Terriquez
Art Director - Anne Marie Horne
Production Manager - Elisabeth Brizzi
Managing Editor - Vy Nguyen
VP of Production - Ron Klamert
Editor-in-Chief - Rob Tokar
Publisher - Mike Kiley
President and C.O.O. - John Parker
C.E.O. and Chief Creative Officer - Stuart Levy

A  Manga

TOKYOPOP and 🐾 are trademarks or registered trademarks of TOKYOPOP Inc.

TOKYOPOP Inc.
5900 Wilshire Blvd. Suite 2000
Los Angeles, CA 90036

E-mail: info@TOKYOPOP.com
Come visit us online at www.TOKYOPOP.com

ISBN: 978-1-59816-882-2

First TOKYOPOP printing: May 2007
10 9 8 7 6 5 4 3 2 1
Printed in the USA

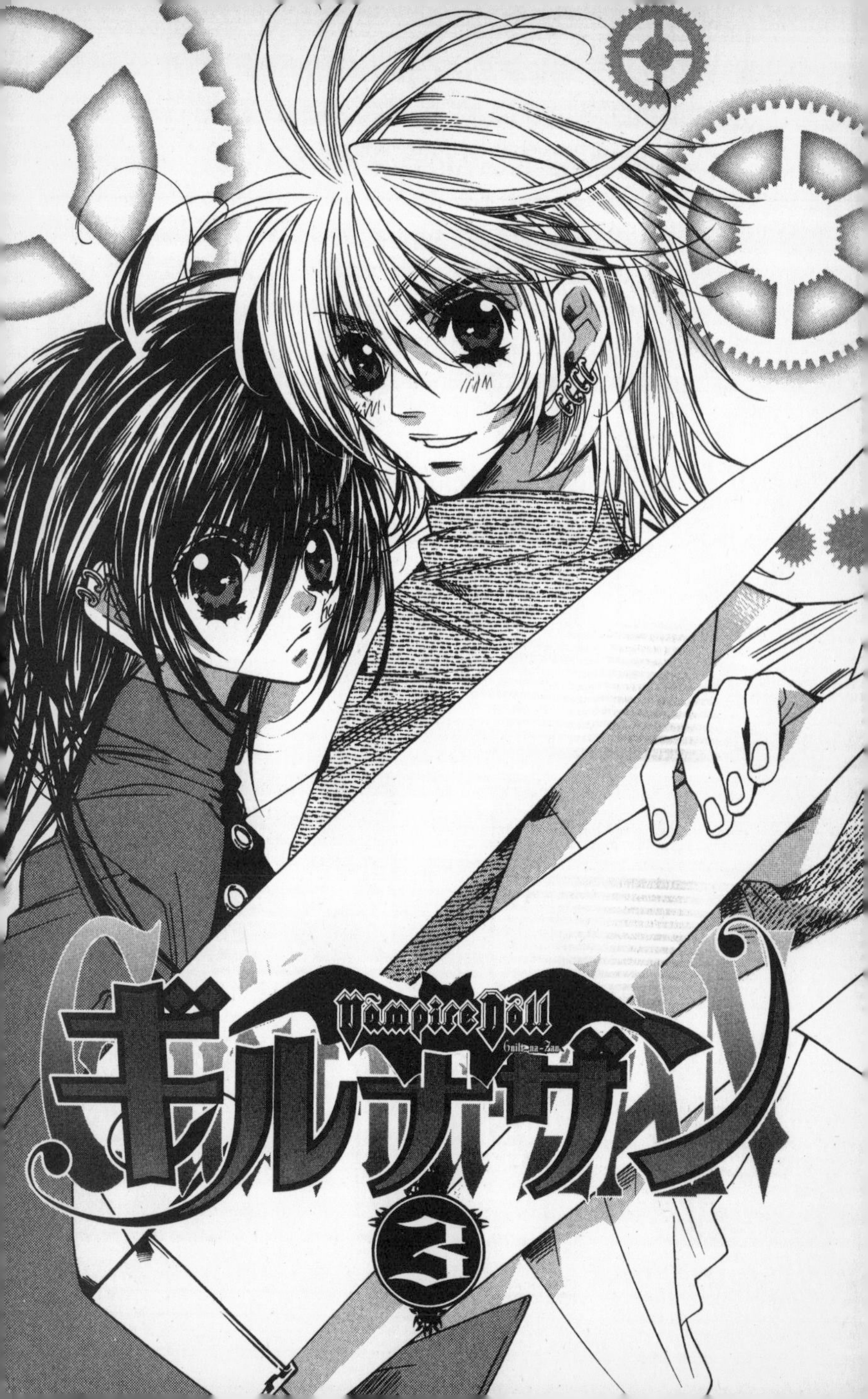
Vampire Doll
Guilt-na-Zan
ギルナザン
3

VAMPIRE DOLL GUILT-NA-ZAN

MAIN CHARACTERS

STORY SO FAR:
THE MOST FEARED VAMPIRE IN THE OLD DAYS OF EUROPE HAS NOW BEEN REVIVED AS A GIRL BY THE HAND OF THE SKILLFUL EXORCIST KYOJI. NOW HE LIVES HIS LIFE AS A MAID FOR THE YOTOBARI FAMILY AND ALSO A MONSTER HUNTER, THE HARDSHIPS OF GUILT-NA-ZAN CONTINUES...

GUILT-NA

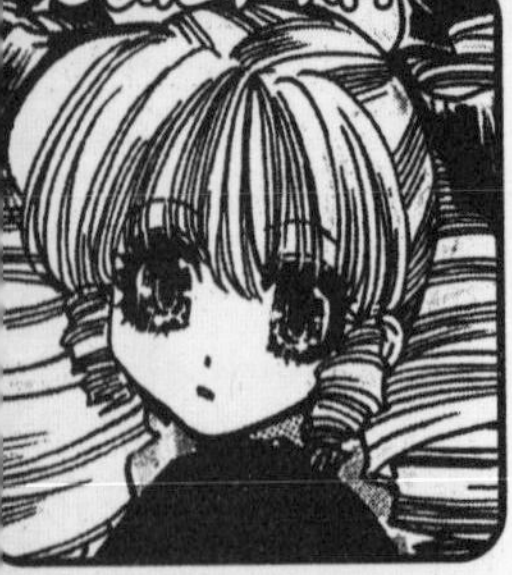

LONG AGO, HE WAS KNOWN AS THE LORD OF VAMPIRES, THE MOST FEARED OF ALL HIS KIND. KYOJI RESURRECTED HIM INTO THE FIGURE OF A WAX DOLL. NOW HE MUST OBEY KYOJI.

GUILT-NA-ZAN

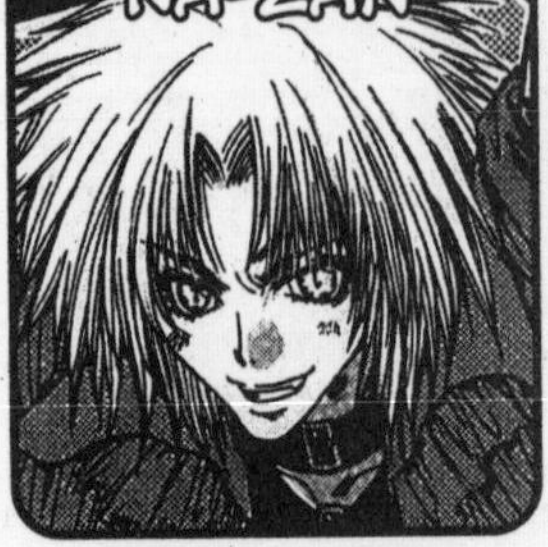

THIS IS WHAT GUILT-NA ORIGINALLY LOOKED LIKE. BY SUCKING 1CC OF TONAE'S BLOOD, HE CAN TRANSFORM INTO HIMSELF--BUT ONLY FOR TEN MINUTES!

KYOJI

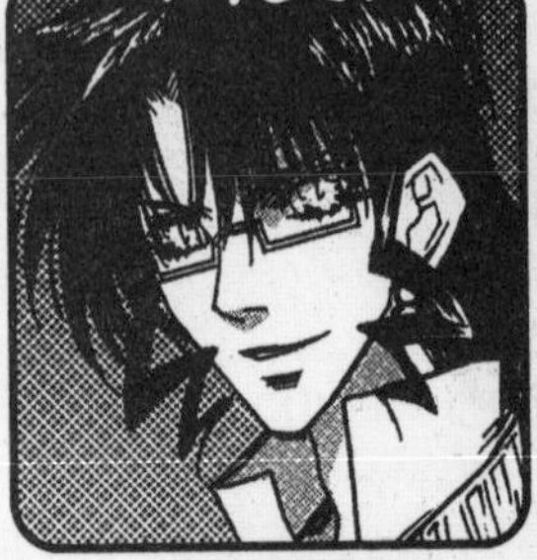

A VERY SKILLED BUT LAZY EXORCIST, HE SPENDS MOST DAYS MAKING FUN OF GUILT-NA.

VINCENT

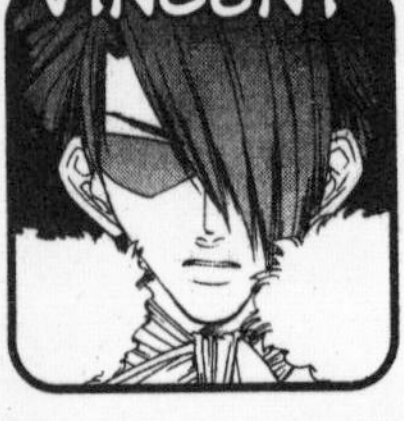

ORIGINALLY A BAT, VINCENT IS A SERVANT OF GUILT-NA-ZAN. HE'S TOO NICE TO BE CALLED A MONSTER.

TONAE

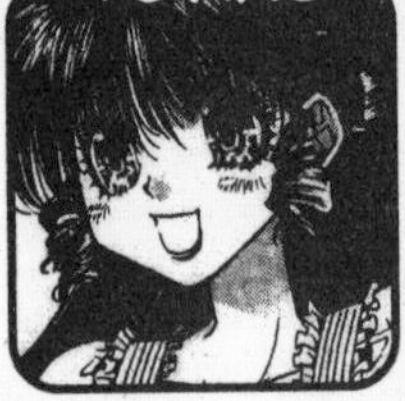

SHE IS THE YOUNGER SISTER OF KYOJI. LIKE VINCENT, SHE IS PURE AND SOMEWHAT SPACEY.

DANTE

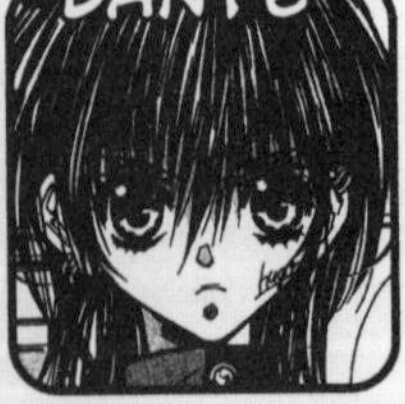

THIS IS NOT HIS ORIGINAL FORM, FOR MARIYA IMPLANTED THIS MONSTER'S SOUL INTO A WAX DOLL. HE NOW HAS HUGE CLAWS AND IS MARIYA'S SERVANT.

MARIYA

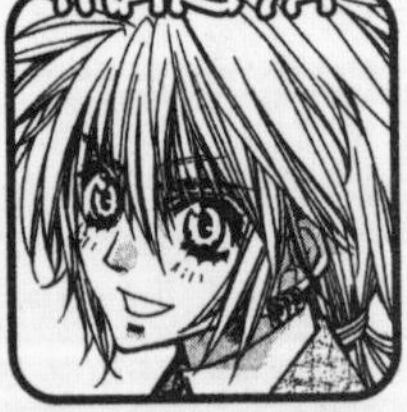

A MASTER AND KYOJI'S WAX DOLL-MAKING MENTOR, MARIYA FOUND DANTE IN THE COUNTRY OF W, WHICH NO LONGER EXISTS. HE SPEAKS IN THE HIROSHIMA DIALECT, AND HIS AGE IS A MYSTERY.

DUNE

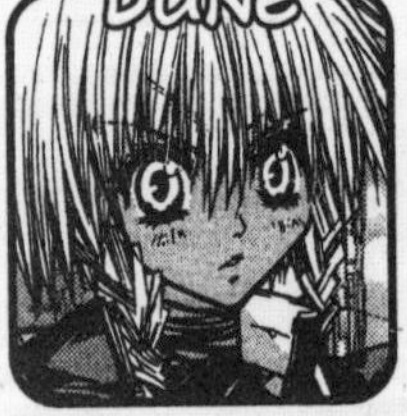

HE FEEDS BY ABSORBING NEGATIVE ENERGY FROM HUMANS AND IS CURRENTLY LIVING AND WORKING AT MITSUHACHI ACADEMY.

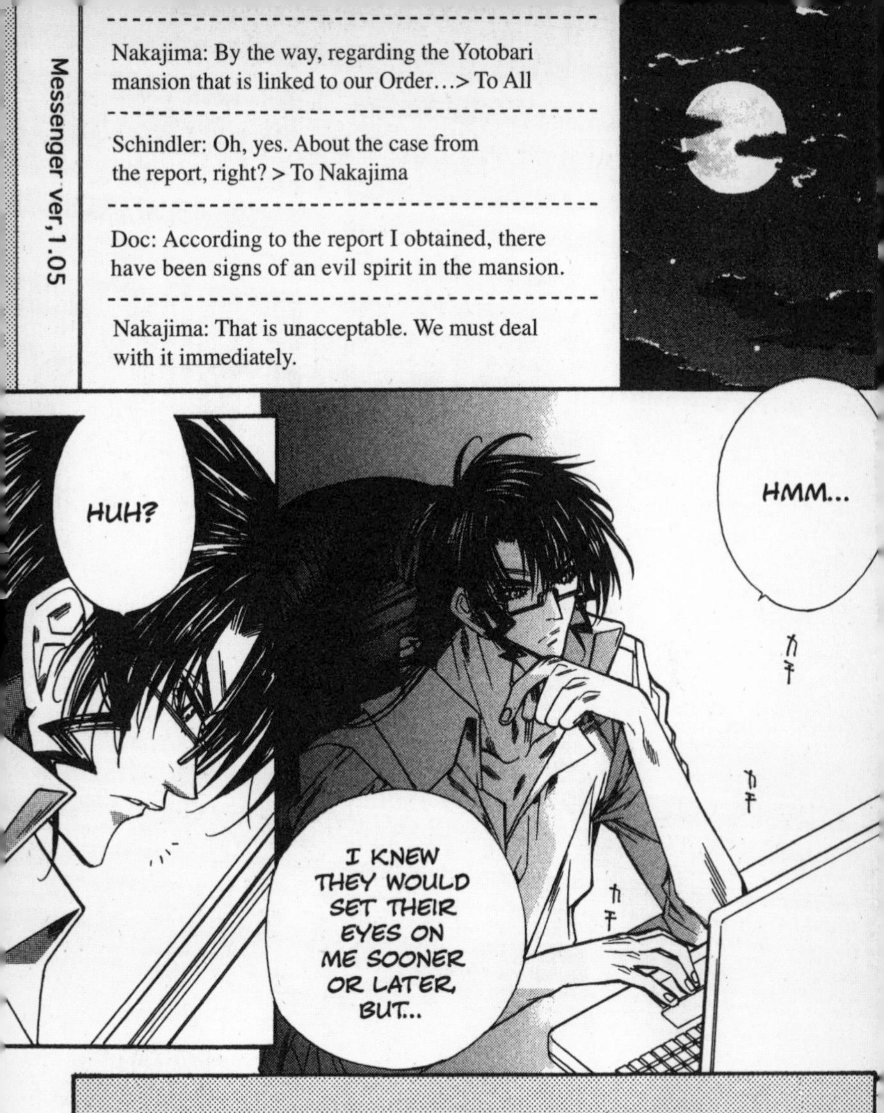
Messenger ver,1.05
Nakajima: By the way, regarding the Yotobari mansion that is linked to our Order…> To All
Schindler: Oh, yes. About the case from the report, right? > To Nakajima
Doc: According to the report I obtained, there have been signs of an evil spirit in the mansion.
Nakajima: That is unacceptable. We must deal with it immediately.
HMM...
カチ
カチ
I KNEW THEY WOULD SET THEIR EYES ON ME SOONER OR LATER, BUT...
カチ
HUH?
Schindler: How should we handle this? > To All
Asu: Leave it to me. Next Sunday, I'll investigate the Yotobari Mansion myself.

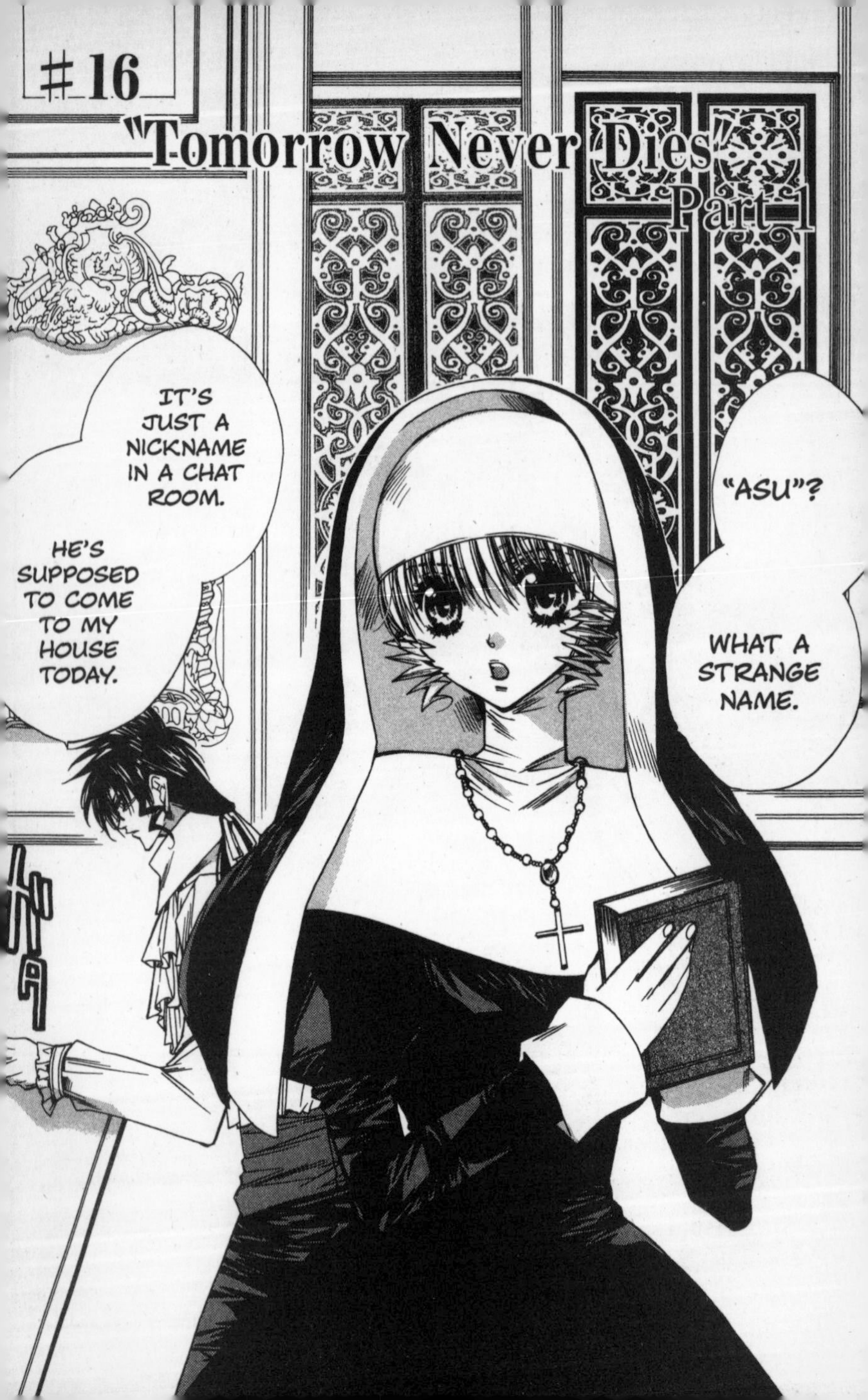

#16
"Tomorrow Never Dies" Part 1
"ASU"?
WHAT A STRANGE NAME.
IT'S JUST A NICKNAME IN A CHAT ROOM.
HE'S SUPPOSED TO COME TO MY HOUSE TODAY.

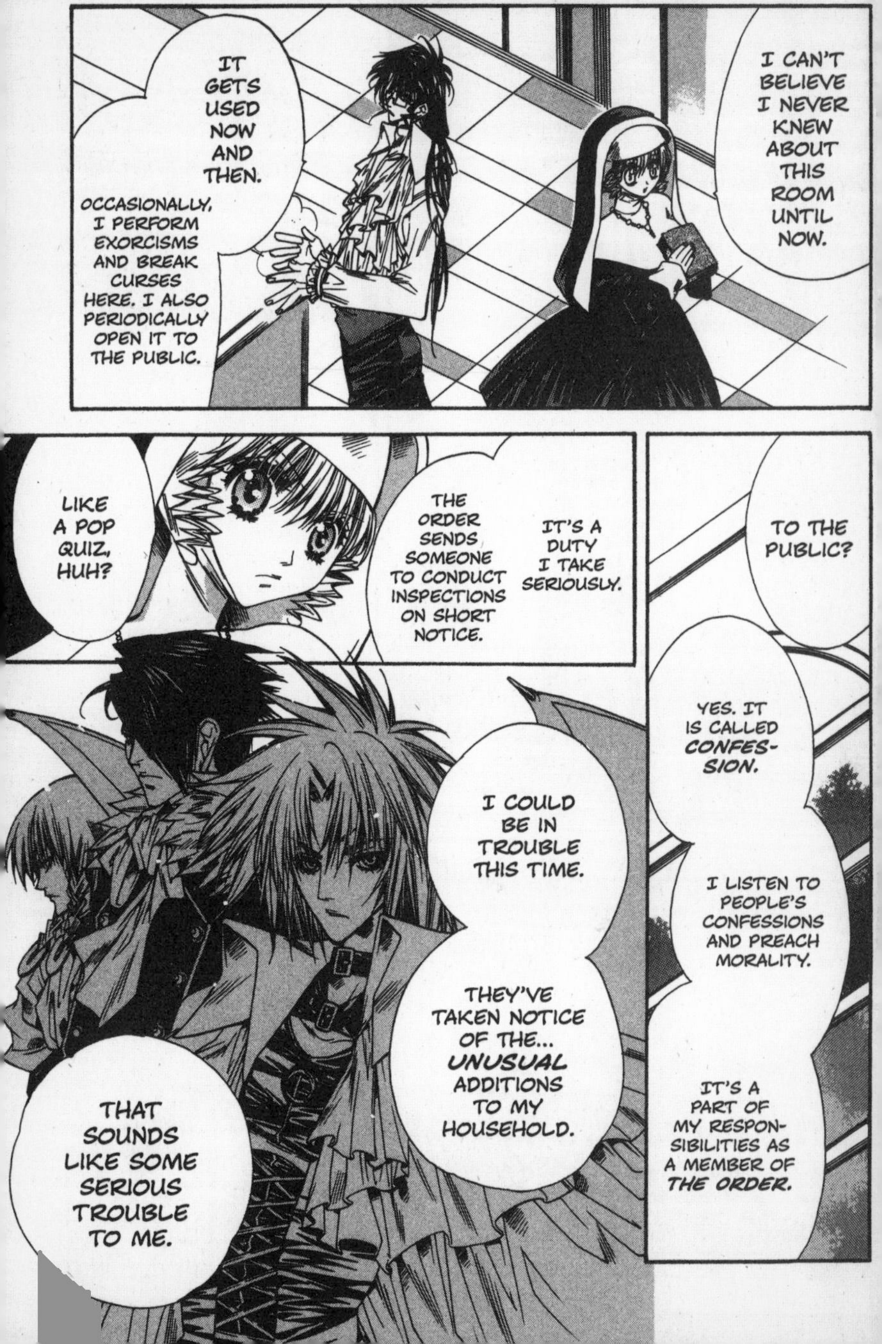
I CAN'T BELIEVE I NEVER KNEW ABOUT THIS ROOM UNTIL NOW.
IT GETS USED NOW AND THEN.
OCCASIONALLY, I PERFORM EXORCISMS AND BREAK CURSES HERE. I ALSO PERIODICALLY OPEN IT TO THE PUBLIC.
TO THE PUBLIC?
YES. IT IS CALLED *CONFESSION.*
I LISTEN TO PEOPLE'S CONFESSIONS AND PREACH MORALITY.
IT'S A PART OF MY RESPONSIBILITIES AS A MEMBER OF *THE ORDER.*
IT'S A DUTY I TAKE SERIOUSLY.
THE ORDER SENDS SOMEONE TO CONDUCT INSPECTIONS ON SHORT NOTICE.
LIKE A POP QUIZ, HUH?
I COULD BE IN TROUBLE THIS TIME.
THEY'VE TAKEN NOTICE OF THE... *UNUSUAL* ADDITIONS TO MY HOUSEHOLD.
THAT SOUNDS LIKE SOME SERIOUS TROUBLE TO ME.

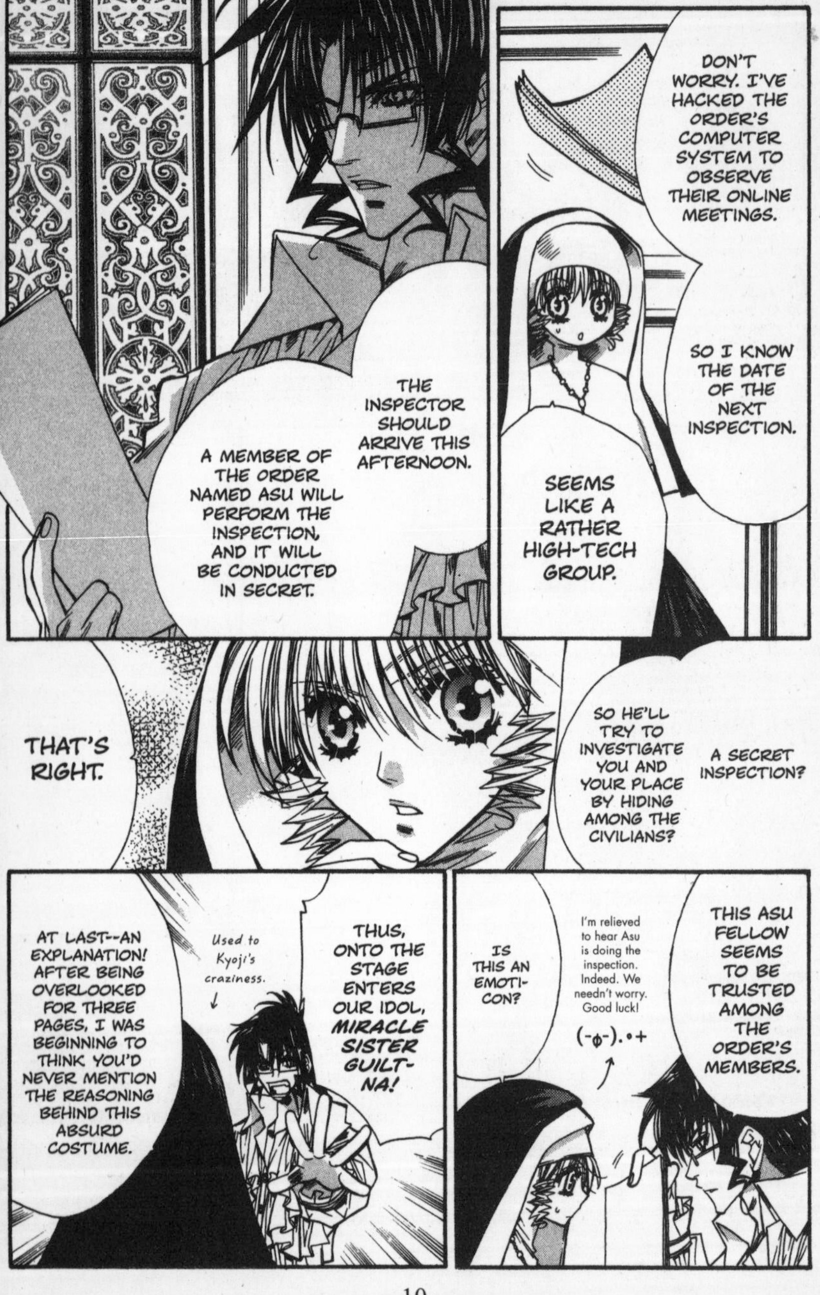
DON'T WORRY. I'VE HACKED THE ORDER'S COMPUTER SYSTEM TO OBSERVE THEIR ONLINE MEETINGS.
SO I KNOW THE DATE OF THE NEXT INSPECTION.
SEEMS LIKE A RATHER HIGH-TECH GROUP.
THE INSPECTOR SHOULD ARRIVE THIS AFTERNOON.
A MEMBER OF THE ORDER NAMED ASU WILL PERFORM THE INSPECTION, AND IT WILL BE CONDUCTED IN SECRET.
A SECRET INSPECTION?
SO HE'LL TRY TO INVESTIGATE YOU AND YOUR PLACE BY HIDING AMONG THE CIVILIANS?
THAT'S RIGHT.
THIS ASU FELLOW SEEMS TO BE TRUSTED AMONG THE ORDER'S MEMBERS.
I'm relieved to hear Asu is doing the inspection. Indeed. We needn't worry. Good luck!
(-ϕ-).∘+
IS THIS AN EMOTI-CON?
THUS, ONTO THE STAGE ENTERS OUR IDOL, ***MIRACLE SISTER GUILT-NA!***
Used to Kyoji's craziness.
AT LAST--AN EXPLANATION! AFTER BEING OVERLOOKED FOR THREE PAGES, I WAS BEGINNING TO THINK YOU'D NEVER MENTION THE REASONING BEHIND THIS ABSURD COSTUME.

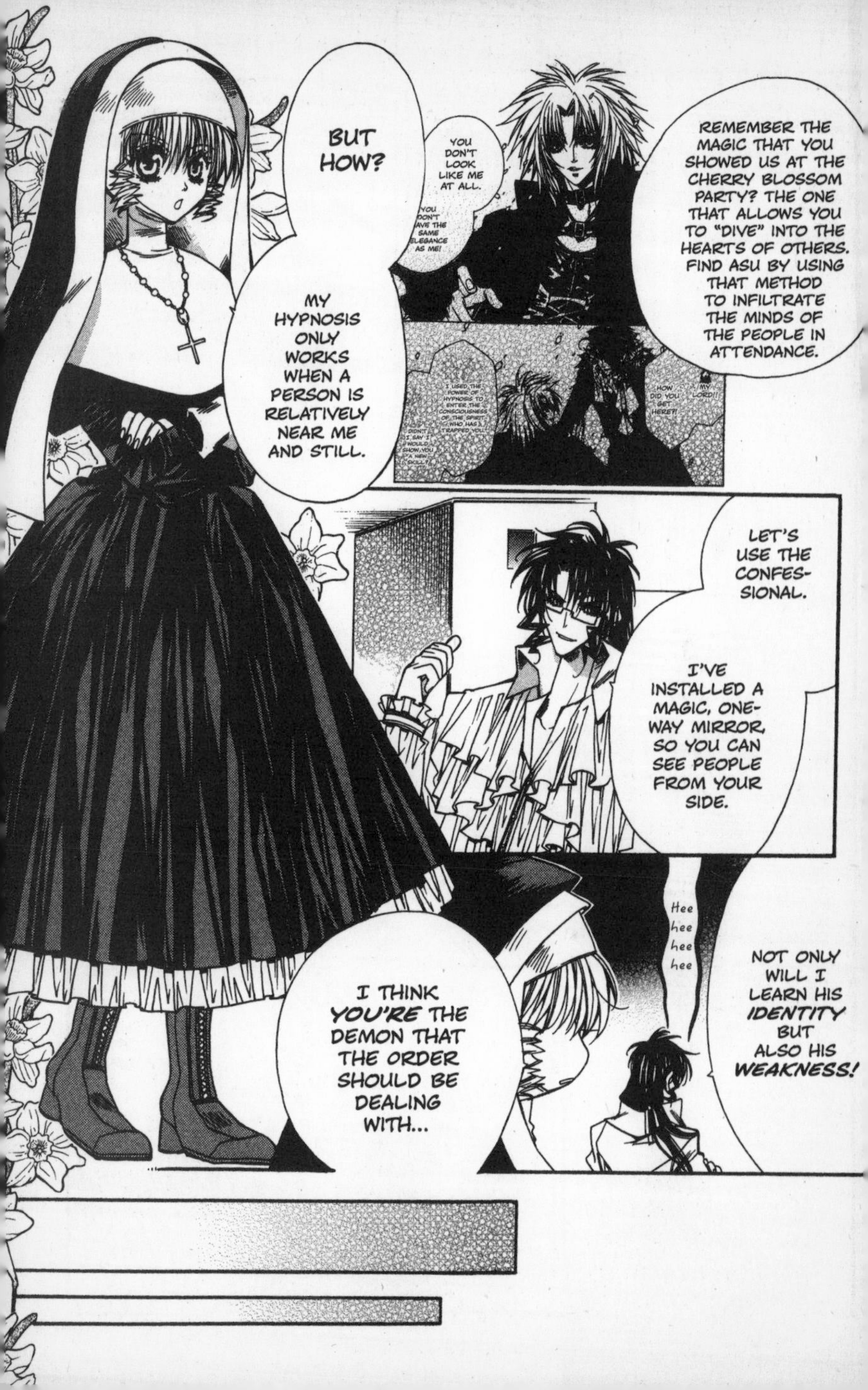
REMEMBER THE MAGIC THAT YOU SHOWED US AT THE CHERRY BLOSSOM PARTY? THE ONE THAT ALLOWS YOU TO "DIVE" INTO THE HEARTS OF OTHERS. FIND ASU BY USING THAT METHOD TO INFILTRATE THE MINDS OF THE PEOPLE IN ATTENDANCE.
YOU DON'T LOOK LIKE ME AT ALL.
YOU DON'T AVE THE SAME ELEGANCE AS ME!
MY LORD!!
HOW DID YOU GET HERE?!
I USED THE POWER OF HYPNOSIS TO ENTER THE CONSCIOUSNESS OF THE SPIRIT WHO HAS TRAPPED YOU.
DIDN'T I SAY I WOULD SHOW YOU A NEW SKILL?
BUT HOW?
MY HYPNOSIS ONLY WORKS WHEN A PERSON IS RELATIVELY NEAR ME AND STILL.
LET'S USE THE CONFES-SIONAL.
I'VE INSTALLED A MAGIC, ONE-WAY MIRROR, SO YOU CAN SEE PEOPLE FROM YOUR SIDE.
Hee hee hee hee
NOT ONLY WILL I LEARN HIS *IDENTITY* BUT ALSO HIS *WEAKNESS!*
I THINK *YOU'RE* THE DEMON THAT THE ORDER SHOULD BE DEALING WITH...

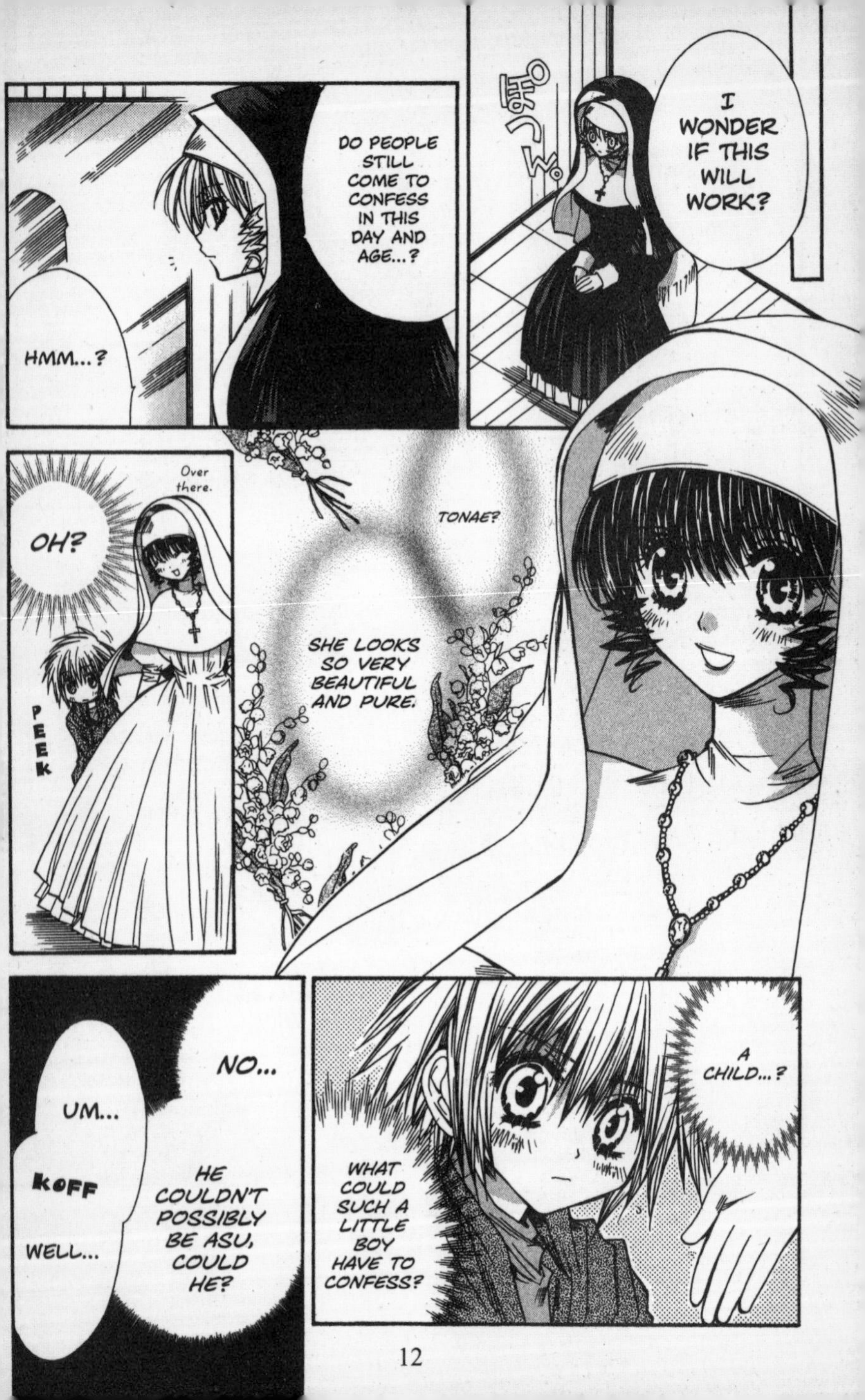
ぽつん。
I WONDER IF THIS WILL WORK?
DO PEOPLE STILL COME TO CONFESS IN THIS DAY AND AGE...?
HMM...?
TONAE?
SHE LOOKS SO VERY BEAUTIFUL AND PURE.
Over there.
OH?
PEEK
A CHILD...?
WHAT COULD SUCH A LITTLE BOY HAVE TO CONFESS?
NO...
HE COULDN'T POSSIBLY BE ASU, COULD HE?
UM...
KOFF
WELL...

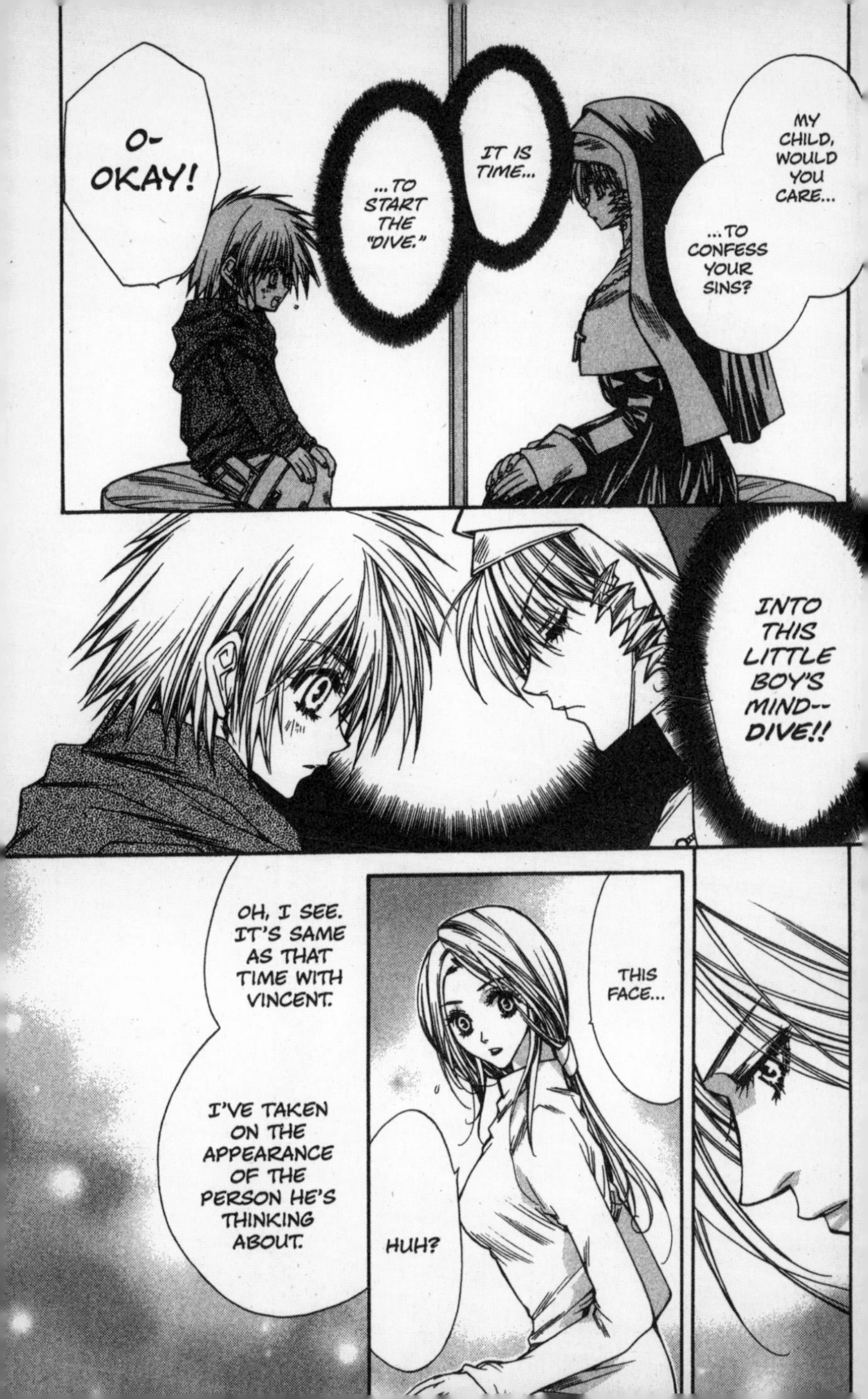
MY CHILD, WOULD YOU CARE...
...TO CONFESS YOUR SINS?
IT IS TIME...
...TO START THE "DIVE."
O- OKAY!
INTO THIS LITTLE BOY'S MIND--DIVE!!
THIS FACE...
HUH?
OH, I SEE. IT'S SAME AS THAT TIME WITH VINCENT.
I'VE TAKEN ON THE APPEARANCE OF THE PERSON HE'S THINKING ABOUT.

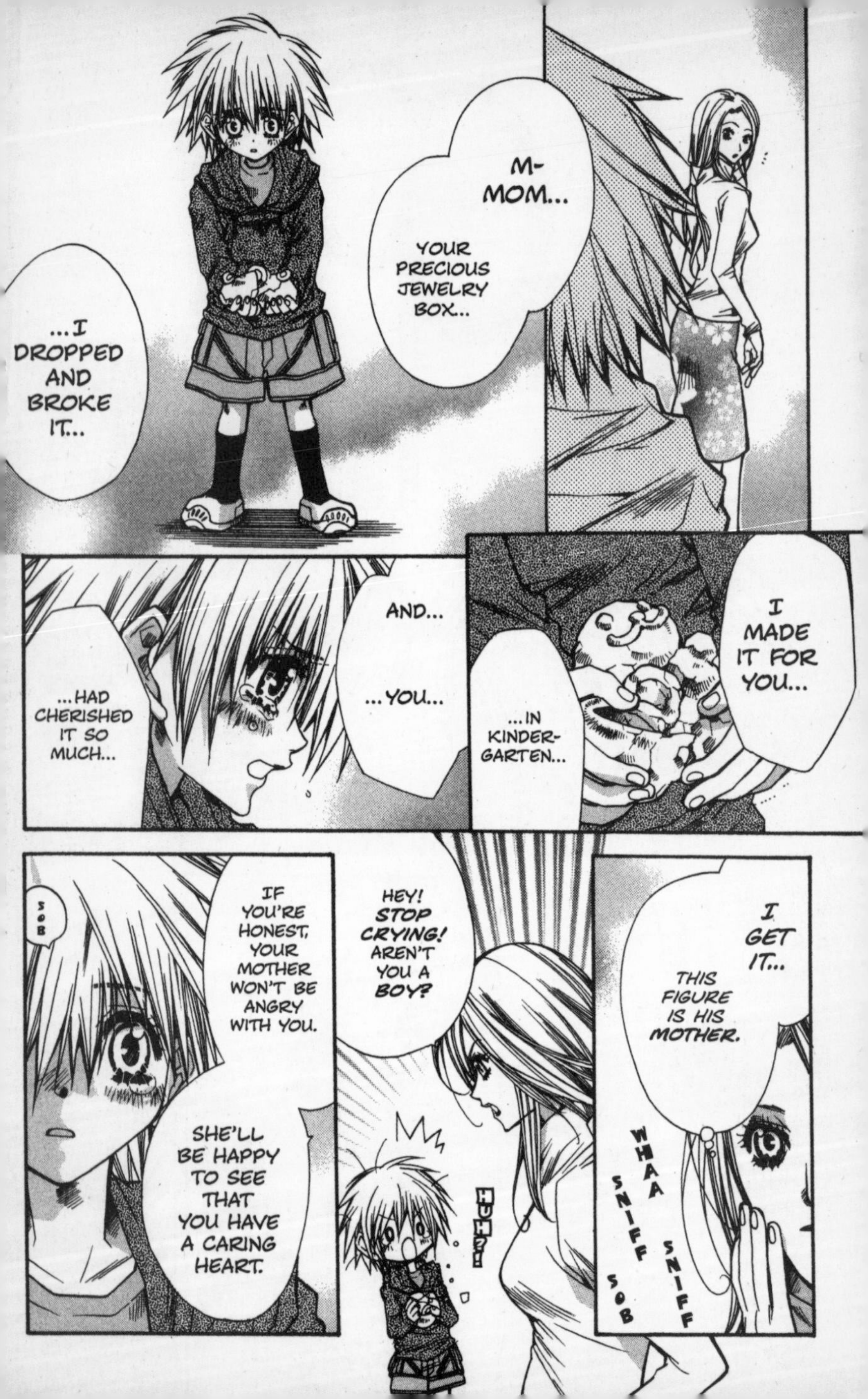
M-MOM...
YOUR PRECIOUS JEWELRY BOX...
...I DROPPED AND BROKE IT...
I MADE IT FOR YOU...
...IN KINDERGARTEN...
AND...
...YOU...
...HAD CHERISHED IT SO MUCH...
I GET IT...
THIS FIGURE IS HIS MOTHER.
WHAA
SNIFF
SNIFF
SOB
HEY! STOP CRYING! AREN'T YOU A BOY?
HUH?!
IF YOU'RE HONEST, YOUR MOTHER WON'T BE ANGRY WITH YOU.
SHE'LL BE HAPPY TO SEE THAT YOU HAVE A CARING HEART.
SOB

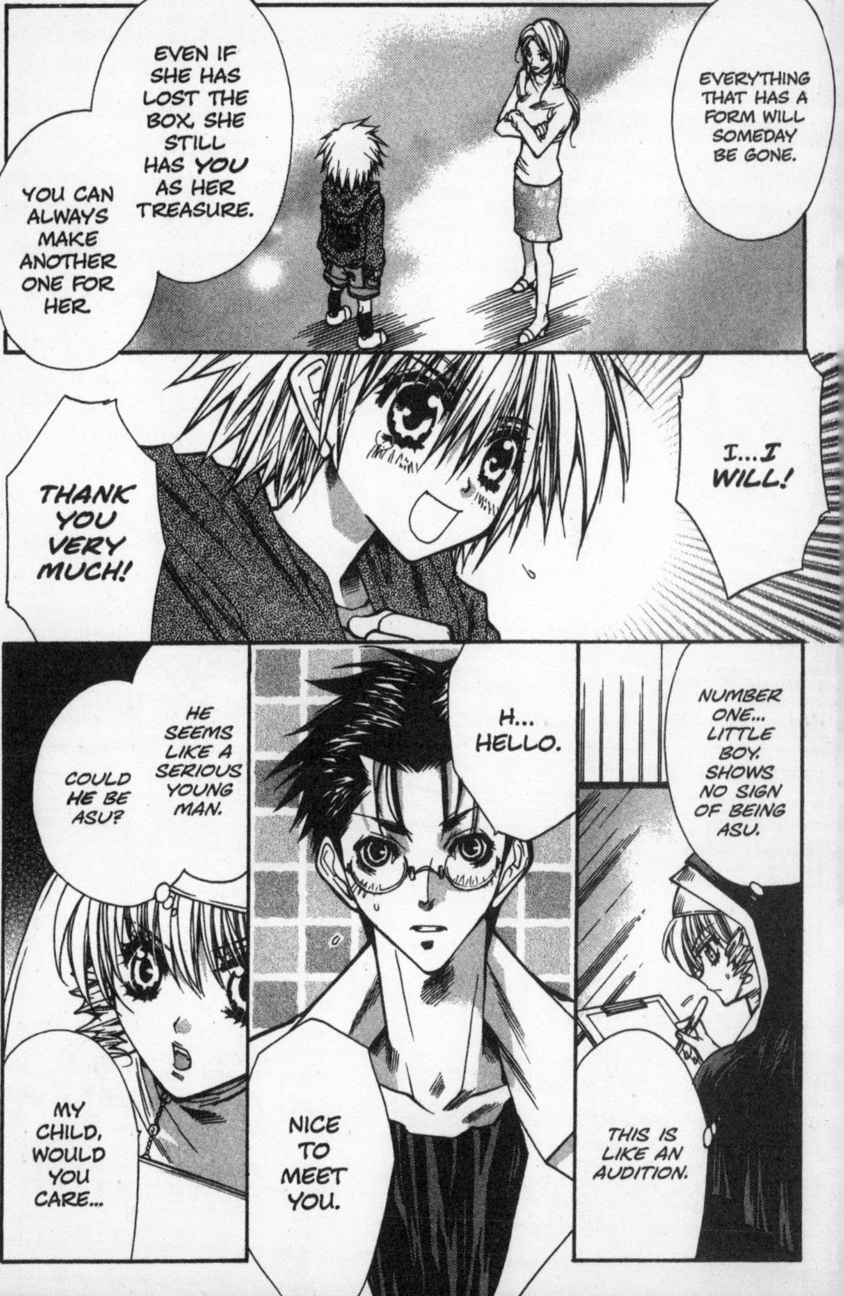
EVERYTHING THAT HAS A FORM WILL SOMEDAY BE GONE.
EVEN IF SHE HAS LOST THE BOX, SHE STILL HAS YOU AS HER TREASURE.
YOU CAN ALWAYS MAKE ANOTHER ONE FOR HER.
I...I WILL!
THANK YOU VERY MUCH!
NUMBER ONE... LITTLE BOY. SHOWS NO SIGN OF BEING ASU.
THIS IS LIKE AN AUDITION.
H... HELLO.
NICE TO MEET YOU.
HE SEEMS LIKE A SERIOUS YOUNG MAN.
COULD HE BE ASU?
MY CHILD, WOULD YOU CARE...

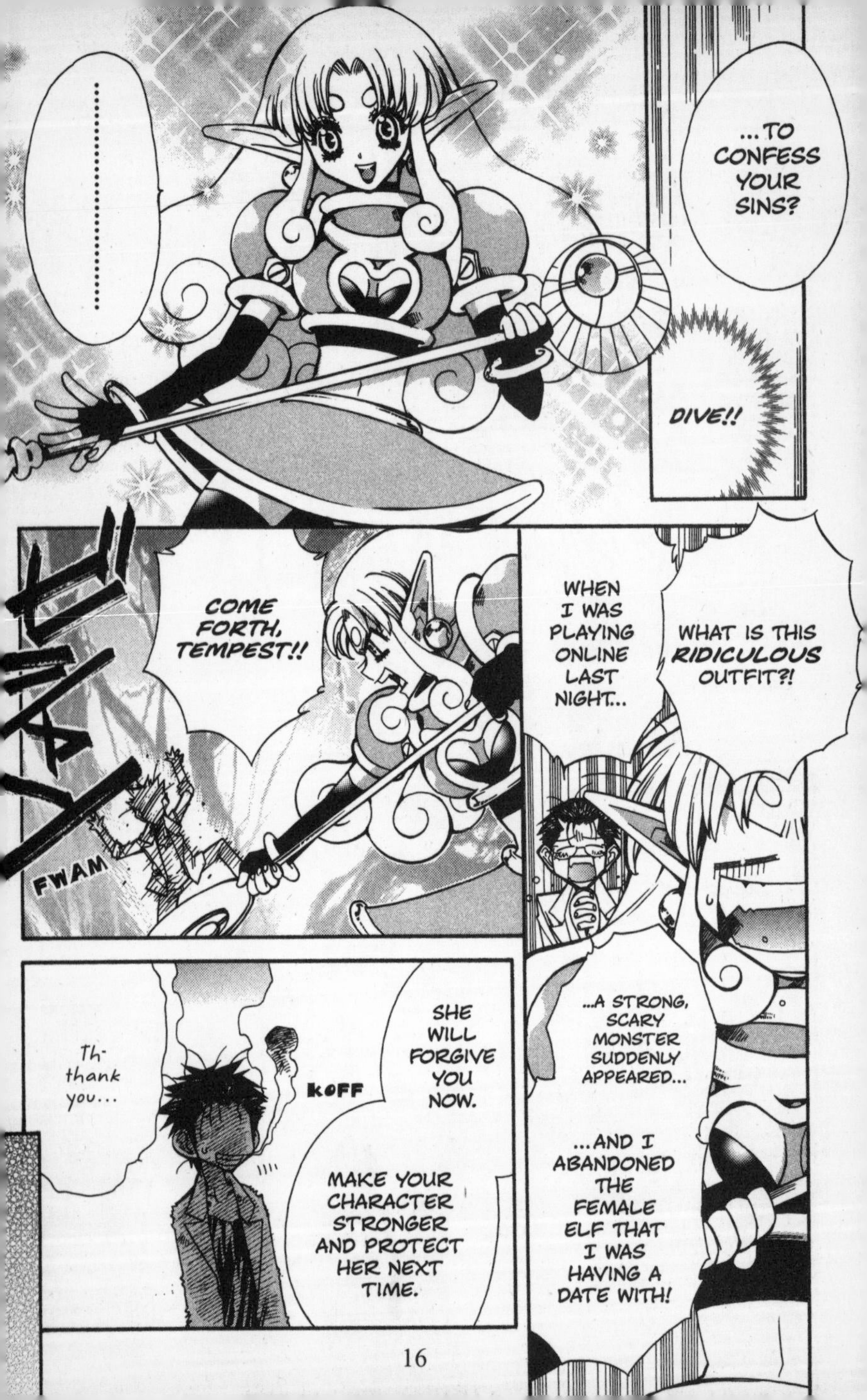
...TO CONFESS YOUR SINS?
DIVE!!
......
WHAT IS THIS RIDICULOUS OUTFIT?!
WHEN I WAS PLAYING ONLINE LAST NIGHT...
...A STRONG, SCARY MONSTER SUDDENLY APPEARED...
...AND I ABANDONED THE FEMALE ELF THAT I WAS HAVING A DATE WITH!
COME FORTH, TEMPEST!!
FLASH
FWAM
SHE WILL FORGIVE YOU NOW.
MAKE YOUR CHARACTER STRONGER AND PROTECT HER NEXT TIME.
KOFF
Th- thank you...

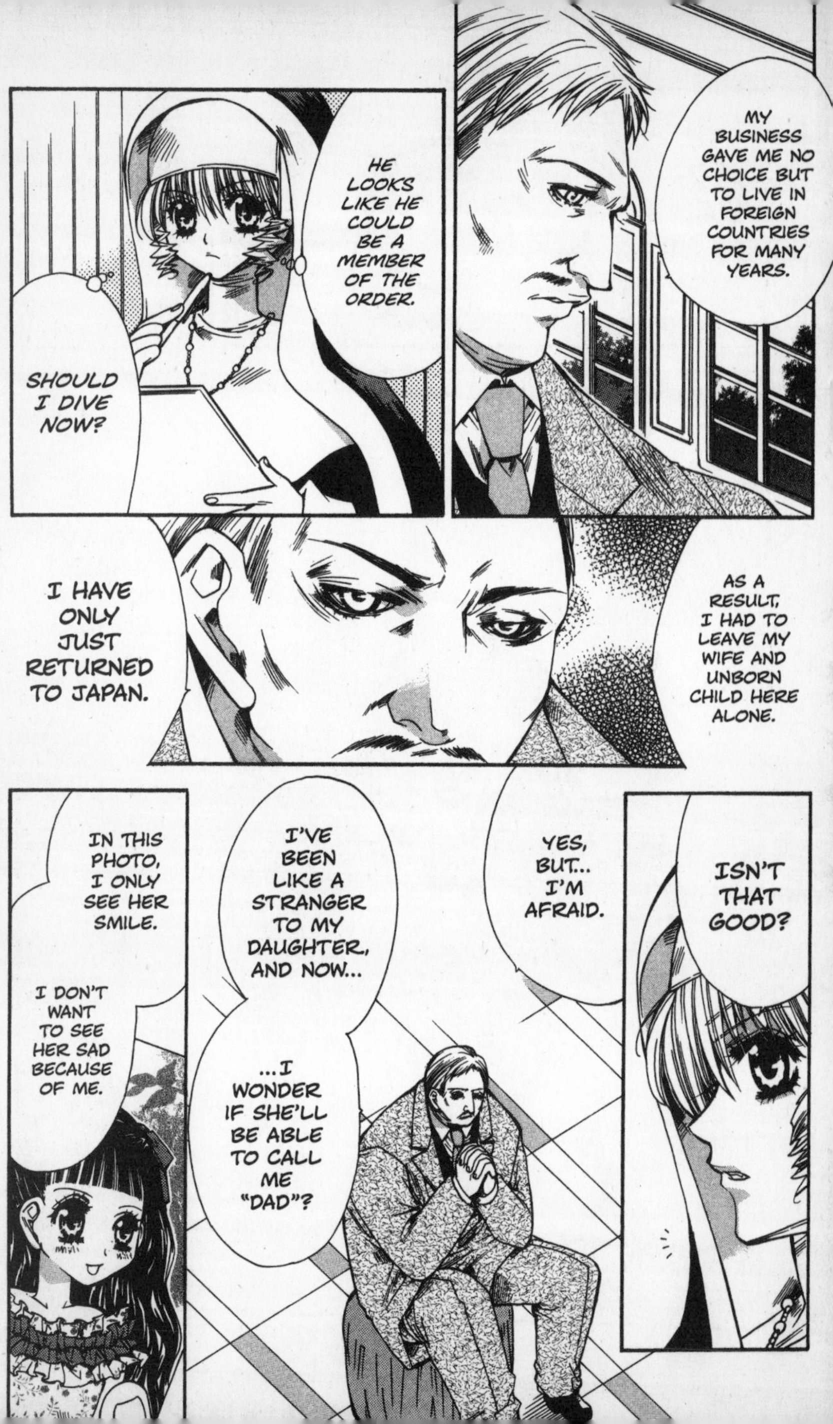
MY BUSINESS GAVE ME NO CHOICE BUT TO LIVE IN FOREIGN COUNTRIES FOR MANY YEARS.
HE LOOKS LIKE HE COULD BE A MEMBER OF THE ORDER.
SHOULD I DIVE NOW?
AS A RESULT, I HAD TO LEAVE MY WIFE AND UNBORN CHILD HERE ALONE.
I HAVE ONLY JUST RETURNED TO JAPAN.
ISN'T THAT GOOD?
YES, BUT... I'M AFRAID.
I'VE BEEN LIKE A STRANGER TO MY DAUGHTER, AND NOW...
...I WONDER IF SHE'LL BE ABLE TO CALL ME "DAD"?
IN THIS PHOTO, I ONLY SEE HER SMILE.
I DON'T WANT TO SEE HER SAD BECAUSE OF ME.

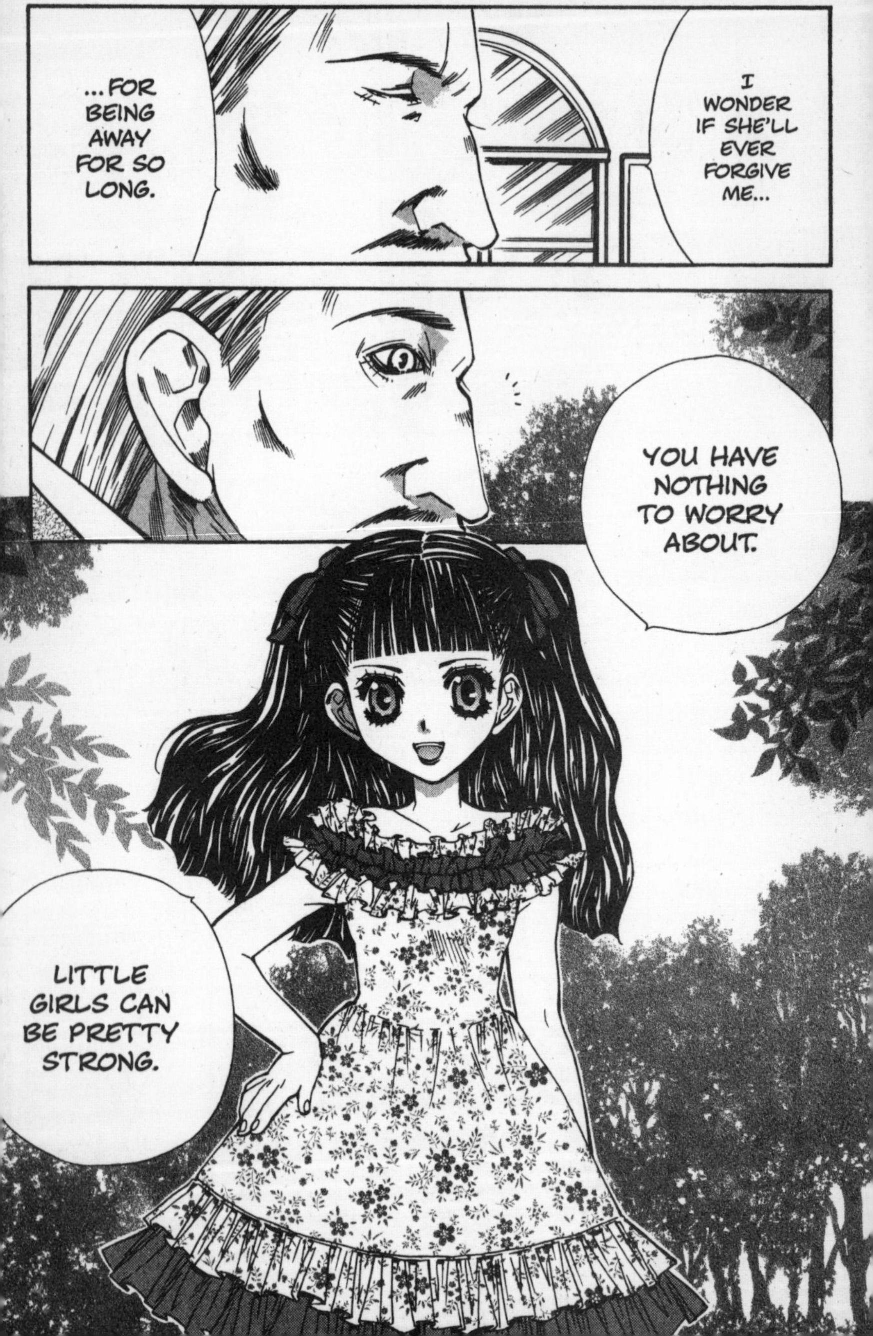
I WONDER IF SHE'LL EVER FORGIVE ME...
...FOR BEING AWAY FOR SO LONG.
YOU HAVE NOTHING TO WORRY ABOUT.
LITTLE GIRLS CAN BE PRETTY STRONG.

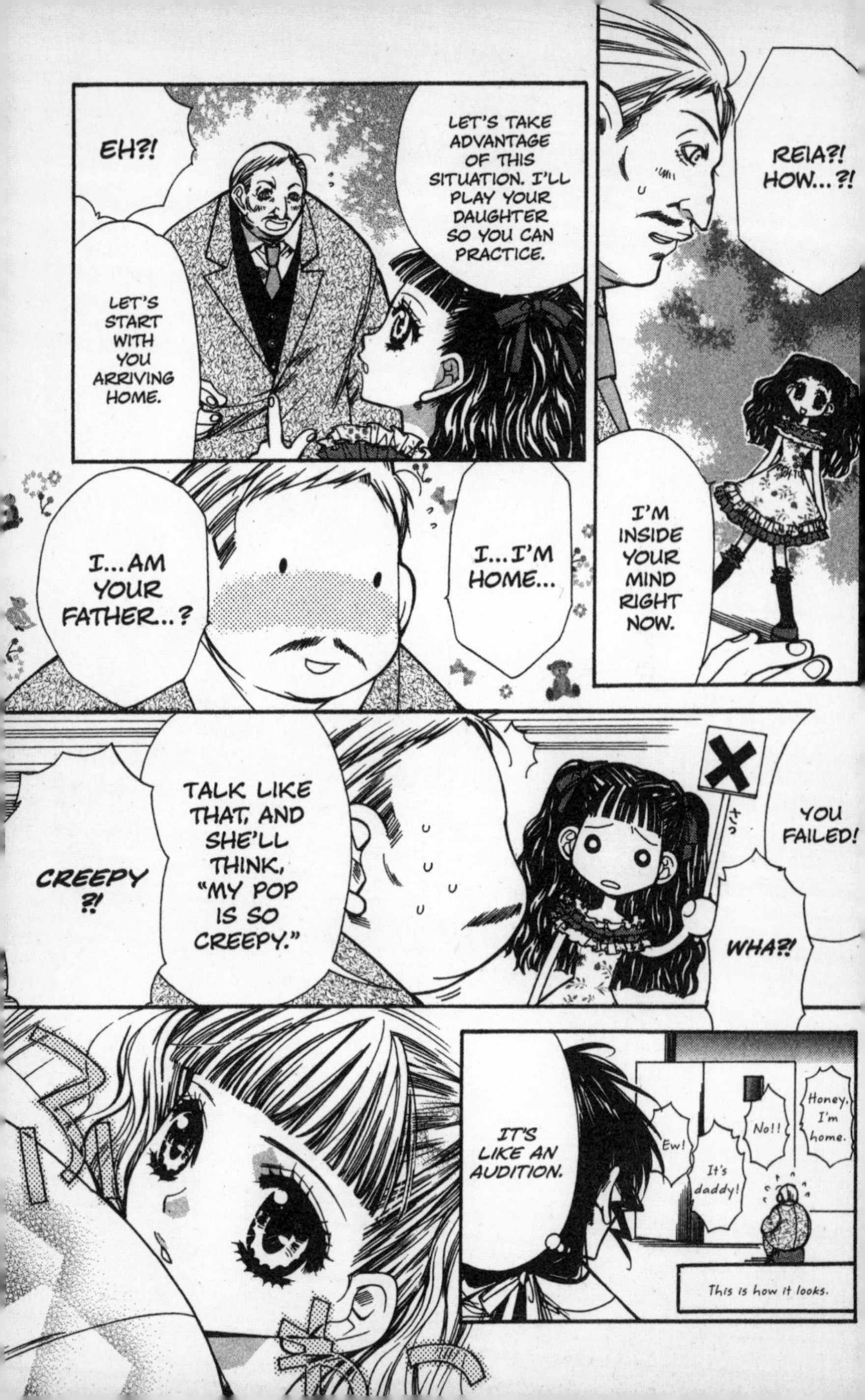
REIA?! HOW...?!
I'M INSIDE YOUR MIND RIGHT NOW.
LET'S TAKE ADVANTAGE OF THIS SITUATION. I'LL PLAY YOUR DAUGHTER SO YOU CAN PRACTICE.
EH?!
LET'S START WITH YOU ARRIVING HOME.
I...I'M HOME...
I...AM YOUR FATHER...?
YOU FAILED!
WHA?!
TALK LIKE THAT, AND SHE'LL THINK, "MY POP IS SO CREEPY."
CREEPY ?!
Honey, I'm home.
No!!
It's daddy!
Ew!
IT'S LIKE AN AUDITION.
This is how it looks.

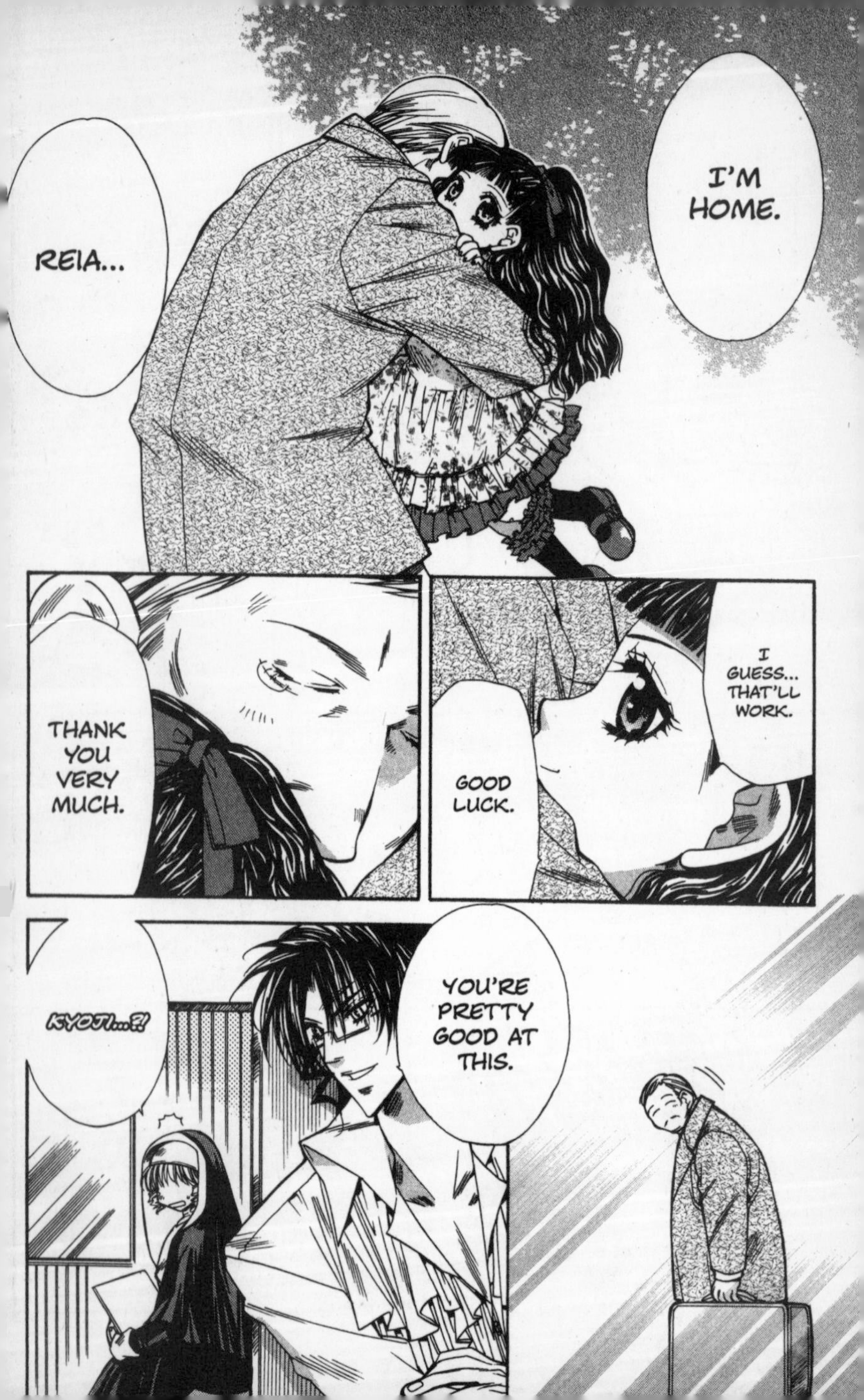
I'M HOME.
REIA...
I GUESS... THAT'LL WORK.
GOOD LUCK.
THANK YOU VERY MUCH.
YOU'RE PRETTY GOOD AT THIS.
KYOJI...?!

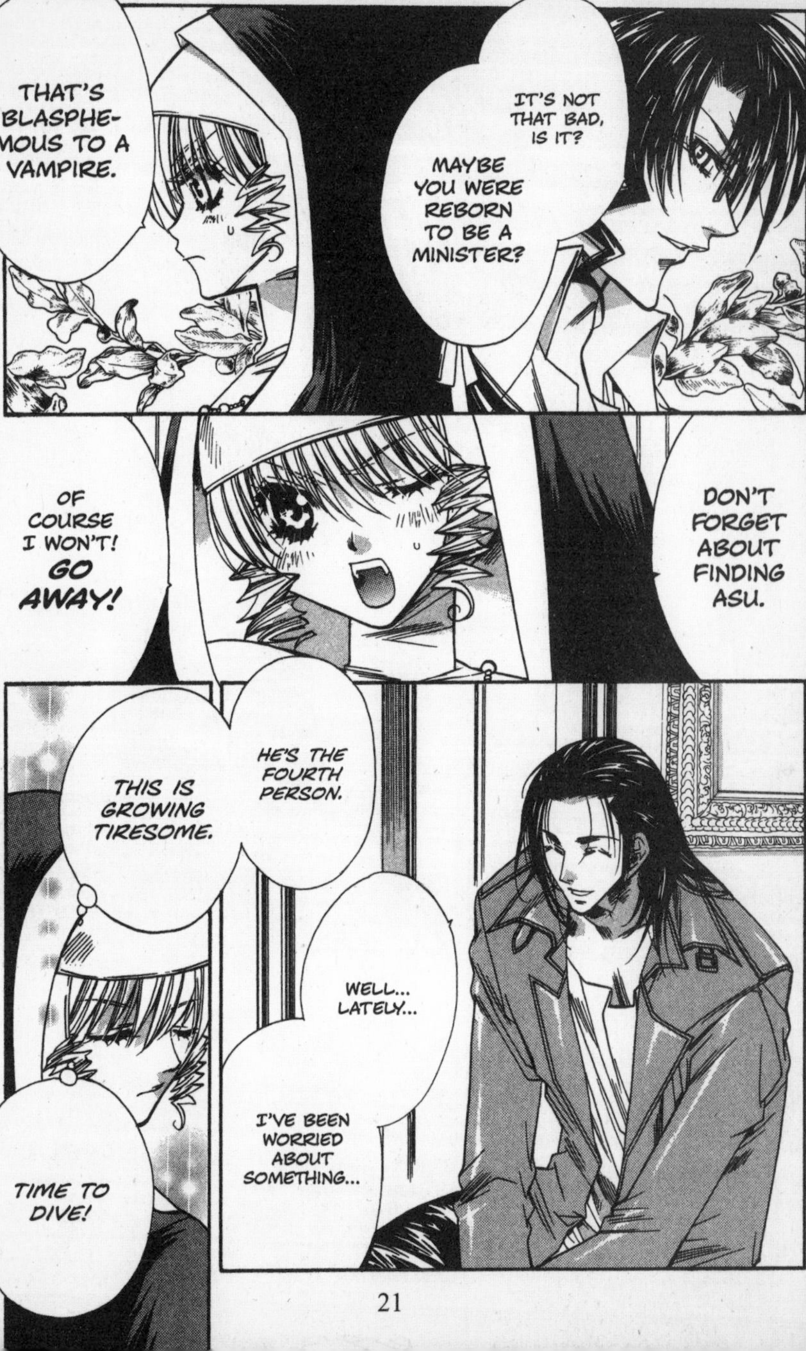
IT'S NOT THAT BAD, IS IT?
MAYBE YOU WERE REBORN TO BE A MINISTER?
THAT'S BLASPHE-MOUS TO A VAMPIRE.
DON'T FORGET ABOUT FINDING ASU.
OF COURSE I WON'T! ***GO AWAY!***
HE'S THE FOURTH PERSON.
THIS IS GROWING TIRESOME.
WELL... LATELY...
I'VE BEEN WORRIED ABOUT SOMETHING...
TIME TO DIVE!

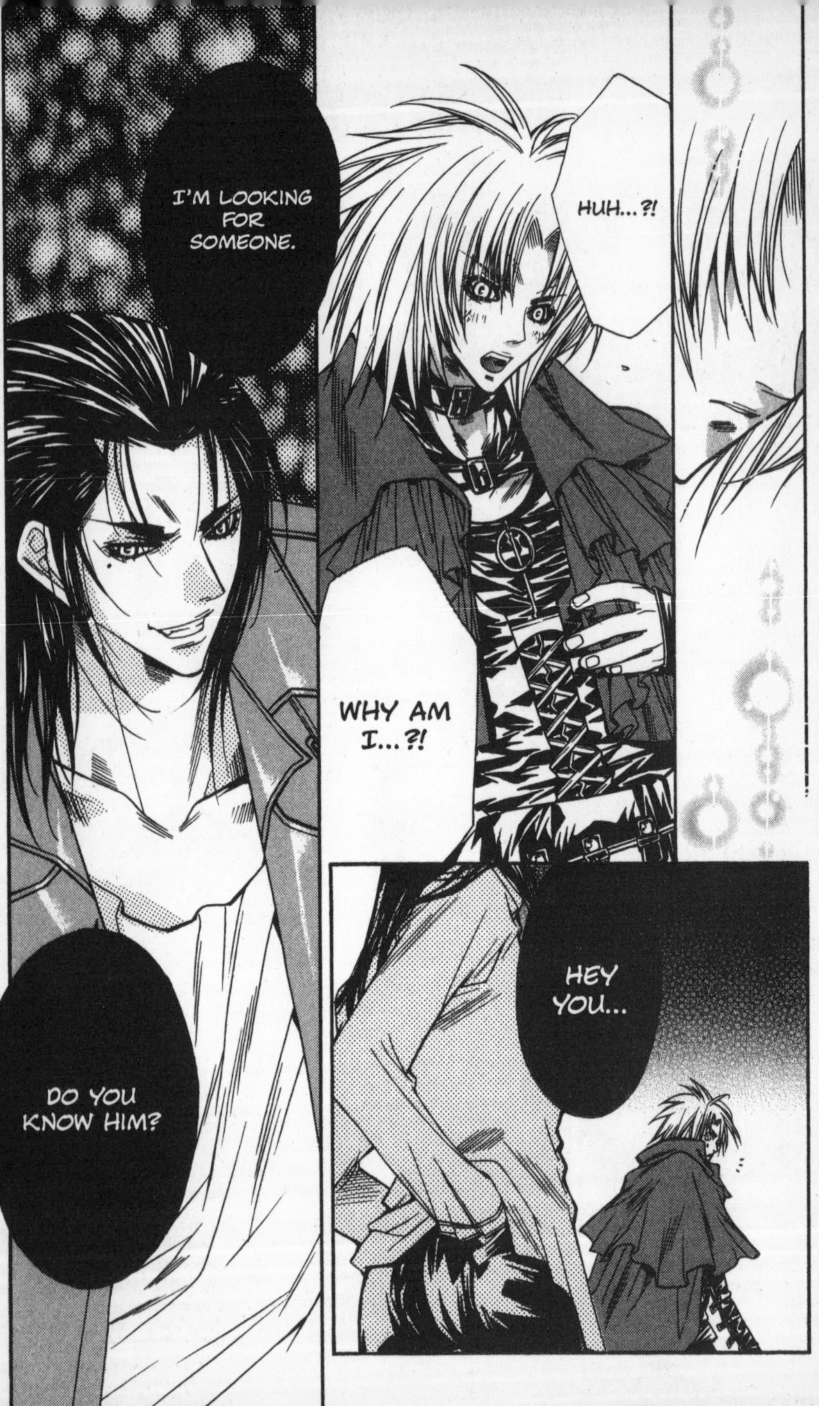
HUH...?!
WHY AM I...?!
HEY YOU...
I'M LOOKING FOR SOMEONE.
DO YOU KNOW HIM?

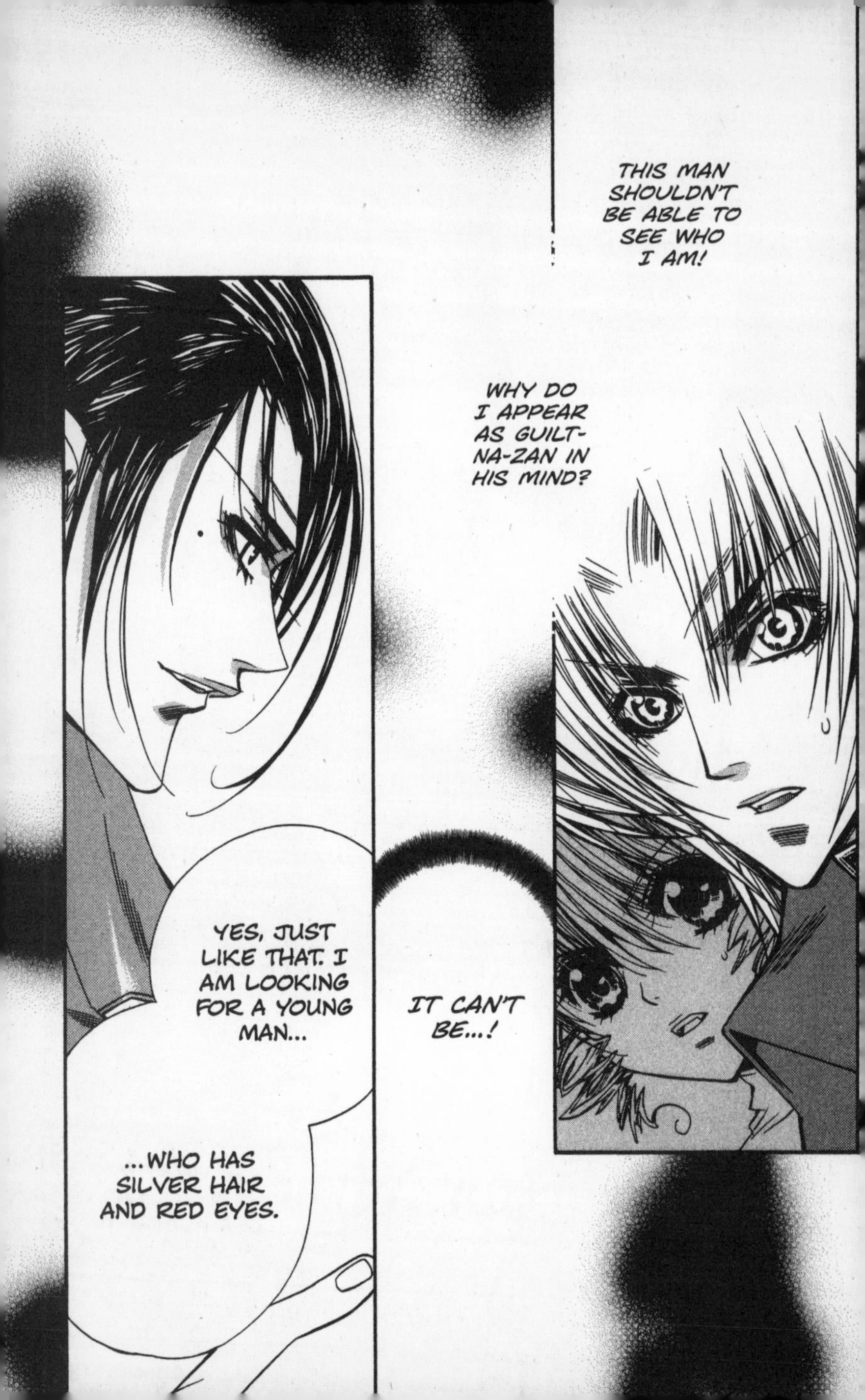
THIS MAN SHOULDN'T BE ABLE TO SEE WHO I AM!
WHY DO I APPEAR AS GUILT-NA-ZAN IN HIS MIND?
YES, JUST LIKE THAT. I AM LOOKING FOR A YOUNG MAN...
...WHO HAS SILVER HAIR AND RED EYES.
IT CAN'T BE...!

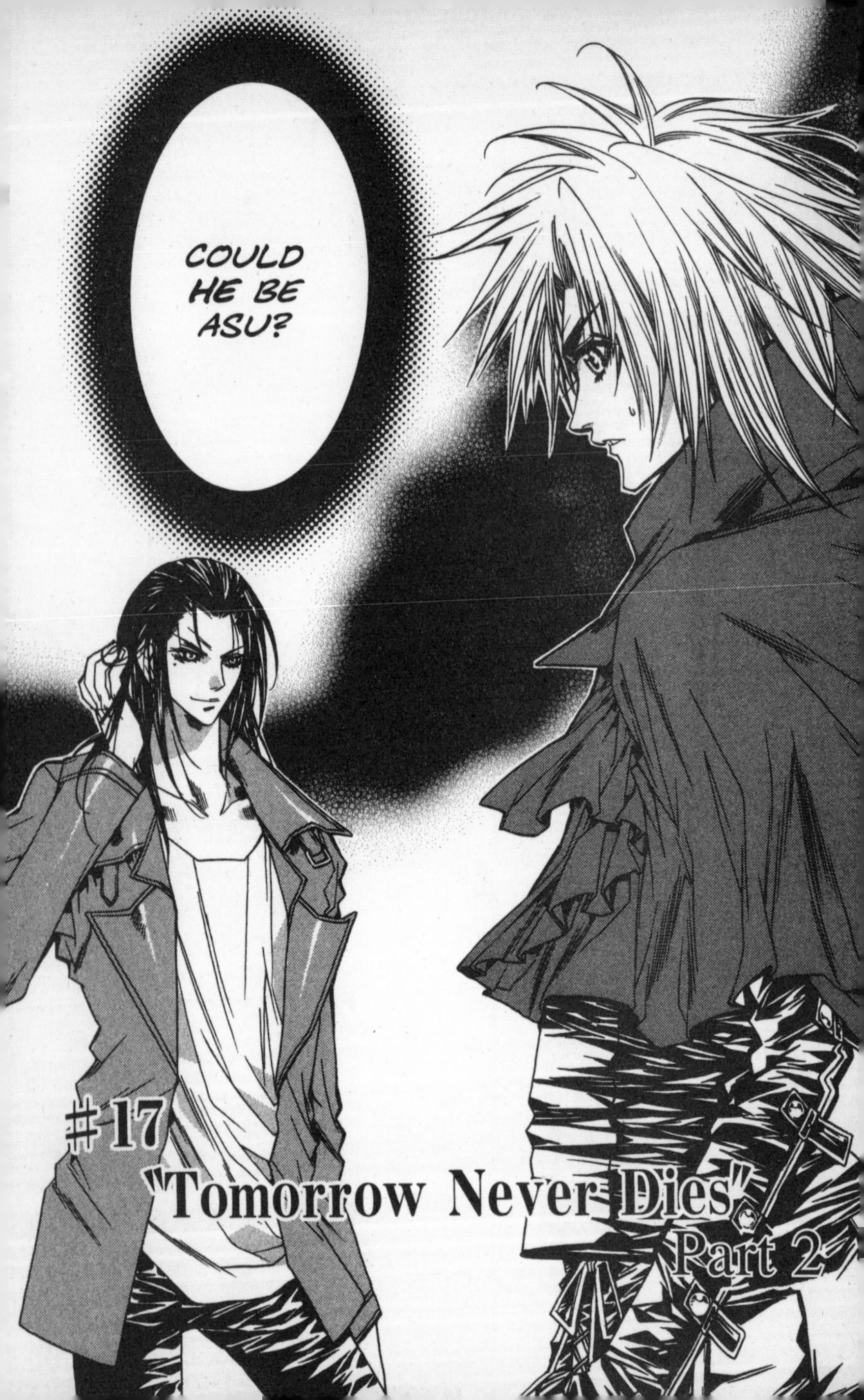
COULD HE BE ASU?
#17
"Tomorrow Never Dies"
Part 2

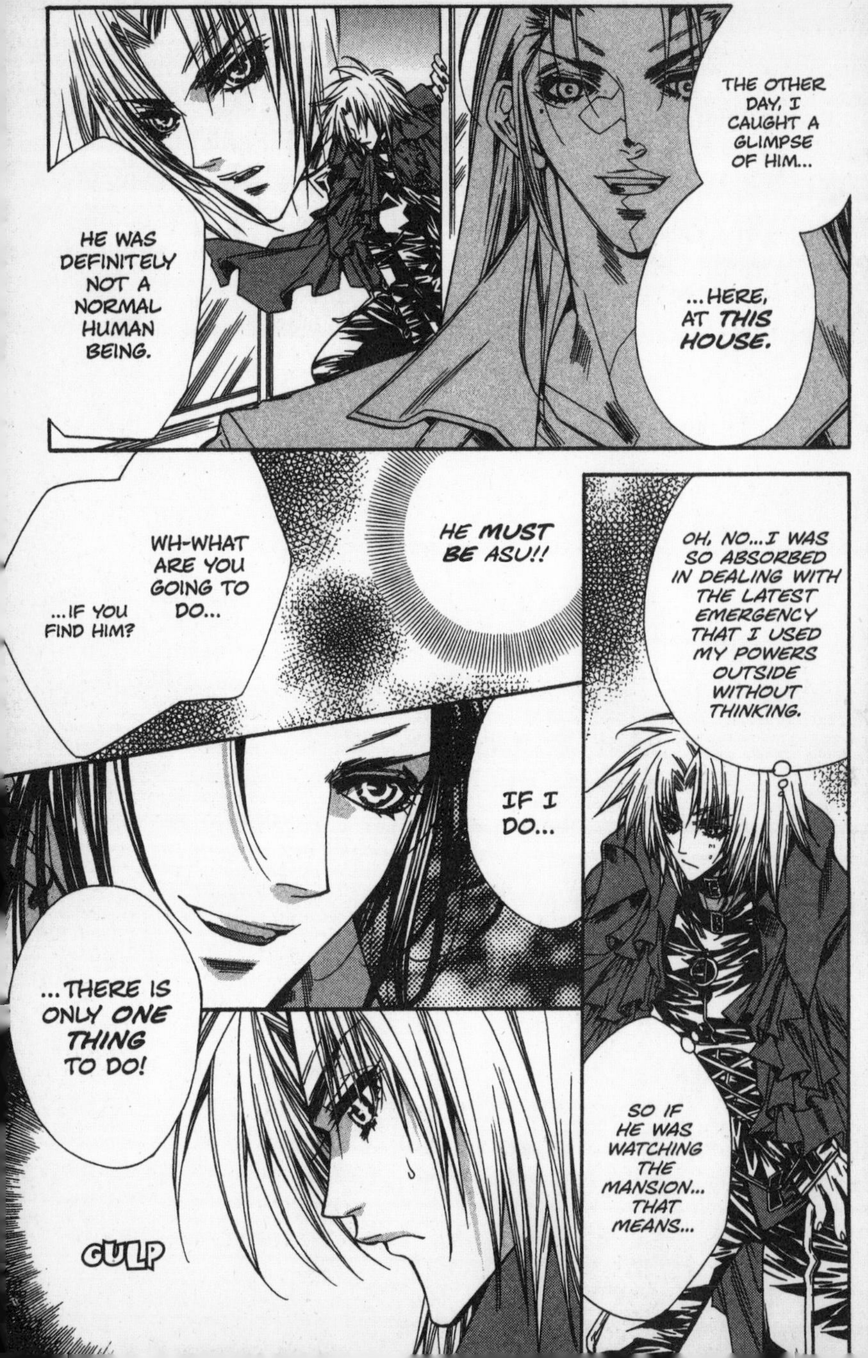
THE OTHER DAY, I CAUGHT A GLIMPSE OF HIM...
...HERE, AT *THIS HOUSE.*
HE WAS DEFINITELY NOT A NORMAL HUMAN BEING.
OH, NO...I WAS SO ABSORBED IN DEALING WITH THE LATEST EMERGENCY THAT I USED MY POWERS OUTSIDE WITHOUT THINKING.
SO IF HE WAS WATCHING THE MANSION... THAT MEANS...
HE *MUST* BE ASU!!
WH-WHAT ARE YOU GOING TO DO...
...IF YOU FIND HIM?
IF I DO...
...THERE IS ONLY *ONE THING* TO DO!
GULP

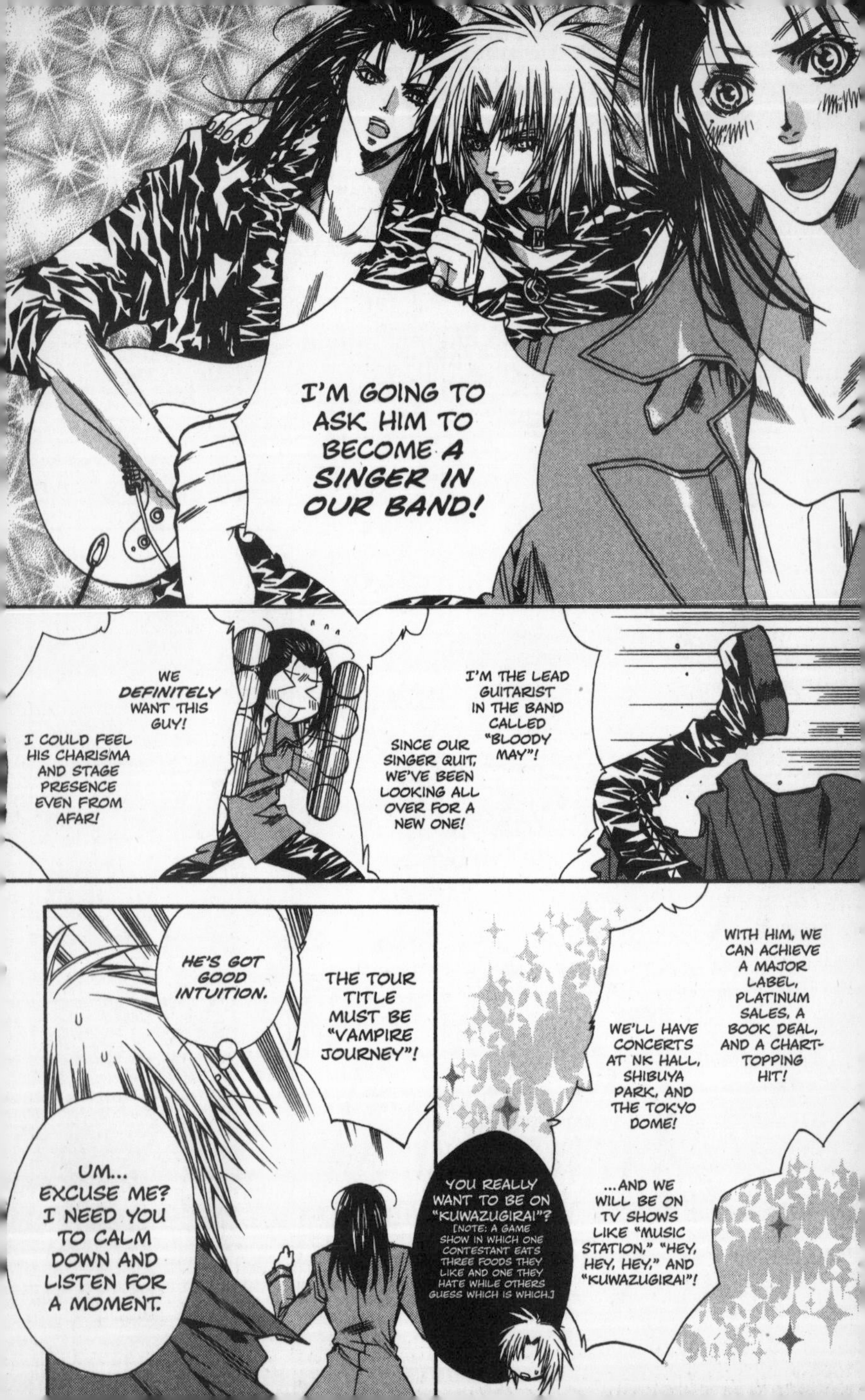
I'M GOING TO ASK HIM TO BECOME A SINGER IN OUR BAND!
I'M THE LEAD GUITARIST IN THE BAND CALLED "BLOODY MAY"!
SINCE OUR SINGER QUIT, WE'VE BEEN LOOKING ALL OVER FOR A NEW ONE!
WE DEFINITELY WANT THIS GUY!
I COULD FEEL HIS CHARISMA AND STAGE PRESENCE EVEN FROM AFAR!
WITH HIM, WE CAN ACHIEVE A MAJOR LABEL, PLATINUM SALES, A BOOK DEAL, AND A CHART-TOPPING HIT!
WE'LL HAVE CONCERTS AT NK HALL, SHIBUYA PARK, AND THE TOKYO DOME!
THE TOUR TITLE MUST BE "VAMPIRE JOURNEY"!
...AND WE WILL BE ON TV SHOWS LIKE "MUSIC STATION," "HEY, HEY, HEY," AND "KUWAZUGIRAI"!
YOU REALLY WANT TO BE ON "KUWAZUGIRAI"? [NOTE: A GAME SHOW IN WHICH ONE CONTESTANT EATS THREE FOODS THEY LIKE AND ONE THEY HATE WHILE OTHERS GUESS WHICH IS WHICH.]
HE'S GOT GOOD INTUITION.
UM... EXCUSE ME? I NEED YOU TO CALM DOWN AND LISTEN FOR A MOMENT.

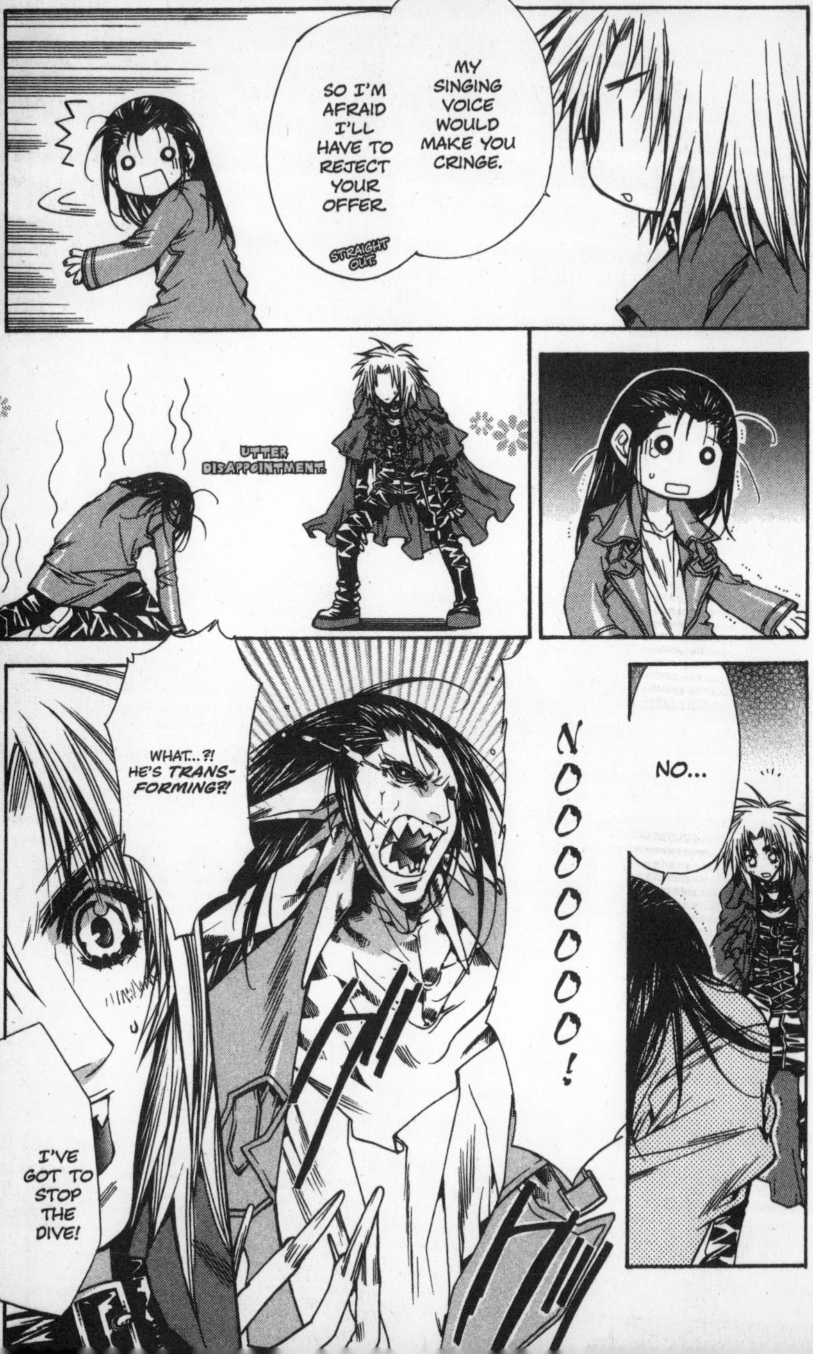
MY SINGING VOICE WOULD MAKE YOU CRINGE.
SO I'M AFRAID I'LL HAVE TO REJECT YOUR OFFER
STRAIGHT OUT.
UTTER DISAPPOINTMENT.
NO...
NOOOOOOOOO!
WHAT...?! HE'S TRANS-FORMING?!
I'VE GOT TO STOP THE DIVE!

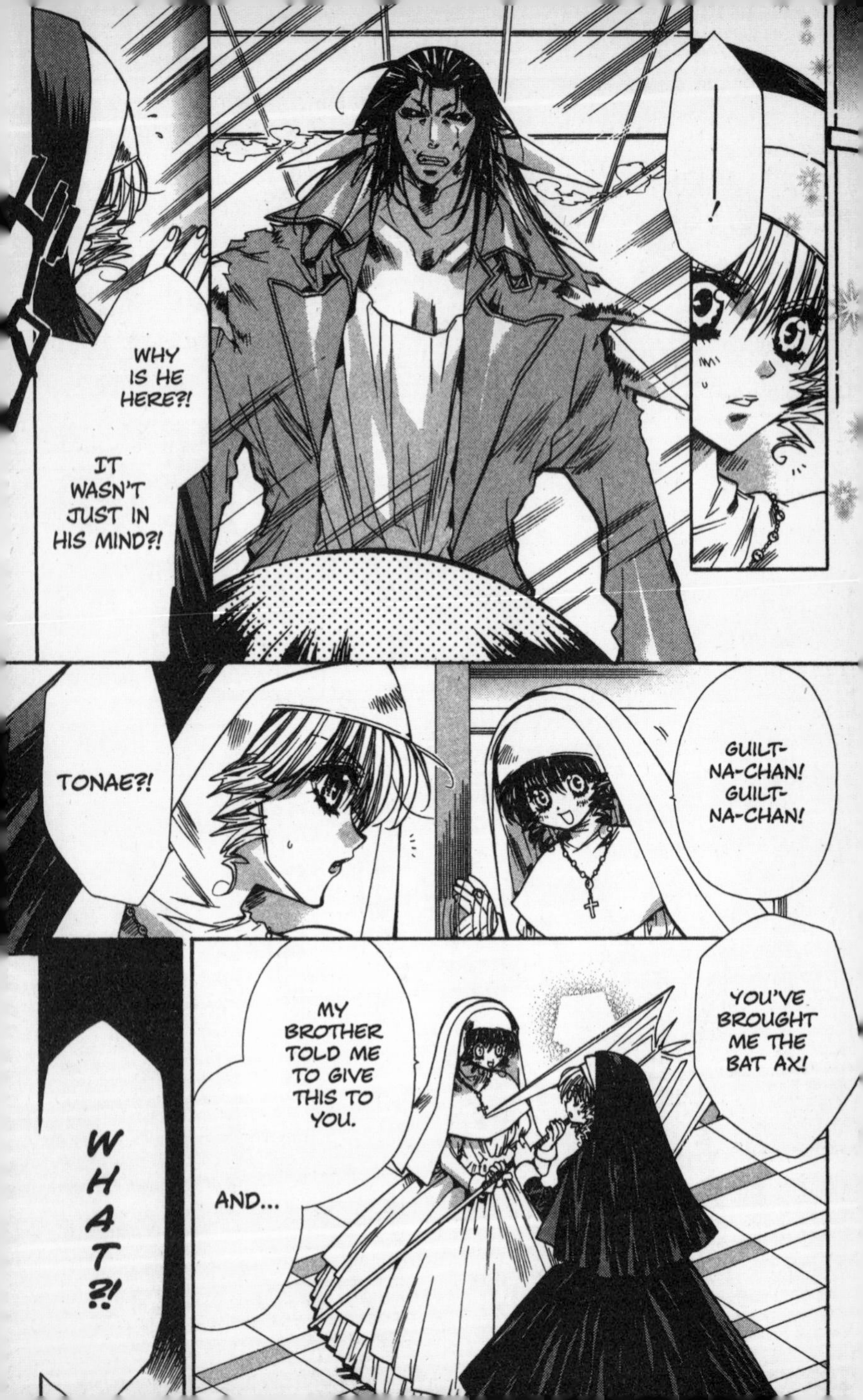

!
WHY IS HE HERE?!
IT WASN'T JUST IN HIS MIND?!
GUILT-NA-CHAN! GUILT-NA-CHAN!
TONAE?!
YOU'VE BROUGHT ME THE BAT AX!
MY BROTHER TOLD ME TO GIVE THIS TO YOU.
AND...
WHAT?!

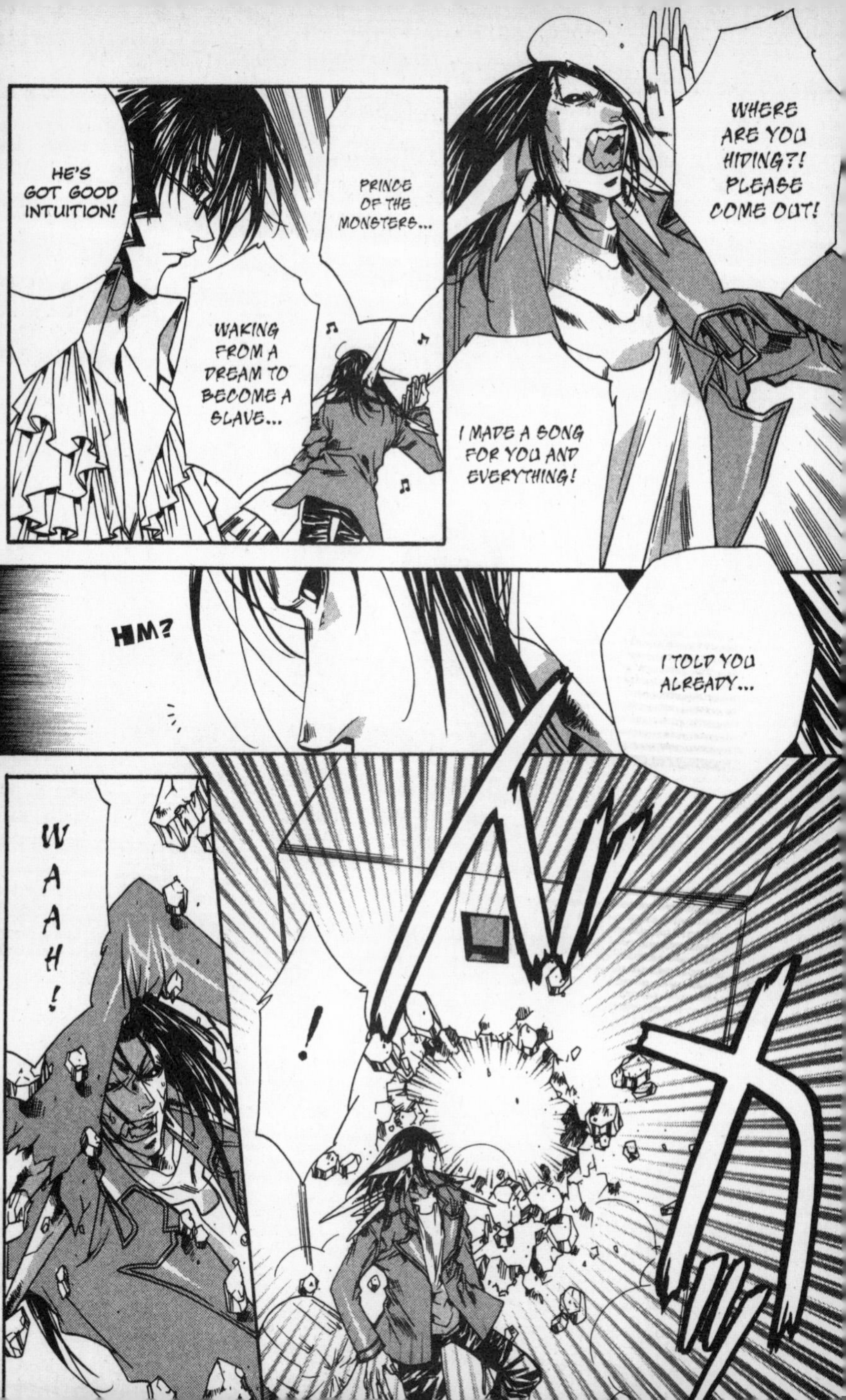
WHERE ARE YOU HIDING?! PLEASE COME OUT!
I MADE A SONG FOR YOU AND EVERYTHING!
PRINCE OF THE MONSTERS...
HE'S GOT GOOD INTUITION!
WAKING FROM A DREAM TO BECOME A SLAVE...
I TOLD YOU ALREADY...
HM?
!
WAAAH!

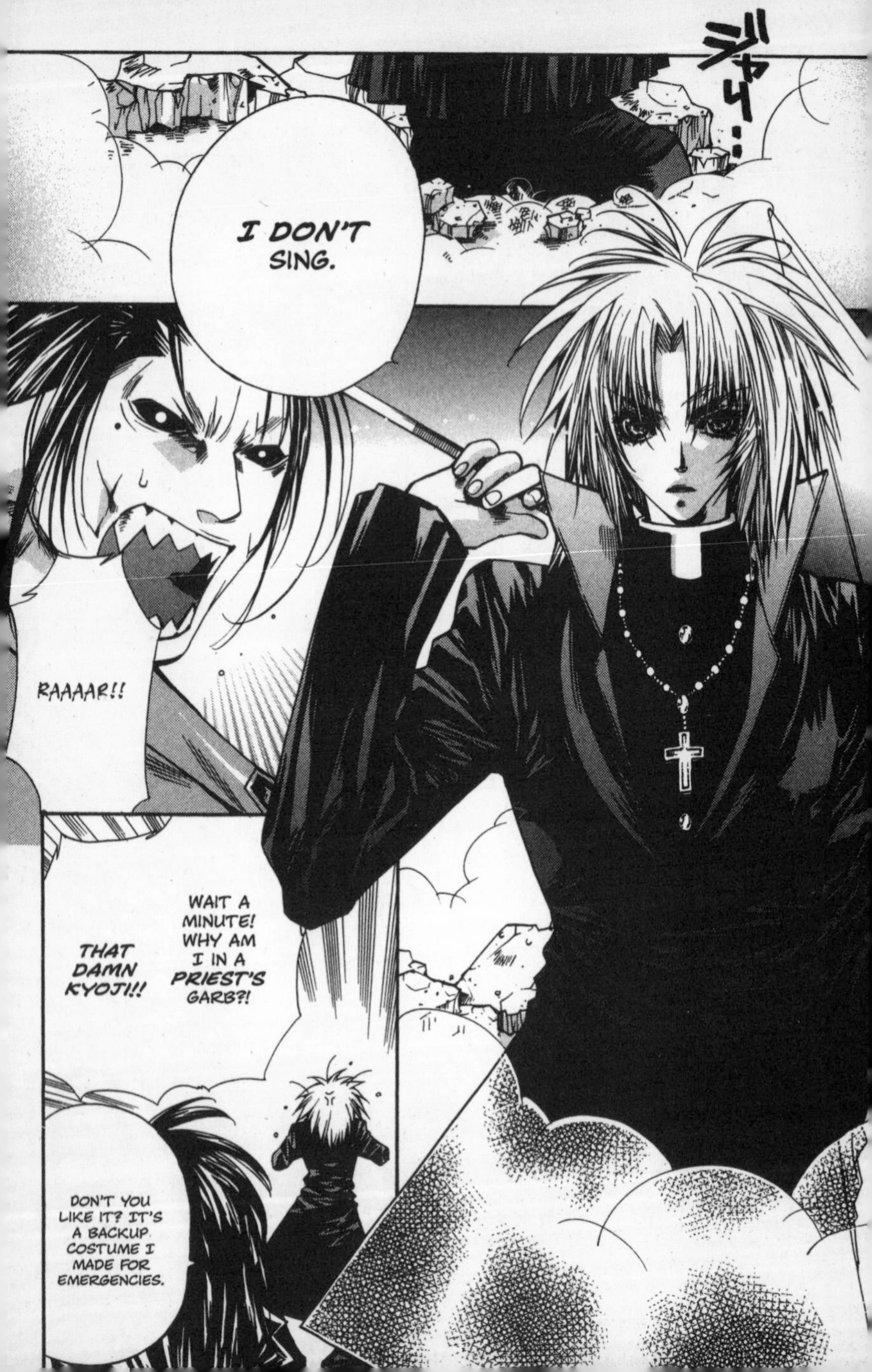
ジャリ…
I DON'T SING.
RAAAAR!!
WAIT A MINUTE! WHY AM I IN A PRIEST'S GARB?!
THAT DAMN KYOJI!!
DON'T YOU LIKE IT? IT'S A BACKUP COSTUME I MADE FOR EMERGENCIES.

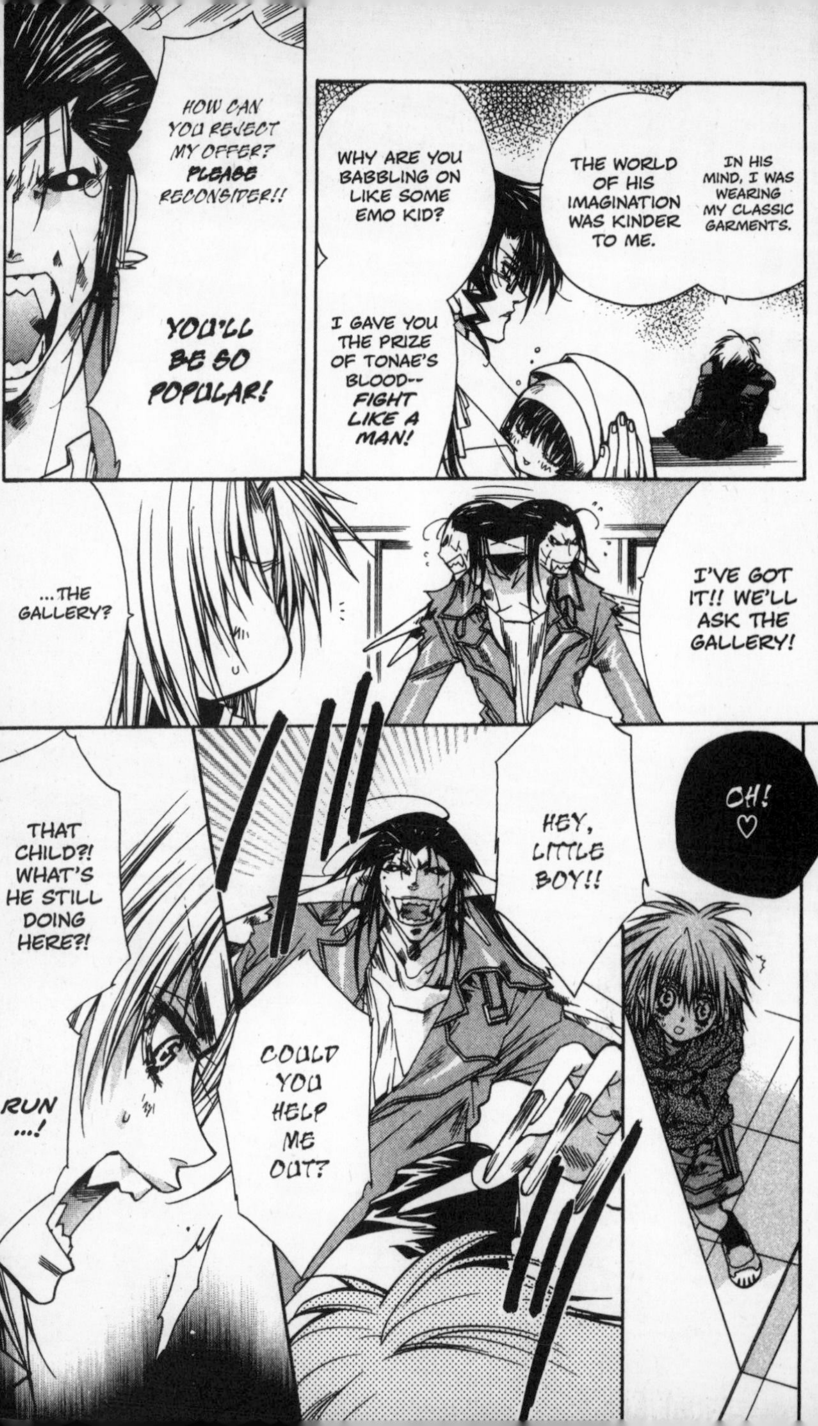
IN HIS MIND, I WAS WEARING MY CLASSIC GARMENTS.
THE WORLD OF HIS IMAGINATION WAS KINDER TO ME.
WHY ARE YOU BABBLING ON LIKE SOME EMO KID?
I GAVE YOU THE PRIZE OF TONAE'S BLOOD-- FIGHT LIKE A MAN!
HOW CAN YOU REJECT MY OFFER? PLEASE RECONSIDER!!
YOU'LL BE SO POPULAR!
I'VE GOT IT!! WE'LL ASK THE GALLERY!
...THE GALLERY?
OH! ♡
HEY, LITTLE BOY!!
COULD YOU HELP ME OUT?
THAT CHILD?! WHAT'S HE STILL DOING HERE?!
RUN ...!

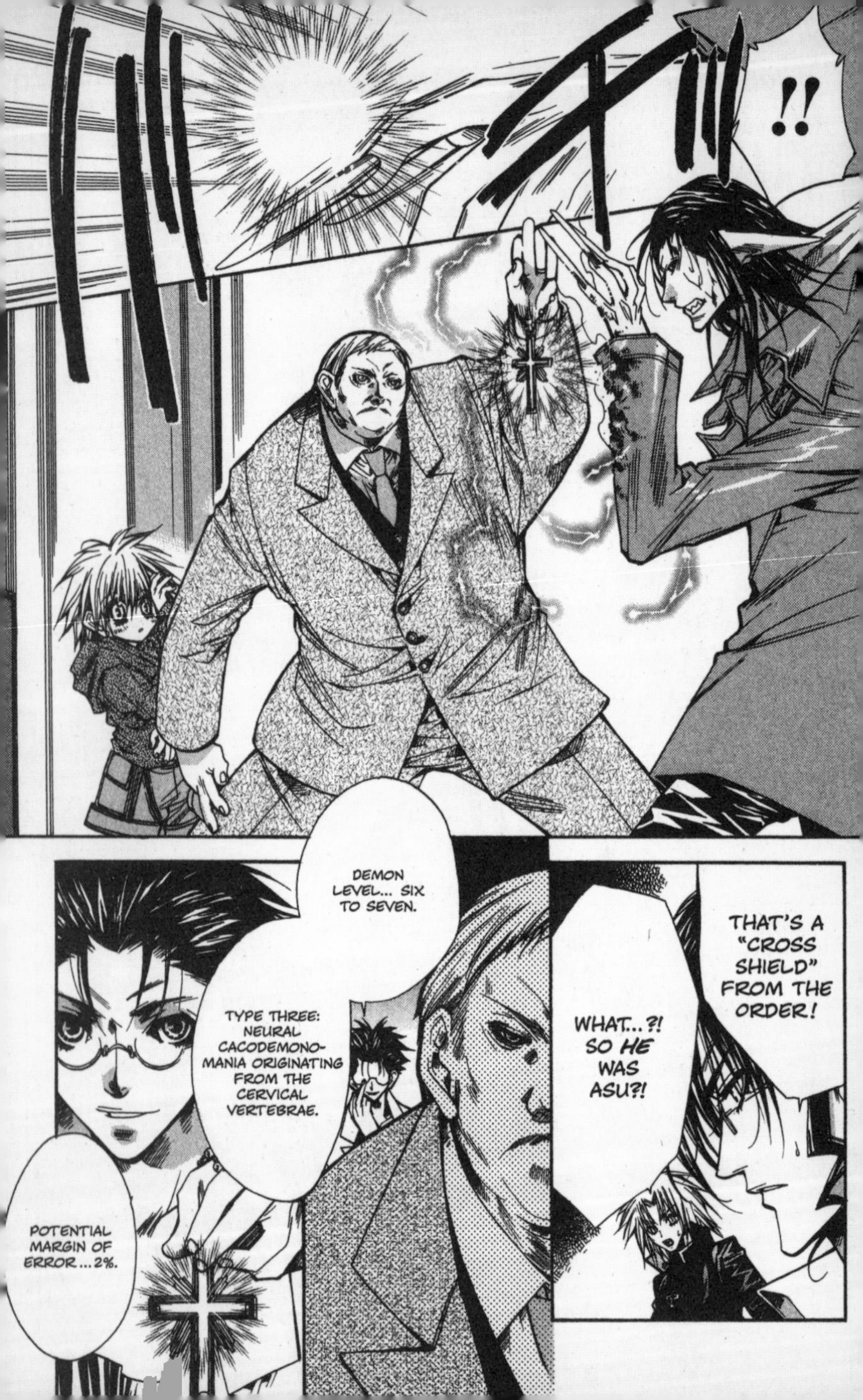
!!
THAT'S A "CROSS SHIELD" FROM THE ORDER!
WHAT...?! SO *HE* WAS ASU?!
DEMON LEVEL... SIX TO SEVEN.
TYPE THREE: NEURAL CACODEMONOMANIA ORIGINATING FROM THE CERVICAL VERTEBRAE.
POTENTIAL MARGIN OF ERROR...2%.

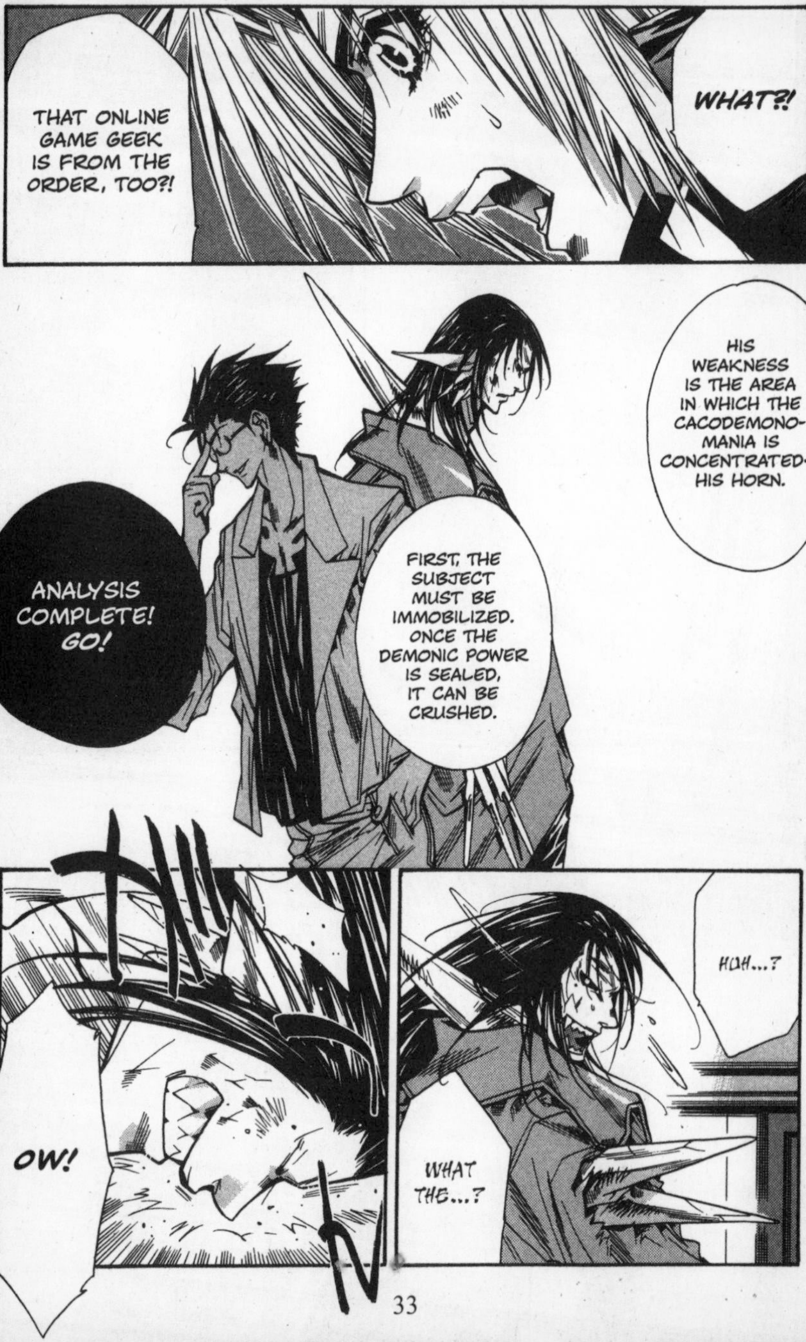
WHAT?!
THAT ONLINE GAME GEEK IS FROM THE ORDER, TOO?!
HIS WEAKNESS IS THE AREA IN WHICH THE CACODEMONO-MANIA IS CONCENTRATED-- HIS HORN.
FIRST, THE SUBJECT MUST BE IMMOBILIZED. ONCE THE DEMONIC POWER IS SEALED, IT CAN BE CRUSHED.
ANALYSIS COMPLETE! GO!
HUH...?
WHAT THE...?
OW!

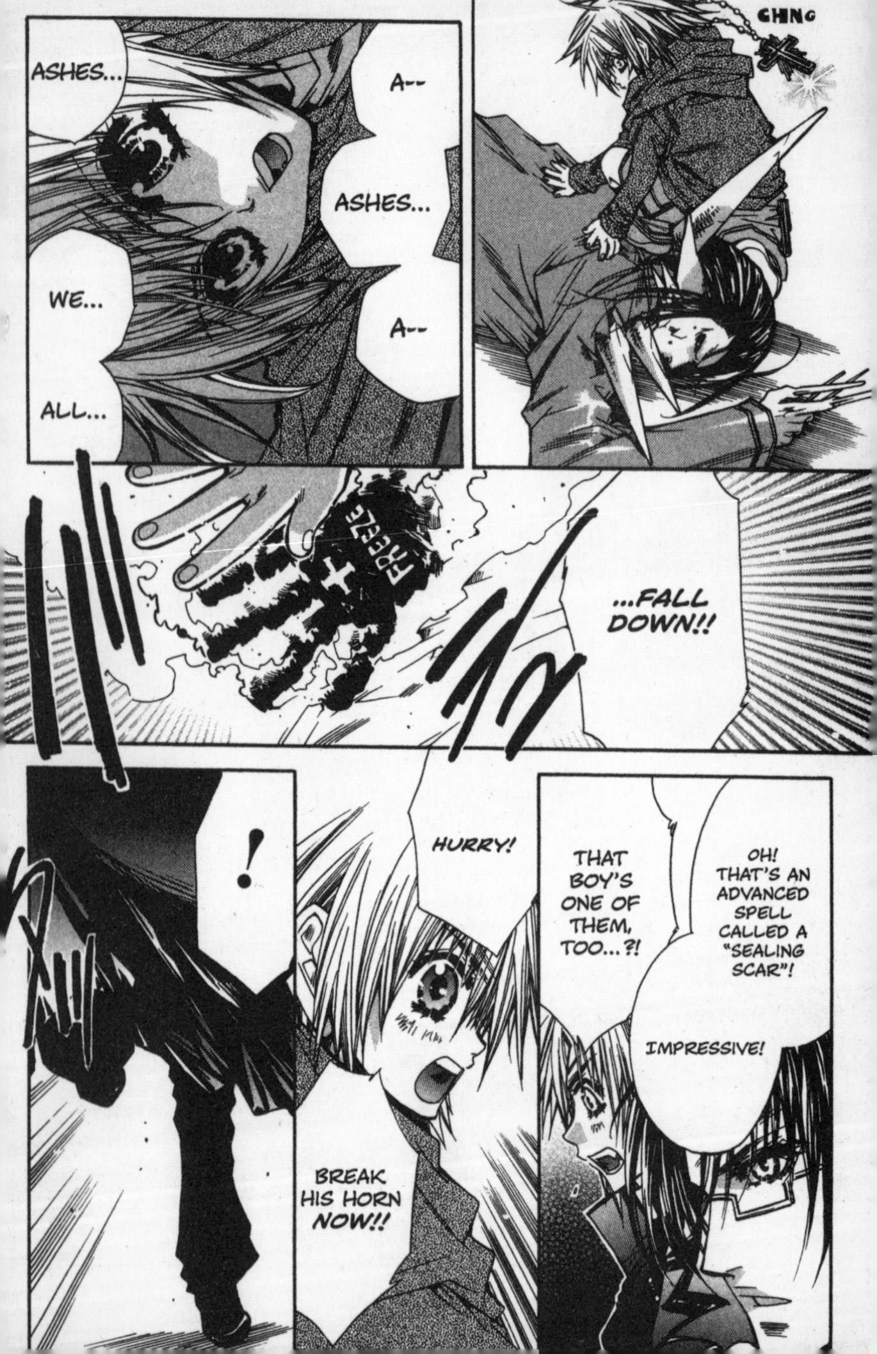
CHING
A--
ASHES...
A--
ASHES...
WE...
ALL...
FREEZE
...FALL DOWN!!
OH! THAT'S AN ADVANCED SPELL CALLED A "SEALING SCAR"!
THAT BOY'S ONE OF THEM, TOO...?!
IMPRESSIVE!
HURRY!
BREAK HIS HORN NOW!!
!

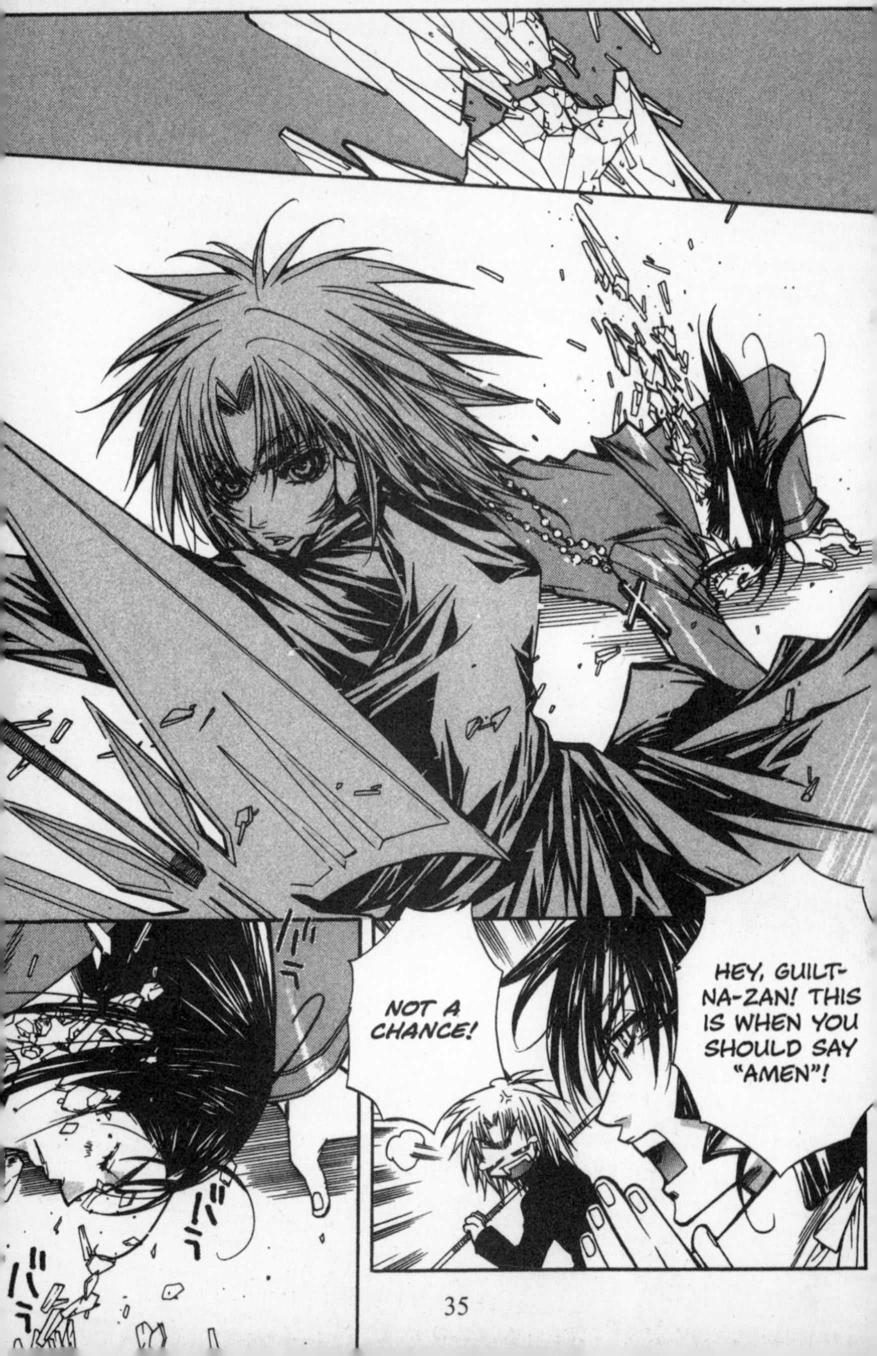
HEY, GUILT-NA-ZAN! THIS IS WHEN YOU SHOULD SAY "AMEN"!
NOT A CHANCE!

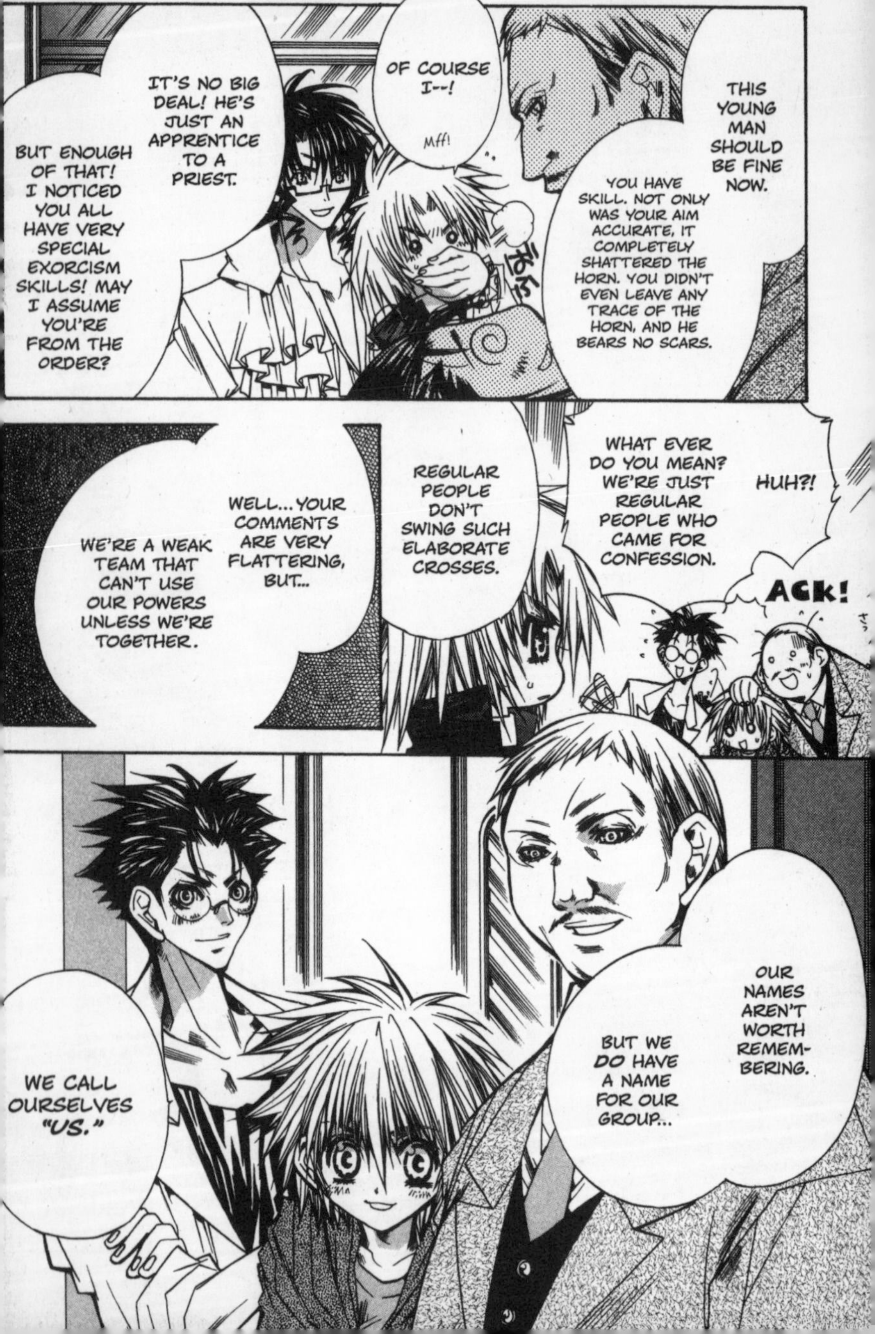
THIS YOUNG MAN SHOULD BE FINE NOW.
YOU HAVE SKILL. NOT ONLY WAS YOUR AIM ACCURATE, IT COMPLETELY SHATTERED THE HORN. YOU DIDN'T EVEN LEAVE ANY TRACE OF THE HORN, AND HE BEARS NO SCARS.
OF COURSE I--!
Mff!
IT'S NO BIG DEAL! HE'S JUST AN APPRENTICE TO A PRIEST.
BUT ENOUGH OF THAT! I NOTICED YOU ALL HAVE VERY SPECIAL EXORCISM SKILLS! MAY I ASSUME YOU'RE FROM THE ORDER?
HUH?!
WHAT EVER DO YOU MEAN? WE'RE JUST REGULAR PEOPLE WHO CAME FOR CONFESSION.
ACK!
REGULAR PEOPLE DON'T SWING SUCH ELABORATE CROSSES.
WELL... YOUR COMMENTS ARE VERY FLATTERING, BUT...
WE'RE A WEAK TEAM THAT CAN'T USE OUR POWERS UNLESS WE'RE TOGETHER.
OUR NAMES AREN'T WORTH REMEMBERING.
BUT WE DO HAVE A NAME FOR OUR GROUP...
WE CALL OURSELVES "US."

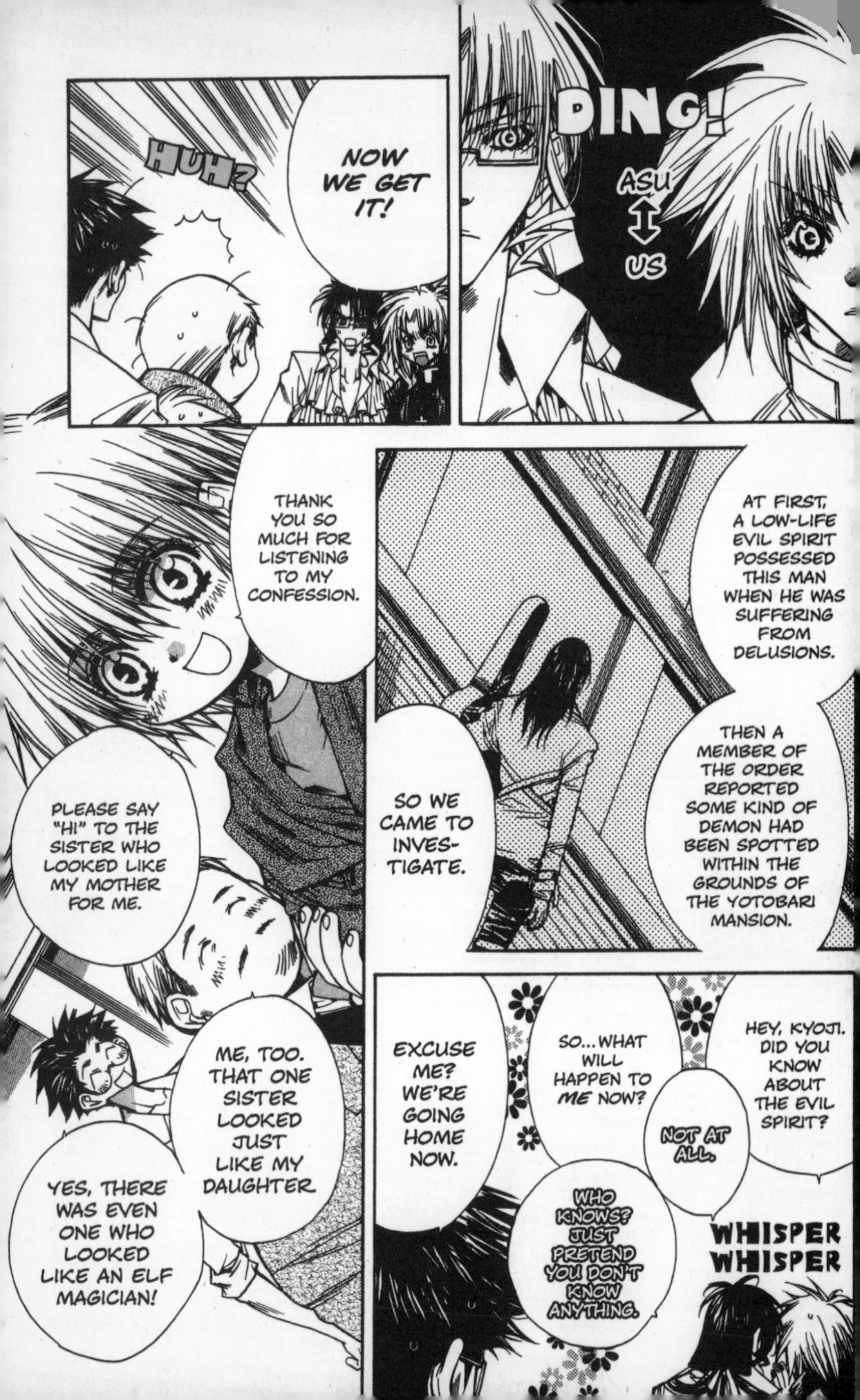
DING!
ASU
US
NOW WE GET IT!
HUH?
AT FIRST, A LOW-LIFE EVIL SPIRIT POSSESSED THIS MAN WHEN HE WAS SUFFERING FROM DELUSIONS.
THEN A MEMBER OF THE ORDER REPORTED SOME KIND OF DEMON HAD BEEN SPOTTED WITHIN THE GROUNDS OF THE YOTOBARI MANSION.
SO WE CAME TO INVES-TIGATE.
HEY, KYOJI. DID YOU KNOW ABOUT THE EVIL SPIRIT?
NOT AT ALL.
WHISPER WHISPER
SO...WHAT WILL HAPPEN TO *ME* NOW?
EXCUSE ME? WE'RE GOING HOME NOW.
WHO KNOWS? JUST PRETEND YOU DON'T KNOW ANYTHING.
THANK YOU SO MUCH FOR LISTENING TO MY CONFESSION.
PLEASE SAY "HI" TO THE SISTER WHO LOOKED LIKE MY MOTHER FOR ME.
ME, TOO. THAT ONE SISTER LOOKED JUST LIKE MY DAUGHTER.
YES, THERE WAS EVEN ONE WHO LOOKED LIKE AN ELF MAGICIAN!

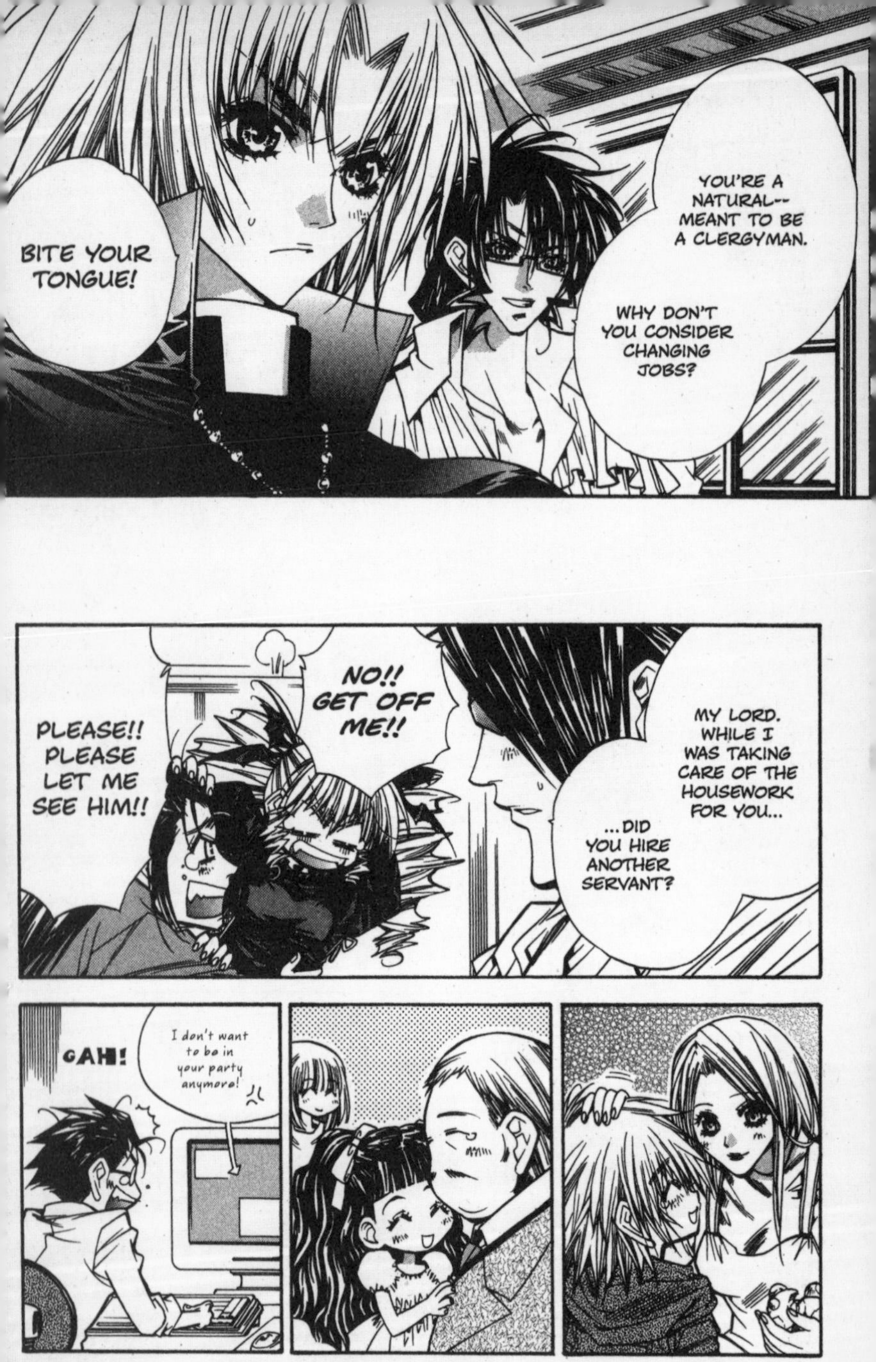
YOU'RE A NATURAL-- MEANT TO BE A CLERGYMAN.
WHY DON'T YOU CONSIDER CHANGING JOBS?
BITE YOUR TONGUE!
MY LORD. WHILE I WAS TAKING CARE OF THE HOUSEWORK FOR YOU...
...DID YOU HIRE ANOTHER SERVANT?
NO!! GET OFF ME!!
PLEASE!! PLEASE LET ME SEE HIM!!
I don't want to be in your party anymore!
GAH!

BONUS COMIC STRIP

VAMPIRE DOLL

REFLECTIONS

Tomorrow Never Dies

WHAT'S YOUR NAME?
~ASU~
YOU MAY HAVE A TEAM NAME, BUT IT WOULD BE HELPFUL IF YOU ALL HAD UNIQUE NAMES WITHIN THE TEAM. HMM...
GOT IT!
ASU-GEEK
ASU-BOY
ASU-DAD
THOSE AREN'T VERY COOL...
I DID MY BEST.
HOW COME I CAN'T JUST BE "ASU-GUY" OR SOMETHING?

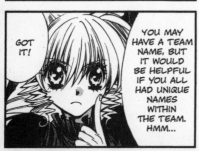

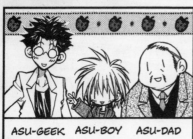

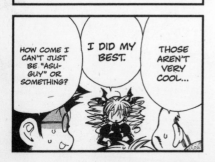

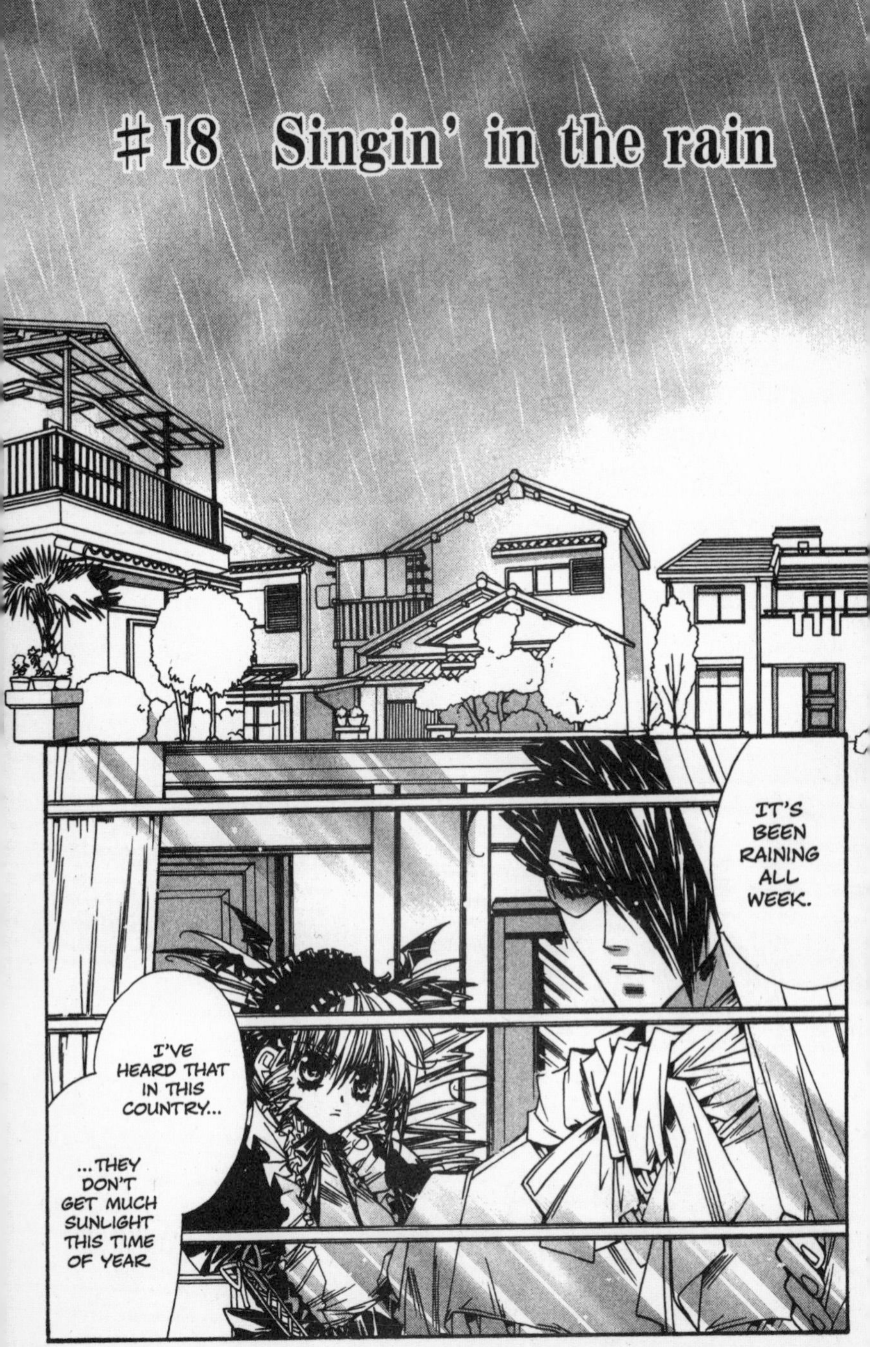
#18 Singin' in the rain
IT'S BEEN RAINING ALL WEEK.
I'VE HEARD THAT IN THIS COUNTRY...
...THEY DON'T GET MUCH SUNLIGHT THIS TIME OF YEAR

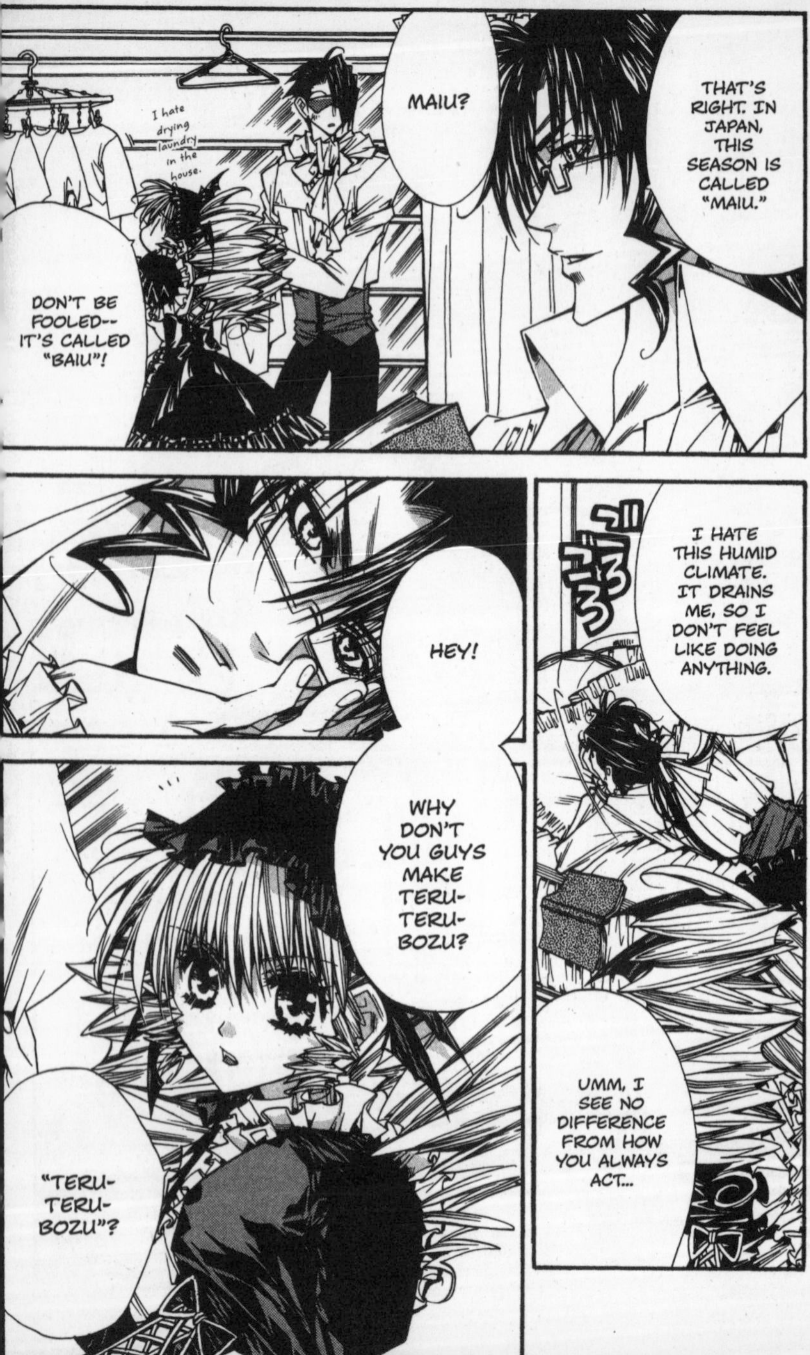
THAT'S RIGHT. IN JAPAN, THIS SEASON IS CALLED "MAIU."
MAIU?
I hate drying laundry in the house.
DON'T BE FOOLED-- IT'S CALLED "BAIU"!
I HATE THIS HUMID CLIMATE. IT DRAINS ME, SO I DON'T FEEL LIKE DOING ANYTHING.
UMM, I SEE NO DIFFERENCE FROM HOW YOU ALWAYS ACT...
HEY!
WHY DON'T YOU GUYS MAKE TERU-TERU-BOZU?
"TERU-TERU-BOZU"?

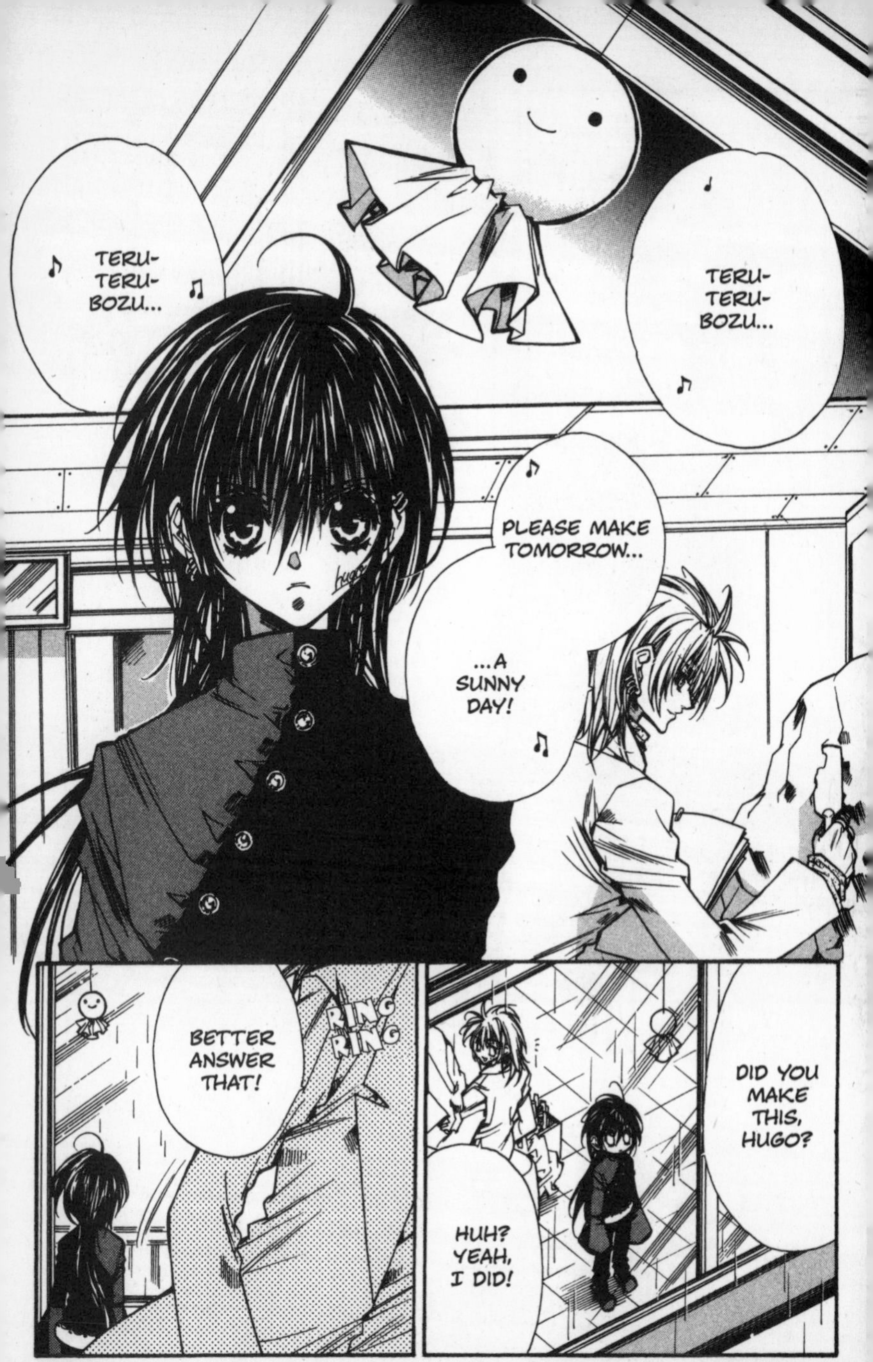
TERU-TERU-BOZU...
TERU-TERU-BOZU...
PLEASE MAKE TOMORROW...
...A SUNNY DAY!
DID YOU MAKE THIS, HUGO?
HUH? YEAH, I DID!
BETTER ANSWER THAT!
RING RING

*NOTE: TERU-TERU-BOZU ARE LITTLE CHARMS THAT ARE SAID TO BRING GOOD WEATHER.

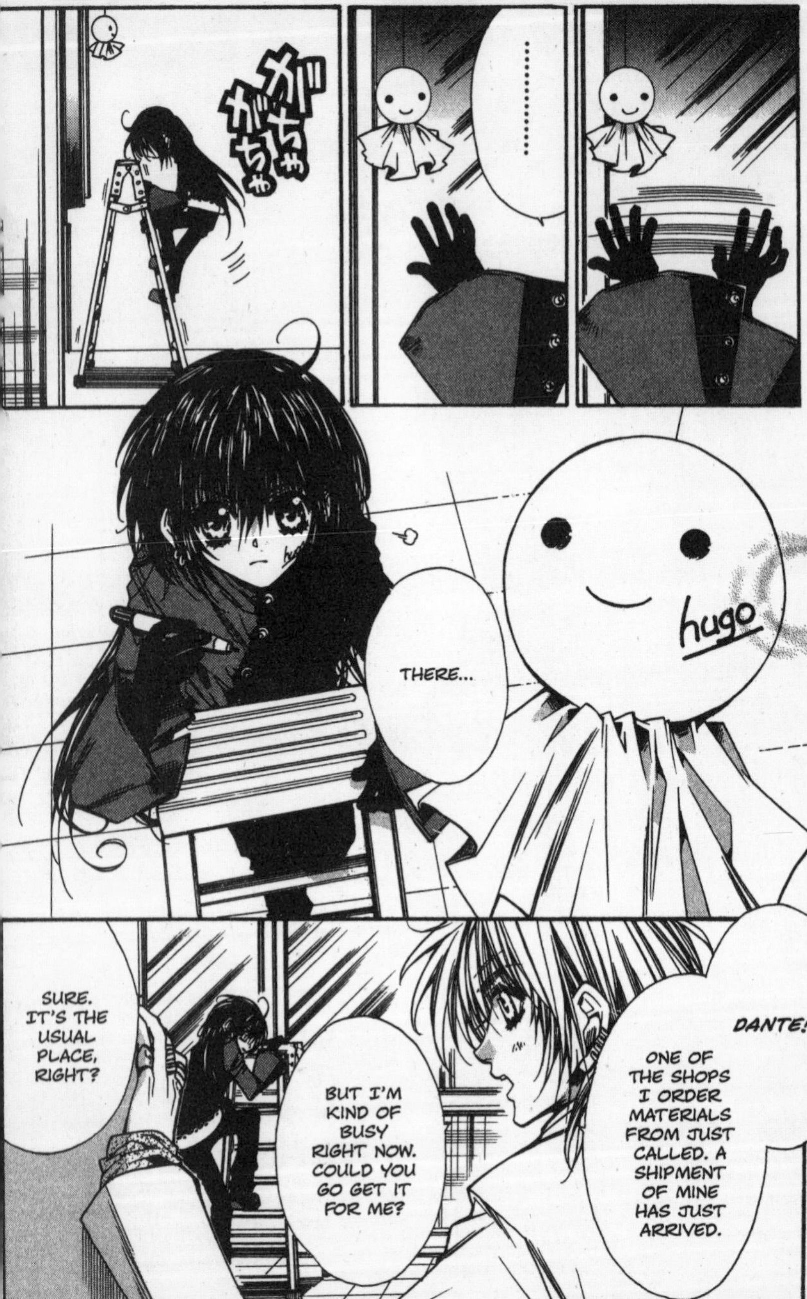
......
がちゃがちゃ
hugo
THERE...
DANTE! ONE OF THE SHOPS I ORDER MATERIALS FROM JUST CALLED. A SHIPMENT OF MINE HAS JUST ARRIVED.
BUT I'M KIND OF BUSY RIGHT NOW. COULD YOU GO GET IT FOR ME?
SURE. IT'S THE USUAL PLACE, RIGHT?

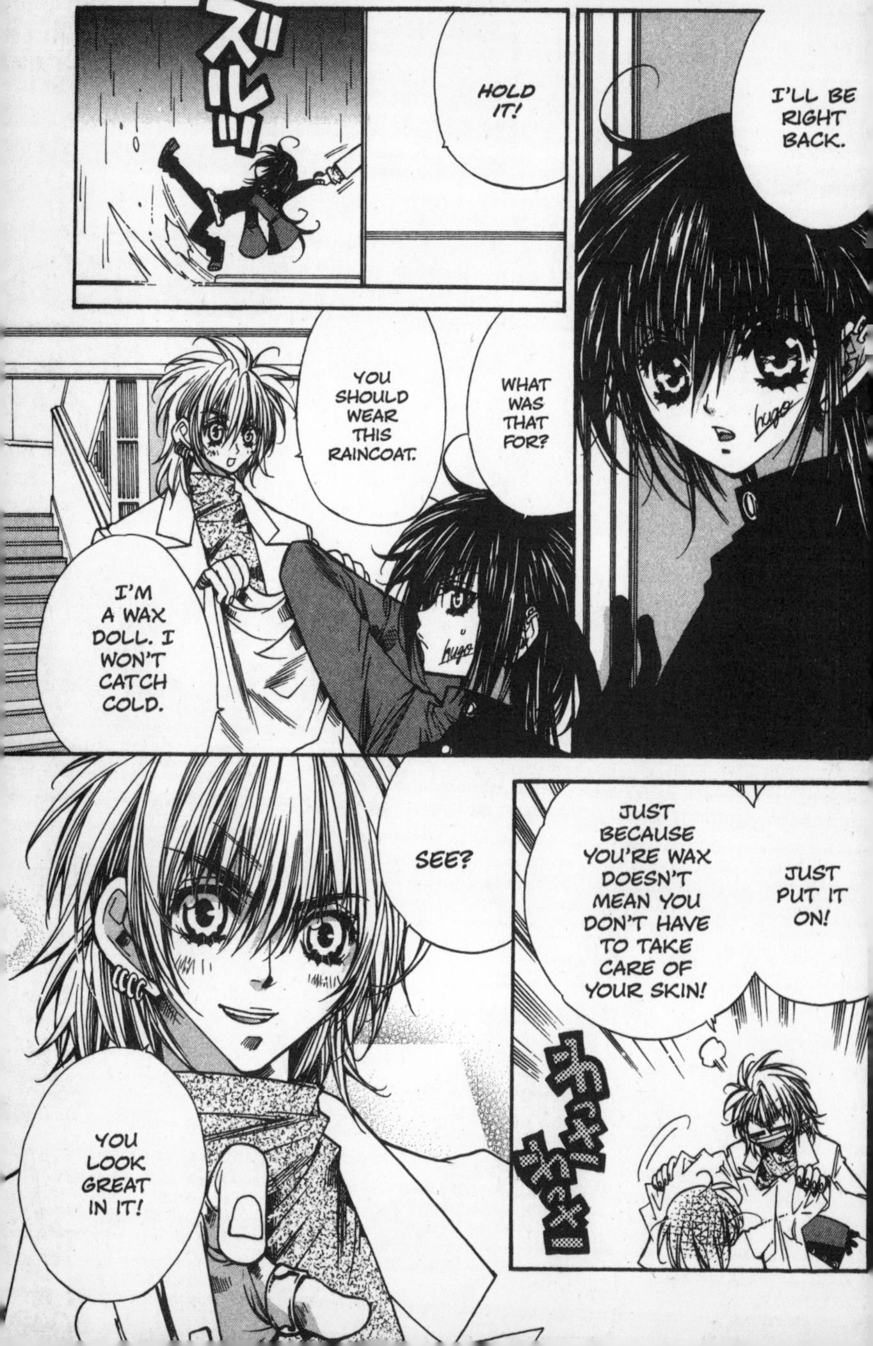
I'LL BE RIGHT BACK.
HOLD IT!
WHAT WAS THAT FOR?
YOU SHOULD WEAR THIS RAINCOAT.
I'M A WAX DOLL. I WON'T CATCH COLD.
JUST PUT IT ON!
JUST BECAUSE YOU'RE WAX DOESN'T MEAN YOU DON'T HAVE TO TAKE CARE OF YOUR SKIN!
SEE?
YOU LOOK GREAT IN IT!

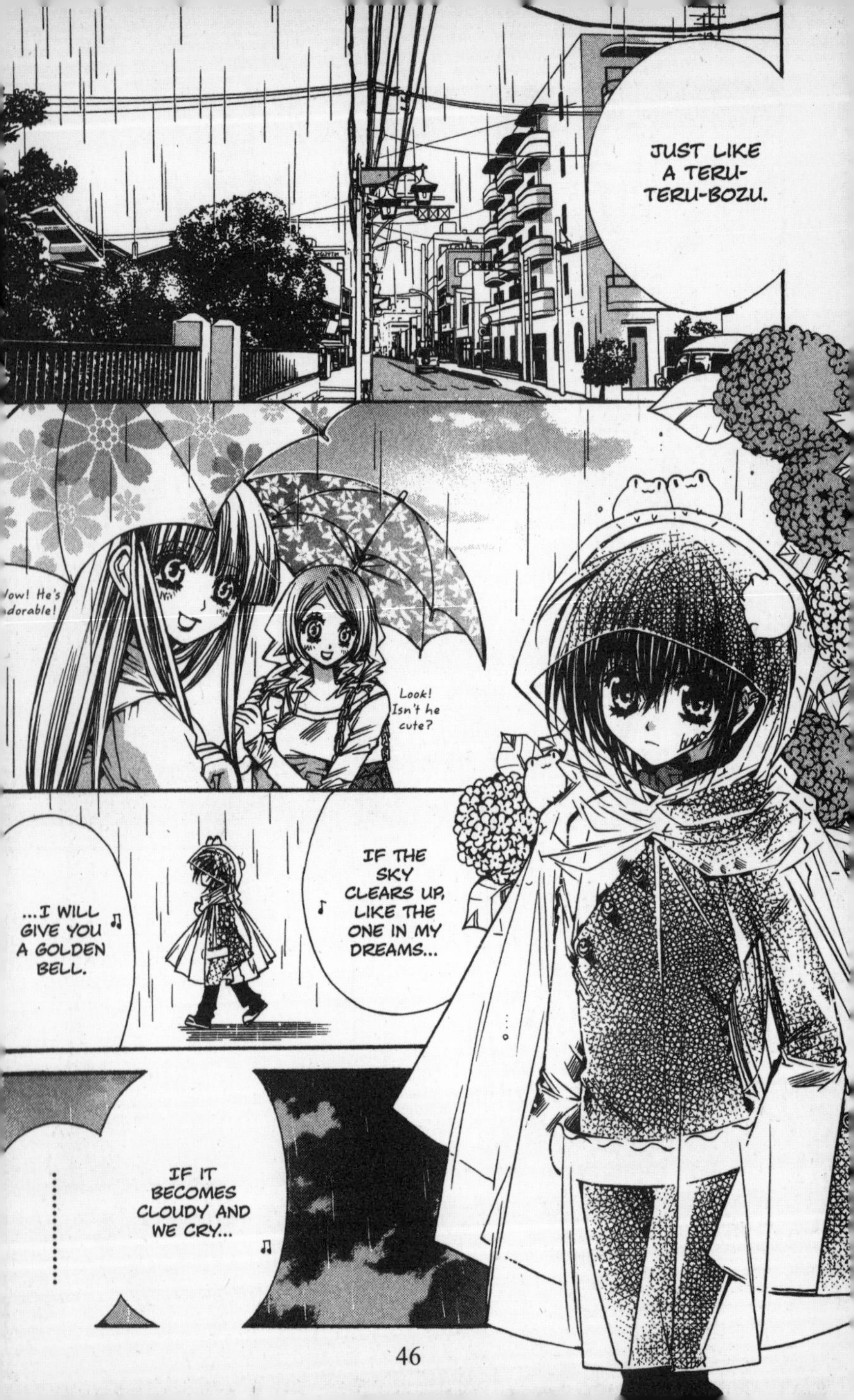

JUST LIKE A TERU-TERU-BOZU.
Look! Isn't he cute?
ow! He's dorable!
IF THE SKY CLEARS UP, LIKE THE ONE IN MY DREAMS... ♪
...I WILL GIVE YOU A GOLDEN BELL. ♫
IF IT BECOMES CLOUDY AND WE CRY... ♫

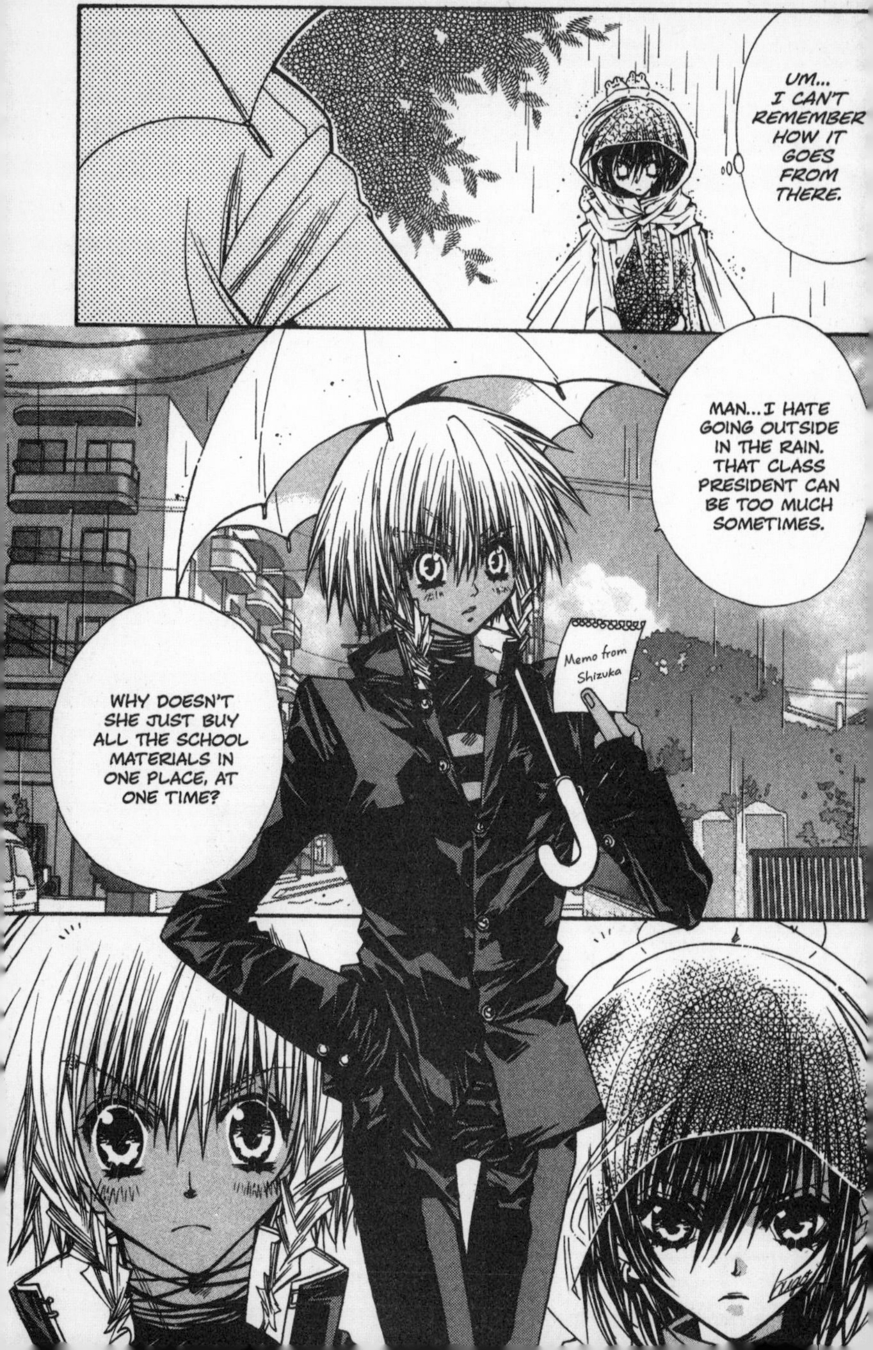
UM... I CAN'T REMEMBER HOW IT GOES FROM THERE.
MAN...I HATE GOING OUTSIDE IN THE RAIN. THAT CLASS PRESIDENT CAN BE TOO MUCH SOMETIMES.
Memo from Shizuka
WHY DOESN'T SHE JUST BUY ALL THE SCHOOL MATERIALS IN ONE PLACE, AT ONE TIME?

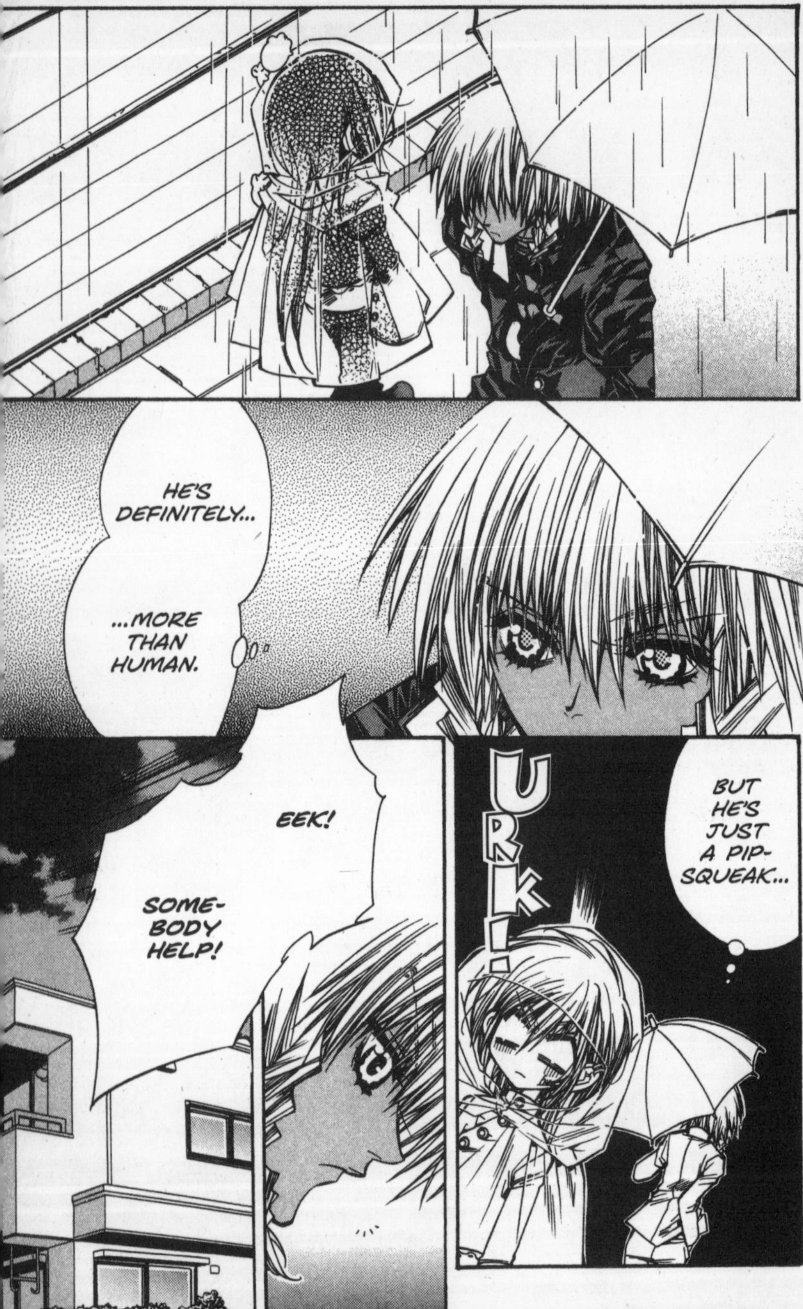
HE'S DEFINITELY...
...MORE THAN HUMAN.
BUT HE'S JUST A PIP-SQUEAK...
URK!
EEK!
SOMEBODY HELP!

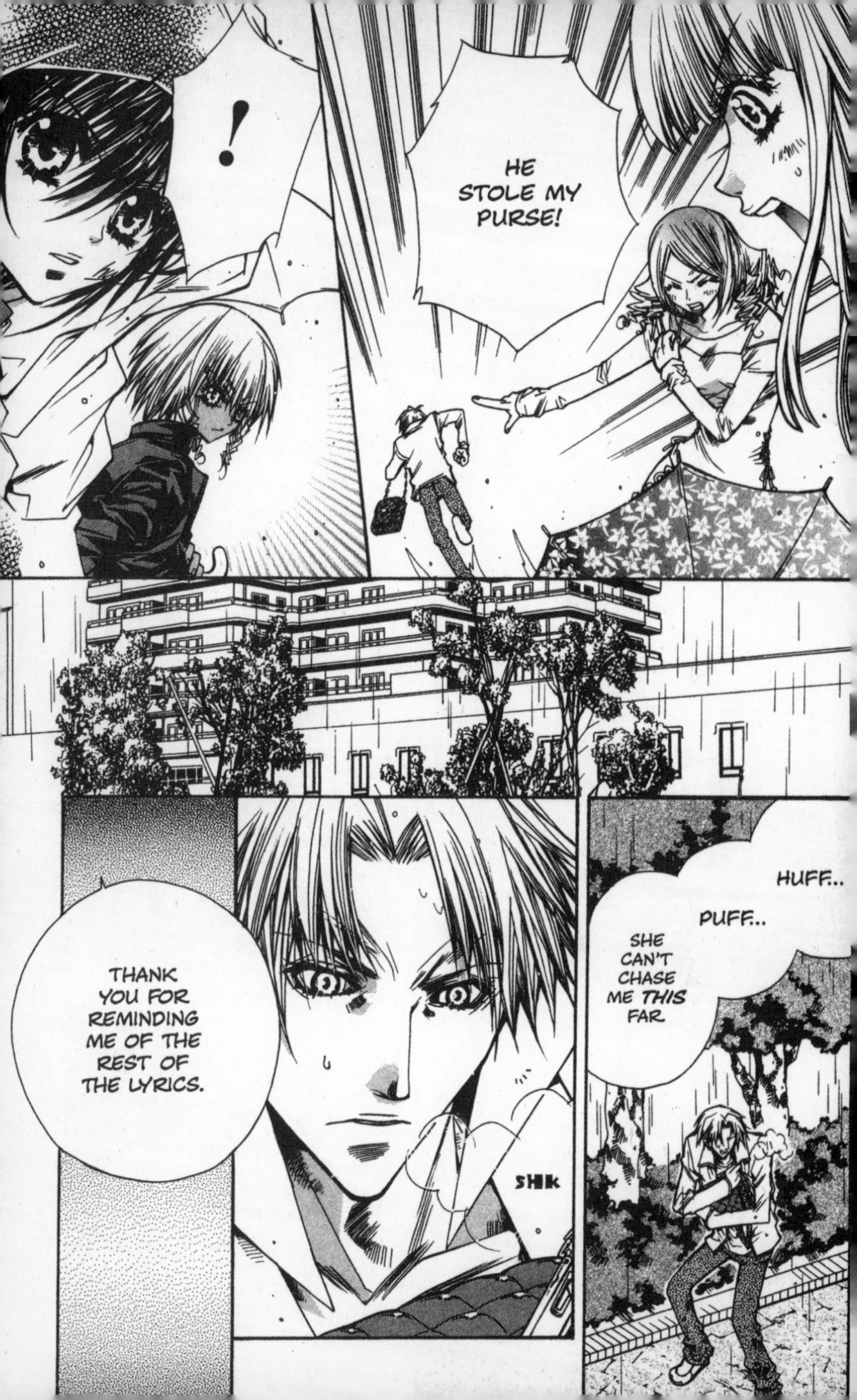
HE STOLE MY PURSE!
!
HUFF..
PUFF..
SHE CAN'T CHASE ME THIS FAR
SHIK
THANK YOU FOR REMINDING ME OF THE REST OF THE LYRICS.

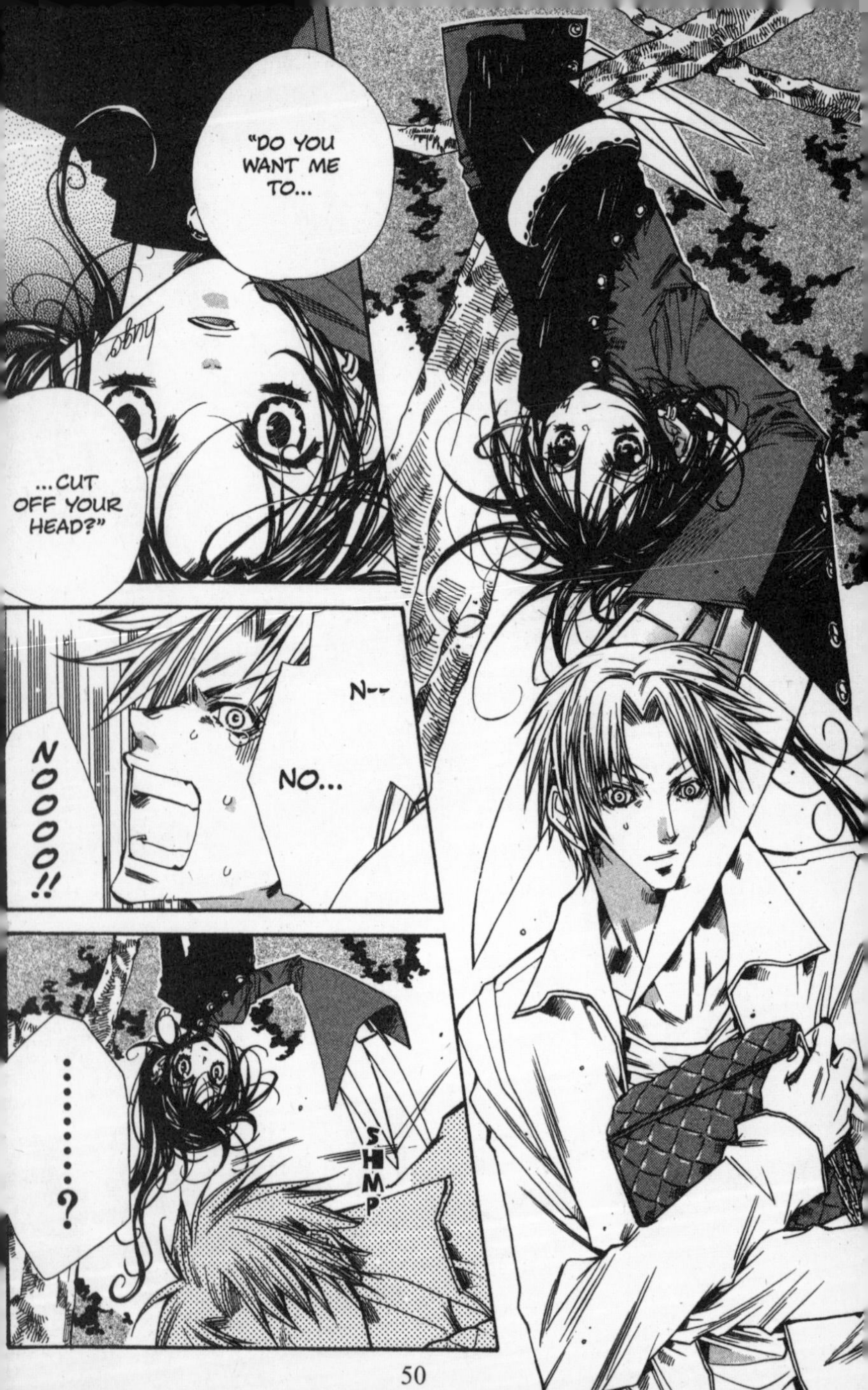
"DO YOU WANT ME TO...
...CUT OFF YOUR HEAD?"
N--
NO...
NOOOOO!!
SHMP
......?

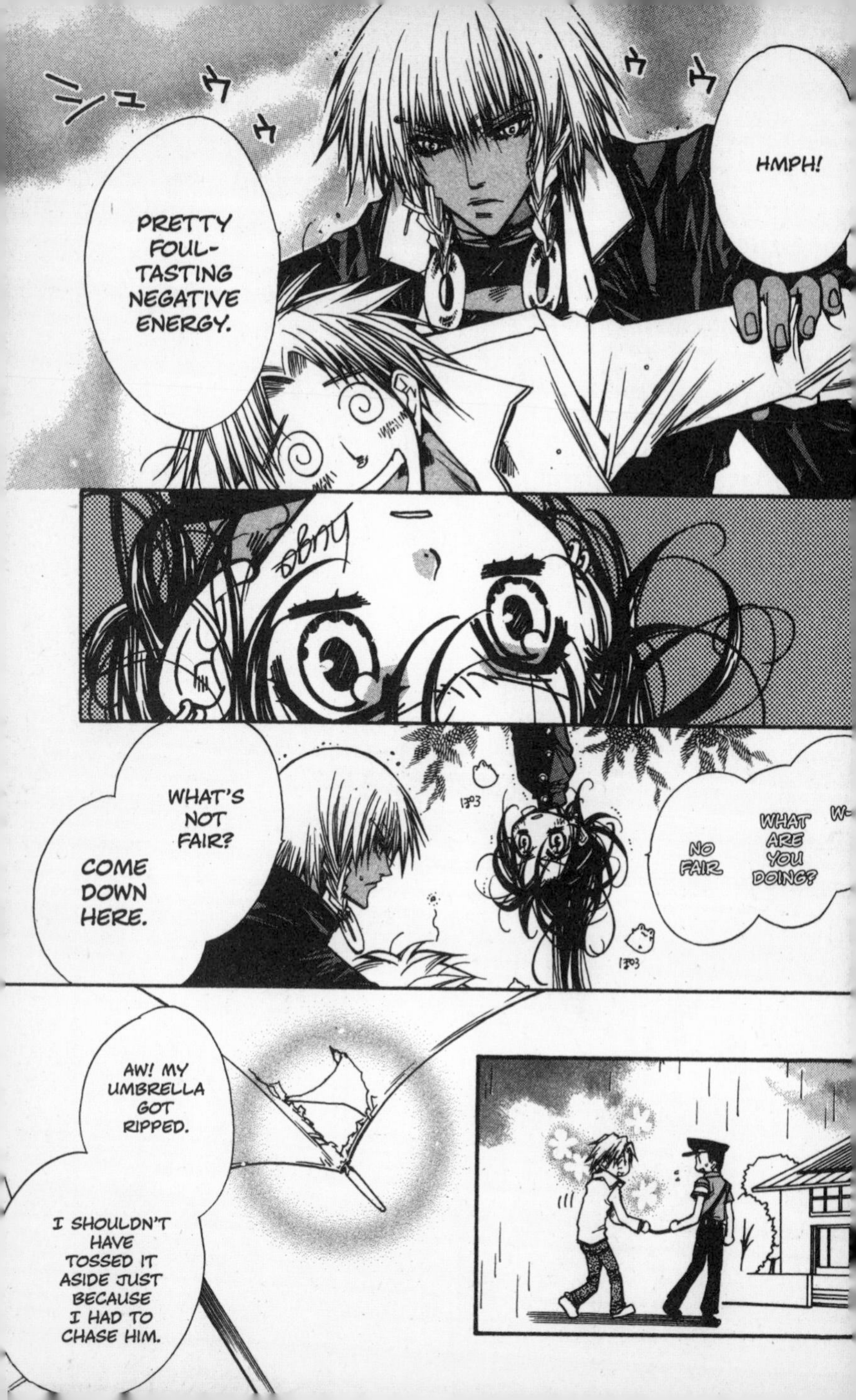
HMPH!
PRETTY FOUL-TASTING NEGATIVE ENERGY.
W-
WHAT ARE YOU DOING?
NO FAIR
WHAT'S NOT FAIR?
COME DOWN HERE.
AW! MY UMBRELLA GOT RIPPED.
I SHOULDN'T HAVE TOSSED IT ASIDE JUST BECAUSE I HAD TO CHASE HIM.

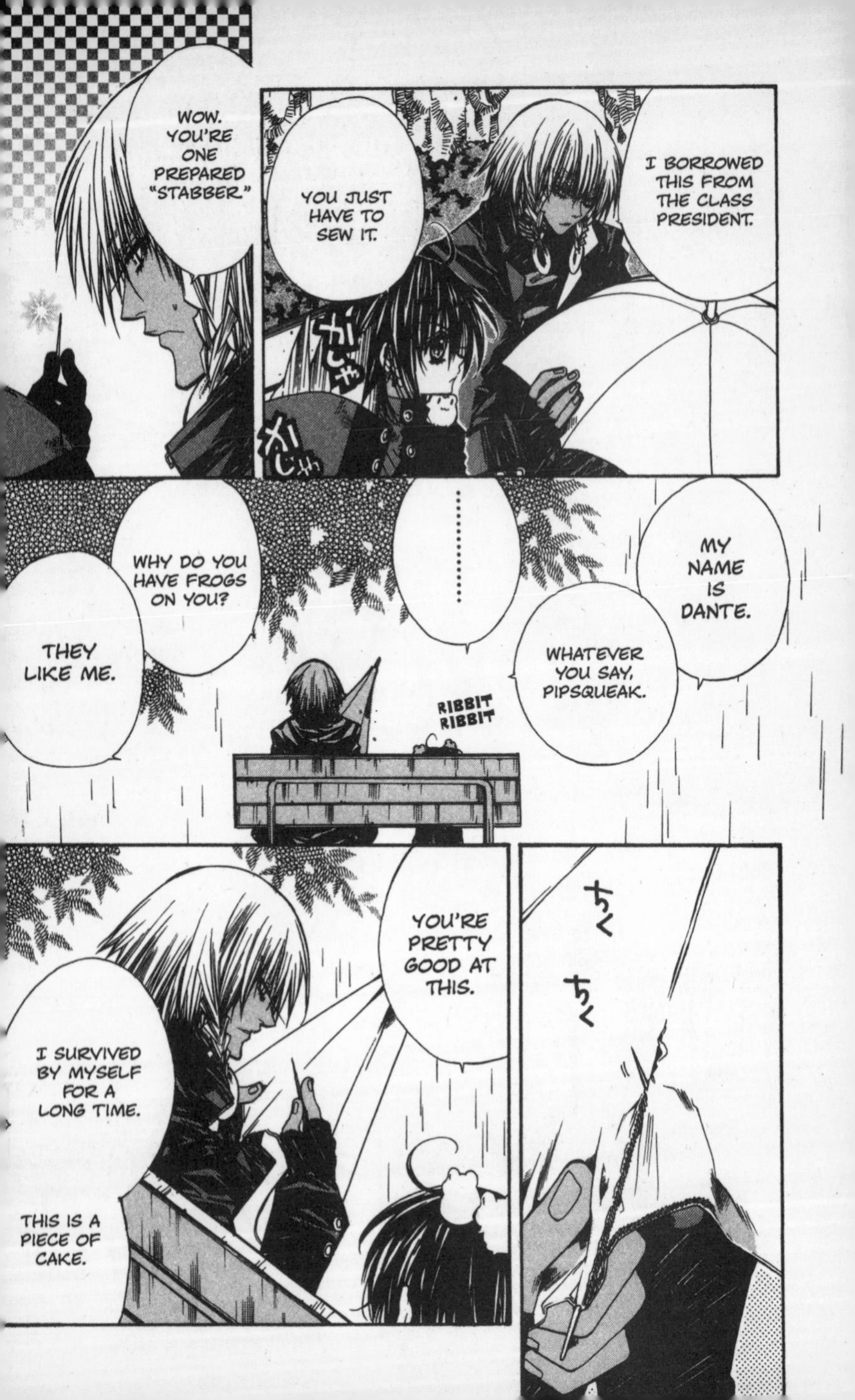
I BORROWED THIS FROM THE CLASS PRESIDENT.
YOU JUST HAVE TO SEW IT.
WOW. YOU'RE ONE PREPARED "STABBER."
MY NAME IS DANTE.
WHATEVER YOU SAY, PIPSQUEAK.
RIBBIT RIBBIT
....
WHY DO YOU HAVE FROGS ON YOU?
THEY LIKE ME.
ちく
ちく
YOU'RE PRETTY GOOD AT THIS.
I SURVIVED BY MYSELF FOR A LONG TIME.
THIS IS A PIECE OF CAKE.

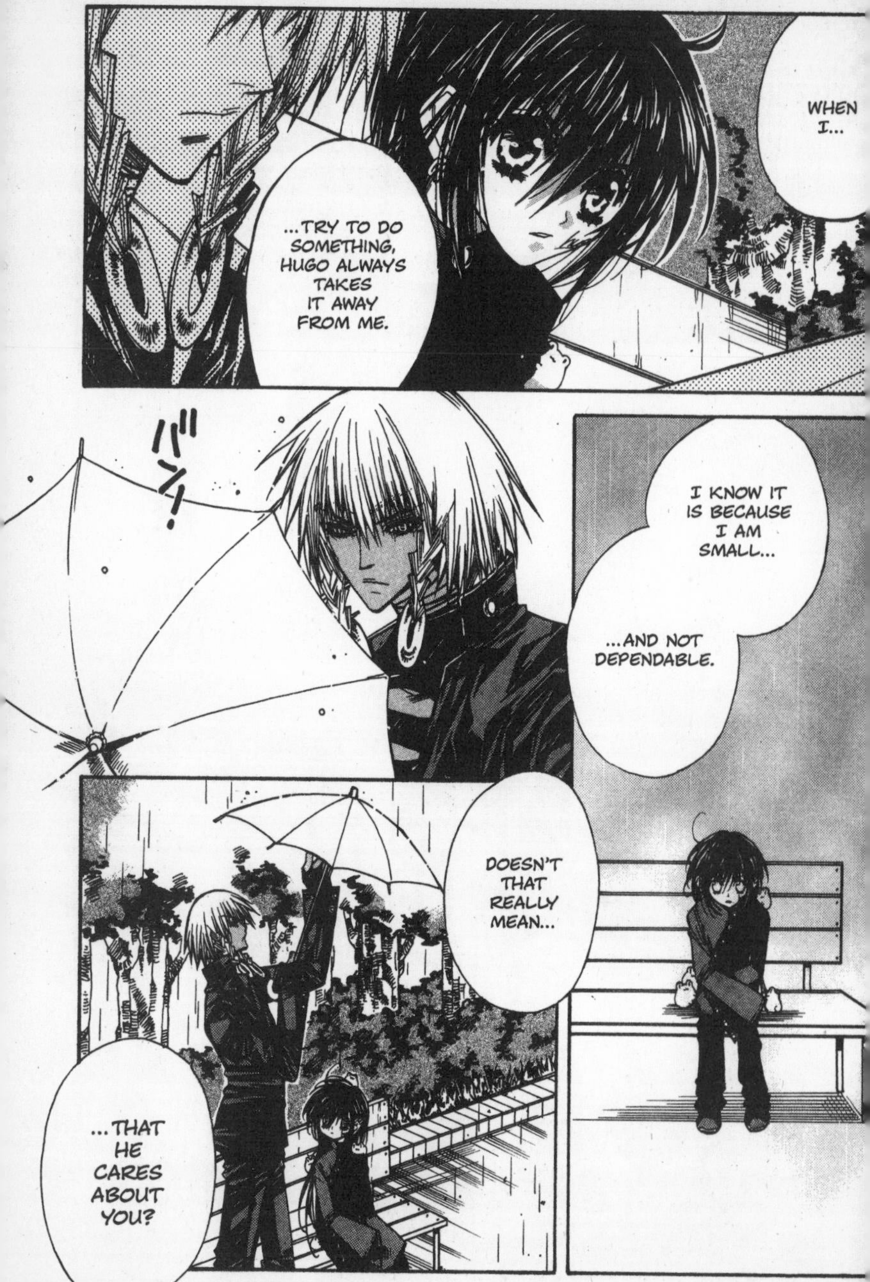
WHEN I...
...TRY TO DO SOMETHING, HUGO ALWAYS TAKES IT AWAY FROM ME.
I KNOW IT IS BECAUSE I AM SMALL...
...AND NOT DEPENDABLE.
バン!
DOESN'T THAT REALLY MEAN...
...THAT HE CARES ABOUT YOU?

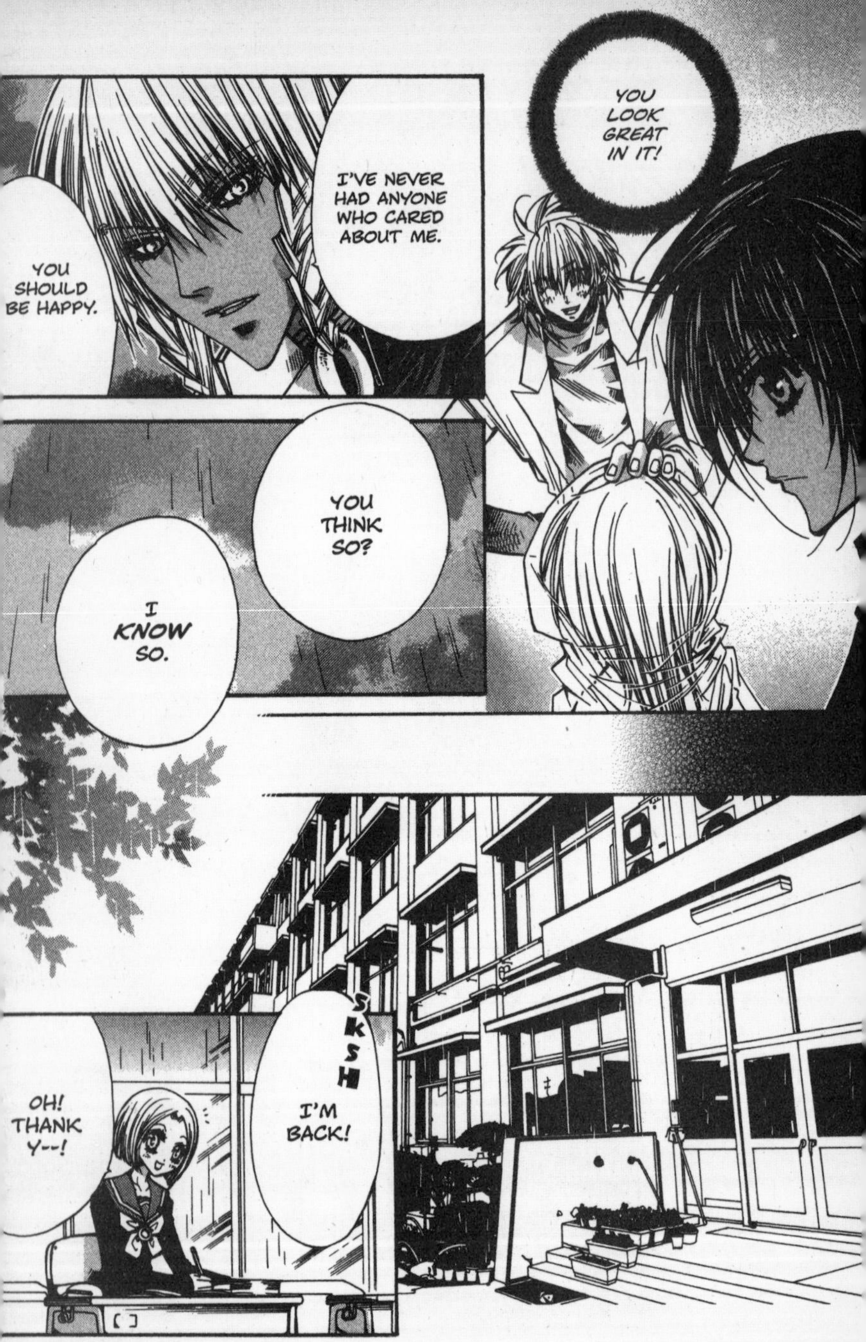
YOU LOOK GREAT IN IT!
I'VE NEVER HAD ANYONE WHO CARED ABOUT ME.
YOU SHOULD BE HAPPY.
YOU THINK SO?
I KNOW SO.
SKSH
I'M BACK!
OH! THANK Y--!

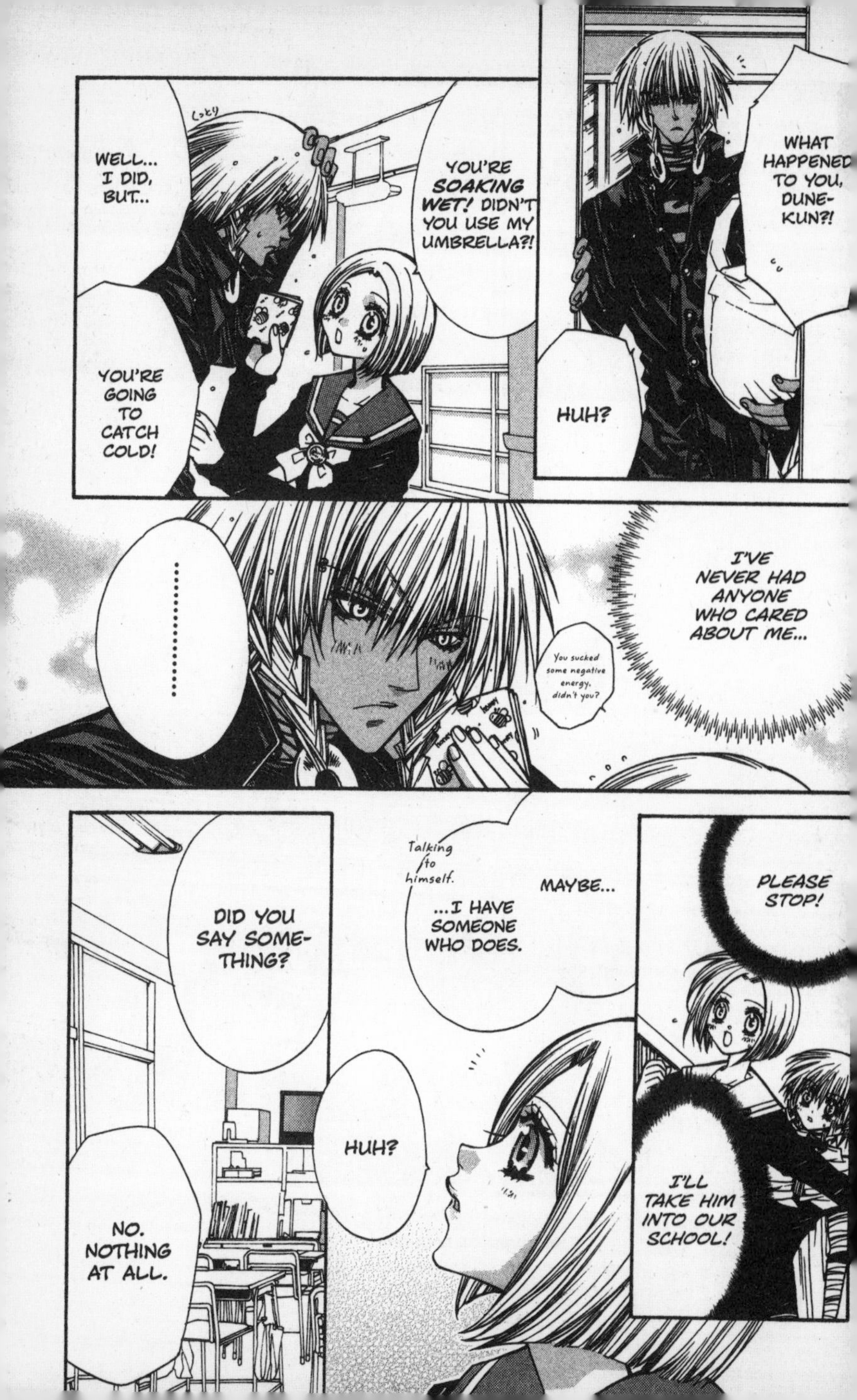
WHAT HAPPENED TO YOU, DUNE-KUN?!
HUH?
YOU'RE SOAKING WET! DIDN'T YOU USE MY UMBRELLA?!
WELL... I DID, BUT...
YOU'RE GOING TO CATCH COLD!
I'VE NEVER HAD ANYONE WHO CARED ABOUT ME...
You sucked some negative energy, didn't you?
......
PLEASE STOP!
I'LL TAKE HIM INTO OUR SCHOOL!
MAYBE...
...I HAVE SOMEONE WHO DOES.
Talking to himself.
DID YOU SAY SOMETHING?
HUH?
NO. NOTHING AT ALL.

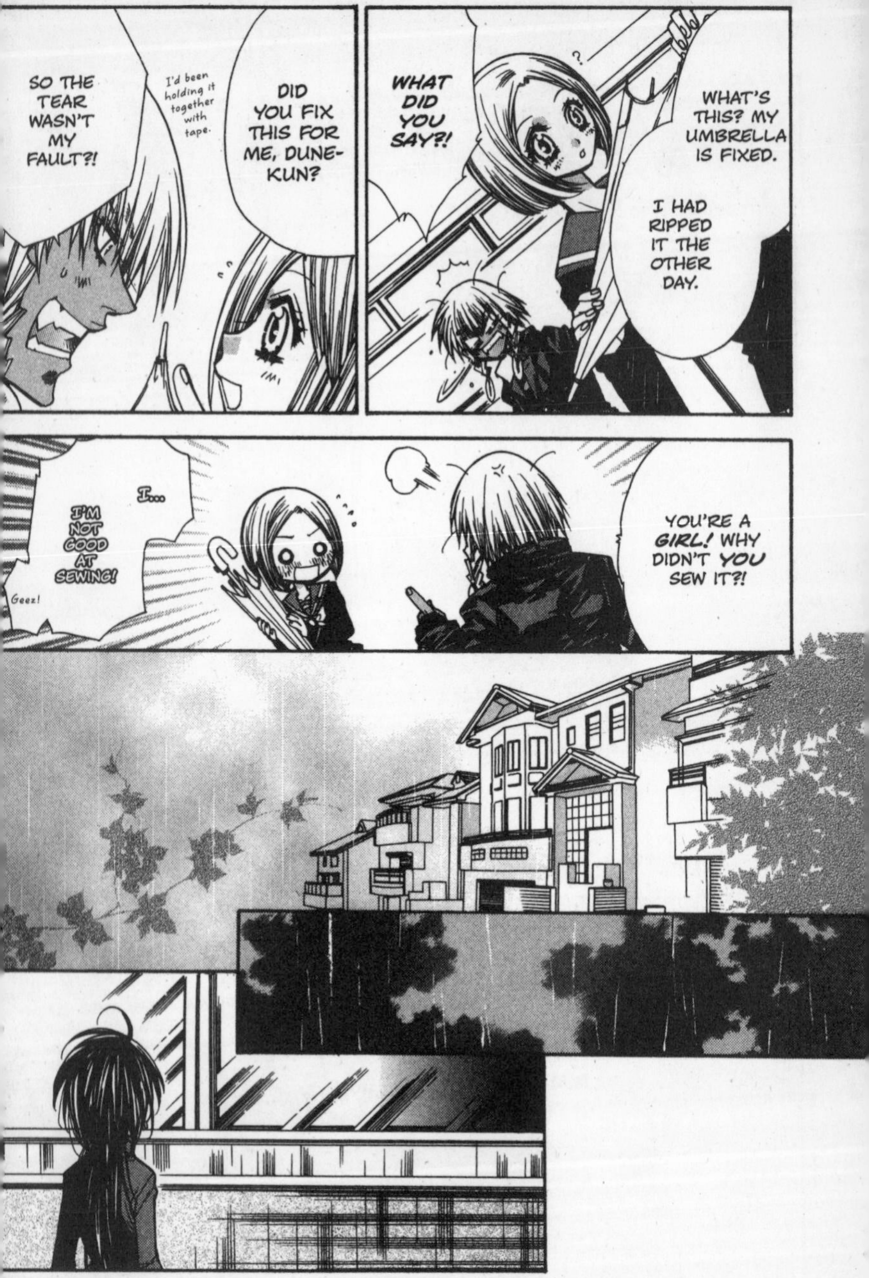

WHAT'S THIS? MY UMBRELLA IS FIXED.
I HAD RIPPED IT THE OTHER DAY.
?
WHAT DID YOU SAY?!
DID YOU FIX THIS FOR ME, DUNE-KUN?
I'd been holding it together with tape.
SO THE TEAR WASN'T MY FAULT?!
YOU'RE A GIRL! WHY DIDN'T YOU SEW IT?!
I...
I'M NOT GOOD AT SEWING!
Geez!

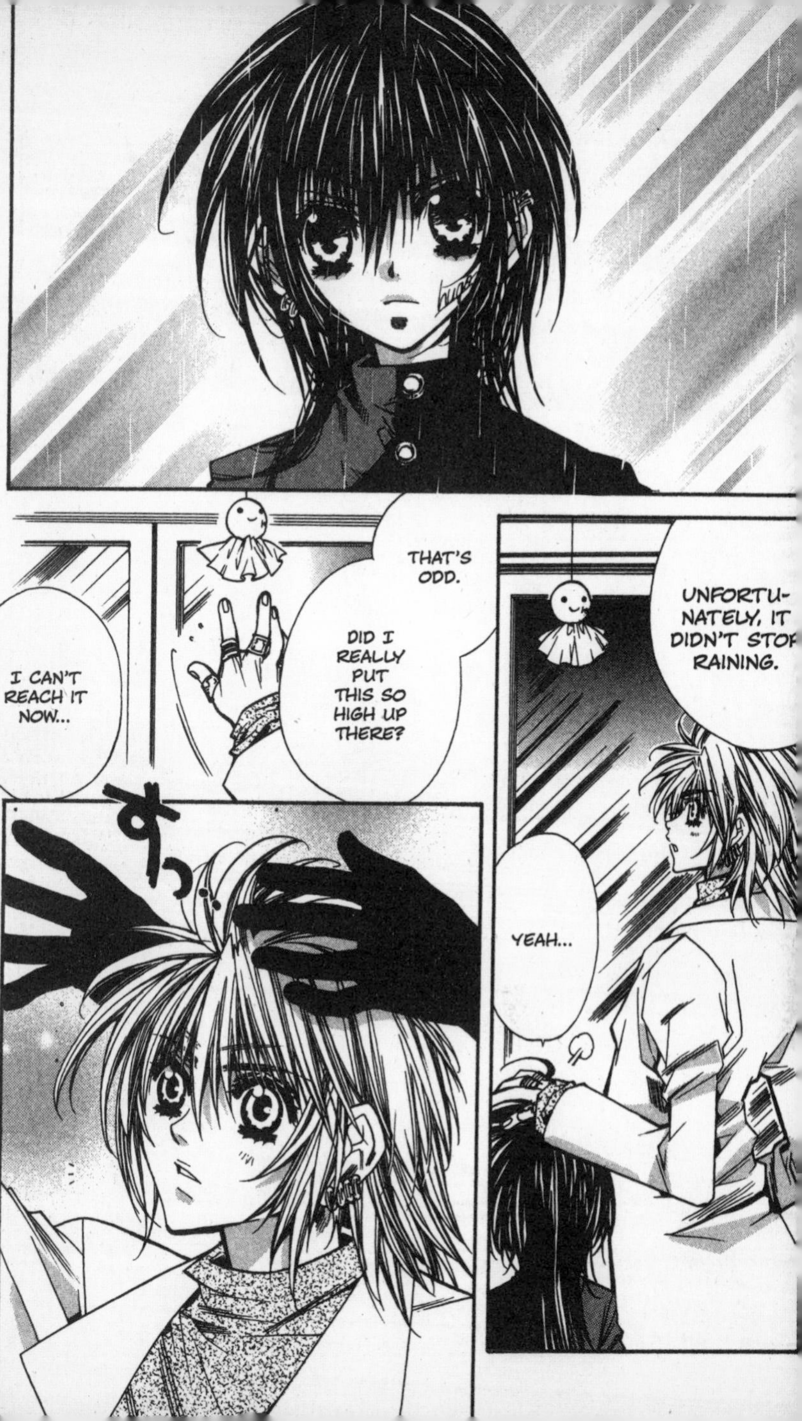
UNFORTUNATELY, IT DIDN'T STOP RAINING.
YEAH...
THAT'S ODD.
DID I REALLY PUT THIS SO HIGH UP THERE?
I CAN'T REACH IT NOW...
すっ

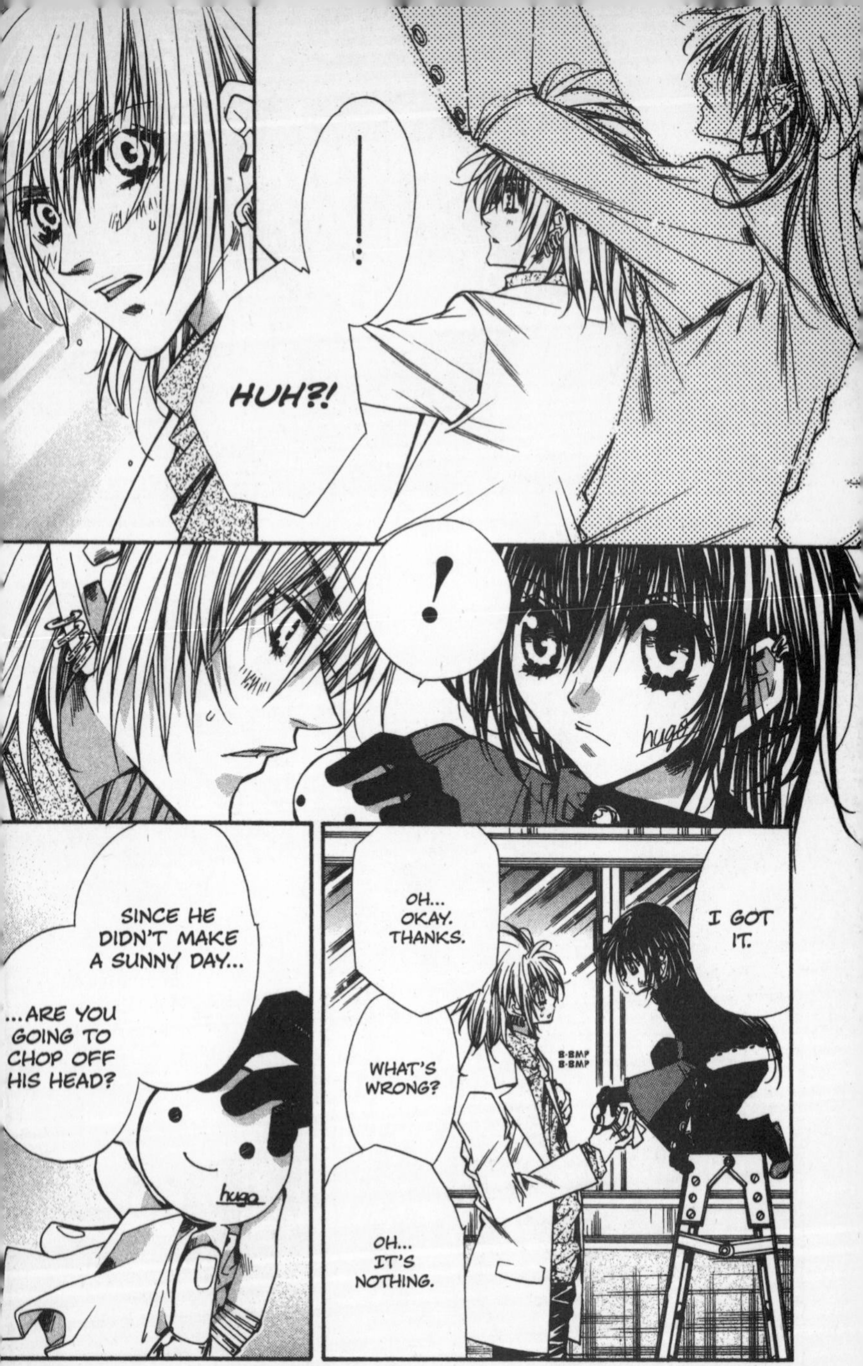
!...
HUH?!
!
hugo
I GOT IT.
OH... OKAY. THANKS.
B-BMP B-BMP
WHAT'S WRONG?
OH... IT'S NOTHING.
SINCE HE DIDN'T MAKE A SUNNY DAY...
...ARE YOU GOING TO CHOP OFF HIS HEAD?
hugo

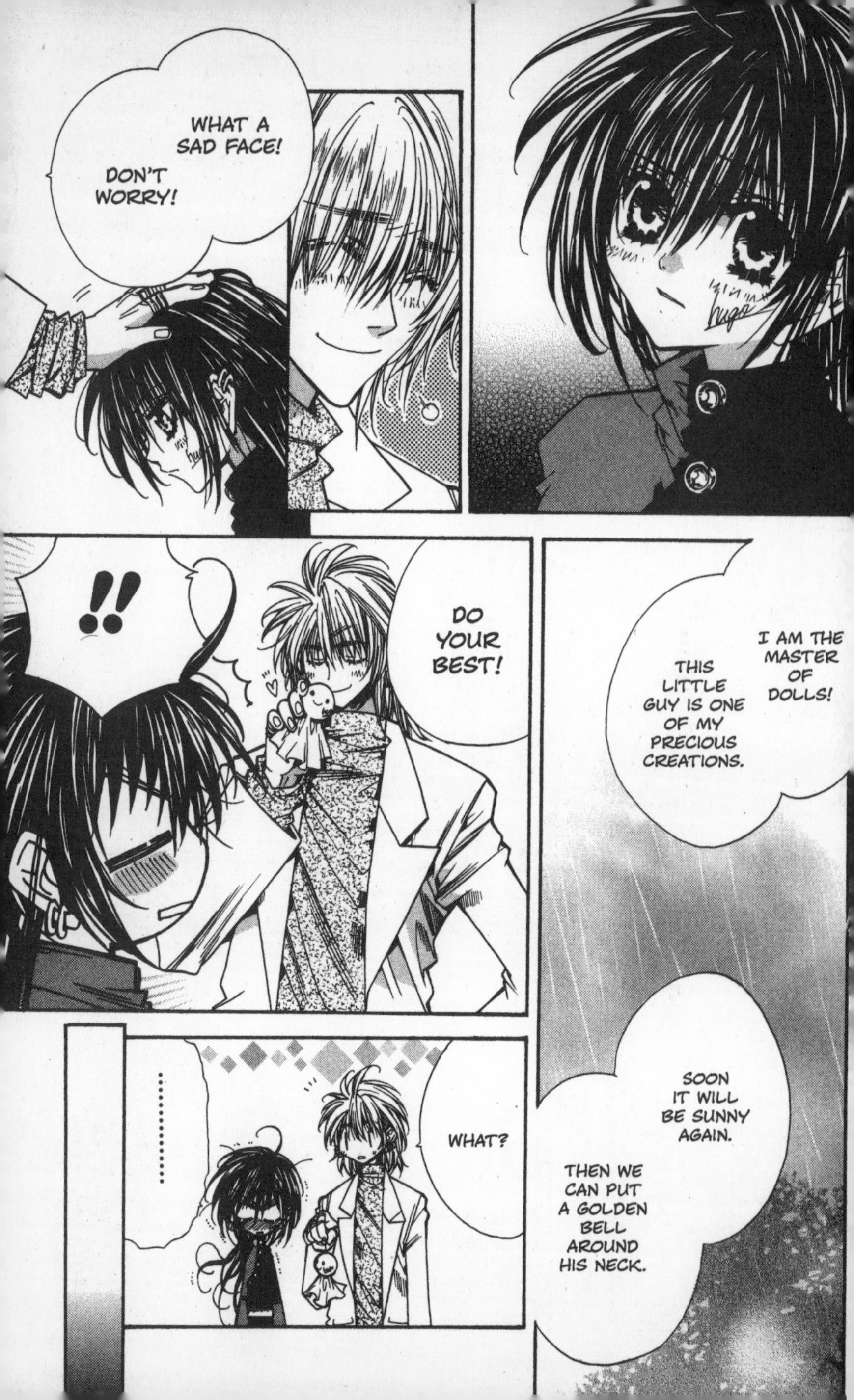
WHAT A SAD FACE!
DON'T WORRY!
I AM THE MASTER OF DOLLS!
THIS LITTLE GUY IS ONE OF MY PRECIOUS CREATIONS.
SOON IT WILL BE SUNNY AGAIN.
THEN WE CAN PUT A GOLDEN BELL AROUND HIS NECK.
DO YOUR BEST!
!!
WHAT?
....

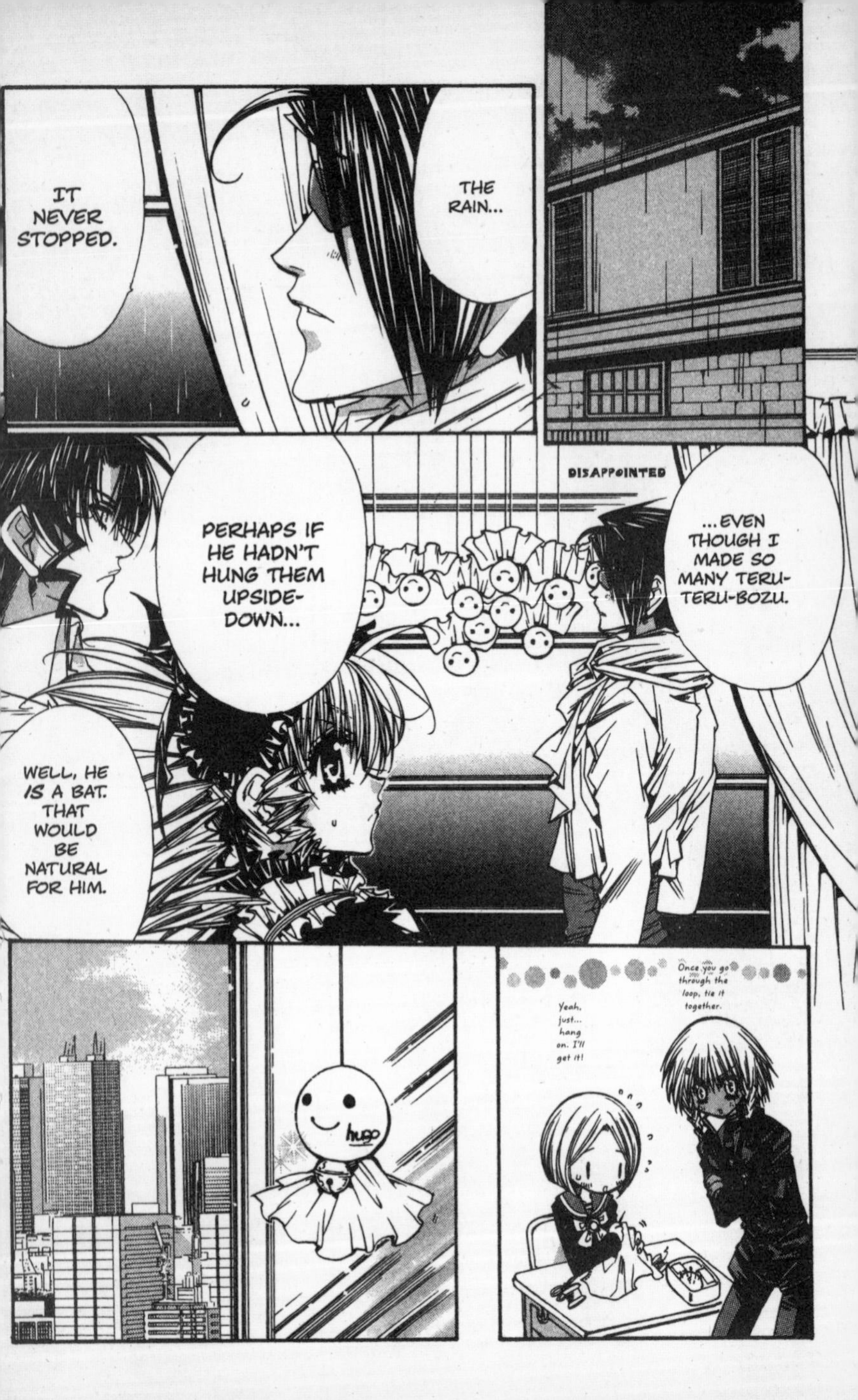
THE RAIN...
IT NEVER STOPPED.
DISAPPOINTED
...EVEN THOUGH I MADE SO MANY TERU-TERU-BOZU.
PERHAPS IF HE HADN'T HUNG THEM UPSIDE-DOWN...
WELL, HE *IS* A BAT. THAT WOULD BE NATURAL FOR HIM.
Once you go through the loop, tie it together.
Yeah, just... hang on. I'll get it!
hugo

BONUS COMIC STRIP

VAMPIRE DOLL REFLECTIONS

Singin' in the rain

WHAT'S YOUR NAME?
~DANTE & DUNE~
I AM NOT A PIPSQUEAK.
MY NAME IS DANTE.
WELL, THE THING IS...
...I DON'T USE PEOPLE'S REAL NAMES. INSTEAD, I PICK ONE BASED ON...
...A UNIQUE TALENT, FEATURE OR TRAIT.
....
OKAY, THEN, MR SUCKER.
THAT'S AN AWFUL NAME!

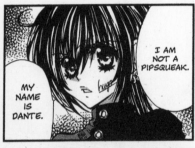

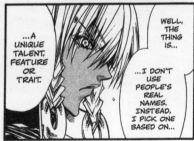

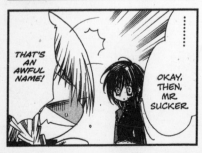

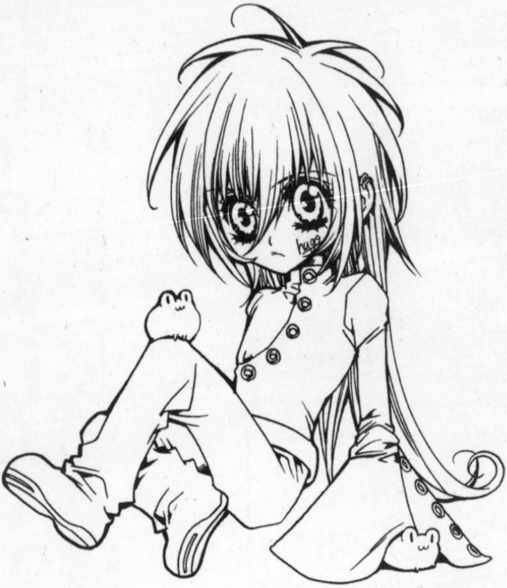
hugs

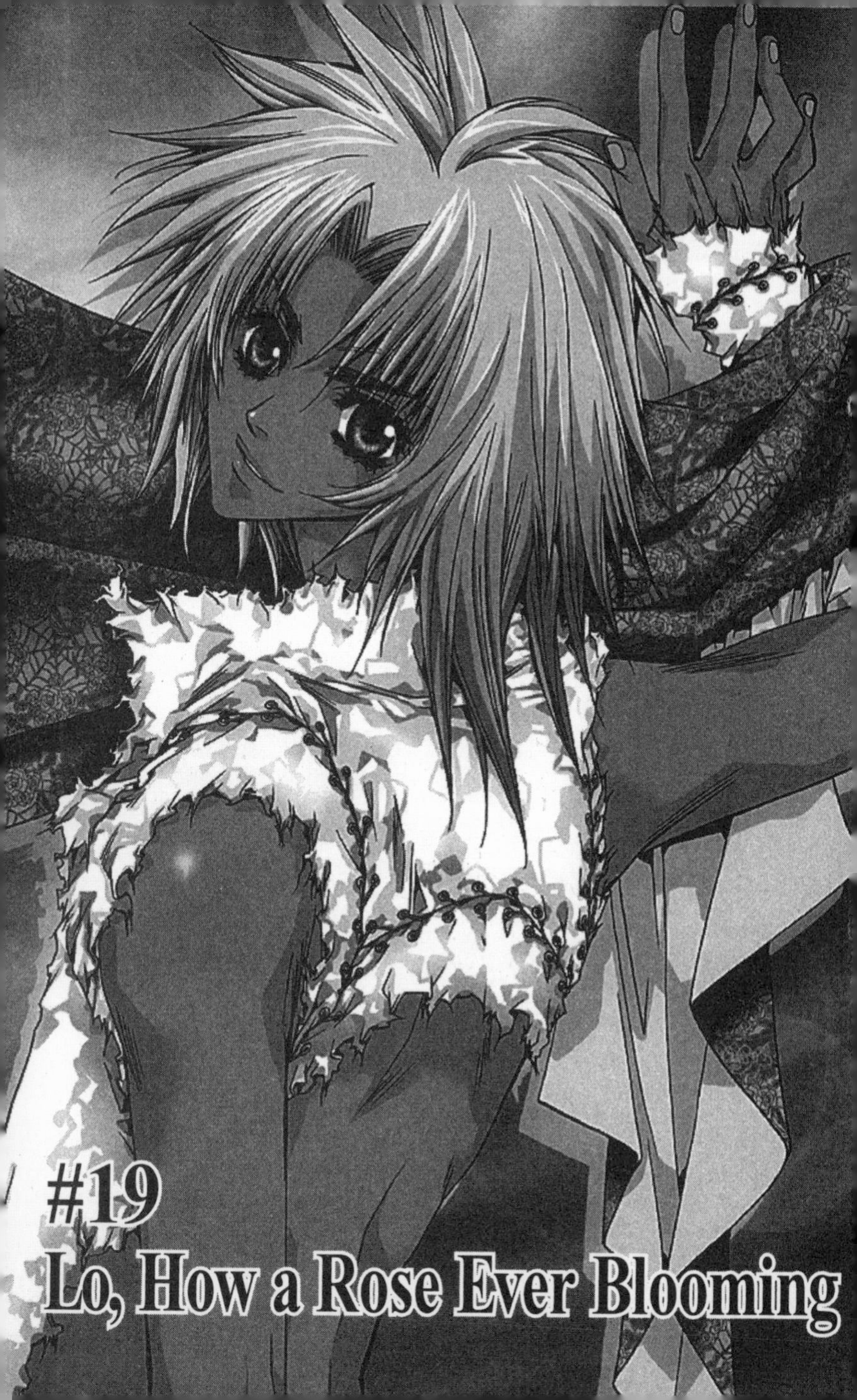

#19
Lo, How a Rose Ever Blooming

Vampire Doll
ギルネサン

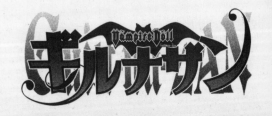

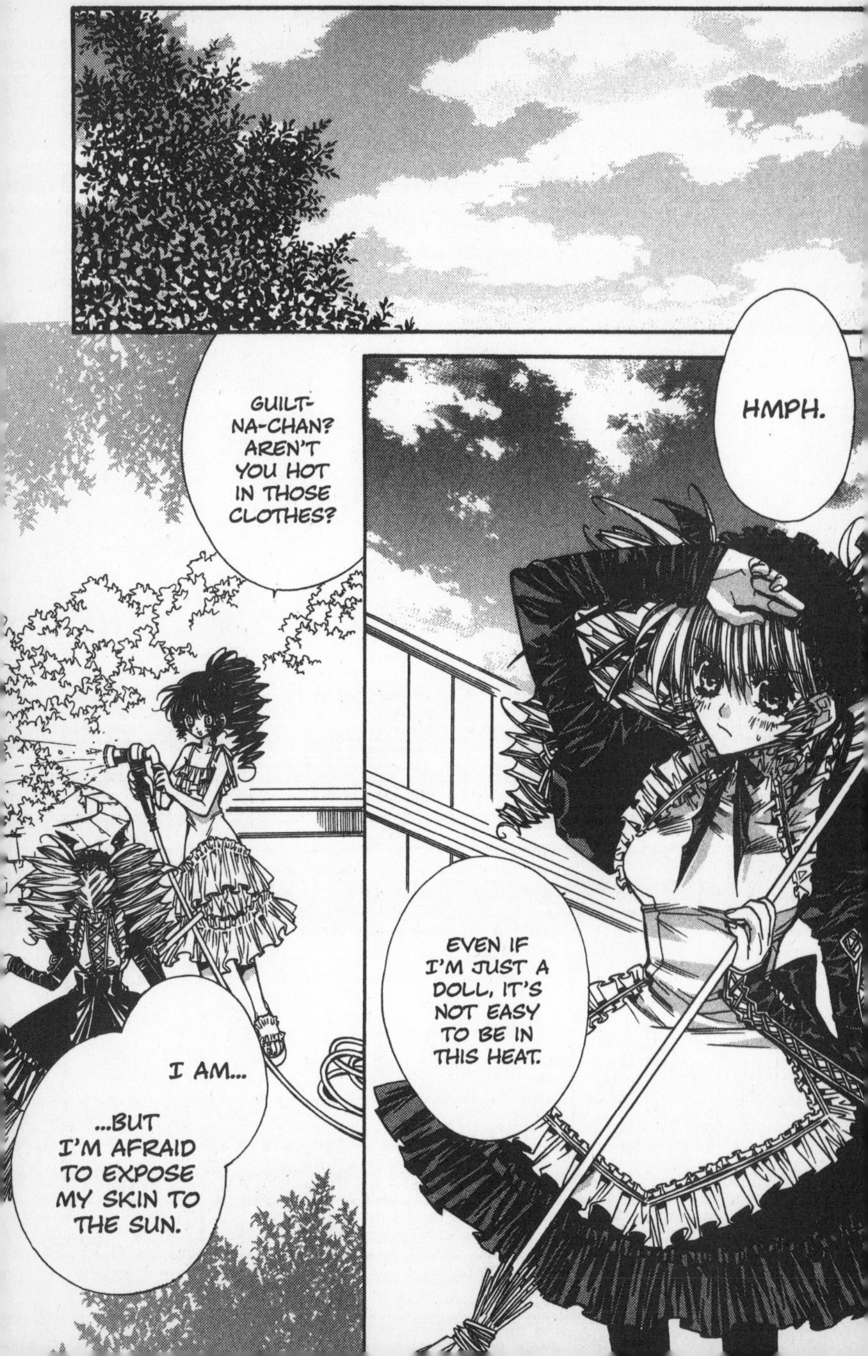
HMPH.
EVEN IF I'M JUST A DOLL, IT'S NOT EASY TO BE IN THIS HEAT.
GUILT-NA-CHAN? AREN'T YOU HOT IN THOSE CLOTHES?
I AM...
...BUT I'M AFRAID TO EXPOSE MY SKIN TO THE SUN.

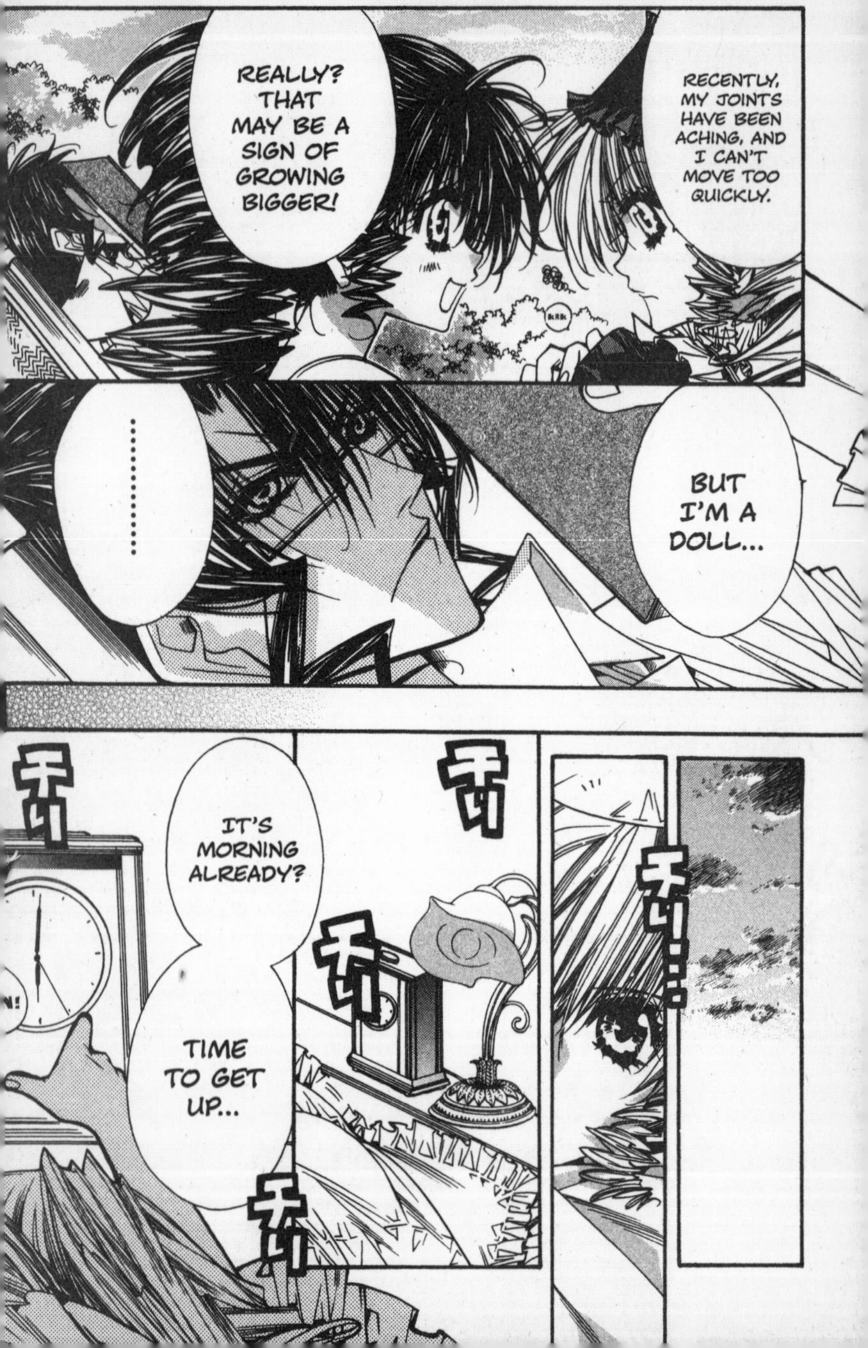
RECENTLY, MY JOINTS HAVE BEEN ACHING, AND I CAN'T MOVE TOO QUICKLY.
REALLY? THAT MAY BE A SIGN OF GROWING BIGGER!
BUT I'M A DOLL...
......
チリ...
チリ
チリ
チリ
IT'S MORNING ALREADY?
TIME TO GET UP...
チリ

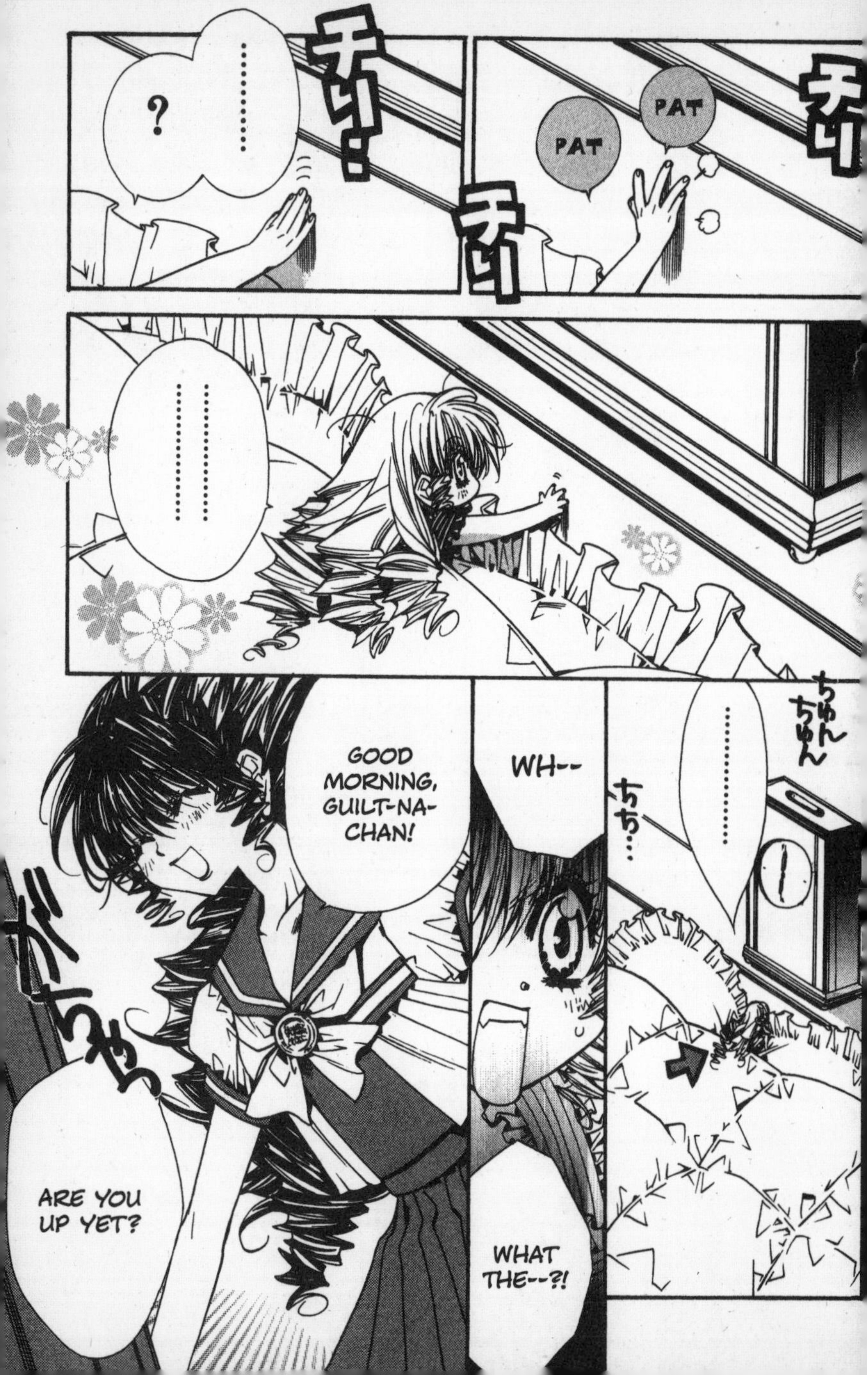

チリ
PAT
PAT
チリ
チリ!
……?
……
ちゅん ちゅん
……!
ちち…
WH--
WHAT THE--?!
GOOD MORNING, GUILT-NA-CHAN!
ARE YOU UP YET?

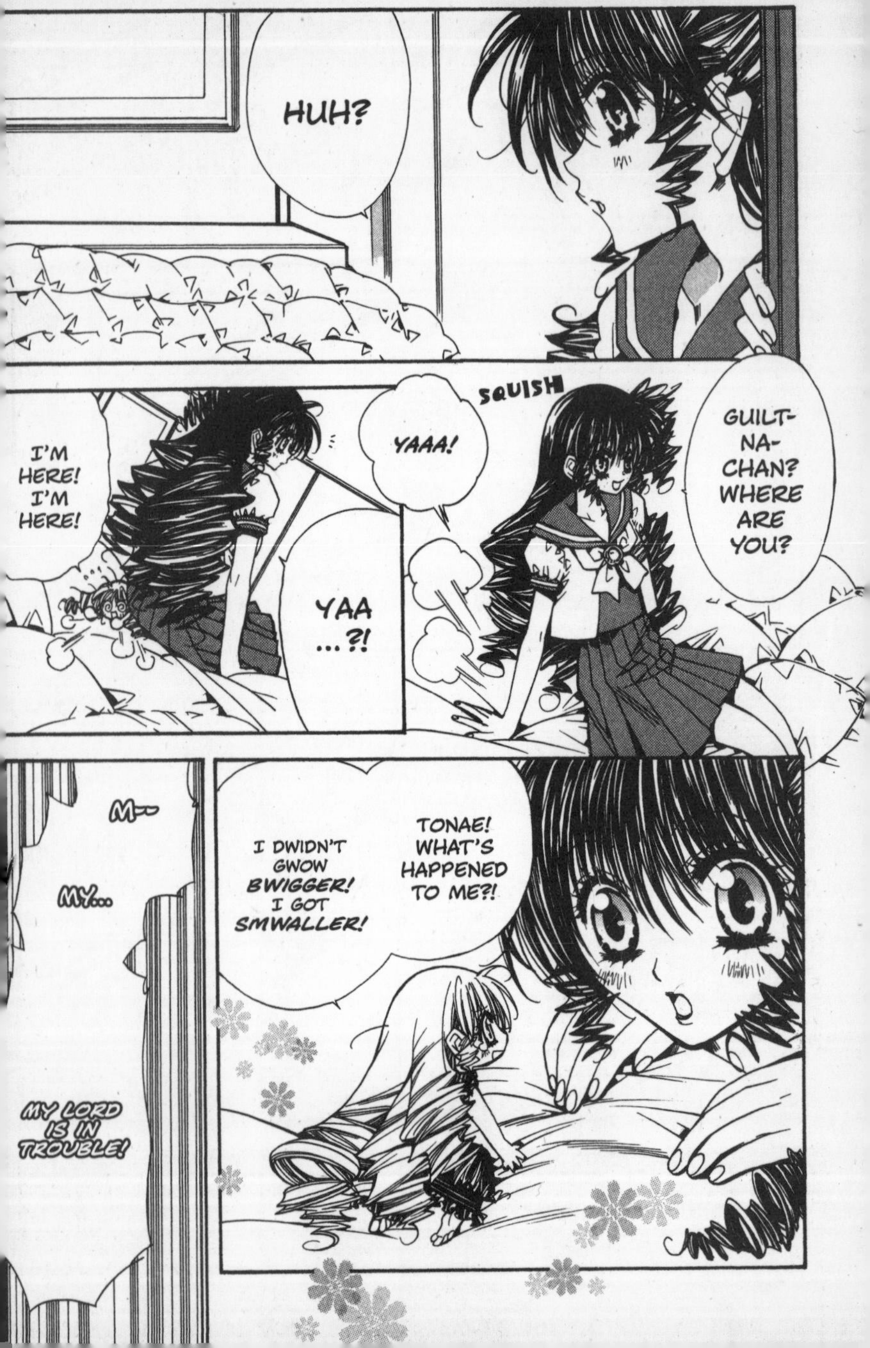
HUH?
GUILT-NA-CHAN? WHERE ARE YOU?
SQUISH
YAAA!
YAA ...?!
I'M HERE! I'M HERE!
TONAE! WHAT'S HAPPENED TO ME?!
I DWIDN'T GWOW BWIGGER! I GOT SMWALLER!
M--
MY...
MY LORD IS IN TROUBLE!

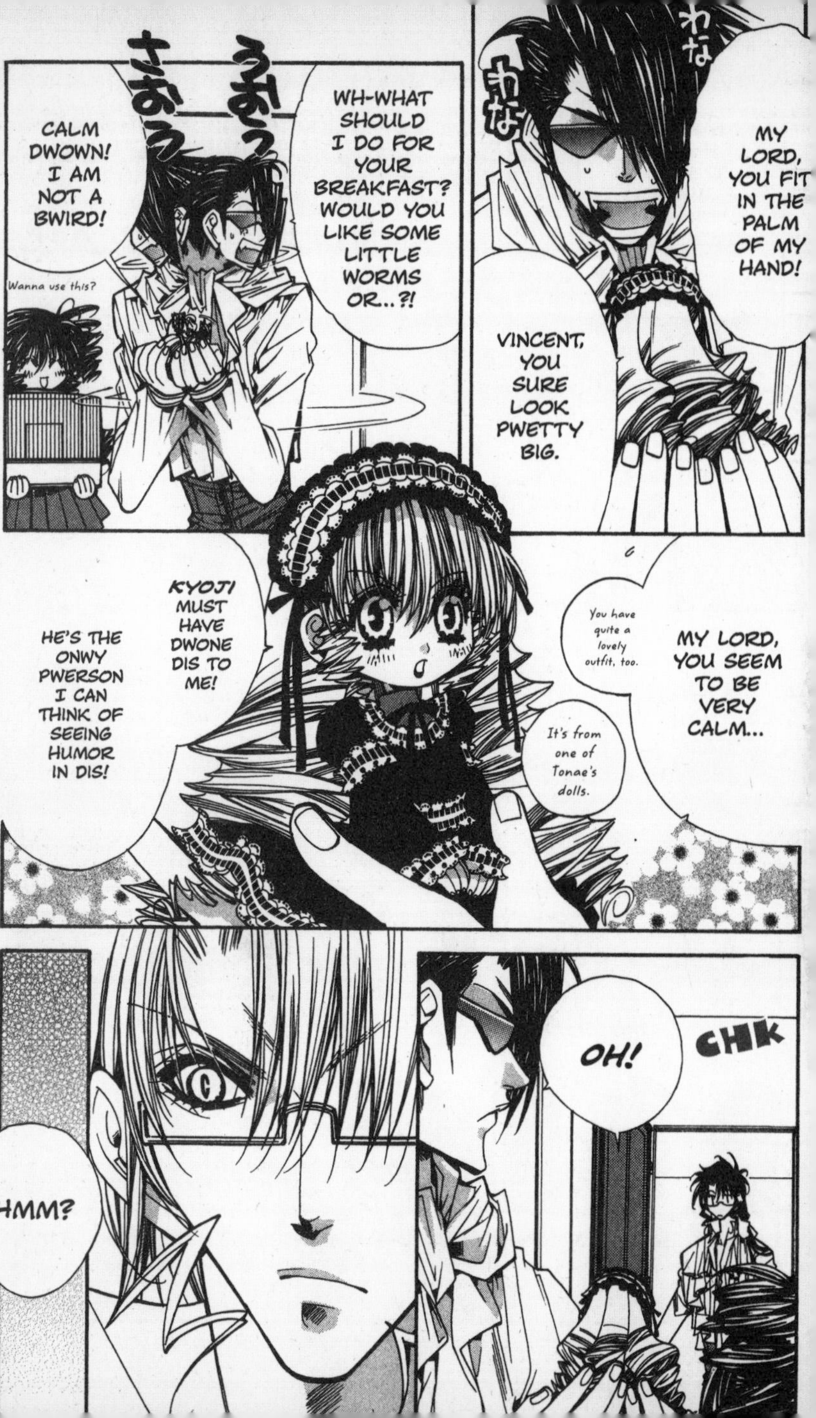

わなわな
MY LORD, YOU FIT IN THE PALM OF MY HAND!
VINCENT, YOU SURE LOOK PWETTY BIG.
WH-WHAT SHOULD I DO FOR YOUR BREAKFAST? WOULD YOU LIKE SOME LITTLE WORMS OR..?!
CALM DWOWN! I AM NOT A BWIRD!
Wanna use this?
MY LORD, YOU SEEM TO BE VERY CALM...
You have quite a lovely outfit, too.
It's from one of Tonae's dolls.
KYOJI MUST HAVE DWONE DIS TO ME!
HE'S THE ONWY PWERSON I CAN THINK OF SEEING HUMOR IN DIS!
CHK
OH!
HMM?

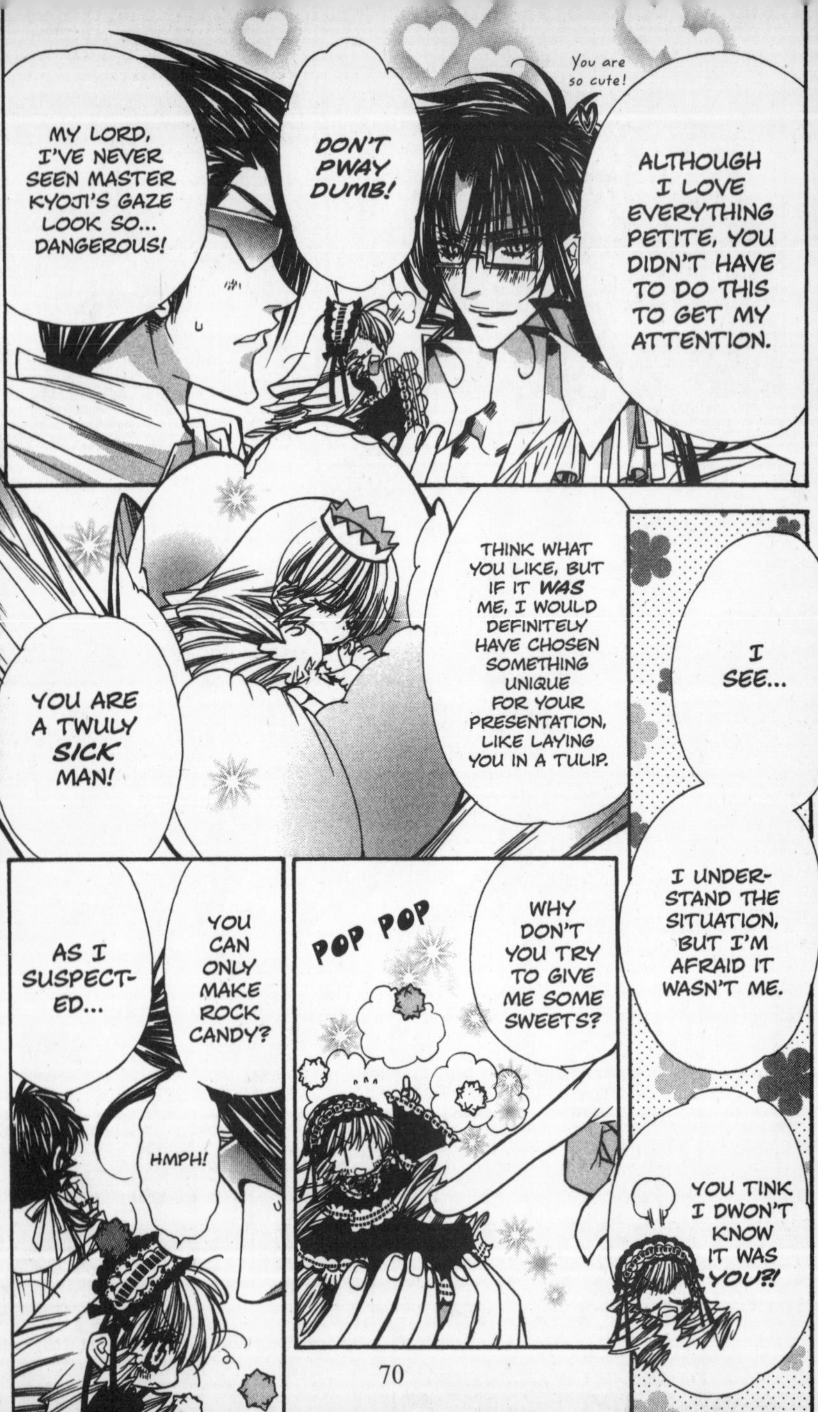
You are so cute!
ALTHOUGH I LOVE EVERYTHING PETITE, YOU DIDN'T HAVE TO DO THIS TO GET MY ATTENTION.
DON'T PWAY DUMB!
MY LORD, I'VE NEVER SEEN MASTER KYOJI'S GAZE LOOK SO... DANGEROUS!
I SEE...
I UNDER-STAND THE SITUATION, BUT I'M AFRAID IT WASN'T ME.
YOU TINK I DWON'T KNOW IT WAS YOU?!
THINK WHAT YOU LIKE, BUT IF IT WAS ME, I WOULD DEFINITELY HAVE CHOSEN SOMETHING UNIQUE FOR YOUR PRESENTATION, LIKE LAYING YOU IN A TULIP.
YOU ARE A TWULY SICK MAN!
WHY DON'T YOU TRY TO GIVE ME SOME SWEETS?
POP POP
YOU CAN ONLY MAKE ROCK CANDY?
AS I SUSPECT-ED...
HMPH!

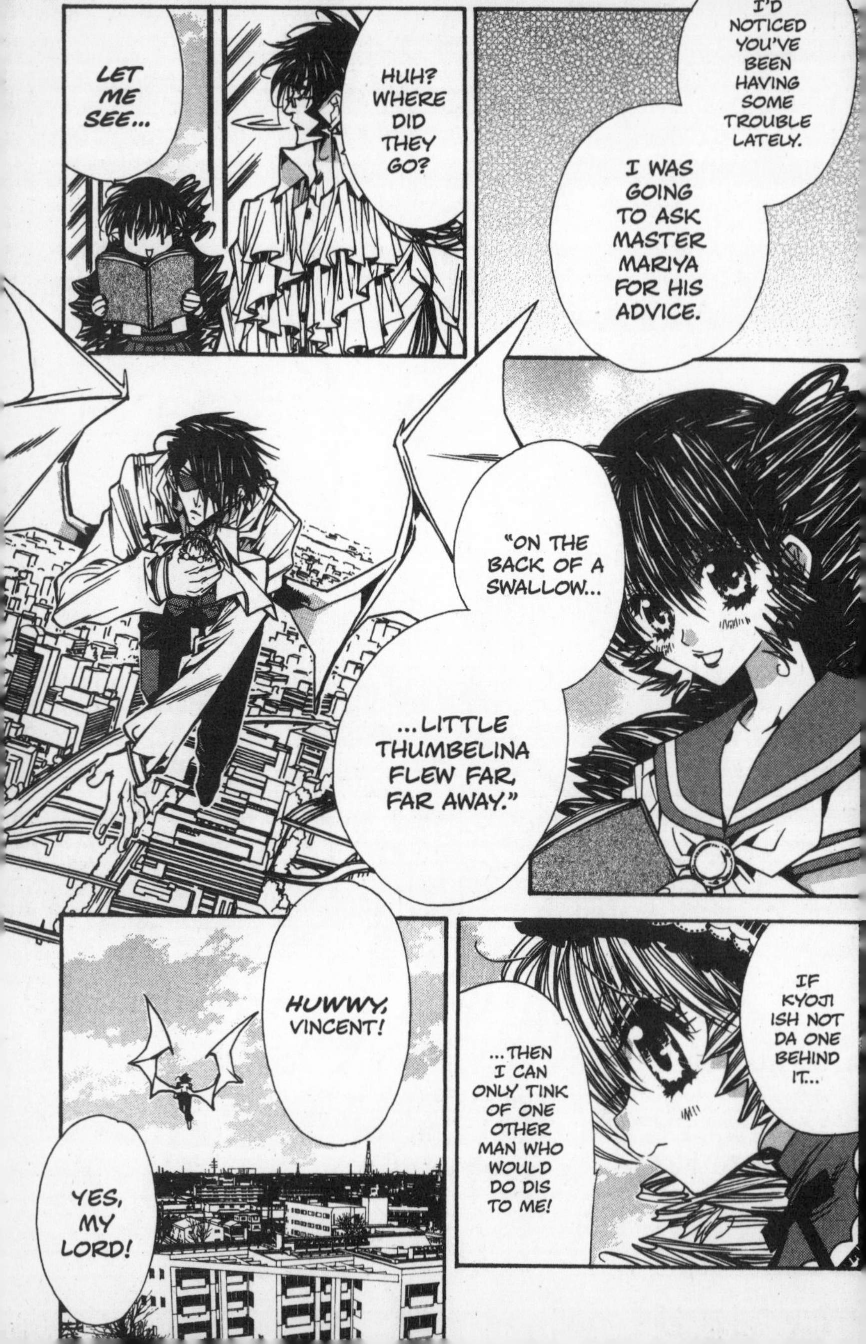
I'D NOTICED YOU'VE BEEN HAVING SOME TROUBLE LATELY.
I WAS GOING TO ASK MASTER MARIYA FOR HIS ADVICE.
HUH? WHERE DID THEY GO?
LET ME SEE...
"ON THE BACK OF A SWALLOW...
...LITTLE THUMBELINA FLEW FAR, FAR AWAY."
IF KYOJI ISH NOT DA ONE BEHIND IT...
...THEN I CAN ONLY TINK OF ONE OTHER MAN WHO WOULD DO DIS TO ME!
HUWWY, VINCENT!
YES, MY LORD!

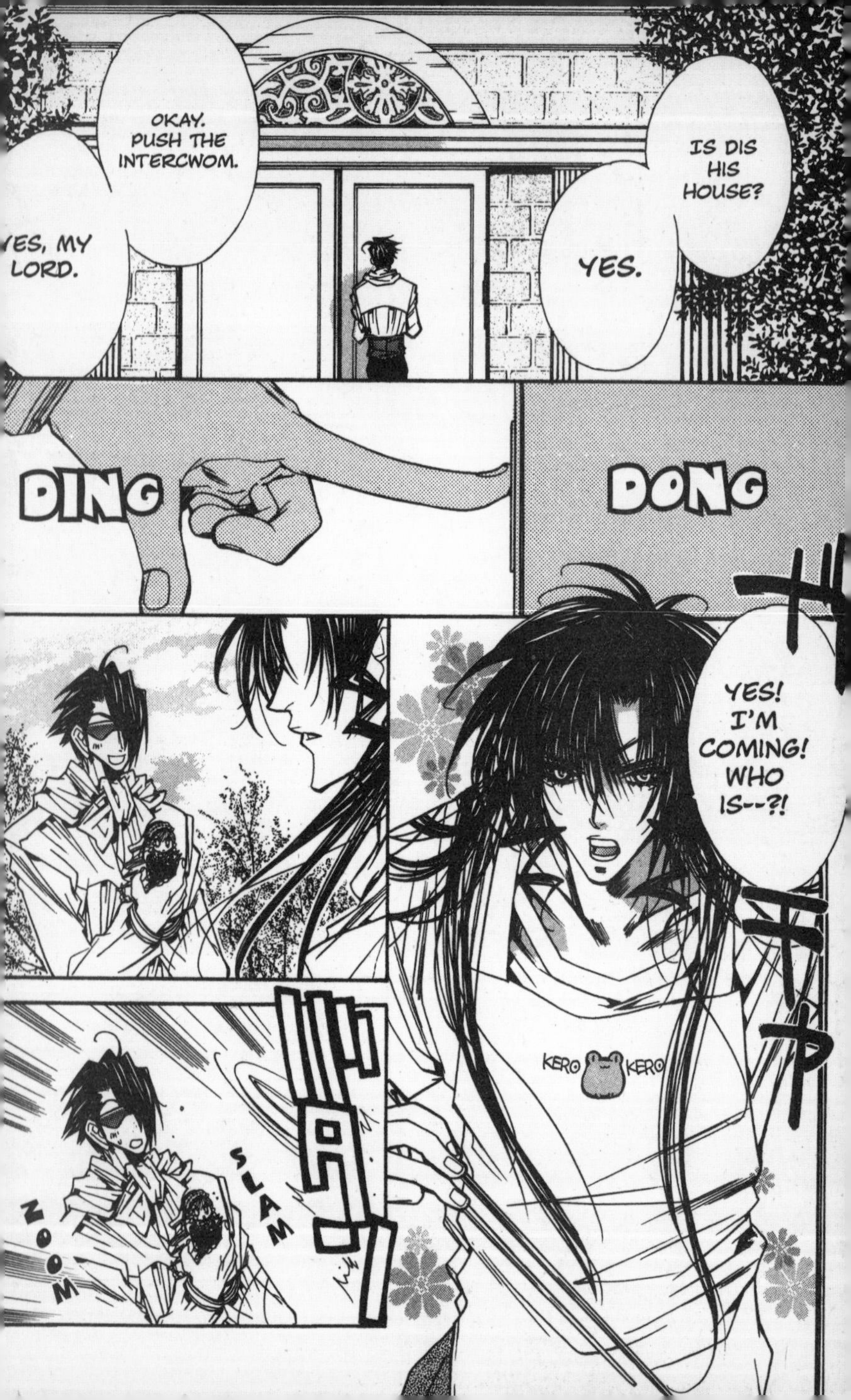
IS DIS HIS HOUSE?
YES.
OKAY. PUSH THE INTERCWOM.
YES, MY LORD.
DONG
DING
YES! I'M COMING! WHO IS--?!
KERO KERO
SLAM
ZOOM

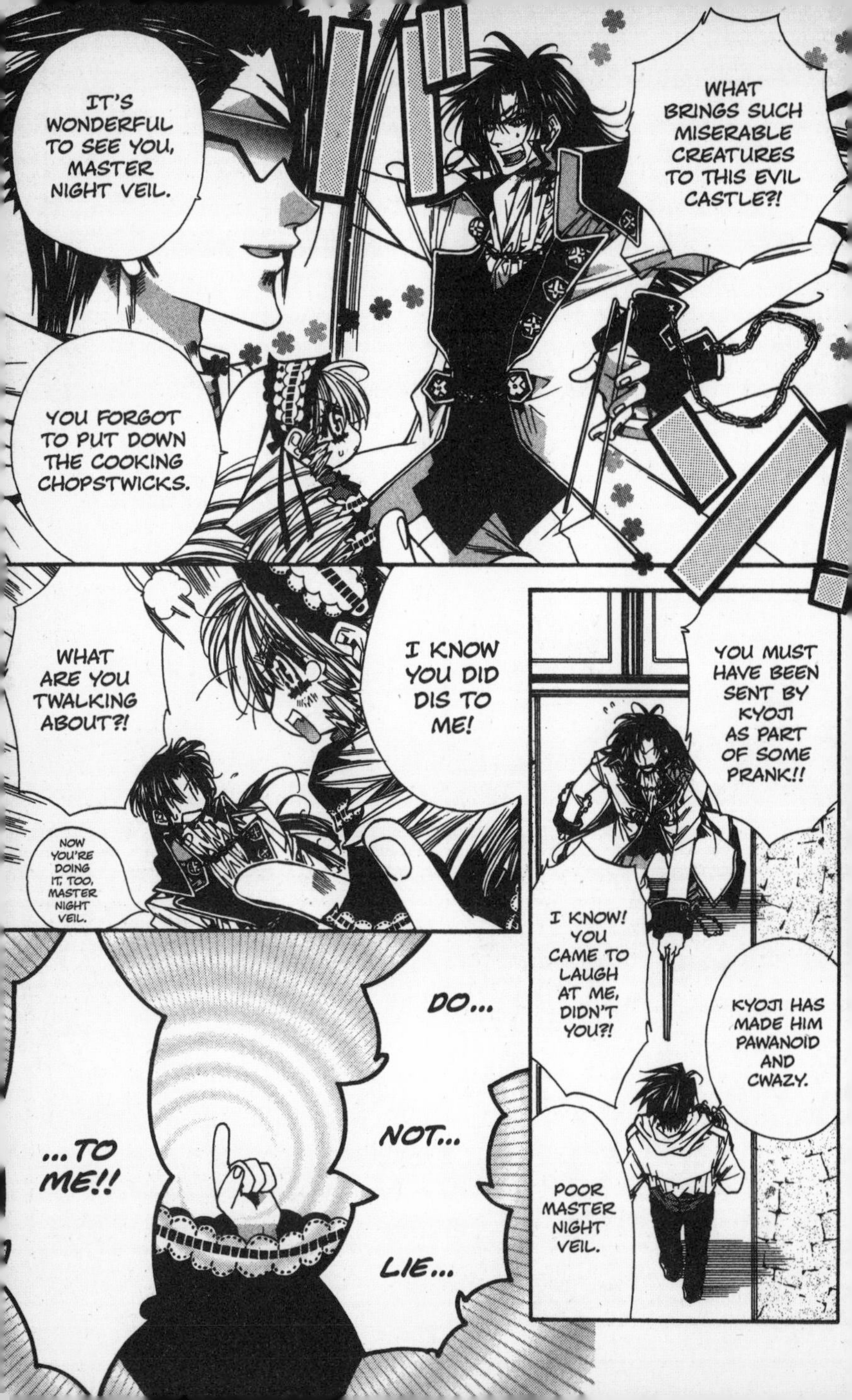
WHAT BRINGS SUCH MISERABLE CREATURES TO THIS EVIL CASTLE?!
IT'S WONDERFUL TO SEE YOU, MASTER NIGHT VEIL.
YOU FORGOT TO PUT DOWN THE COOKING CHOPSTWICKS.
YOU MUST HAVE BEEN SENT BY KYOJI AS PART OF SOME PRANK!!
I KNOW! YOU CAME TO LAUGH AT ME, DIDN'T YOU?!
KYOJI HAS MADE HIM PAWANOID AND CWAZY.
POOR MASTER NIGHT VEIL.
I KNOW YOU DID DIS TO ME!
WHAT ARE YOU TWALKING ABOUT?!
NOW YOU'RE DOING IT, TOO, MASTER NIGHT VEIL.
DO...
NOT...
LIE...
...TO ME!!

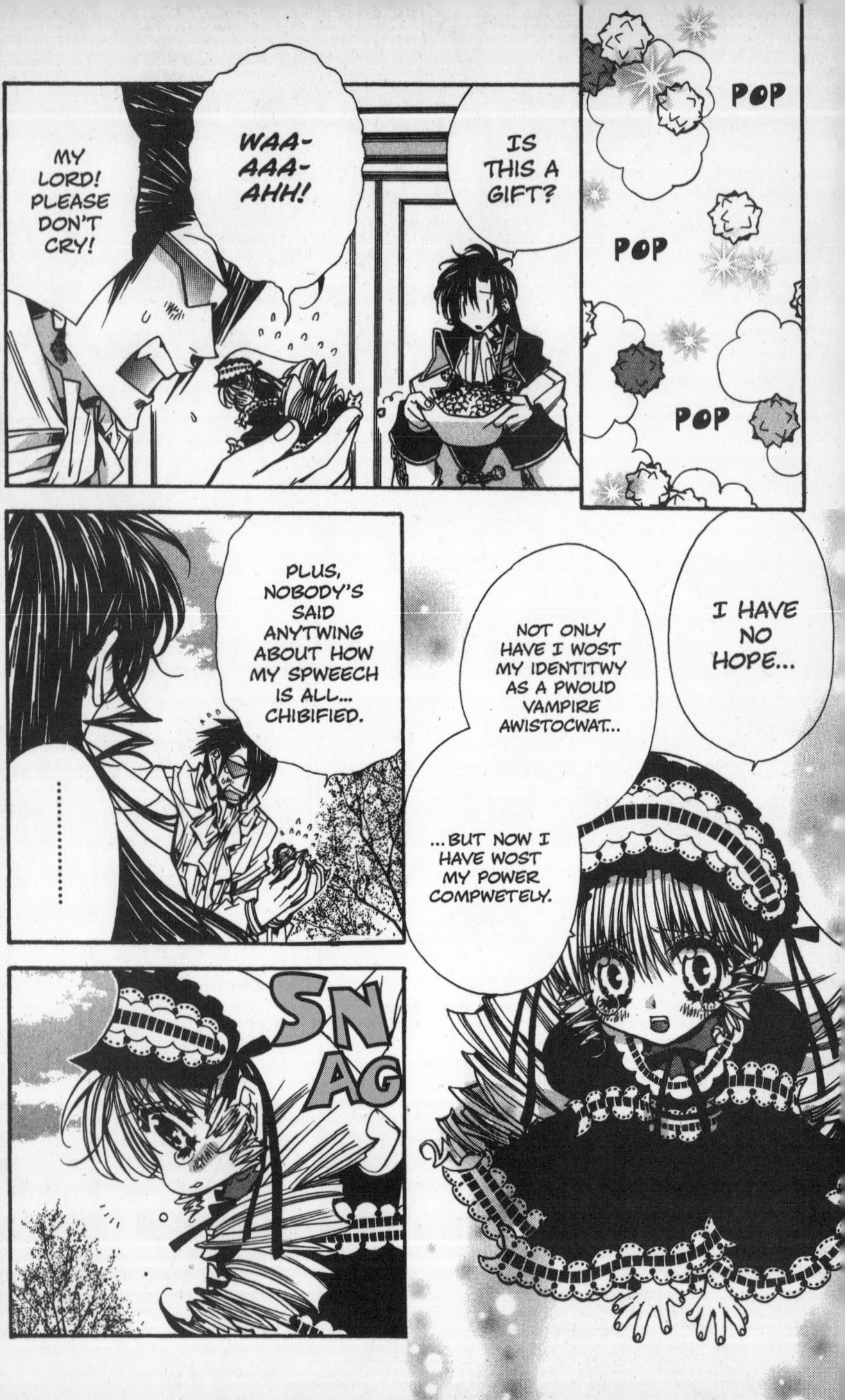
POP
POP
POP
IS THIS A GIFT?
WAA-AAA-AHH!
MY LORD! PLEASE DON'T CRY!
I HAVE NO HOPE...
NOT ONLY HAVE I WOST MY IDENTITWY AS A PWOUD VAMPIRE AWISTOCWAT...
...BUT NOW I HAVE WOST MY POWER COMPWETELY.
PLUS, NOBODY'S SAID ANYTWING ABOUT HOW MY SPWEECH IS ALL... CHIBIFIED.
....
SNAG

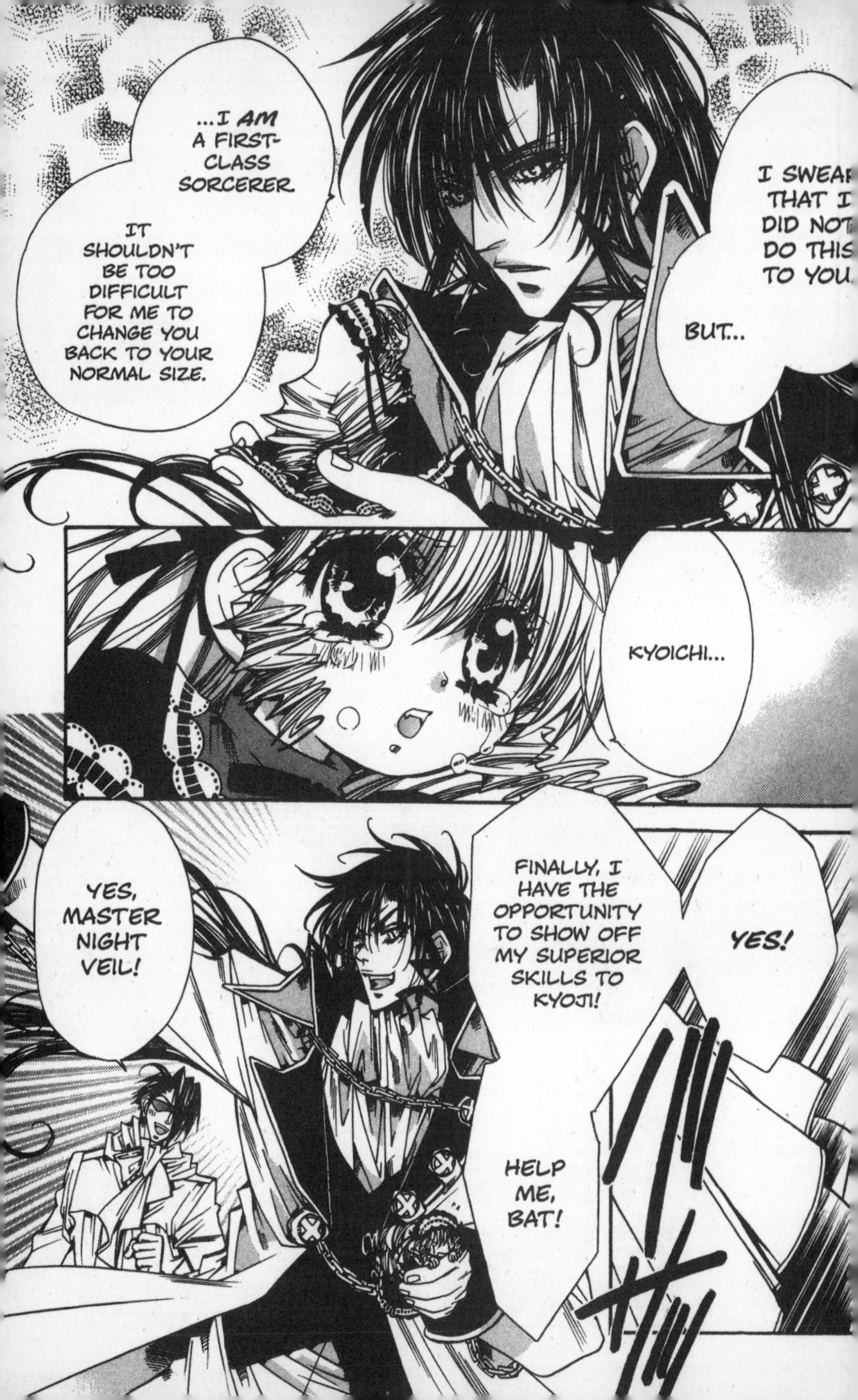
I SWEAR THAT I DID NOT DO THIS TO YOU.
BUT...
...I AM A FIRST-CLASS SORCERER.
IT SHOULDN'T BE TOO DIFFICULT FOR ME TO CHANGE YOU BACK TO YOUR NORMAL SIZE.
KYOICHI...
YES!
FINALLY, I HAVE THE OPPORTUNITY TO SHOW OFF MY SUPERIOR SKILLS TO KYOJI!
HELP ME, BAT!
YES, MASTER NIGHT VEIL!

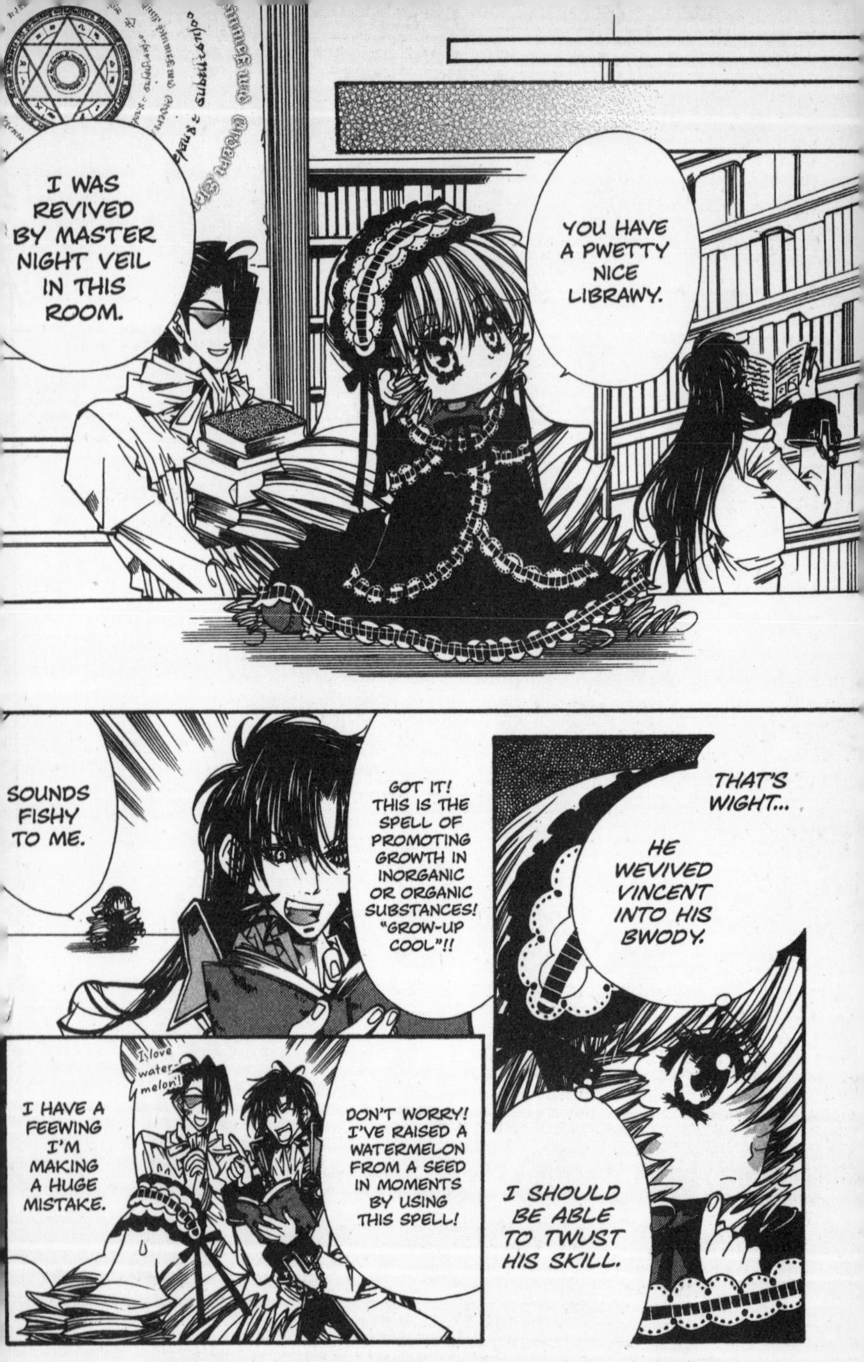
YOU HAVE A PWETTY NICE LIBRAWY.
I WAS REVIVED BY MASTER NIGHT VEIL IN THIS ROOM.
THAT'S WIGHT...
HE WEVIVED VINCENT INTO HIS BWODY.
I SHOULD BE ABLE TO TWUST HIS SKILL.
GOT IT! THIS IS THE SPELL OF PROMOTING GROWTH IN INORGANIC OR ORGANIC SUBSTANCES! "GROW-UP COOL"!!
SOUNDS FISHY TO ME.
DON'T WORRY! I'VE RAISED A WATERMELON FROM A SEED IN MOMENTS BY USING THIS SPELL!
I love watermelon!
I HAVE A FEEWING I'M MAKING A HUGE MISTAKE.

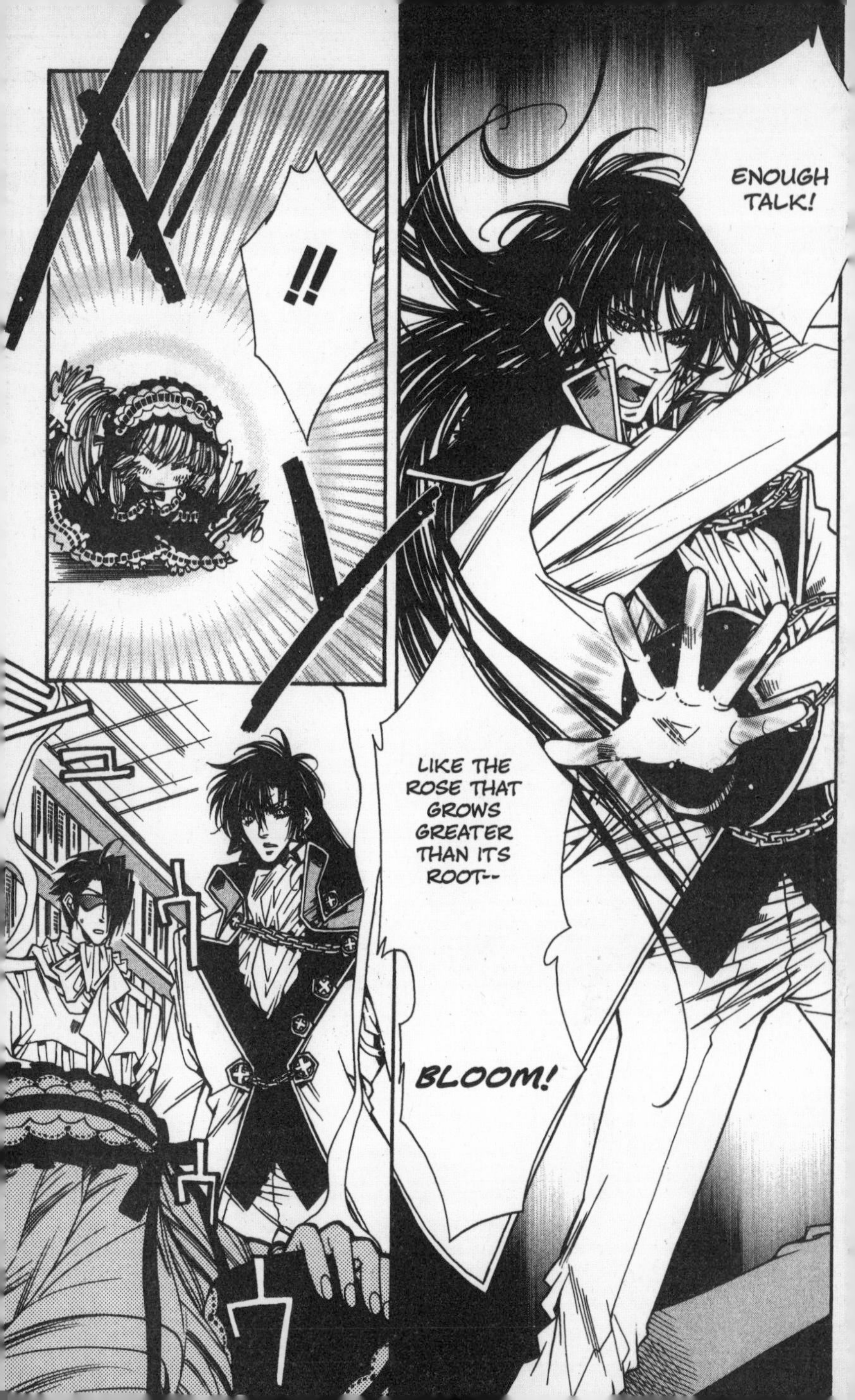
ENOUGH TALK!
LIKE THE ROSE THAT GROWS GREATER THAN ITS ROOT--
BLOOM!
!!

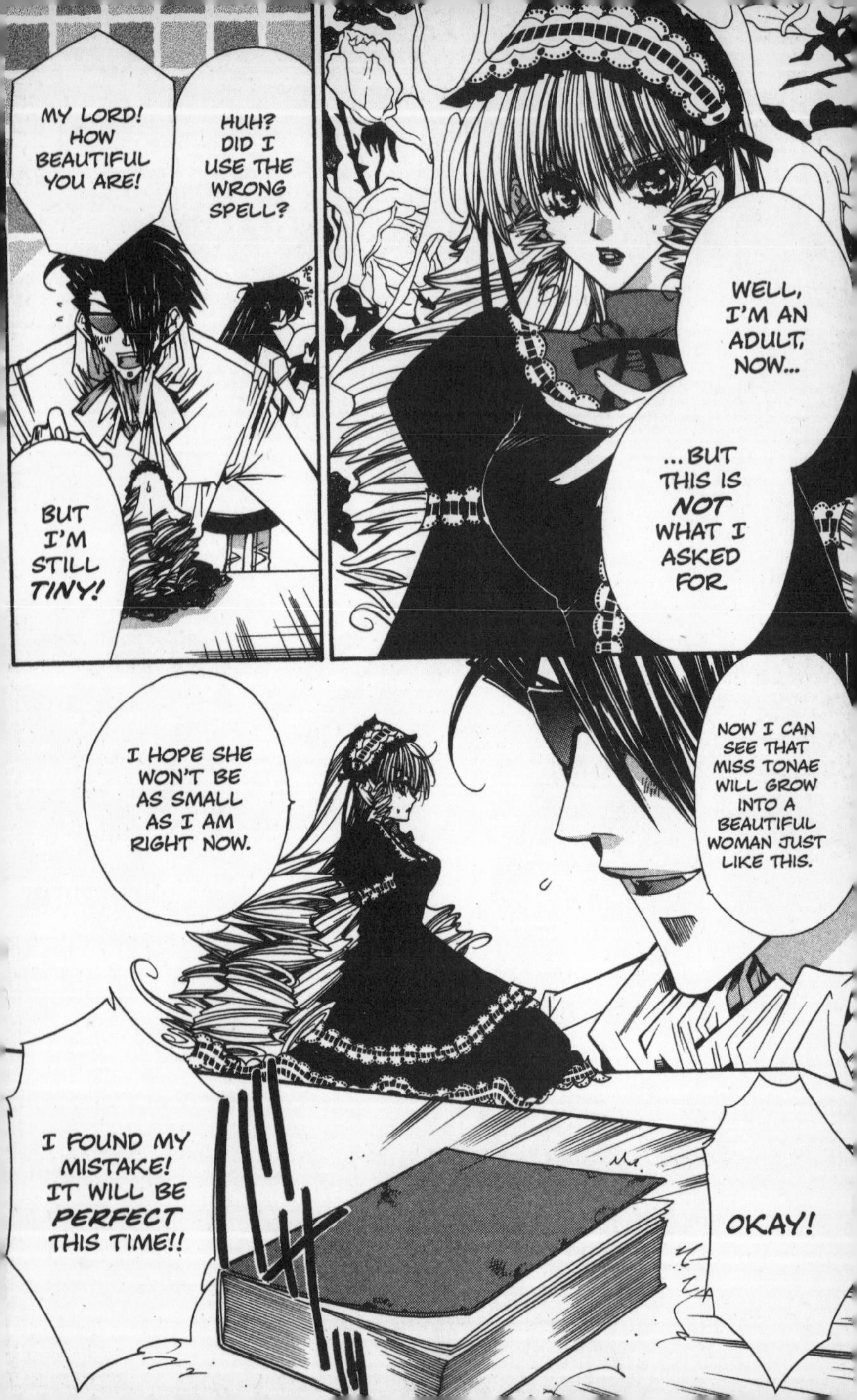
WELL, I'M AN ADULT, NOW...
...BUT THIS IS *NOT* WHAT I ASKED FOR
HUH? DID I USE THE WRONG SPELL?
MY LORD! HOW BEAUTIFUL YOU ARE!
BUT I'M STILL *TINY!*
NOW I CAN SEE THAT MISS TONAE WILL GROW INTO A BEAUTIFUL WOMAN JUST LIKE THIS.
I HOPE SHE WON'T BE AS SMALL AS I AM RIGHT NOW.
I FOUND MY MISTAKE! IT WILL BE *PERFECT* THIS TIME!!
OKAY!

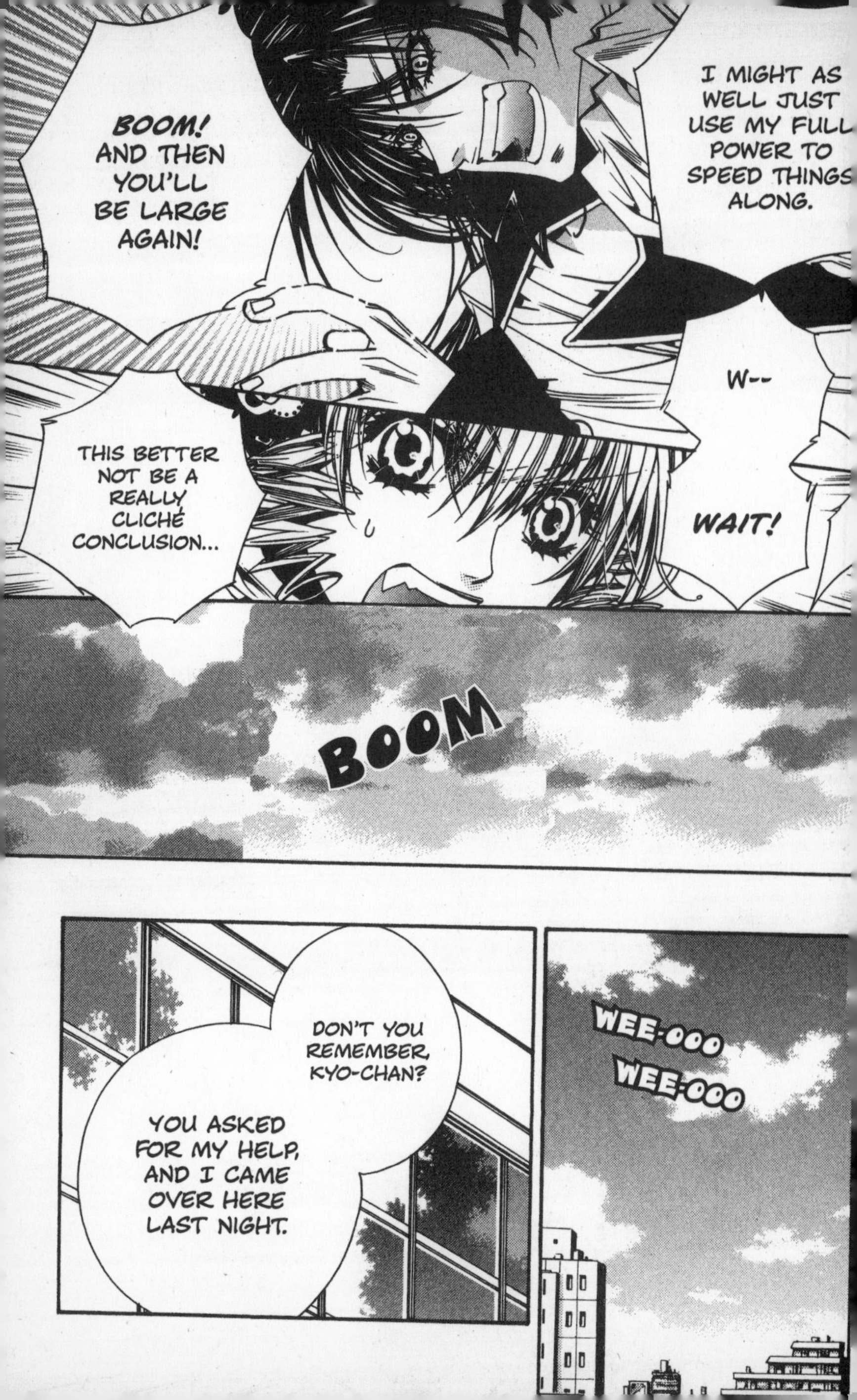
I MIGHT AS WELL JUST USE MY FULL POWER TO SPEED THINGS ALONG.
BOOM! AND THEN YOU'LL BE LARGE AGAIN!
W-- WAIT!
THIS BETTER NOT BE A REALLY CLICHÉ CONCLUSION...
BOOM
WEE-OOO WEE-OOO
DON'T YOU REMEMBER, KYO-CHAN?
YOU ASKED FOR MY HELP, AND I CAME OVER HERE LAST NIGHT.

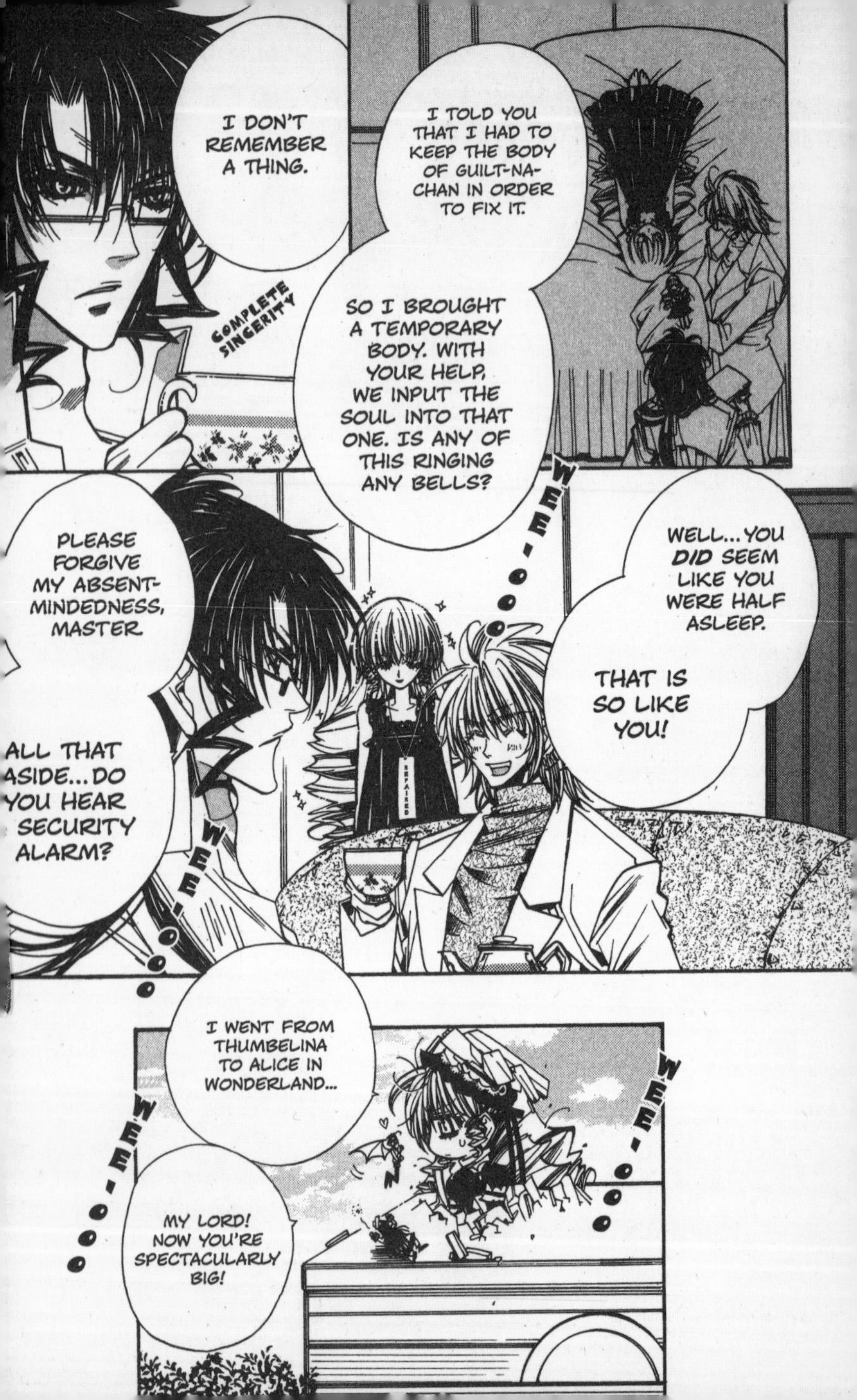
I TOLD YOU THAT I HAD TO KEEP THE BODY OF GUILT-NA-CHAN IN ORDER TO FIX IT.
SO I BROUGHT A TEMPORARY BODY. WITH YOUR HELP, WE INPUT THE SOUL INTO THAT ONE. IS ANY OF THIS RINGING ANY BELLS?
I DON'T REMEMBER A THING.
COMPLETE SINCERITY
WEE...
WELL...YOU DID SEEM LIKE YOU WERE HALF ASLEEP.
THAT IS SO LIKE YOU!
PLEASE FORGIVE MY ABSENT-MINDEDNESS, MASTER
ALL THAT ASIDE...DO YOU HEAR SECURITY ALARM?
WEE...
WEE...
I WENT FROM THUMBELINA TO ALICE IN WONDERLAND...
MY LORD! NOW YOU'RE SPECTACULARLY BIG!
WEE...

BONUS COMIC STRIP

VAMPIRE DOLL REFLECTIONS

Lo, How a Rose Ever Blooming

WHAT'S YOUR NAME?
~NIGHT VEIL~
WHAT A STWANGE NAME FOR A SPELL.
"GROW-UP COOL"?
THERE ARE MORE... THE "COROLLA CURSE" AND "ROTTEN ROOT OFF COURSE"
WHO INVENTED THWEM?
SPECIAL GUEST APPEARANCE.
THE EDO-PERIOD SCIENTIST WHO MADE THAT A LEGENDARY DEAD CHERRY TREE BLOOM.
"AYASHIGE SHOJIKI."
HIS ISH THE *WEIRD-EST* NAME OF ALL!

[NOTE: AYASHIGE MEANS FISHY. SHOJIKI MEANS HONEST.]

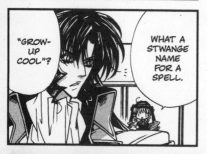

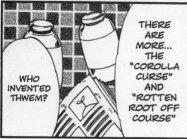

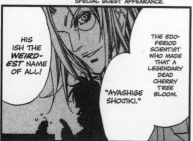

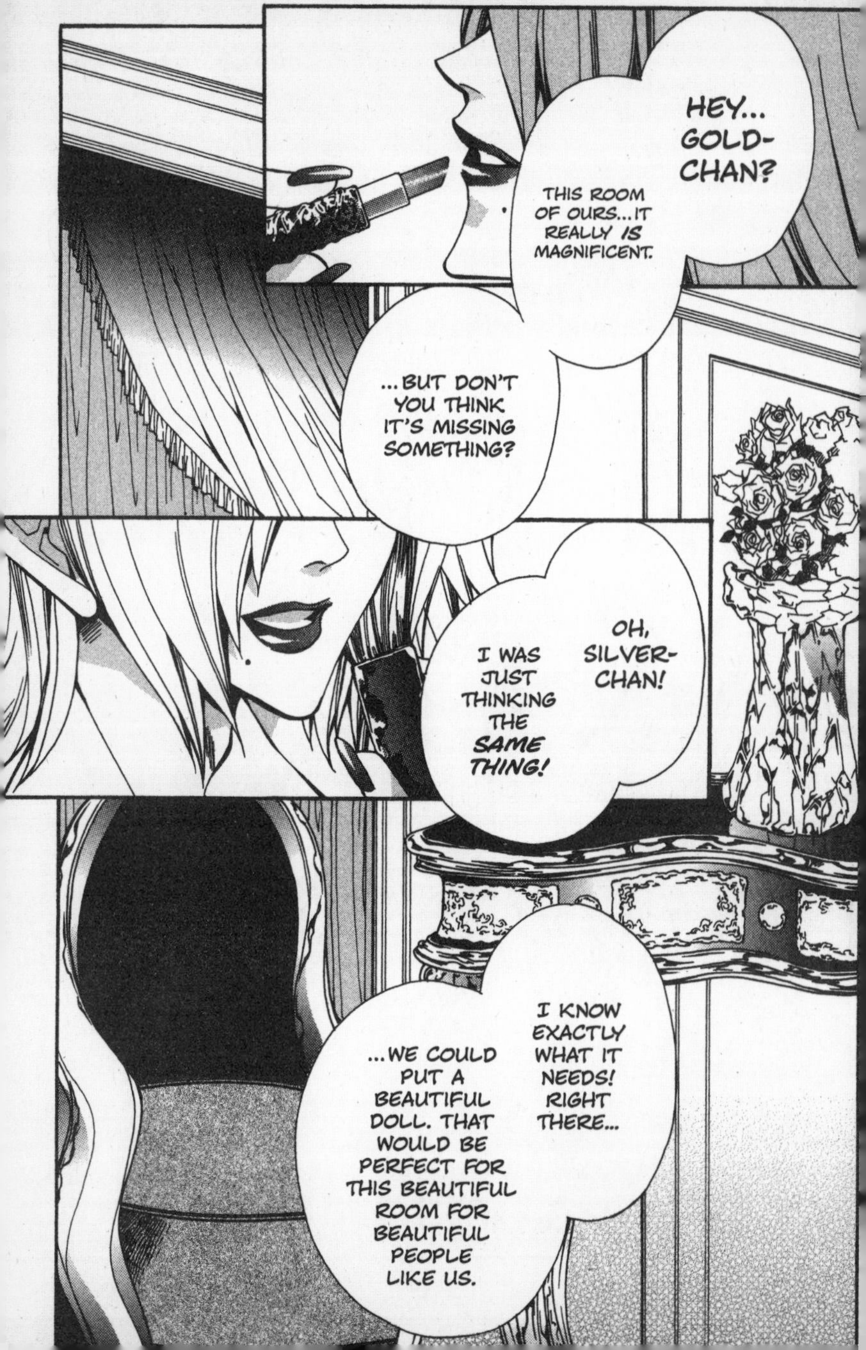
HEY... GOLD-CHAN?
THIS ROOM OF OURS...IT REALLY *IS* MAGNIFICENT.
...BUT DON'T YOU THINK IT'S MISSING SOMETHING?
OH, SILVER-CHAN!
I WAS JUST THINKING THE *SAME THING!*
I KNOW EXACTLY WHAT IT NEEDS! RIGHT THERE...
...WE COULD PUT A BEAUTIFUL DOLL. THAT WOULD BE PERFECT FOR THIS BEAUTIFUL ROOM FOR BEAUTIFUL PEOPLE LIKE US.

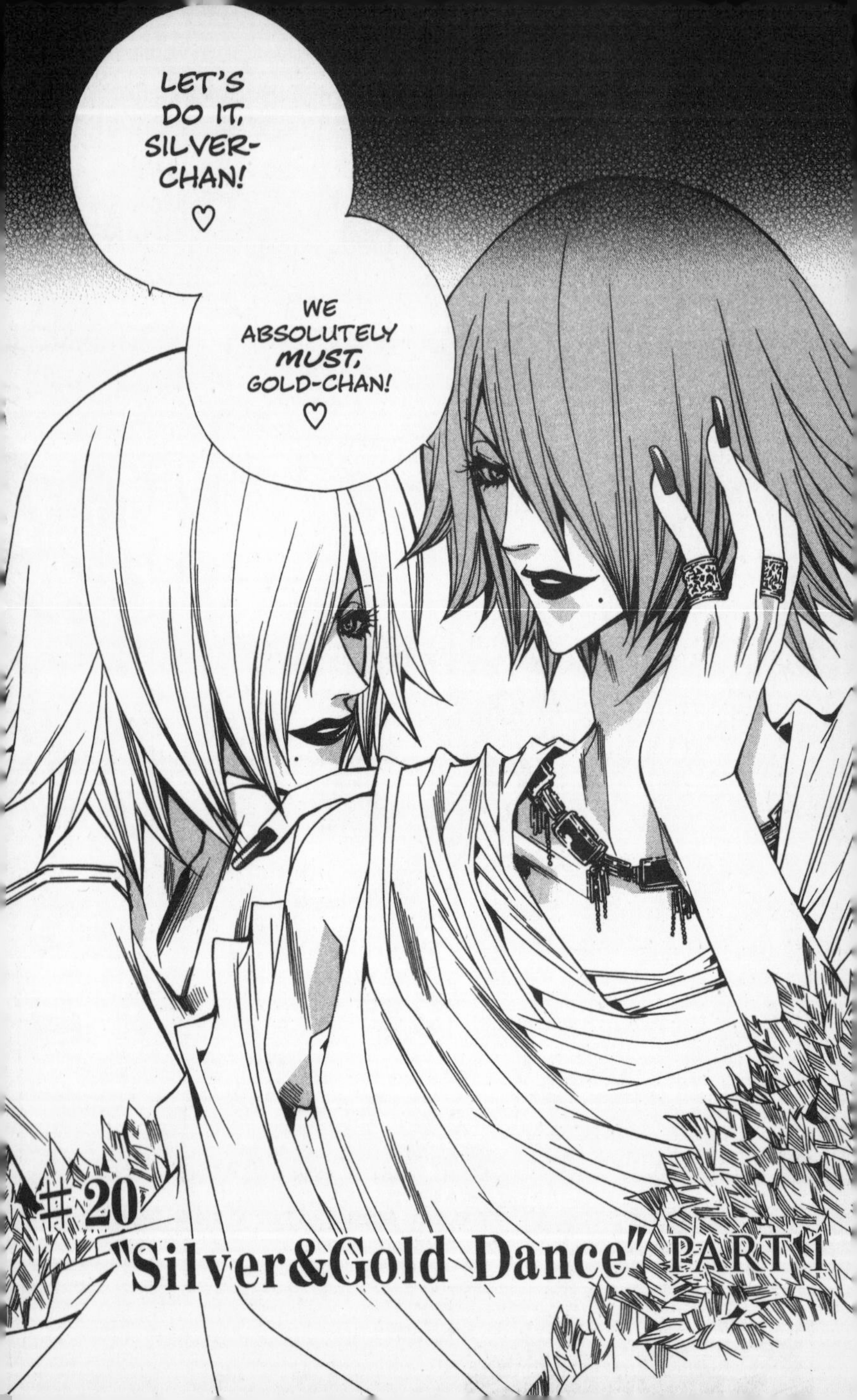
LET'S DO IT, SILVER-CHAN! ♡
WE ABSOLUTELY MUST, GOLD-CHAN! ♡

#20 "Silver&Gold Dance" PART 1

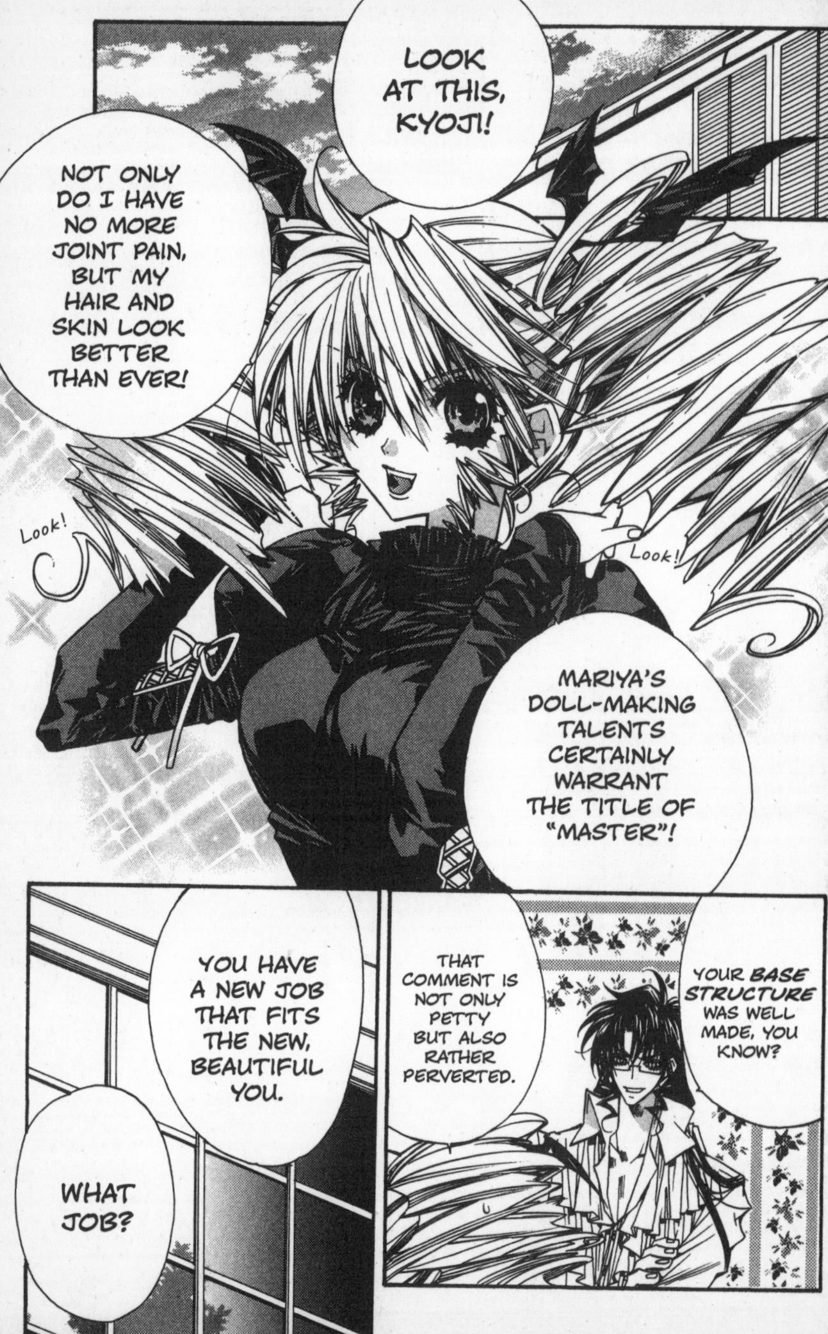
LOOK AT THIS, KYOJI!
NOT ONLY DO I HAVE NO MORE JOINT PAIN, BUT MY HAIR AND SKIN LOOK BETTER THAN EVER!
Look!
Look!
MARIYA'S DOLL-MAKING TALENTS CERTAINLY WARRANT THE TITLE OF "MASTER"!
YOUR *BASE STRUCTURE* WAS WELL MADE, YOU KNOW?
THAT COMMENT IS NOT ONLY PETTY BUT ALSO RATHER PERVERTED.
YOU HAVE A NEW JOB THAT FITS THE NEW, BEAUTIFUL YOU.
WHAT JOB?

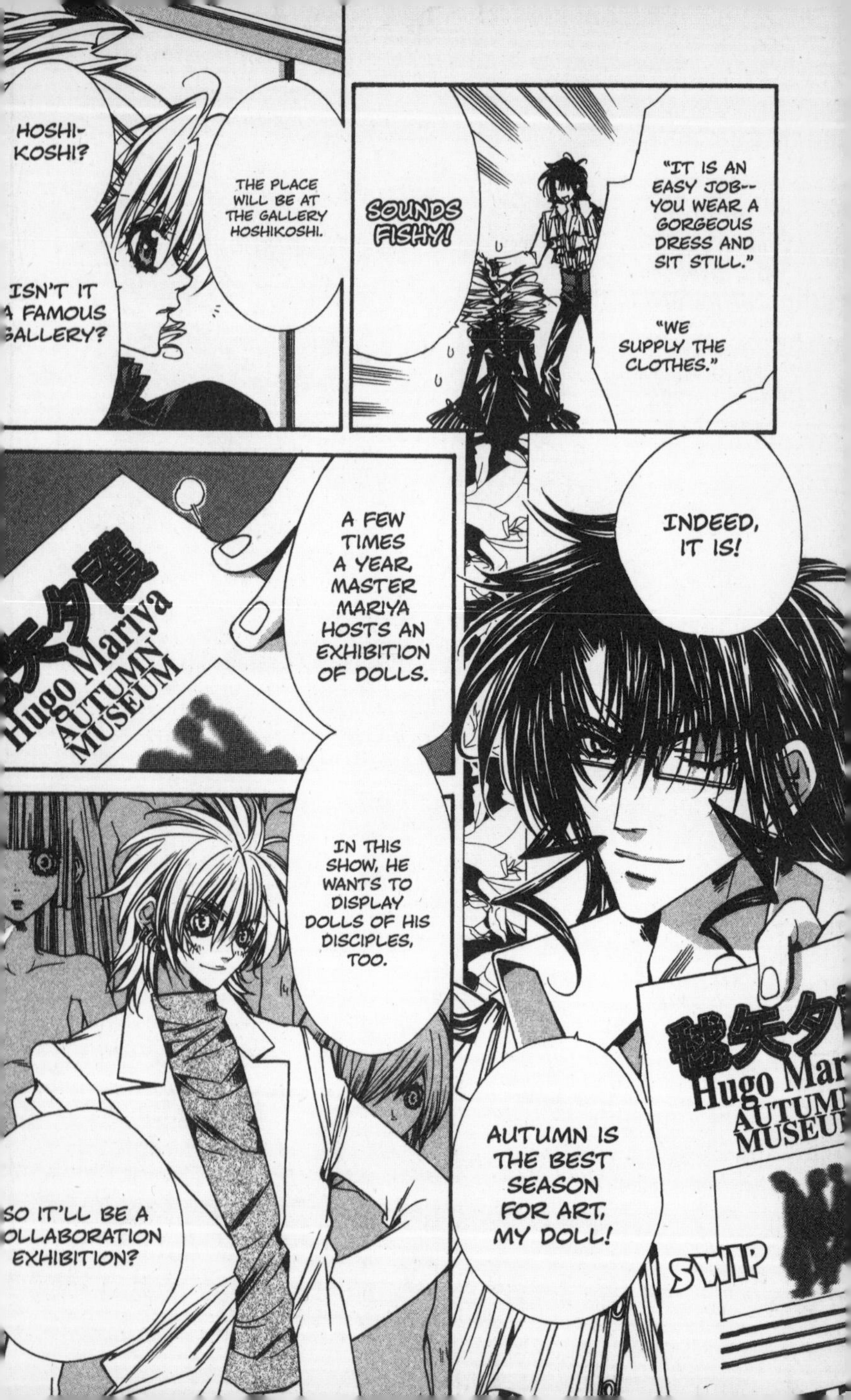
"IT IS AN EASY JOB-- YOU WEAR A GORGEOUS DRESS AND SIT STILL."
"WE SUPPLY THE CLOTHES."
SOUNDS FISHY!
THE PLACE WILL BE AT THE GALLERY HOSHIKOSHI.
HOSHI-KOSHI?
ISN'T IT A FAMOUS GALLERY?
INDEED, IT IS!
AUTUMN IS THE BEST SEASON FOR ART, MY DOLL!
SWIP
A FEW TIMES A YEAR, MASTER MARIYA HOSTS AN EXHIBITION OF DOLLS.
Hugo Mariya
AUTUMN MUSEUM
IN THIS SHOW, HE WANTS TO DISPLAY DOLLS OF HIS DISCIPLES, TOO.
SO IT'LL BE A COLLABORATION EXHIBITION?

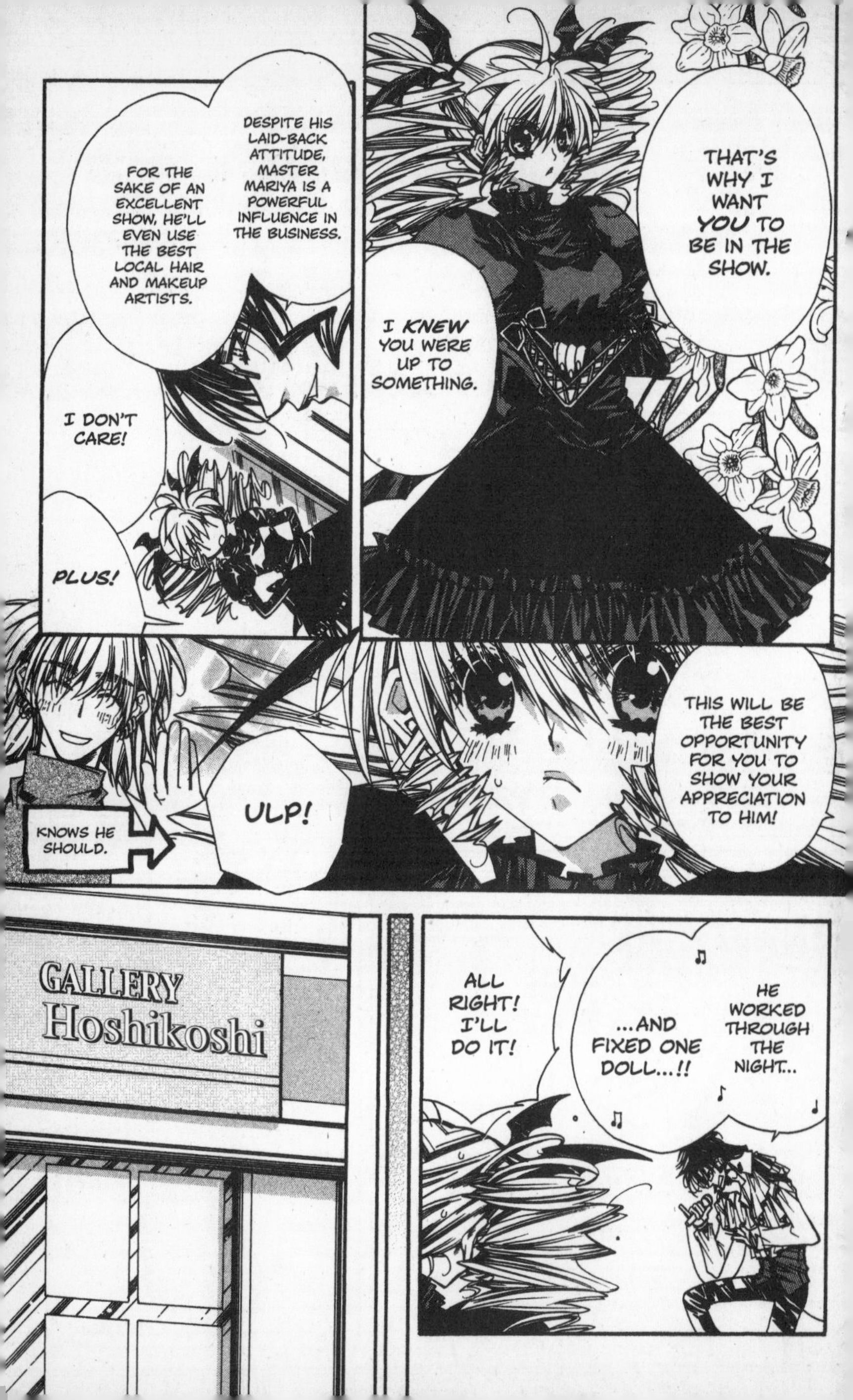
THAT'S WHY I WANT *YOU* TO BE IN THE SHOW.
I *KNEW* YOU WERE UP TO SOMETHING.
DESPITE HIS LAID-BACK ATTITUDE, MASTER MARIYA IS A POWERFUL INFLUENCE IN THE BUSINESS.
FOR THE SAKE OF AN EXCELLENT SHOW, HE'LL EVEN USE THE BEST LOCAL HAIR AND MAKEUP ARTISTS.
I DON'T CARE!
PLUS!
THIS WILL BE THE BEST OPPORTUNITY FOR YOU TO SHOW YOUR APPRECIATION TO HIM!
ULP!
KNOWS HE SHOULD.
HE WORKED THROUGH THE NIGHT...
...AND FIXED ONE DOLL...!!
ALL RIGHT! I'LL DO IT!
GALLERY Hoshikoshi

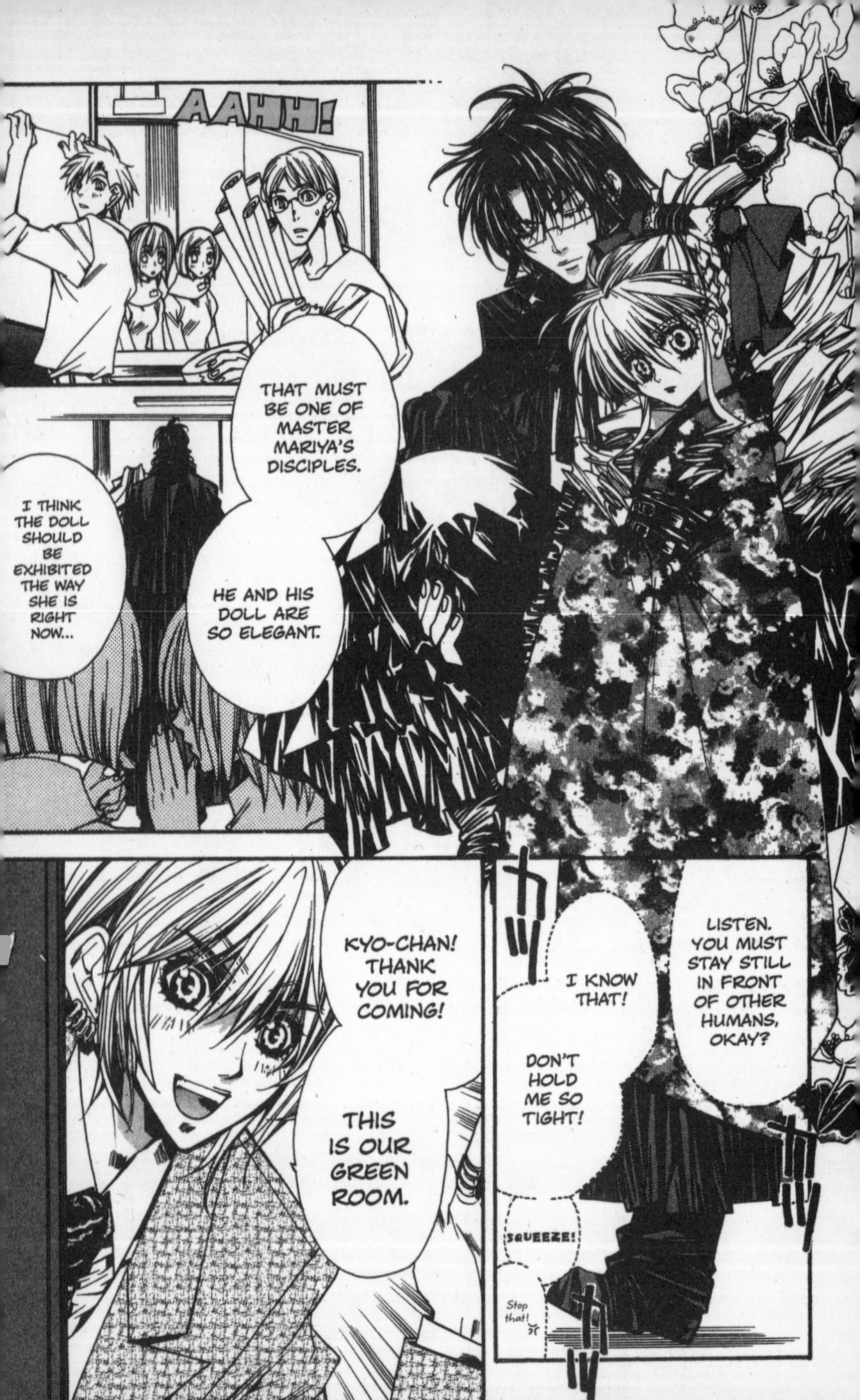
AAHH!
THAT MUST BE ONE OF MASTER MARIYA'S DISCIPLES.
HE AND HIS DOLL ARE SO ELEGANT.
I THINK THE DOLL SHOULD BE EXHIBITED THE WAY SHE IS RIGHT NOW...
LISTEN. YOU MUST STAY STILL IN FRONT OF OTHER HUMANS, OKAY?
I KNOW THAT!
DON'T HOLD ME SO TIGHT!
SQUEEZE!
Stop that!
KYO-CHAN! THANK YOU FOR COMING!
THIS IS OUR GREEN ROOM.

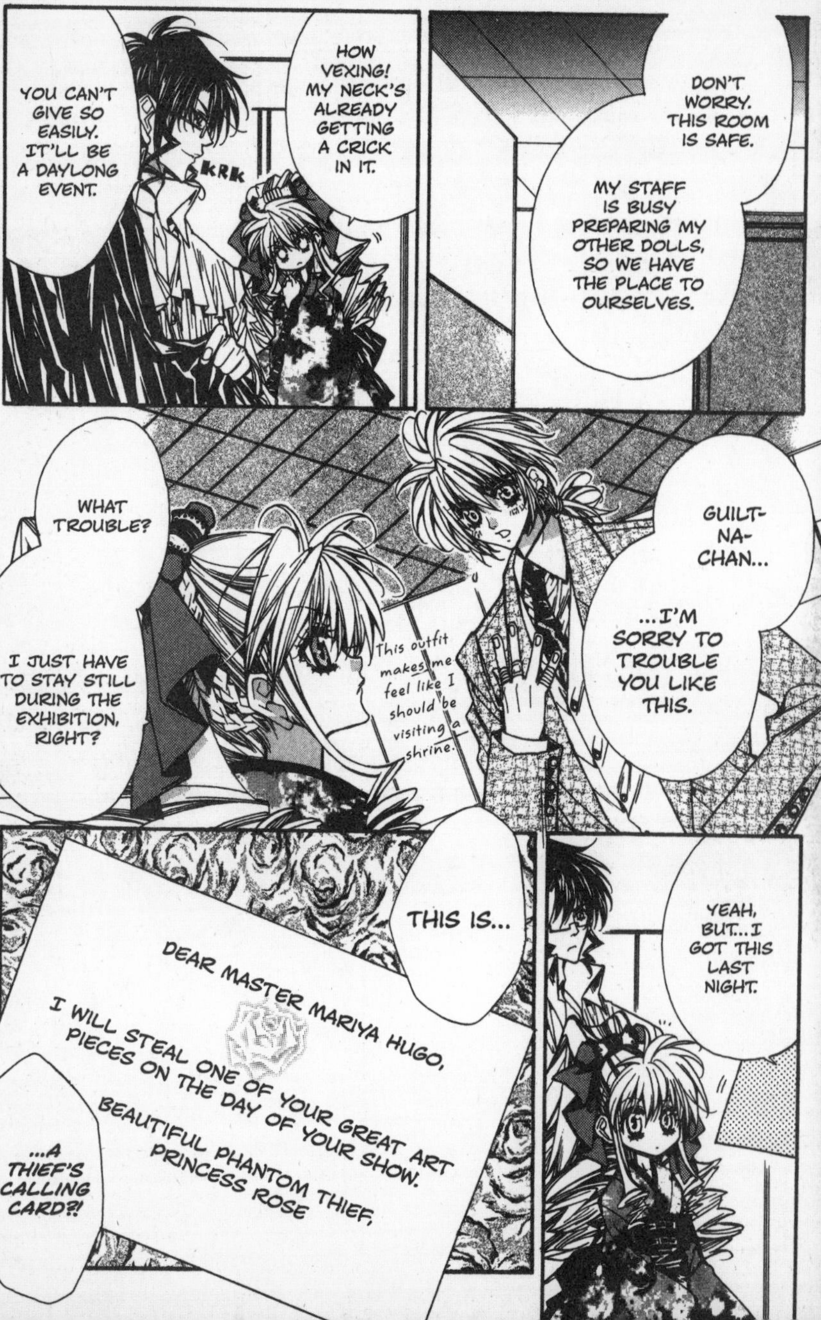
DON'T WORRY. THIS ROOM IS SAFE.
MY STAFF IS BUSY PREPARING MY OTHER DOLLS, SO WE HAVE THE PLACE TO OURSELVES.
HOW VEXING! MY NECK'S ALREADY GETTING A CRICK IN IT.
KRK
YOU CAN'T GIVE SO EASILY. IT'LL BE A DAYLONG EVENT.
GUILT-NA-CHAN...
...I'M SORRY TO TROUBLE YOU LIKE THIS.
This outfit makes me feel like I should be visiting a shrine.
WHAT TROUBLE?
I JUST HAVE TO STAY STILL DURING THE EXHIBITION, RIGHT?
YEAH, BUT...I GOT THIS LAST NIGHT.
THIS IS...
DEAR MASTER MARIYA HUGO,
I WILL STEAL ONE OF YOUR GREAT ART PIECES ON THE DAY OF YOUR SHOW.
BEAUTIFUL PHANTOM THIEF, PRINCESS ROSE
...A THIEF'S CALLING CARD?!

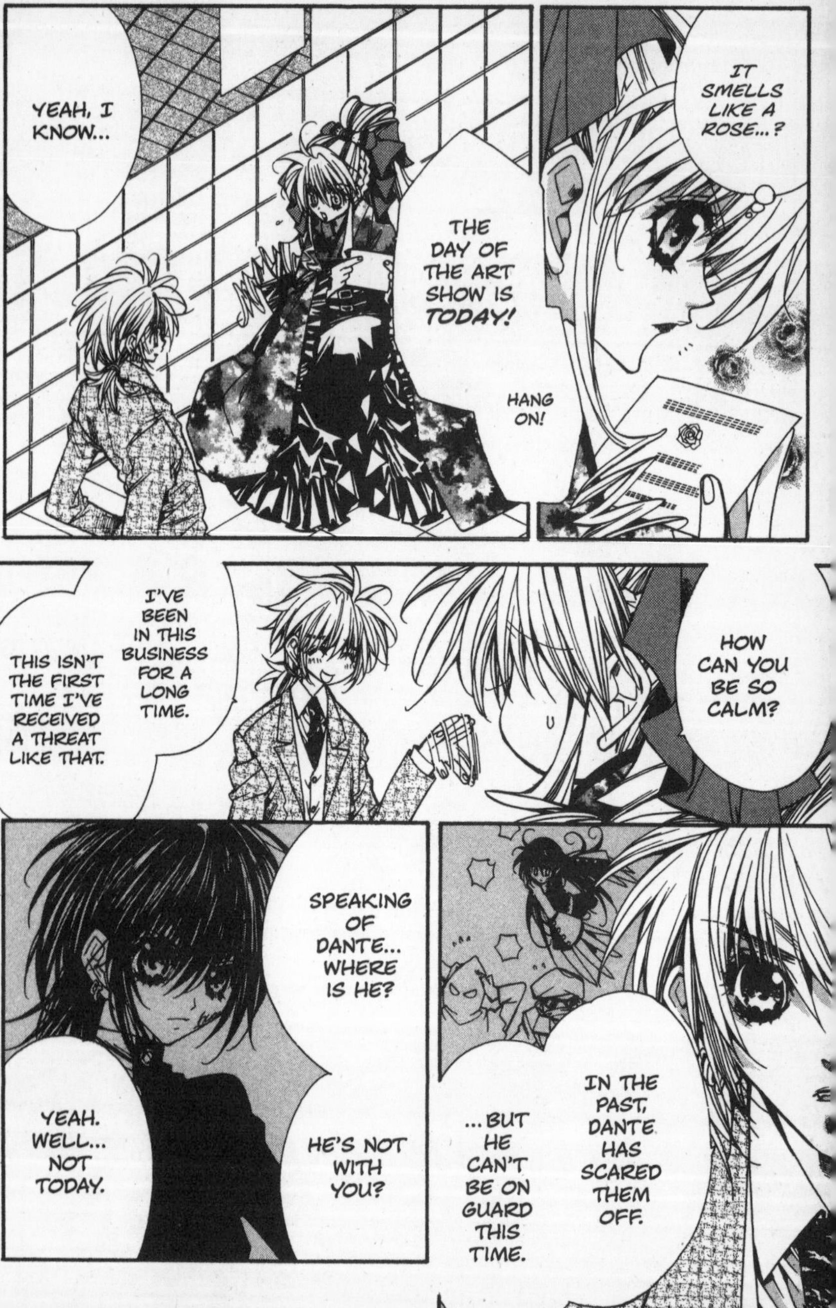
IT SMELLS LIKE A ROSE...?
THE DAY OF THE ART SHOW IS *TODAY!*
HANG ON!
YEAH, I KNOW...
HOW CAN YOU BE SO CALM?
I'VE BEEN IN THIS BUSINESS FOR A LONG TIME.
THIS ISN'T THE FIRST TIME I'VE RECEIVED A THREAT LIKE THAT.
IN THE PAST, DANTE HAS SCARED THEM OFF.
...BUT HE CAN'T BE ON GUARD THIS TIME.
SPEAKING OF DANTE... WHERE IS HE?
HE'S NOT WITH YOU?
YEAH. WELL... NOT TODAY.

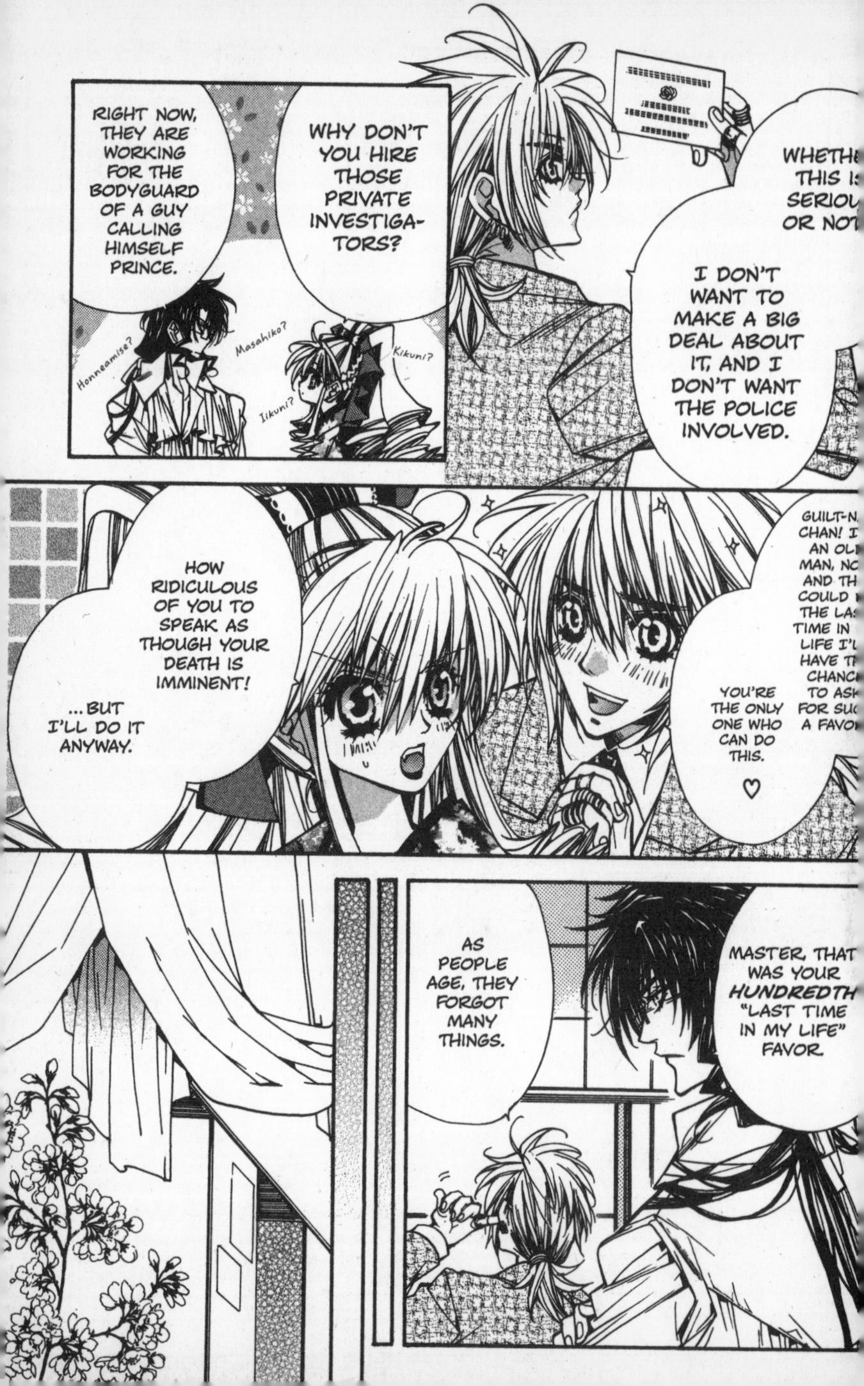
WHETH THIS IS SERIOU OR NOT
I DON'T WANT TO MAKE A BIG DEAL ABOUT IT, AND I DON'T WANT THE POLICE INVOLVED.
WHY DON'T YOU HIRE THOSE PRIVATE INVESTIGA-TORS?
RIGHT NOW, THEY ARE WORKING FOR THE BODYGUARD OF A GUY CALLING HIMSELF PRINCE.
Kikuni?
Ikuni?
Masahiko?
Honneamise?
GUILT-N CHAN! I AN OL MAN, NO AND TH COULD THE LA TIME IN LIFE I'L HAVE T CHANC TO ASK FOR SU A FAVO
YOU'RE THE ONLY ONE WHO CAN DO THIS. ♡
HOW RIDICULOUS OF YOU TO SPEAK AS THOUGH YOUR DEATH IS IMMINENT!
...BUT I'LL DO IT ANYWAY.
MASTER, THAT WAS YOUR *HUNDREDTH* "LAST TIME IN MY LIFE" FAVOR
AS PEOPLE AGE, THEY FORGOT MANY THINGS.

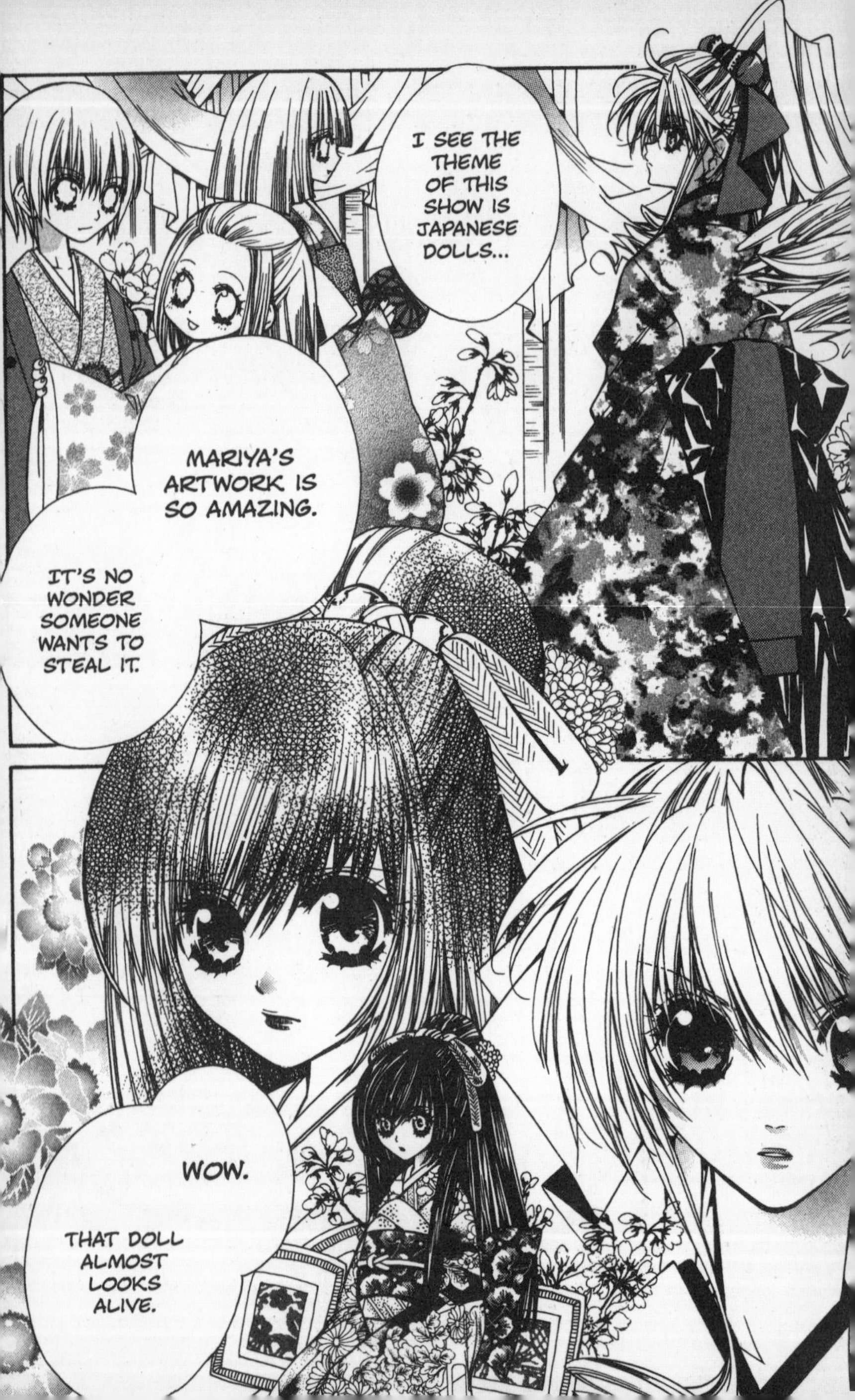
I SEE THE THEME OF THIS SHOW IS JAPANESE DOLLS...
MARIYA'S ARTWORK IS SO AMAZING.
IT'S NO WONDER SOMEONE WANTS TO STEAL IT.
WOW.
THAT DOLL ALMOST LOOKS ALIVE.

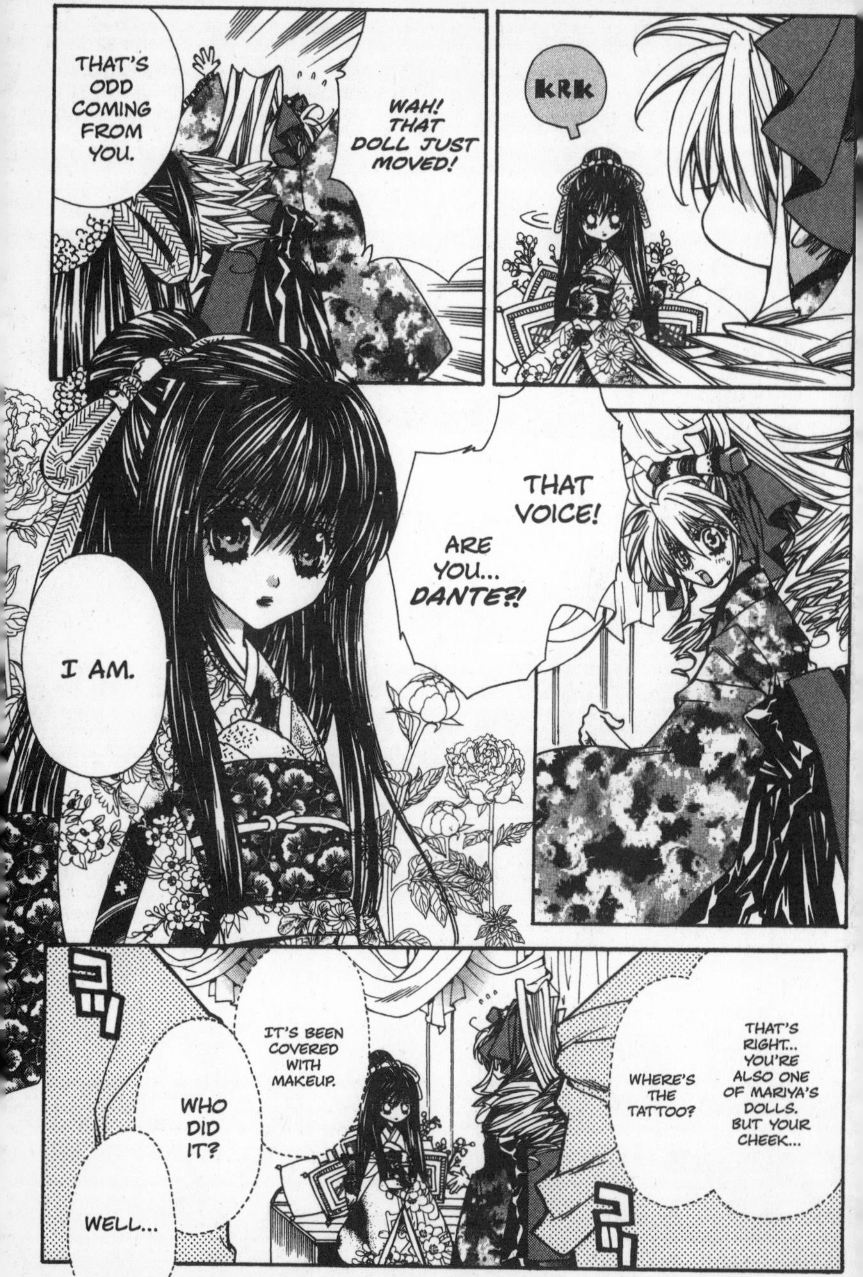
KRK
WAH! THAT DOLL JUST MOVED!
THAT'S ODD COMING FROM YOU.
THAT VOICE!
ARE YOU... DANTE?!
I AM.
THAT'S RIGHT... YOU'RE ALSO ONE OF MARIYA'S DOLLS. BUT YOUR CHEEK...
WHERE'S THE TATTOO?
IT'S BEEN COVERED WITH MAKEUP.
WHO DID IT?
WELL...

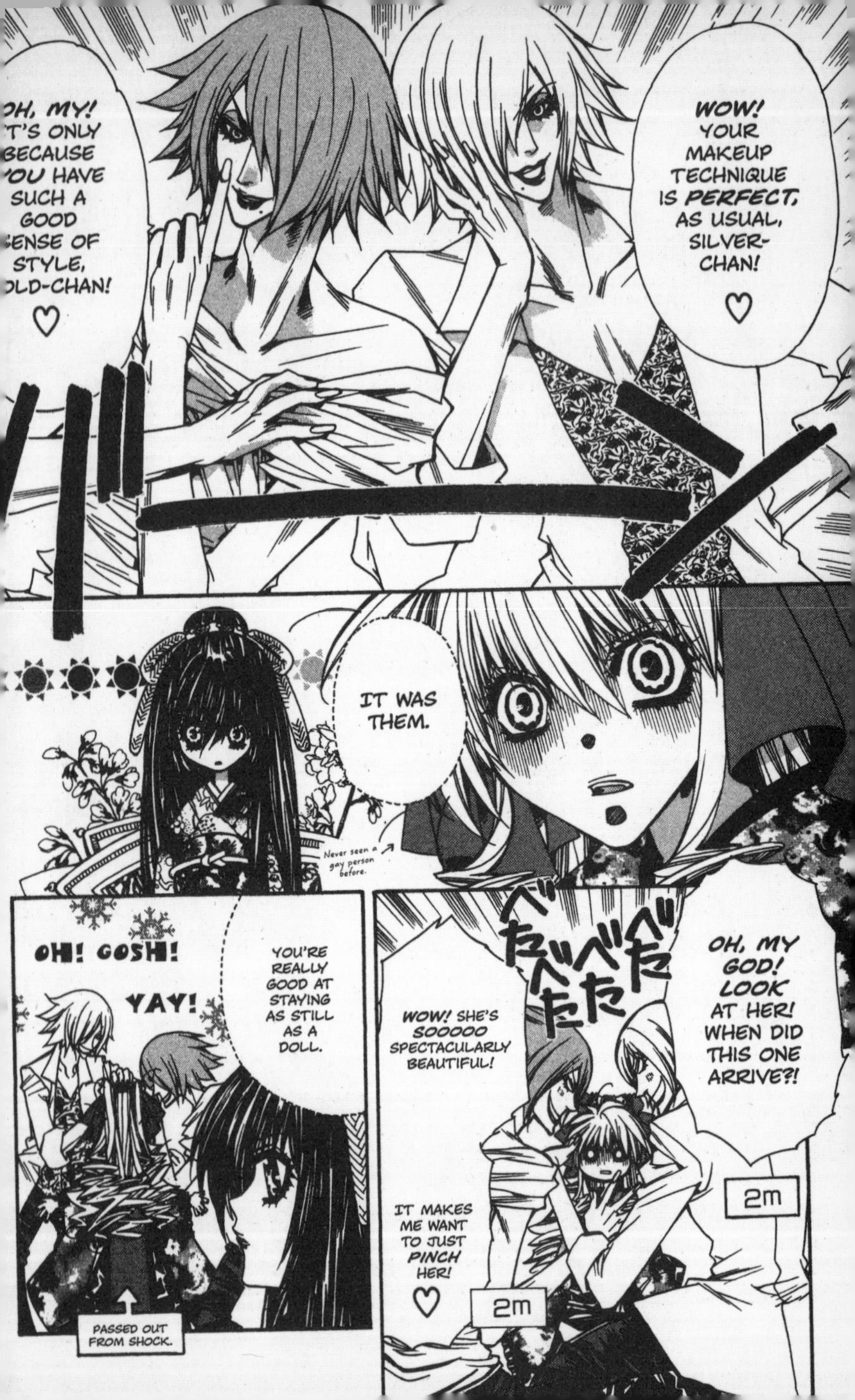
WOW! YOUR MAKEUP TECHNIQUE IS PERFECT, AS USUAL, SILVER-CHAN! ♡
OH, MY! T'S ONLY BECAUSE YOU HAVE SUCH A GOOD SENSE OF STYLE, OLD-CHAN! ♡
IT WAS THEM.
Never seen a gay person before.
OH, MY GOD! LOOK AT HER! WHEN DID THIS ONE ARRIVE?!
WOW! SHE'S SOOOOO SPECTACULARLY BEAUTIFUL!
2m
IT MAKES ME WANT TO JUST PINCH HER! ♡
2m
YOU'RE REALLY GOOD AT STAYING AS STILL AS A DOLL.
OH! GOSH!
YAY!
PASSED OUT FROM SHOCK.

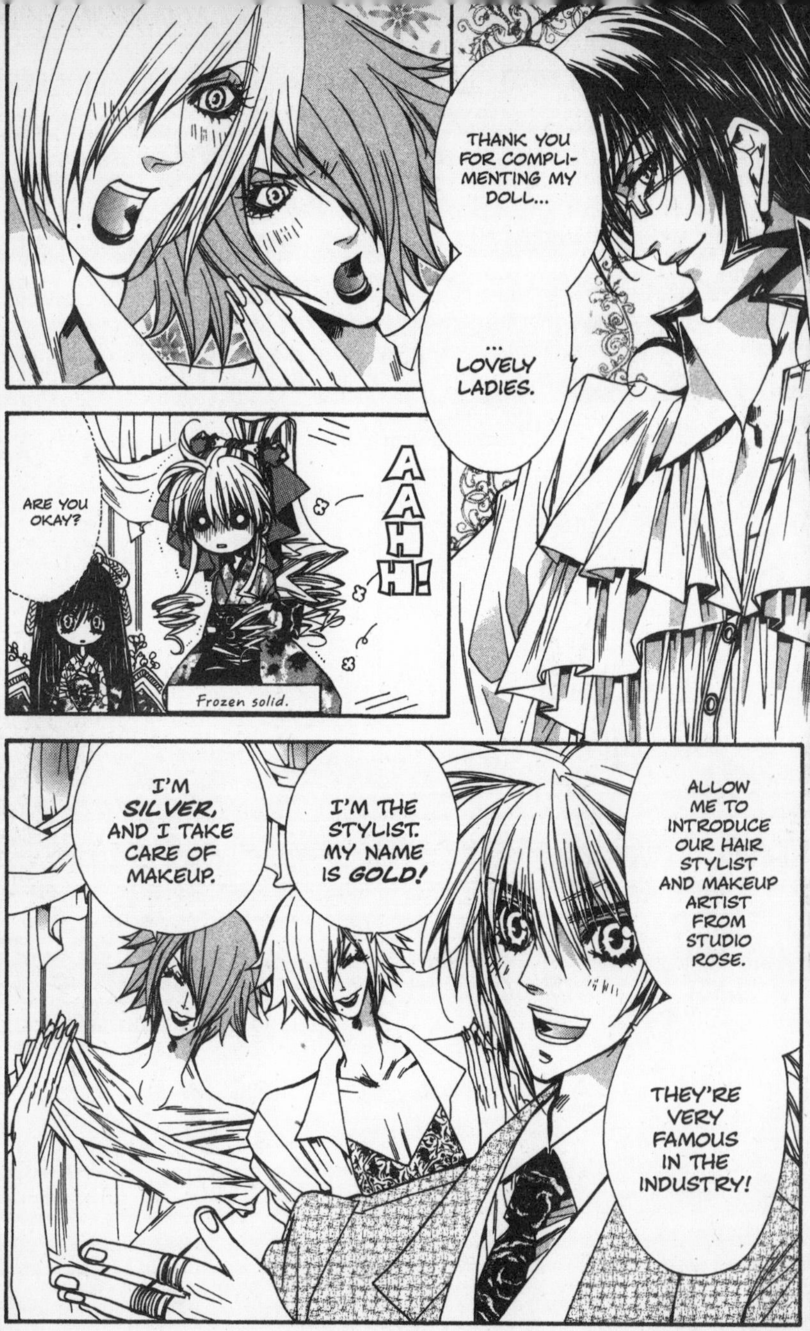
THANK YOU FOR COMPLIMENTING MY DOLL...
... LOVELY LADIES.
AAAHH!
ARE YOU OKAY?
Frozen solid.
ALLOW ME TO INTRODUCE OUR HAIR STYLIST AND MAKEUP ARTIST FROM STUDIO ROSE.
THEY'RE VERY FAMOUS IN THE INDUSTRY!
I'M THE STYLIST. MY NAME IS GOLD!
I'M SILVER, AND I TAKE CARE OF MAKEUP.

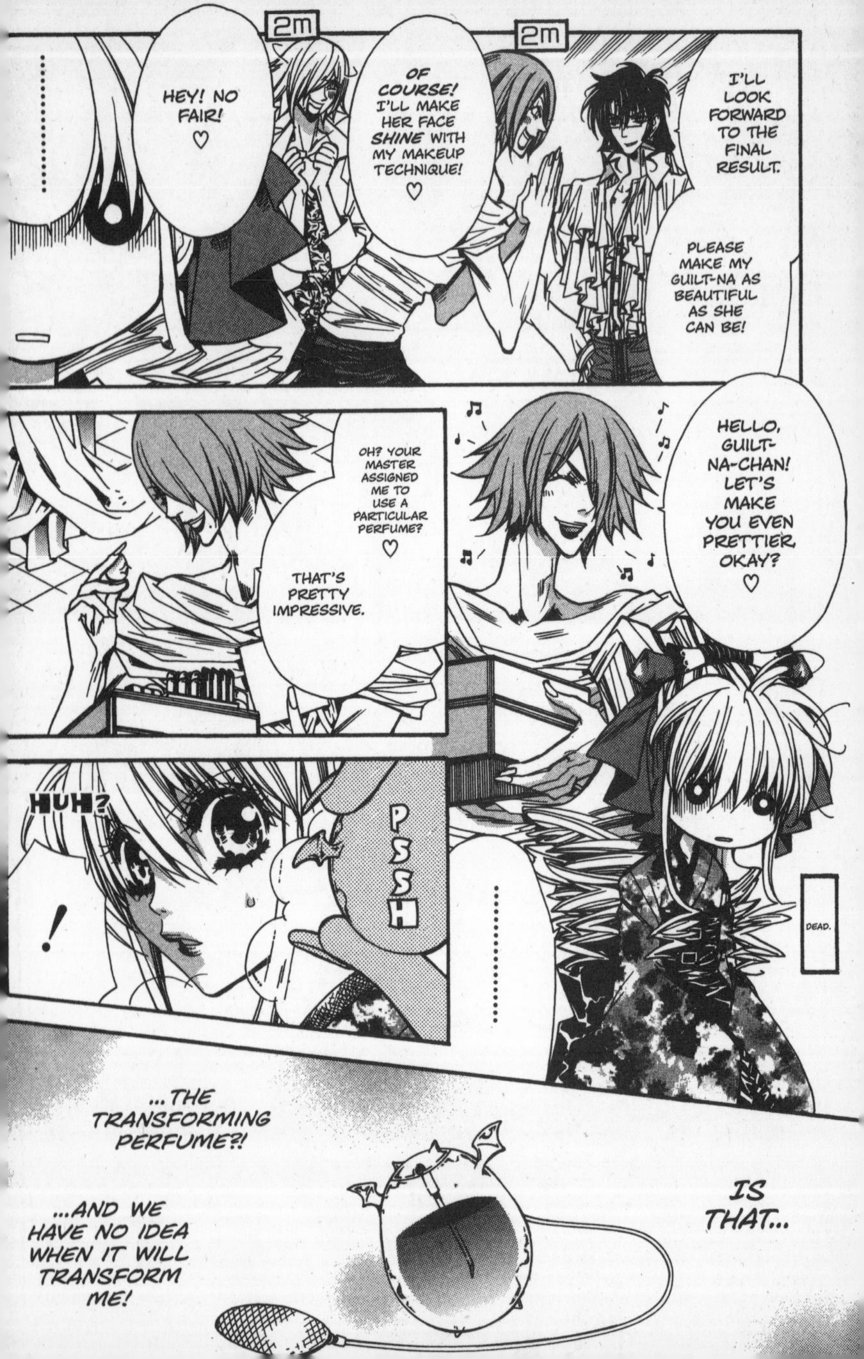
2m
I'LL LOOK FORWARD TO THE FINAL RESULT.
PLEASE MAKE MY GUILT-NA AS BEAUTIFUL AS SHE CAN BE!
2m
OF COURSE! I'LL MAKE HER FACE SHINE WITH MY MAKEUP TECHNIQUE! ♡
HEY! NO FAIR! ♡
......
HELLO, GUILT-NA-CHAN! LET'S MAKE YOU EVEN PRETTIER, OKAY? ♡
OH? YOUR MASTER ASSIGNED ME TO USE A PARTICULAR PERFUME? ♡
THAT'S PRETTY IMPRESSIVE.
DEAD.
......
PSSH
HUH?
!
IS THAT...
...THE TRANSFORMING PERFUME?!
...AND WE HAVE NO IDEA WHEN IT WILL TRANSFORM ME!

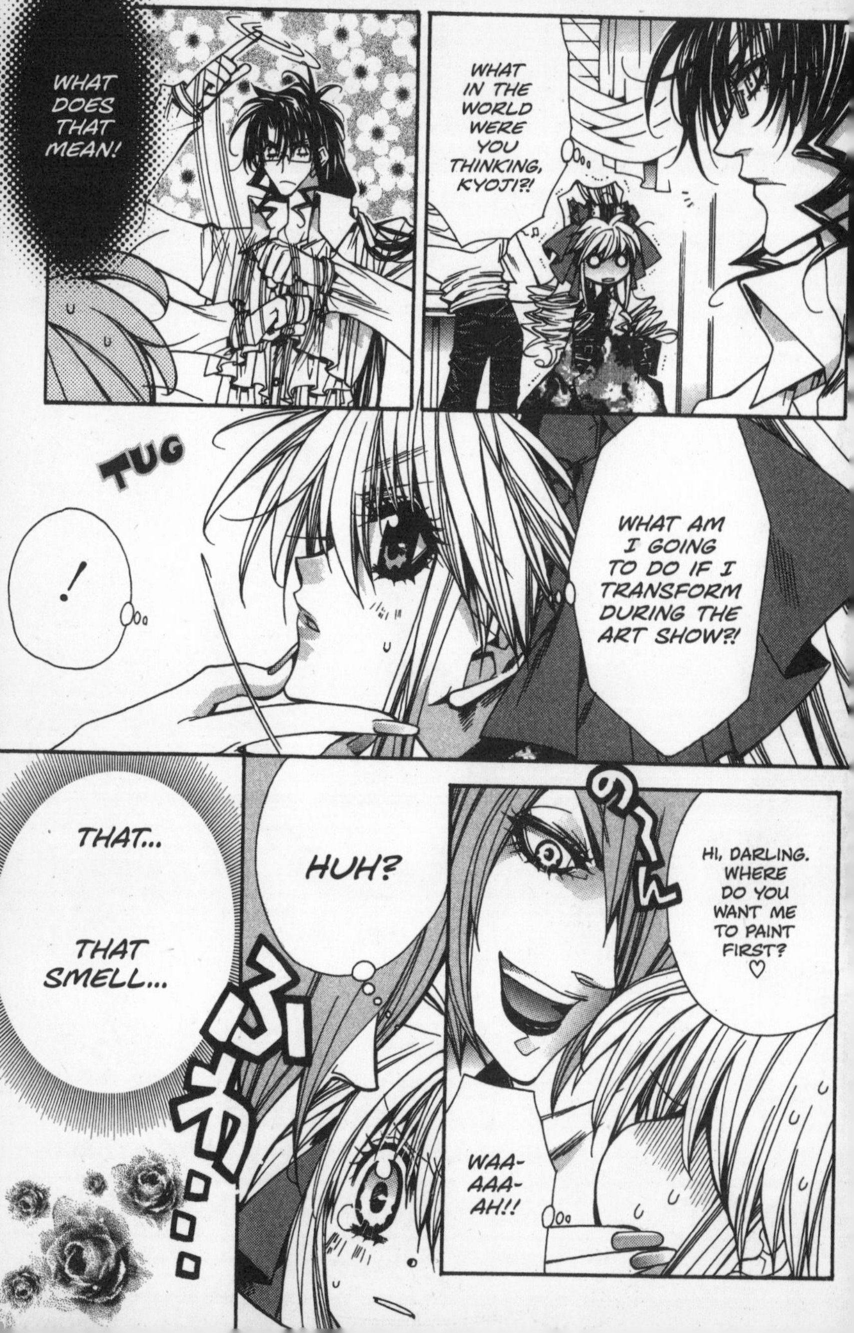
WHAT IN THE WORLD WERE YOU THINKING, KYOJI?!
WHAT DOES THAT MEAN!
WHAT AM I GOING TO DO IF I TRANSFORM DURING THE ART SHOW?!
TUG
!
HI, DARLING. WHERE DO YOU WANT ME TO PAINT FIRST? ♡
WAA-AAA-AH!!
HUH?
THAT...
THAT SMELL...

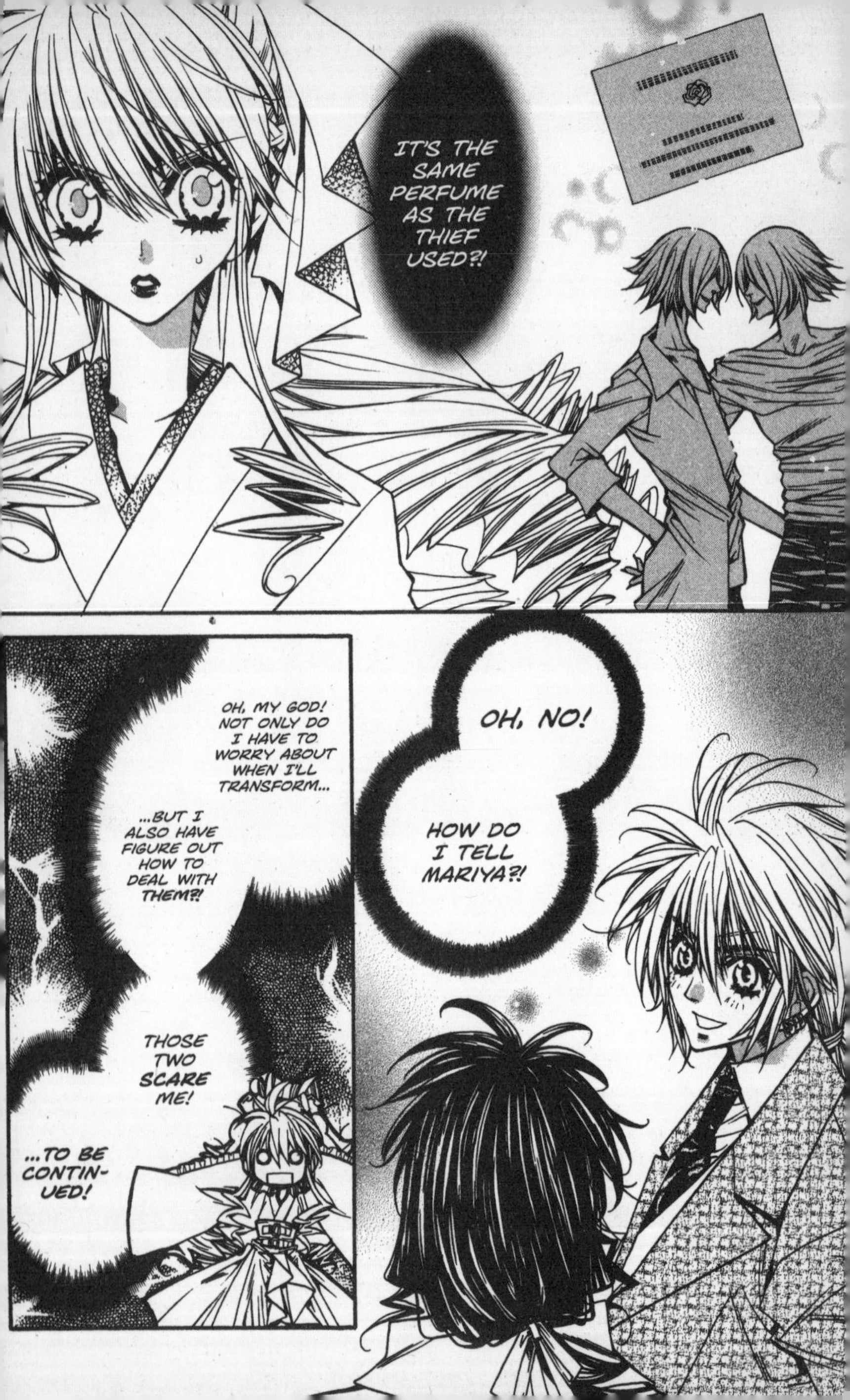
IT'S THE SAME PERFUME AS THE THIEF USED?!
OH, NO!
HOW DO I TELL MARIYA?!
OH, MY GOD! NOT ONLY DO I HAVE TO WORRY ABOUT WHEN I'LL TRANSFORM...
...BUT I ALSO HAVE FIGURE OUT HOW TO DEAL WITH THEM?!
THOSE TWO SCARE ME!
...TO BE CONTIN-UED!

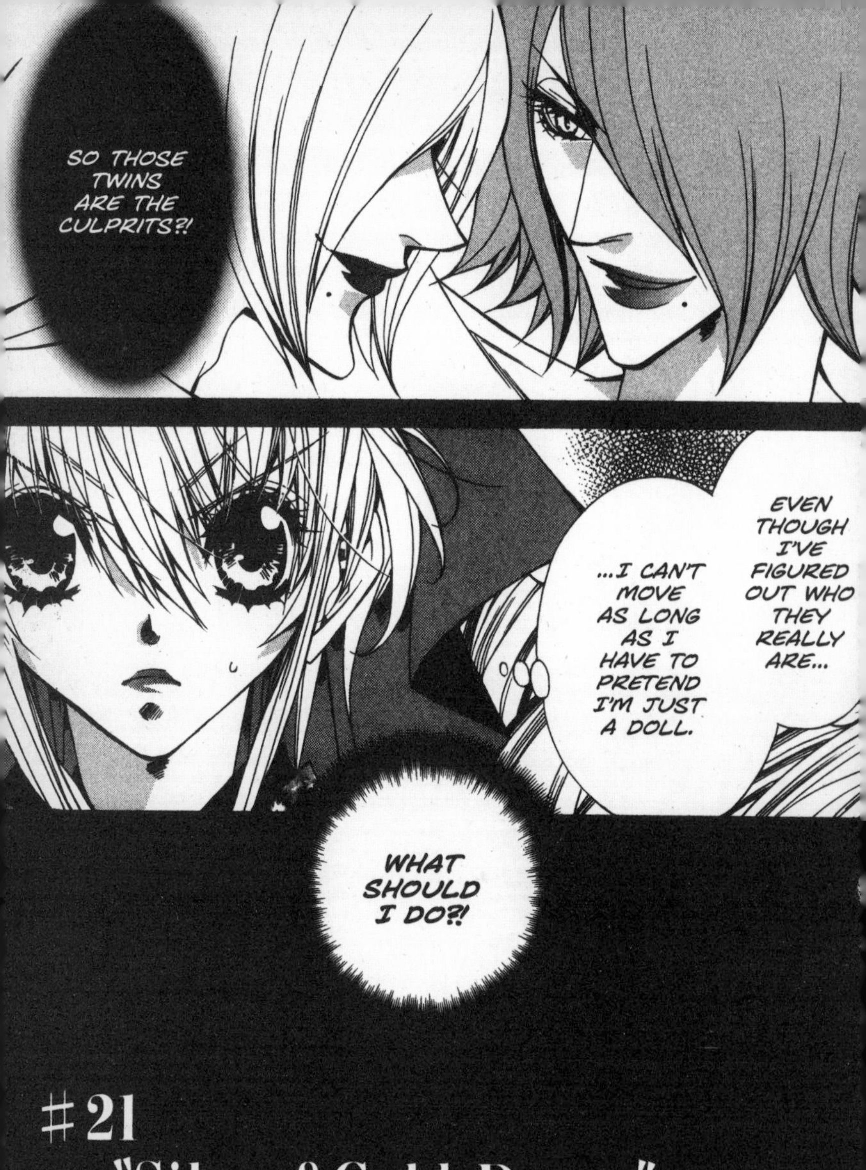
SO THOSE TWINS ARE THE CULPRITS?!
EVEN THOUGH I'VE FIGURED OUT WHO THEY REALLY ARE...
...I CAN'T MOVE AS LONG AS I HAVE TO PRETEND I'M JUST A DOLL.
WHAT SHOULD I DO?!

♯21 "Silver&Gold Dance" PART 2

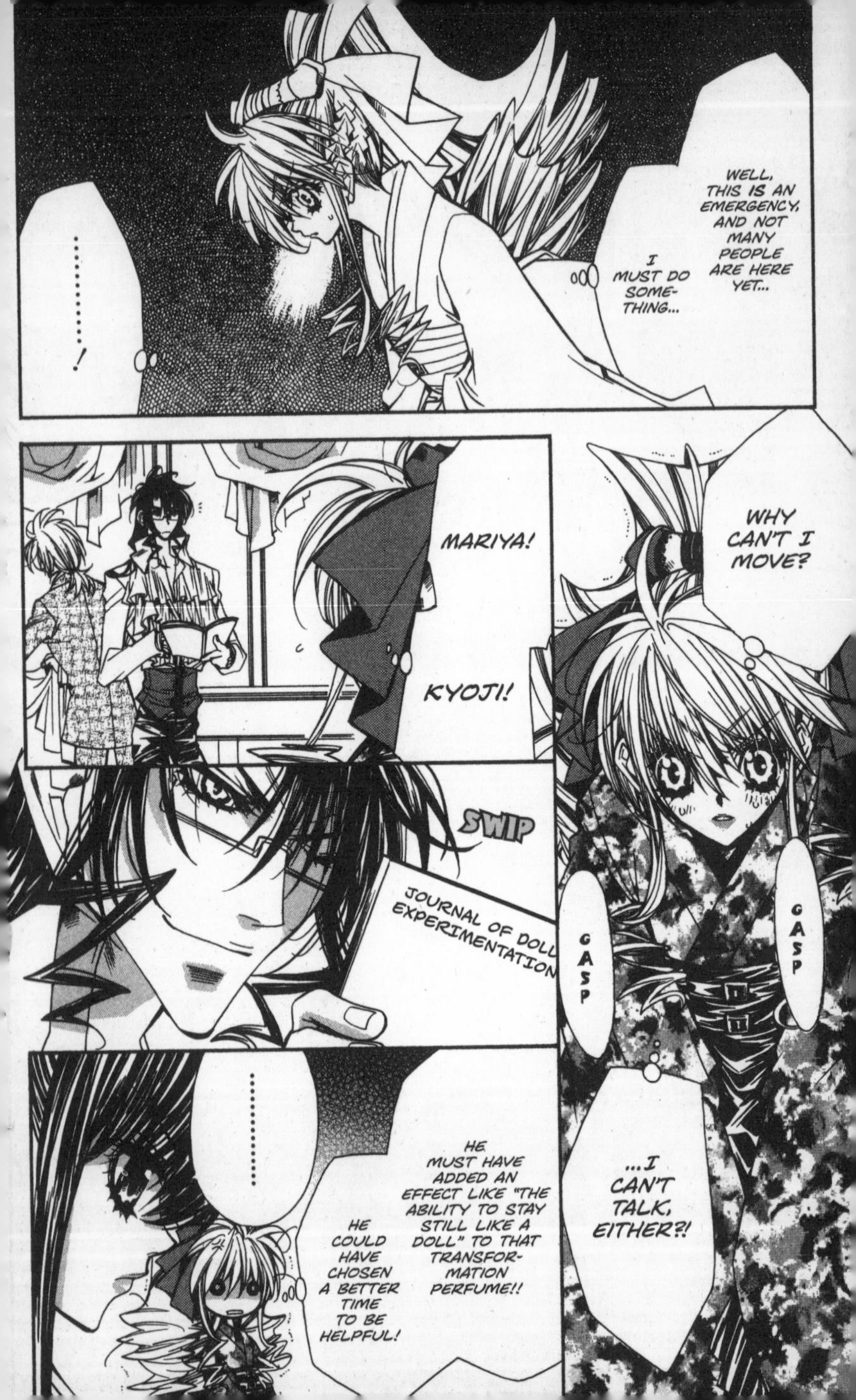
WELL, THIS IS AN EMERGENCY, AND NOT MANY PEOPLE ARE HERE YET...
I MUST DO SOME-THING...
......!
WHY CAN'T I MOVE?
GASP
GASP
...I CAN'T TALK, EITHER?!
MARIYA!
KYOJI!
SWIP
JOURNAL OF DOLL EXPERIMENTATION
HE MUST HAVE ADDED AN EFFECT LIKE "THE ABILITY TO STAY STILL LIKE A DOLL" TO THAT TRANSFOR-MATION PERFUME!!
HE COULD HAVE CHOSEN A BETTER TIME TO BE HELPFUL!
......

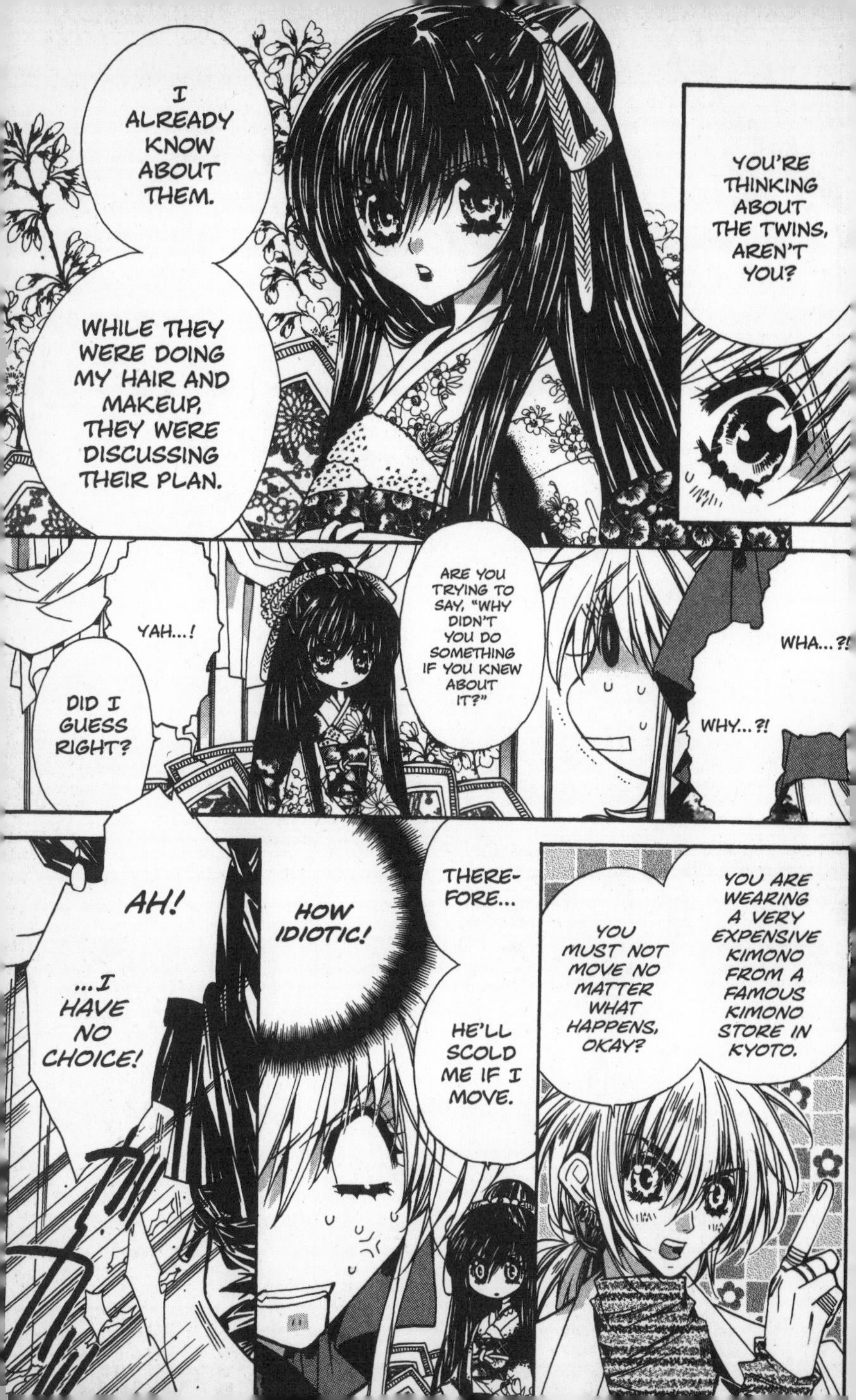

YOU'RE THINKING ABOUT THE TWINS, AREN'T YOU?
I ALREADY KNOW ABOUT THEM.
WHILE THEY WERE DOING MY HAIR AND MAKEUP, THEY WERE DISCUSSING THEIR PLAN.
WHA...?!
WHY...?!
ARE YOU TRYING TO SAY, "WHY DIDN'T YOU DO SOMETHING IF YOU KNEW ABOUT IT?"
YAH...!
DID I GUESS RIGHT?
YOU ARE WEARING A VERY EXPENSIVE KIMONO FROM A FAMOUS KIMONO STORE IN KYOTO.
YOU MUST NOT MOVE NO MATTER WHAT HAPPENS, OKAY?
THERE-FORE...
HOW IDIOTIC!
HE'LL SCOLD ME IF I MOVE.
AH!
...I HAVE NO CHOICE!

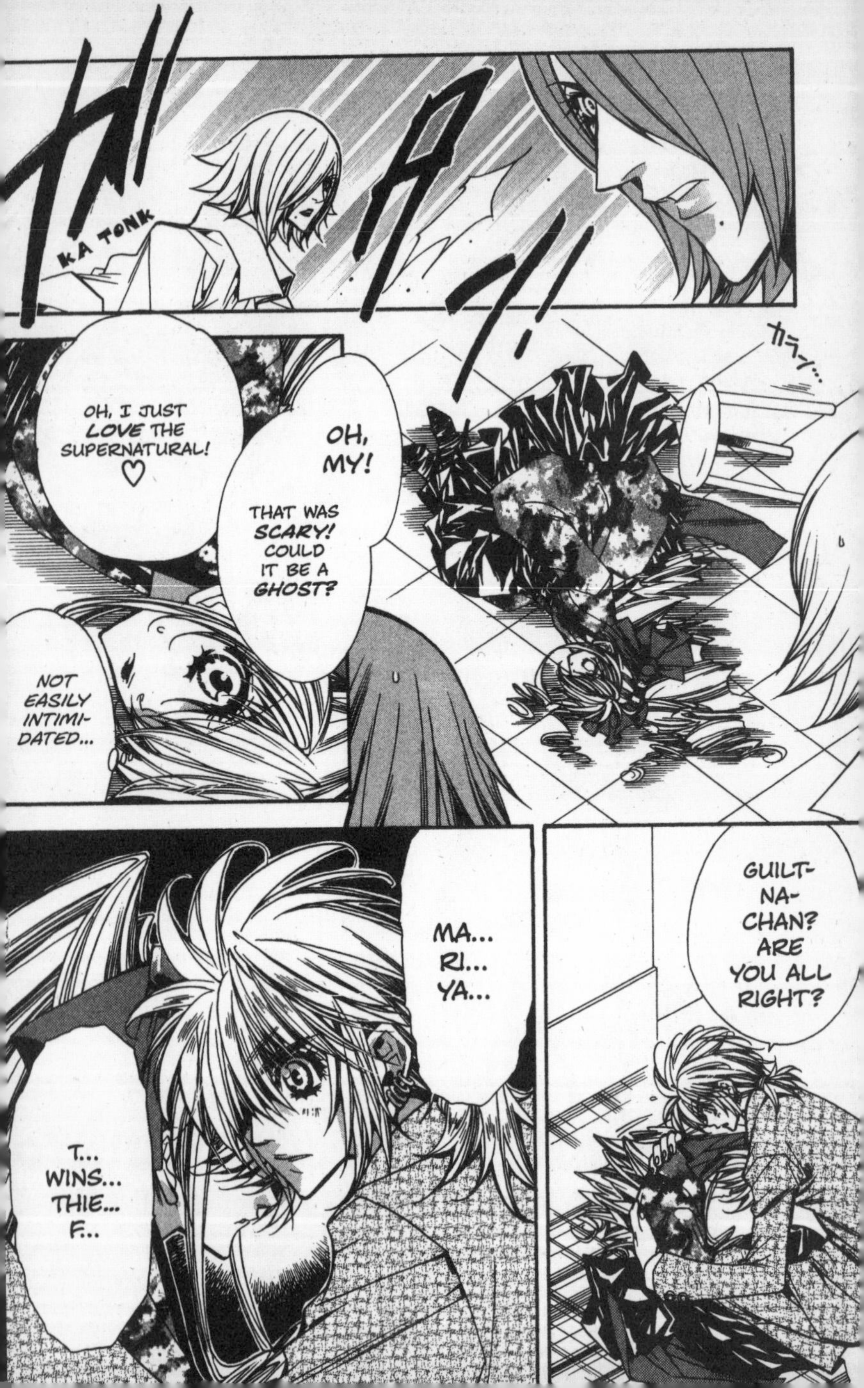
KA TONK
OH, MY! THAT WAS SCARY! COULD IT BE A GHOST?
OH, I JUST LOVE THE SUPERNATURAL! ♡
NOT EASILY INTIMIDATED...
GUILT-NA-CHAN? ARE YOU ALL RIGHT?
MA... RI... YA...
T... WINS... THIE... F...

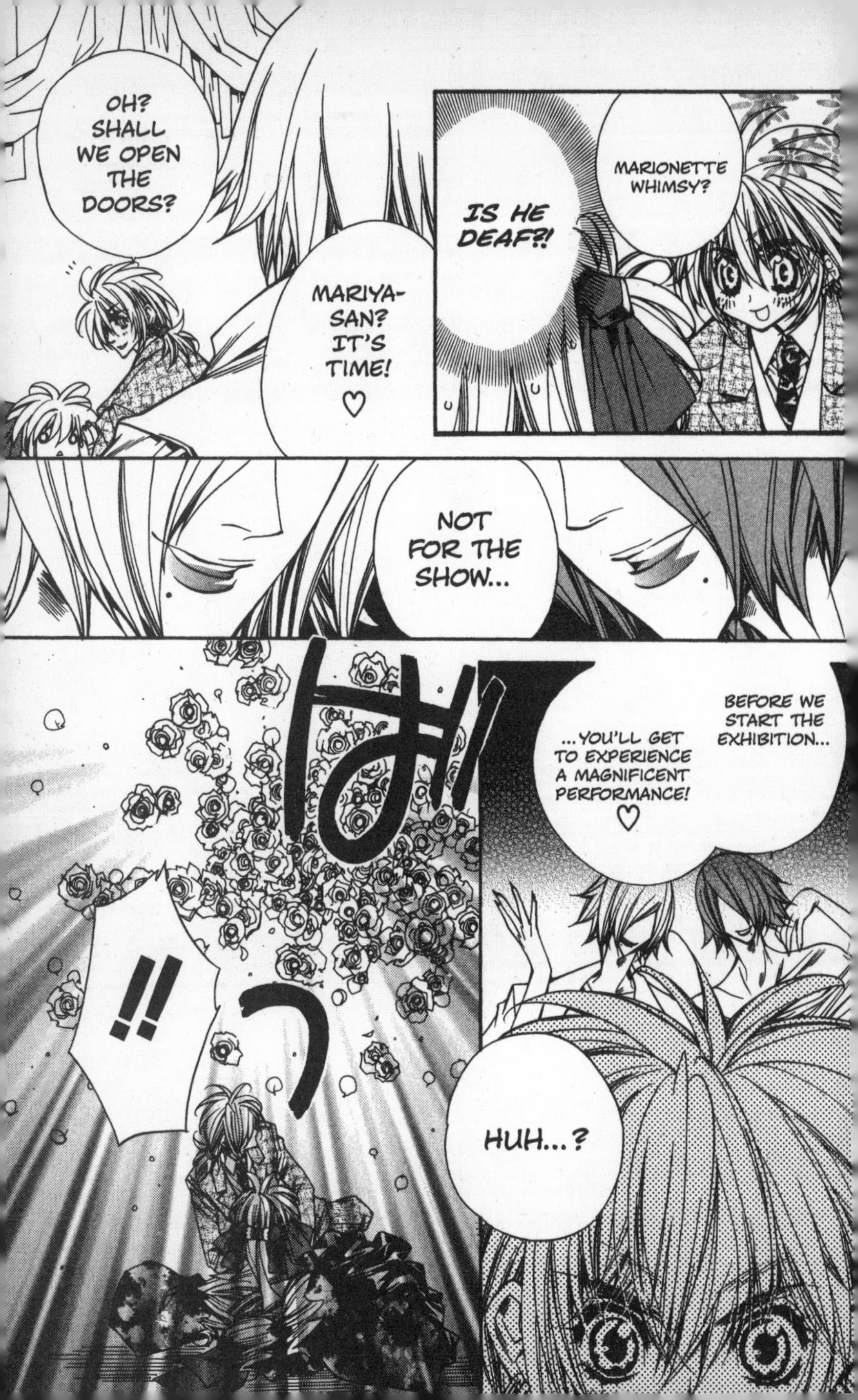
MARIONETTE WHIMSY?
IS HE DEAF?!
MARIYA-SAN? IT'S TIME! ♡
OH? SHALL WE OPEN THE DOORS?
NOT FOR THE SHOW...
BEFORE WE START THE EXHIBITION...
...YOU'LL GET TO EXPERIENCE A MAGNIFICENT PERFORMANCE! ♡
HUH...?
ばっ
!!

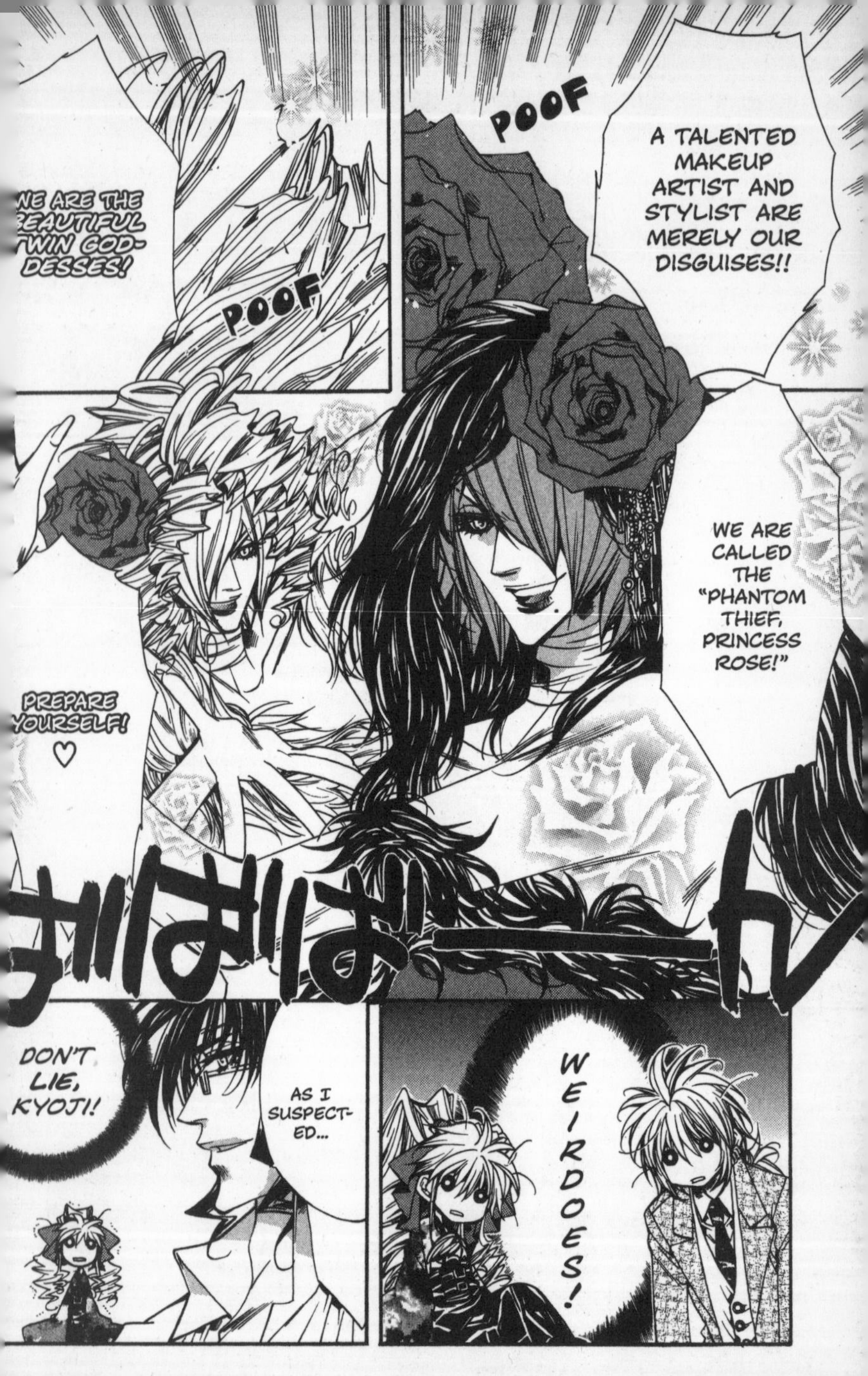
POOF
A TALENTED MAKEUP ARTIST AND STYLIST ARE MERELY OUR DISGUISES!!
WE ARE THE BEAUTIFUL TWIN GOD-DESSES!
POOF
WE ARE CALLED THE "PHANTOM THIEF, PRINCESS ROSE!"
PREPARE YOURSELF! ♡
WEIRDOES!
AS I SUSPECT-ED...
DON'T LIE, KYOJI!

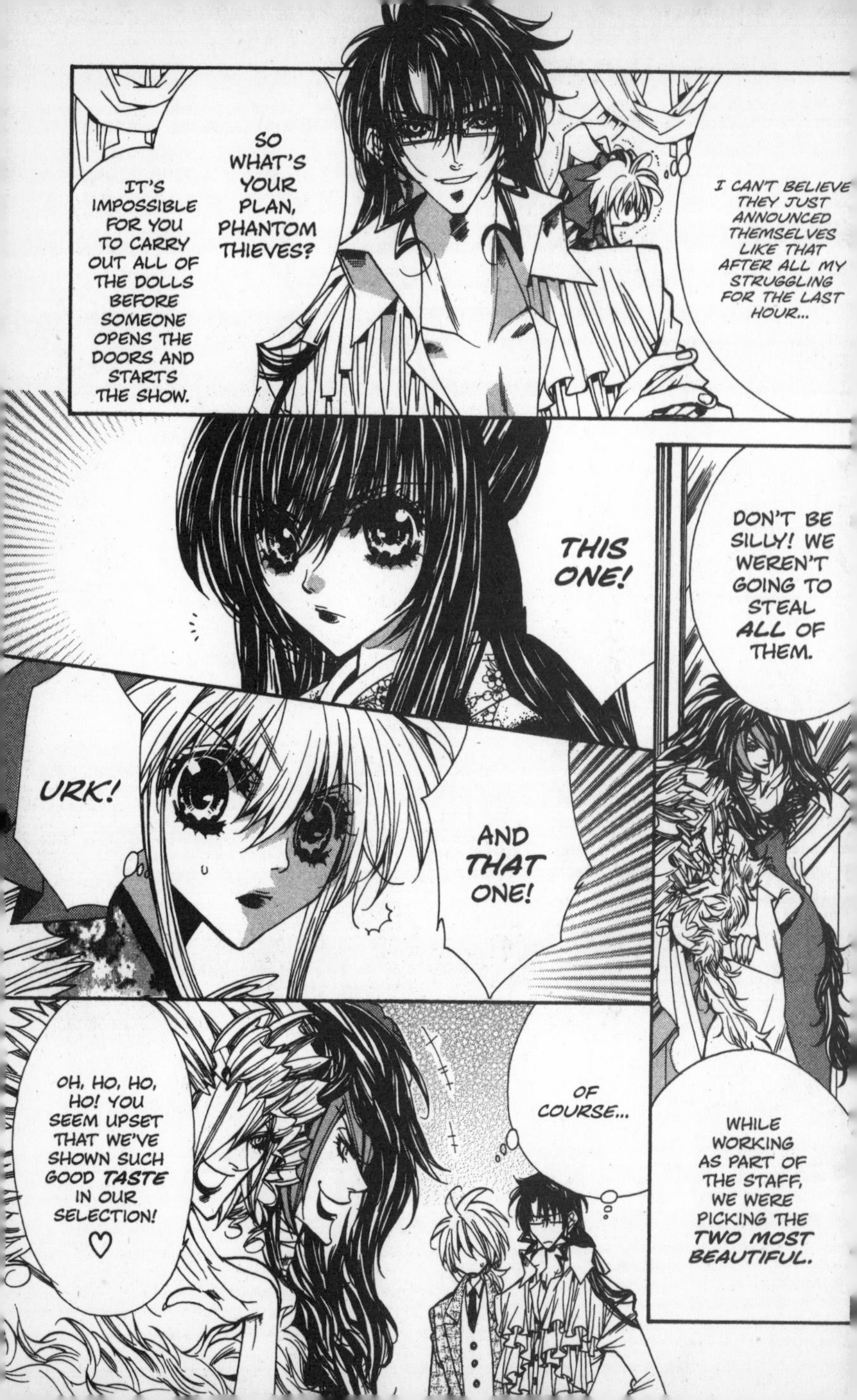
I CAN'T BELIEVE THEY JUST ANNOUNCED THEMSELVES LIKE THAT AFTER ALL MY STRUGGLING FOR THE LAST HOUR...
SO WHAT'S YOUR PLAN, PHANTOM THIEVES?
IT'S IMPOSSIBLE FOR YOU TO CARRY OUT ALL OF THE DOLLS BEFORE SOMEONE OPENS THE DOORS AND STARTS THE SHOW.
DON'T BE SILLY! WE WEREN'T GOING TO STEAL ALL OF THEM.
WHILE WORKING AS PART OF THE STAFF, WE WERE PICKING THE TWO MOST BEAUTIFUL.
THIS ONE!
AND THAT ONE!
URK!
OF COURSE...
OH, HO, HO, HO! YOU SEEM UPSET THAT WE'VE SHOWN SUCH GOOD TASTE IN OUR SELECTION! ♡

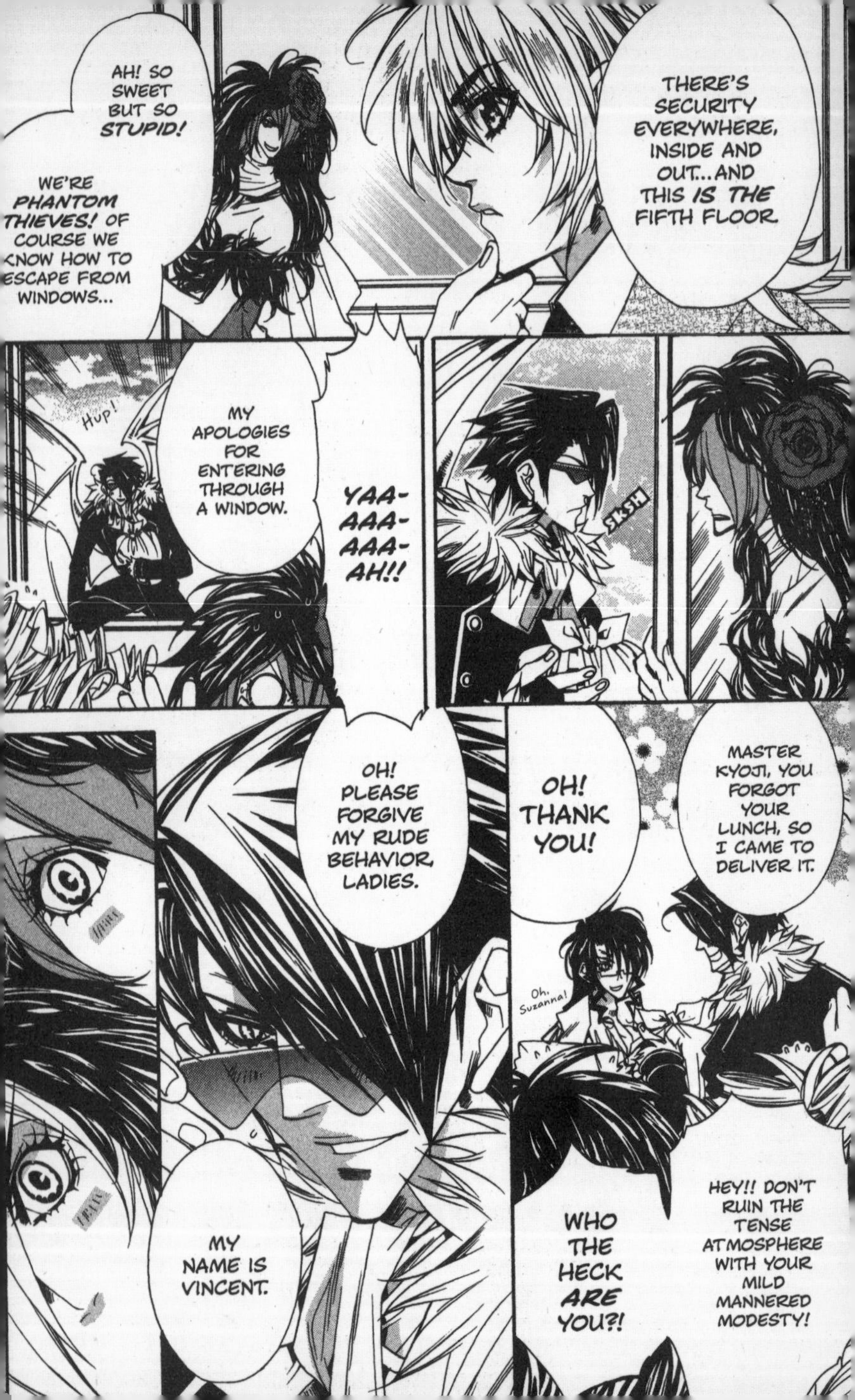

THERE'S SECURITY EVERYWHERE, INSIDE AND OUT...AND THIS *IS THE* FIFTH FLOOR
AH! SO SWEET BUT SO *STUPID!*
WE'RE *PHANTOM THIEVES!* OF COURSE WE KNOW HOW TO ESCAPE FROM WINDOWS...
SKSH
Hup!
MY APOLOGIES FOR ENTERING THROUGH A WINDOW.
YAA-AAA-AAA-AH!!
MASTER KYOJI, YOU FORGOT YOUR LUNCH, SO I CAME TO DELIVER IT.
OH! THANK YOU!
Oh, Suzanna!
HEY!! DON'T RUIN THE TENSE ATMOSPHERE WITH YOUR MILD MANNERED MODESTY!
WHO THE HECK *ARE* YOU?!
OH! PLEASE FORGIVE MY RUDE BEHAVIOR, LADIES.
MY NAME IS VINCENT.

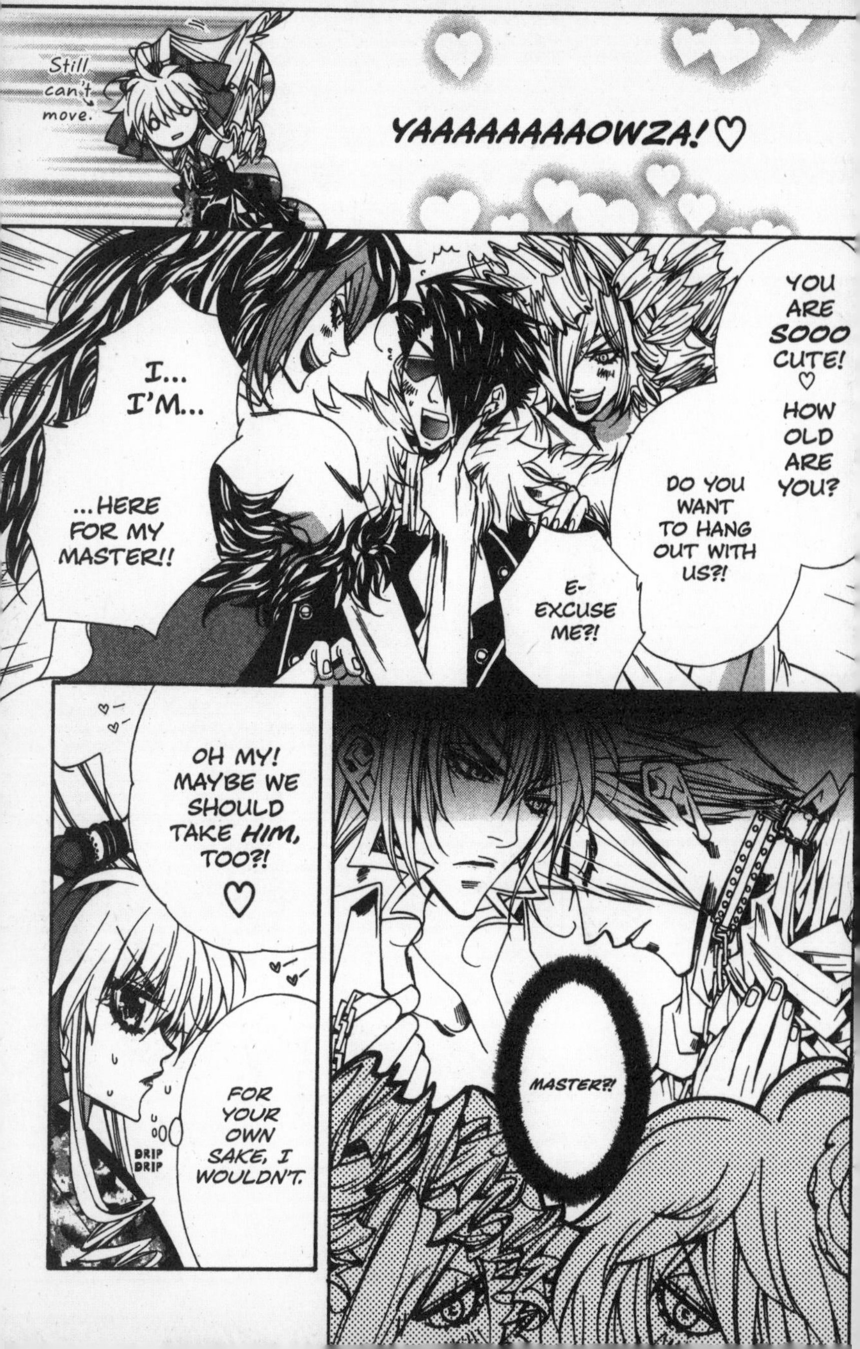
YAAAAAAAAOWZA! ♡
Still can't move.
YOU ARE SOOO CUTE! ♡ HOW OLD ARE YOU?
DO YOU WANT TO HANG OUT WITH US?!
E-EXCUSE ME?!
I... I'M...
...HERE FOR MY MASTER!!
MASTER?!
OH MY! MAYBE WE SHOULD TAKE HIM, TOO?! ♡
FOR YOUR OWN SAKE, I WOULDN'T.
DRIP DRIP

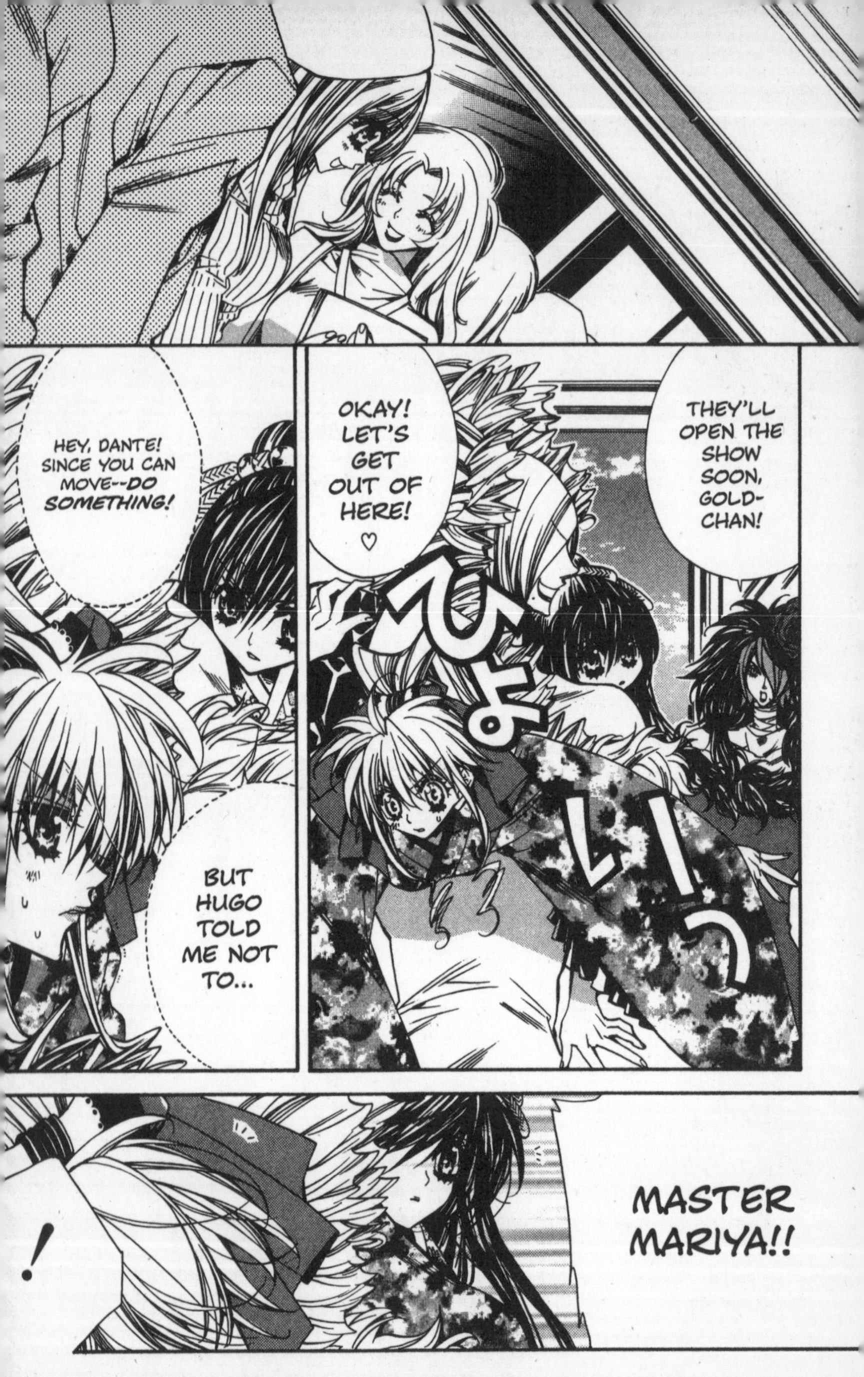
THEY'LL OPEN THE SHOW SOON, GOLD-CHAN!
OKAY! LET'S GET OUT OF HERE! ♡
HEY, DANTE! SINCE YOU CAN MOVE--DO SOMETHING!
BUT HUGO TOLD ME NOT TO...
MASTER MARIYA!!
!

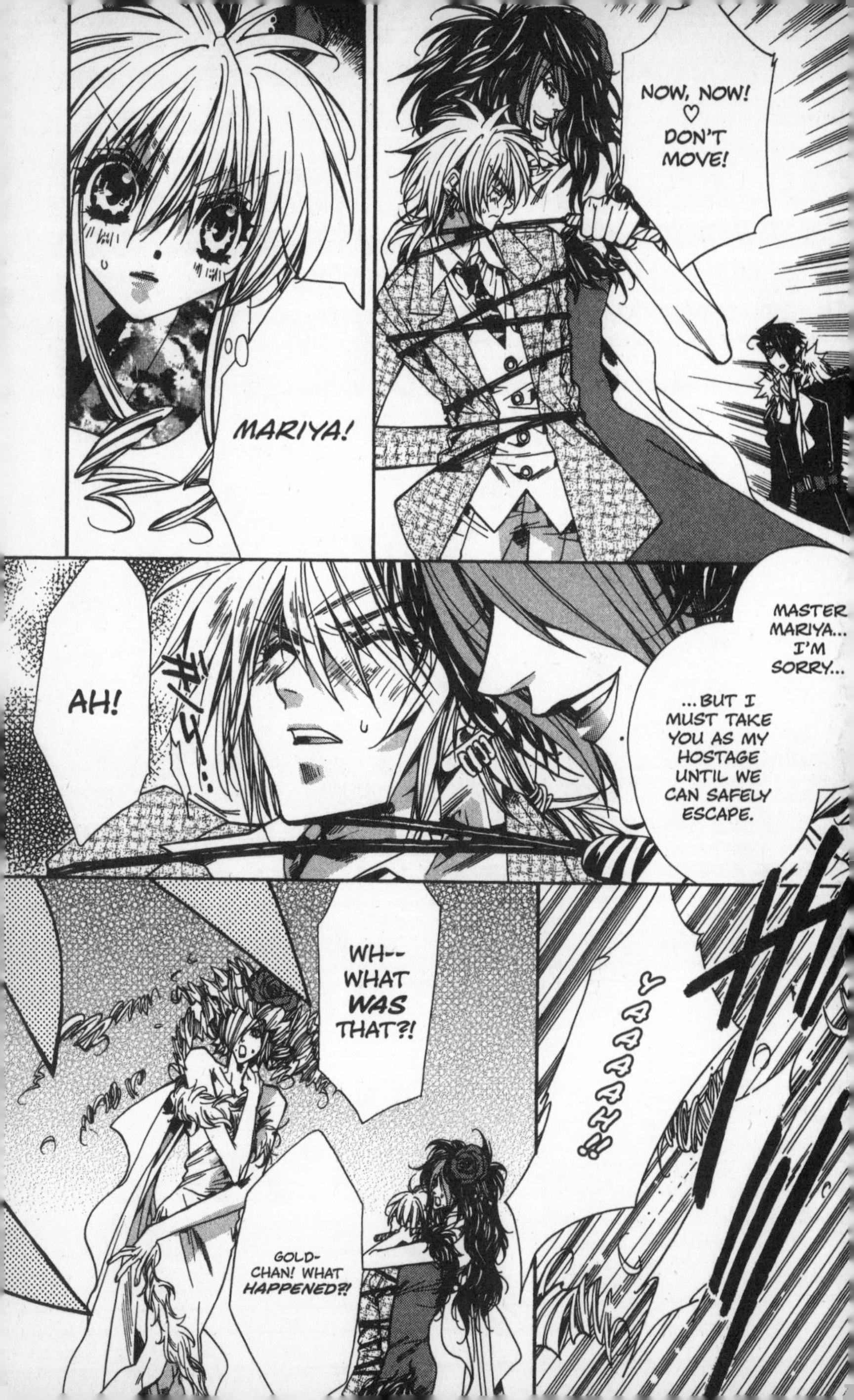
NOW, NOW! ♡ DON'T MOVE!
MARIYA!
MASTER MARIYA... I'M SORRY...
...BUT I MUST TAKE YOU AS MY HOSTAGE UNTIL WE CAN SAFELY ESCAPE.
AH!
YAAAAAH!!
WH-- WHAT *WAS* THAT?!
GOLD-CHAN! WHAT *HAPPENED*?!

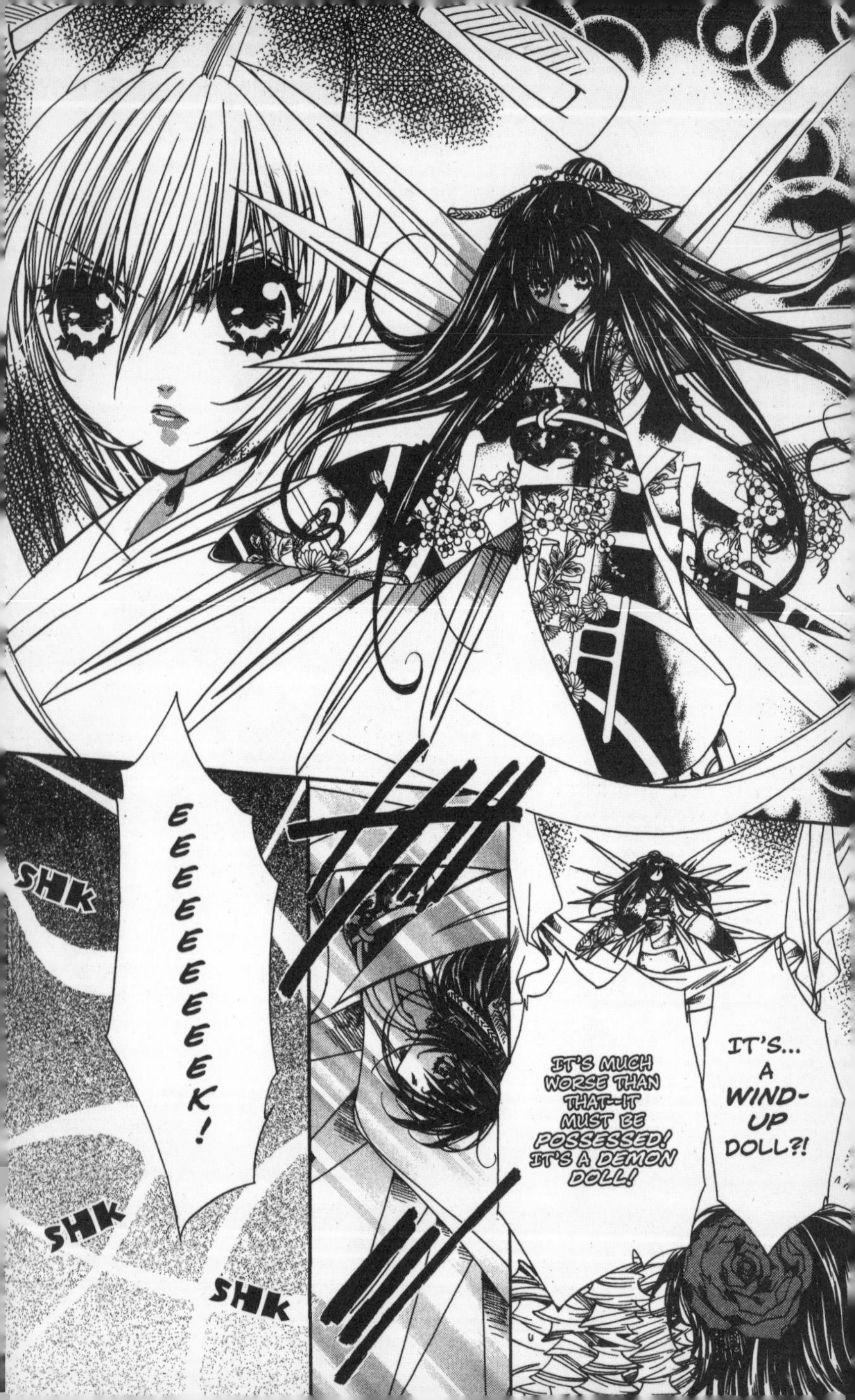
IT'S... A WIND-UP DOLL?!
IT'S MUCH WORSE THAN THAT--IT MUST BE POSSESSED! IT'S A DEMON DOLL!
EEEEEEEEEEK!
SHK
SHK
SHK

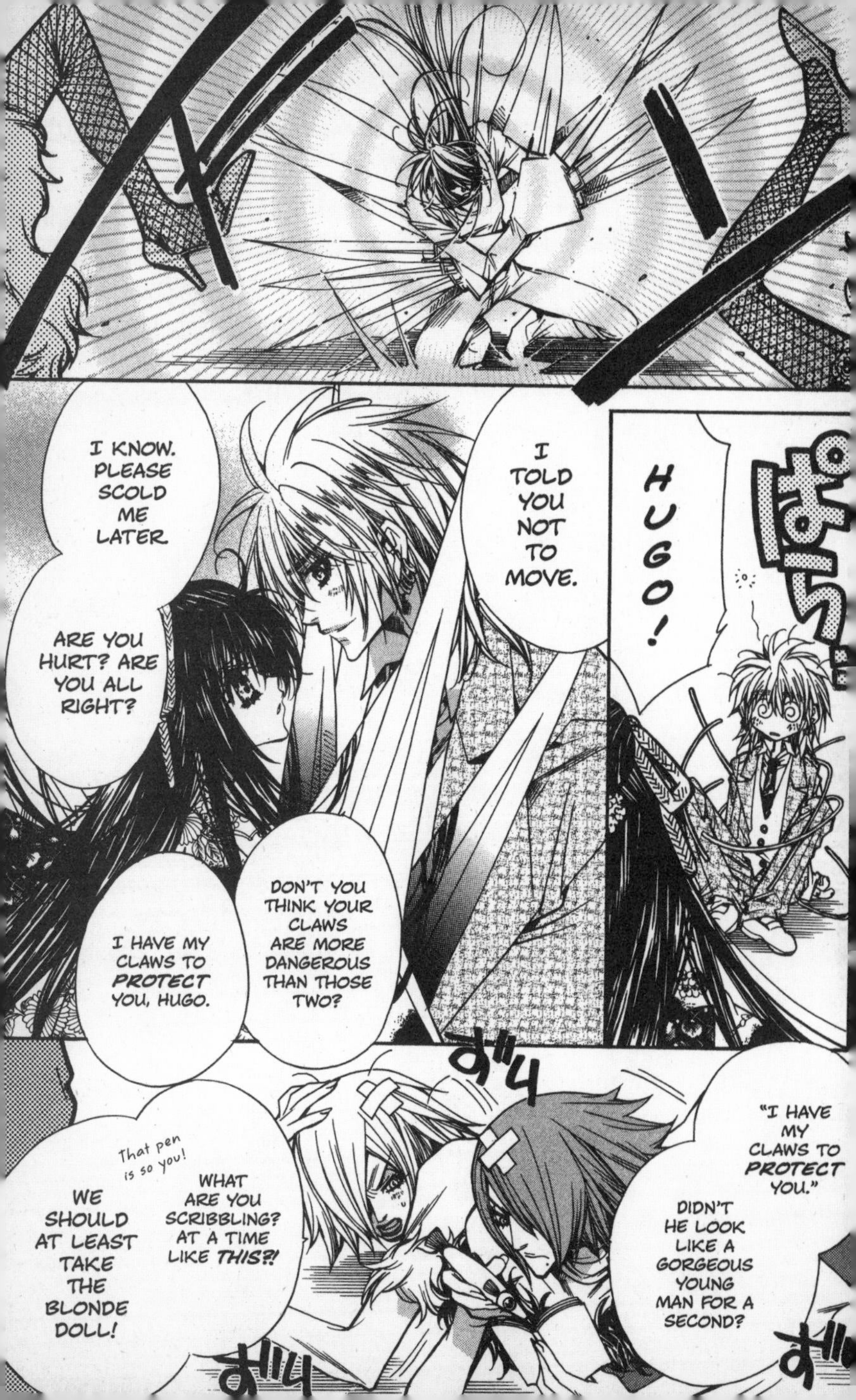

HUGO!
I TOLD YOU NOT TO MOVE.
I KNOW. PLEASE SCOLD ME LATER
ARE YOU HURT? ARE YOU ALL RIGHT?
DON'T YOU THINK YOUR CLAWS ARE MORE DANGEROUS THAN THOSE TWO?
I HAVE MY CLAWS TO *PROTECT* YOU, HUGO.
"I HAVE MY CLAWS TO *PROTECT* YOU."
DIDN'T HE LOOK LIKE A GORGEOUS YOUNG MAN FOR A SECOND?
WHAT ARE YOU SCRIBBLING? AT A TIME LIKE *THIS?!*
That pen is so you!
WE SHOULD AT LEAST TAKE THE BLONDE DOLL!

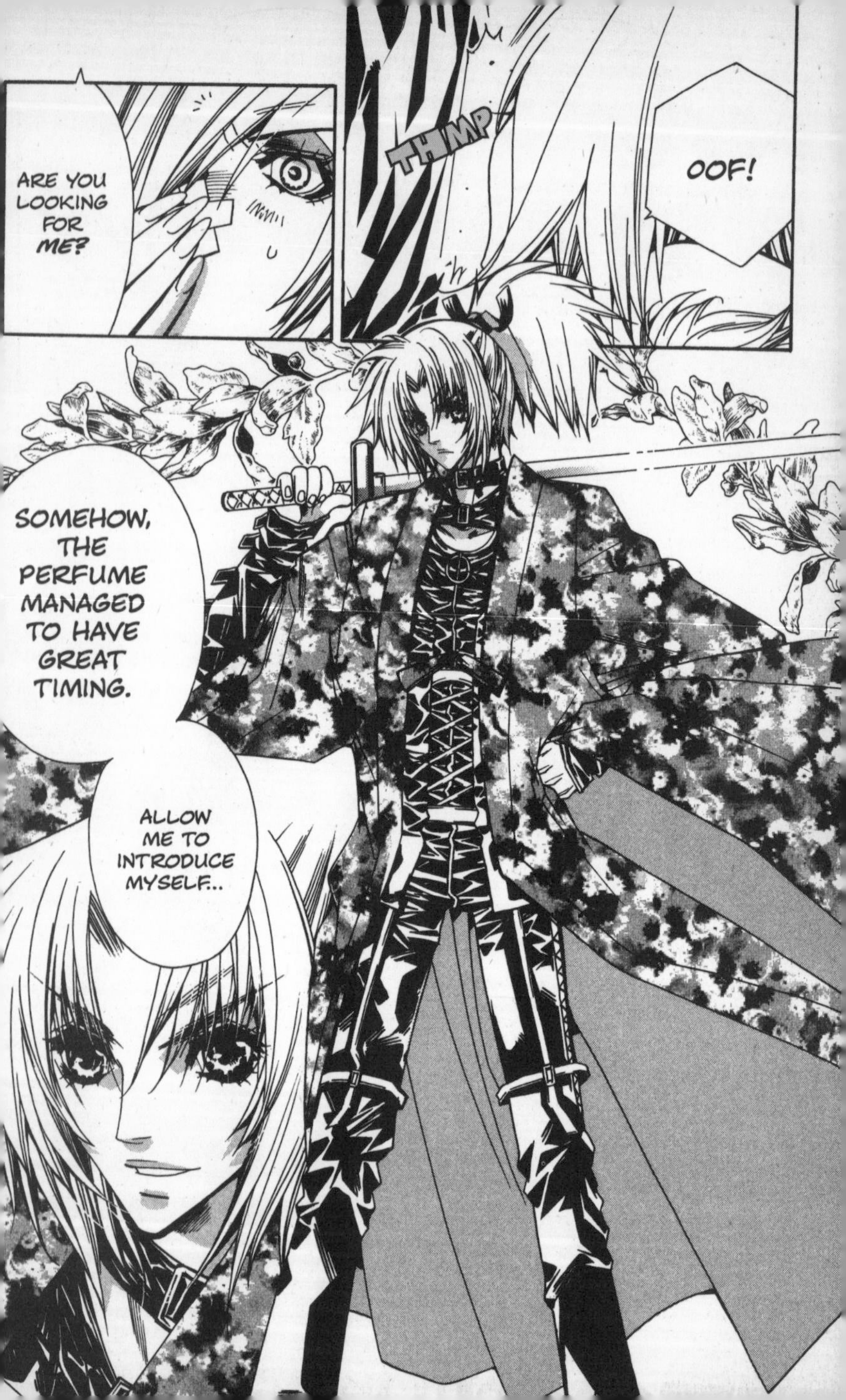
THMP
OOF!
ARE YOU LOOKING FOR ME?
SOMEHOW, THE PERFUME MANAGED TO HAVE GREAT TIMING.
ALLOW ME TO INTRODUCE MYSELF...

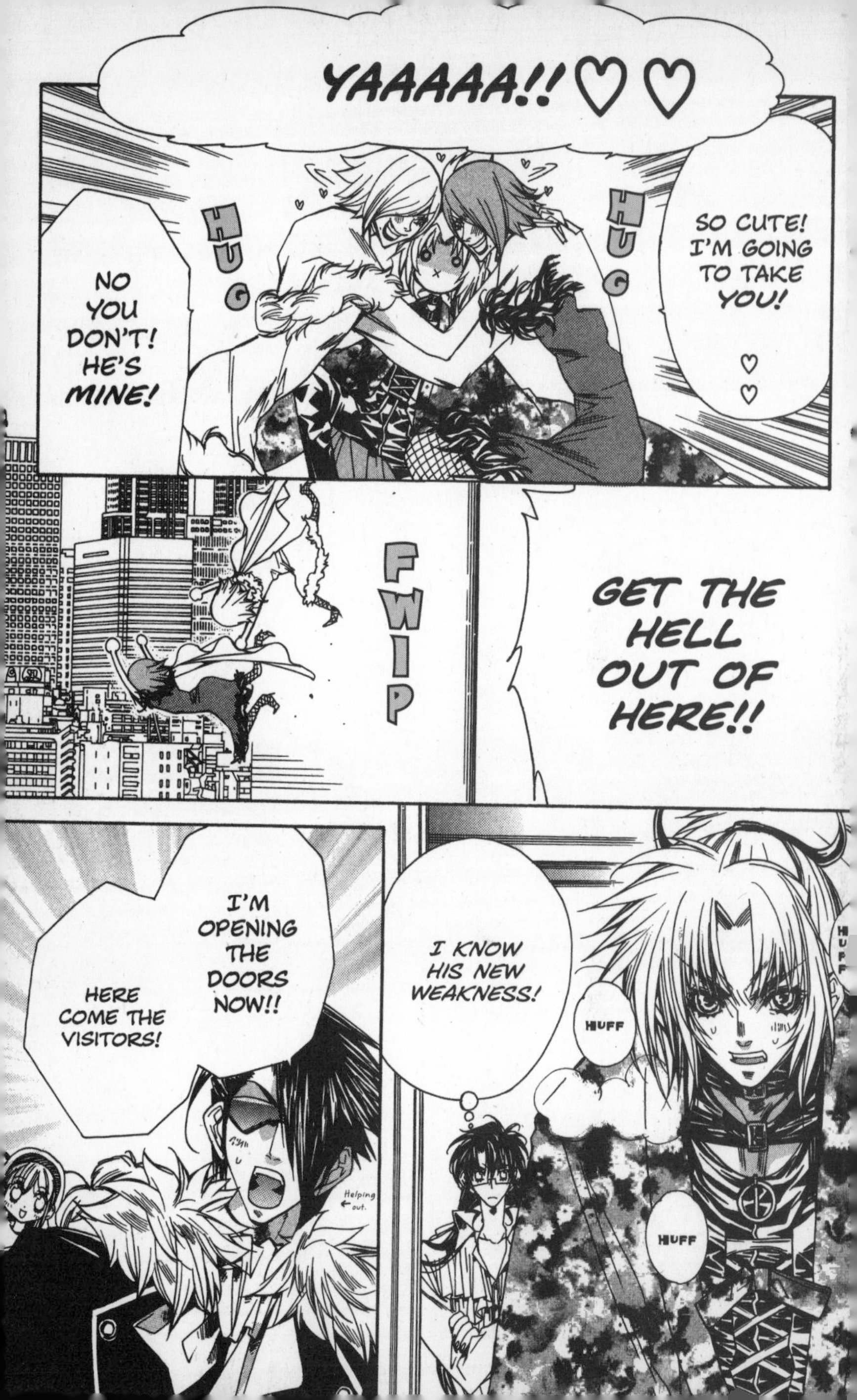
YAAAAA!! ♡ ♡
SO CUTE! I'M GOING TO TAKE YOU! ♡ ♡
HUG
HUG
NO YOU DON'T! HE'S MINE!
GET THE HELL OUT OF HERE!!
FWIP
HUFF
I KNOW HIS NEW WEAKNESS!
HUFF
HUFF
I'M OPENING THE DOORS NOW!!
HERE COME THE VISITORS!
Helping out.

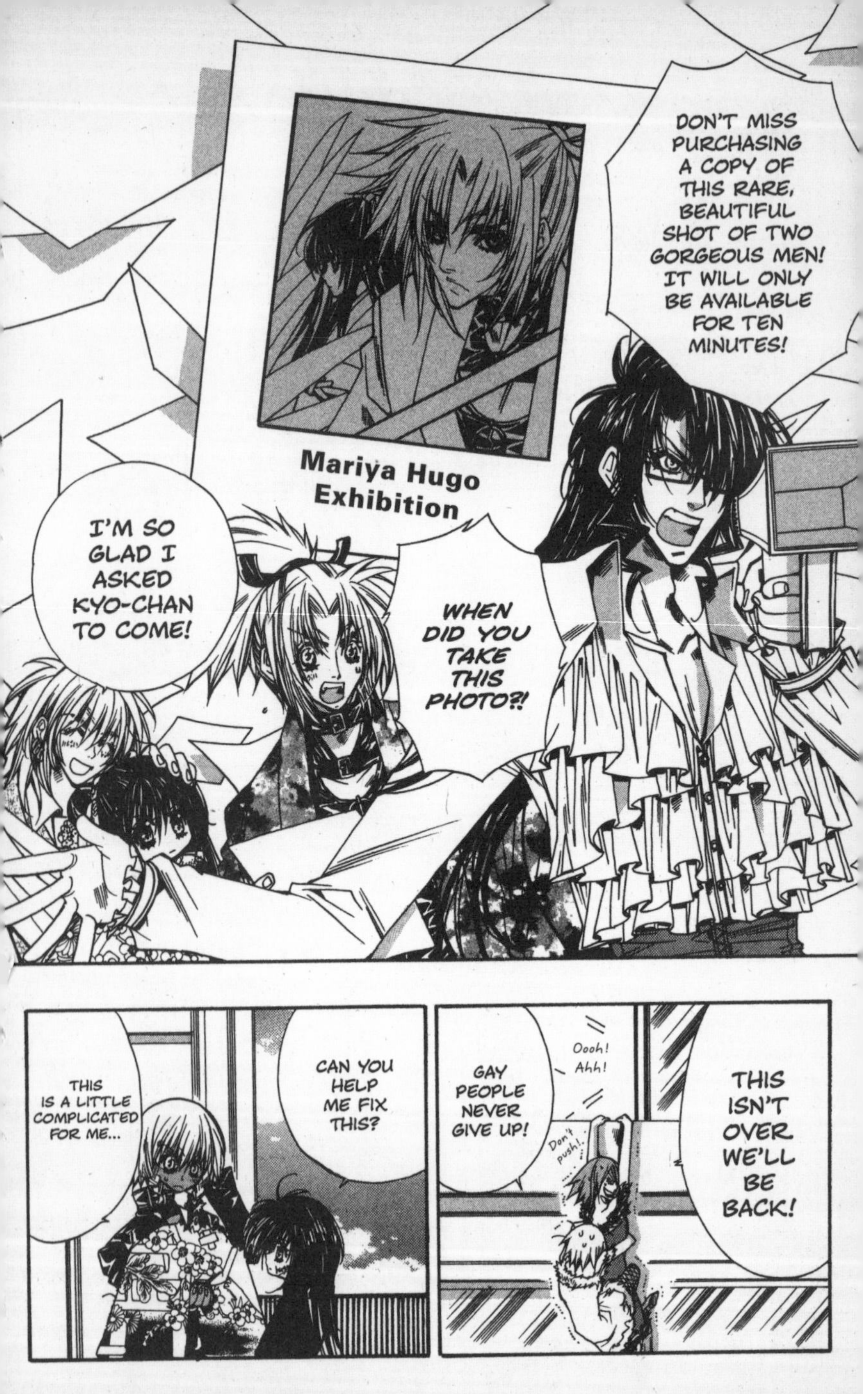
DON'T MISS PURCHASING A COPY OF THIS RARE, BEAUTIFUL SHOT OF TWO GORGEOUS MEN! IT WILL ONLY BE AVAILABLE FOR TEN MINUTES!
Mariya Hugo Exhibition
WHEN DID YOU TAKE THIS PHOTO?!
I'M SO GLAD I ASKED KYO-CHAN TO COME!
THIS ISN'T OVER WE'LL BE BACK!
Oooh! Ahh!
GAY PEOPLE NEVER GIVE UP!
Don't push!
CAN YOU HELP ME FIX THIS?
THIS IS A LITTLE COMPLICATED FOR ME...

BONUS COMIC STRIP

VAMPIRE DOLL REFLECTIONS

Silver&Gold Dance

WHAT'S YOUR NAME?
~SILVER & GOLD~
KI--
HOLD IT RIGHT THERE!
DO *NOT* CALL US "GIN-SAN" AND "KIN-SAN" LIKE THOSE OLD GRANNIES FROM JAPANESE FOLK TALES!
WE *INSIST* ON BEING CALLED BY MORE GORGEOUS, SOPHISTICATED NAMES!
KINKAKU AND GINKAKU?
OH, GOOD ONE!
WE NEVER CONSIDERED THAT!

(NOTE: KINKAKU AND GINKAKU ARE FAMOUS TEMPLES IN KYOTO.)

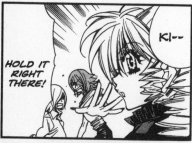

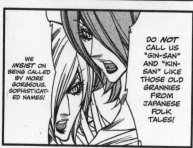

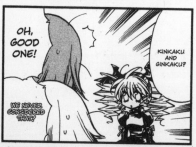

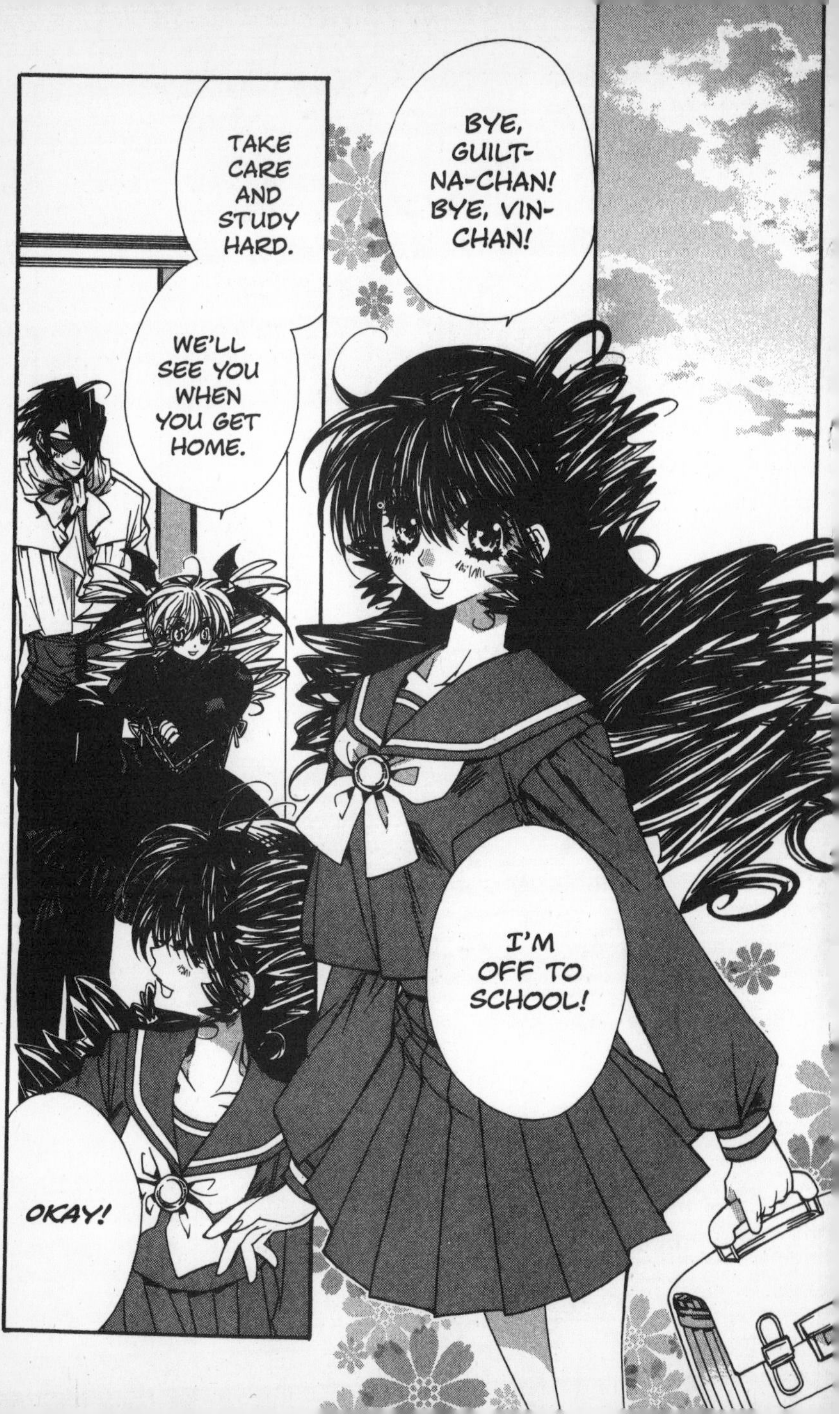
BYE, GUILT-NA-CHAN! BYE, VIN-CHAN!
I'M OFF TO SCHOOL!
TAKE CARE AND STUDY HARD.
WE'LL SEE YOU WHEN YOU GET HOME.
OKAY!

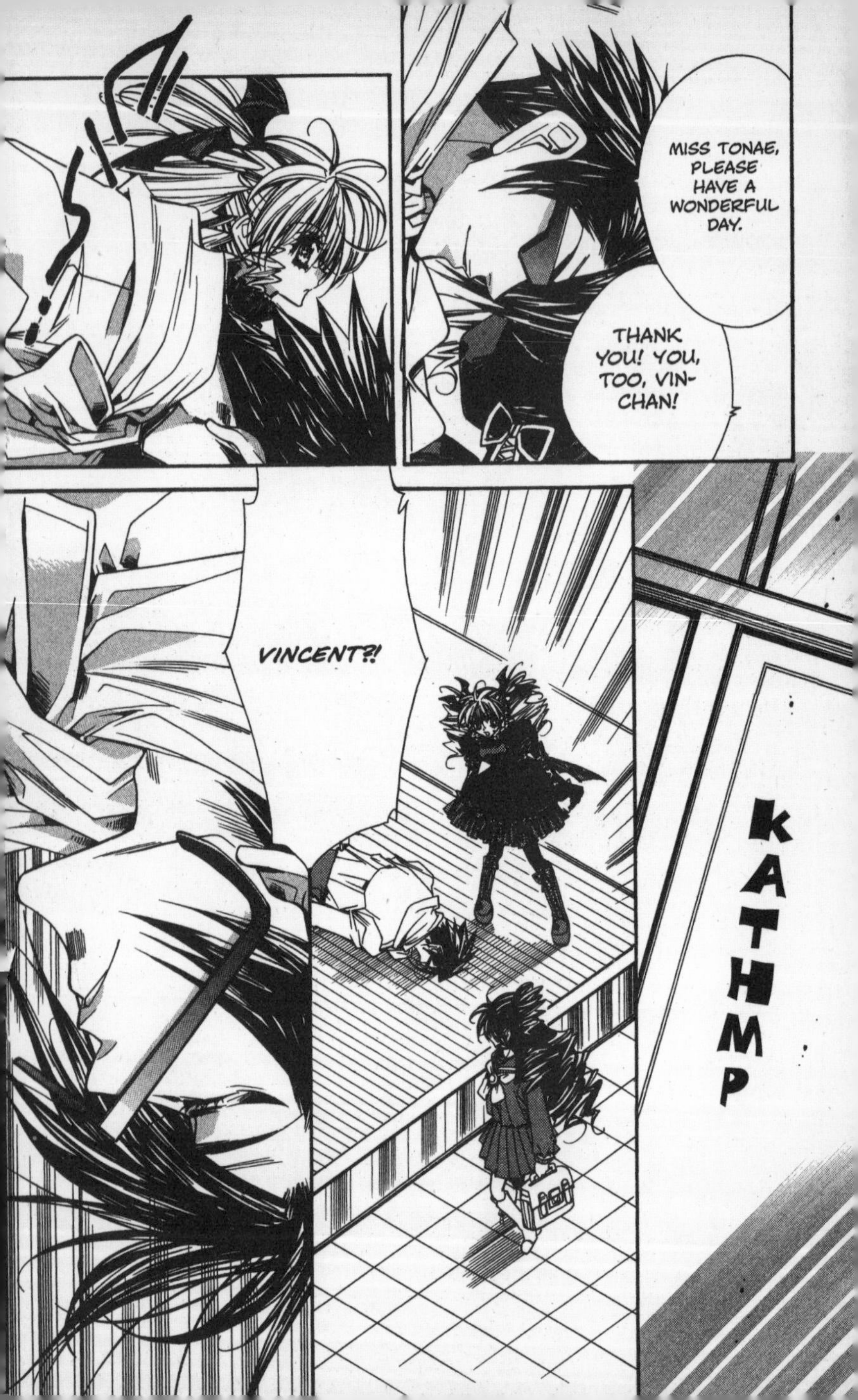
MISS TONAE, PLEASE HAVE A WONDERFUL DAY.
THANK YOU! YOU, TOO, VIN-CHAN!
KATHMP
VINCENT?!

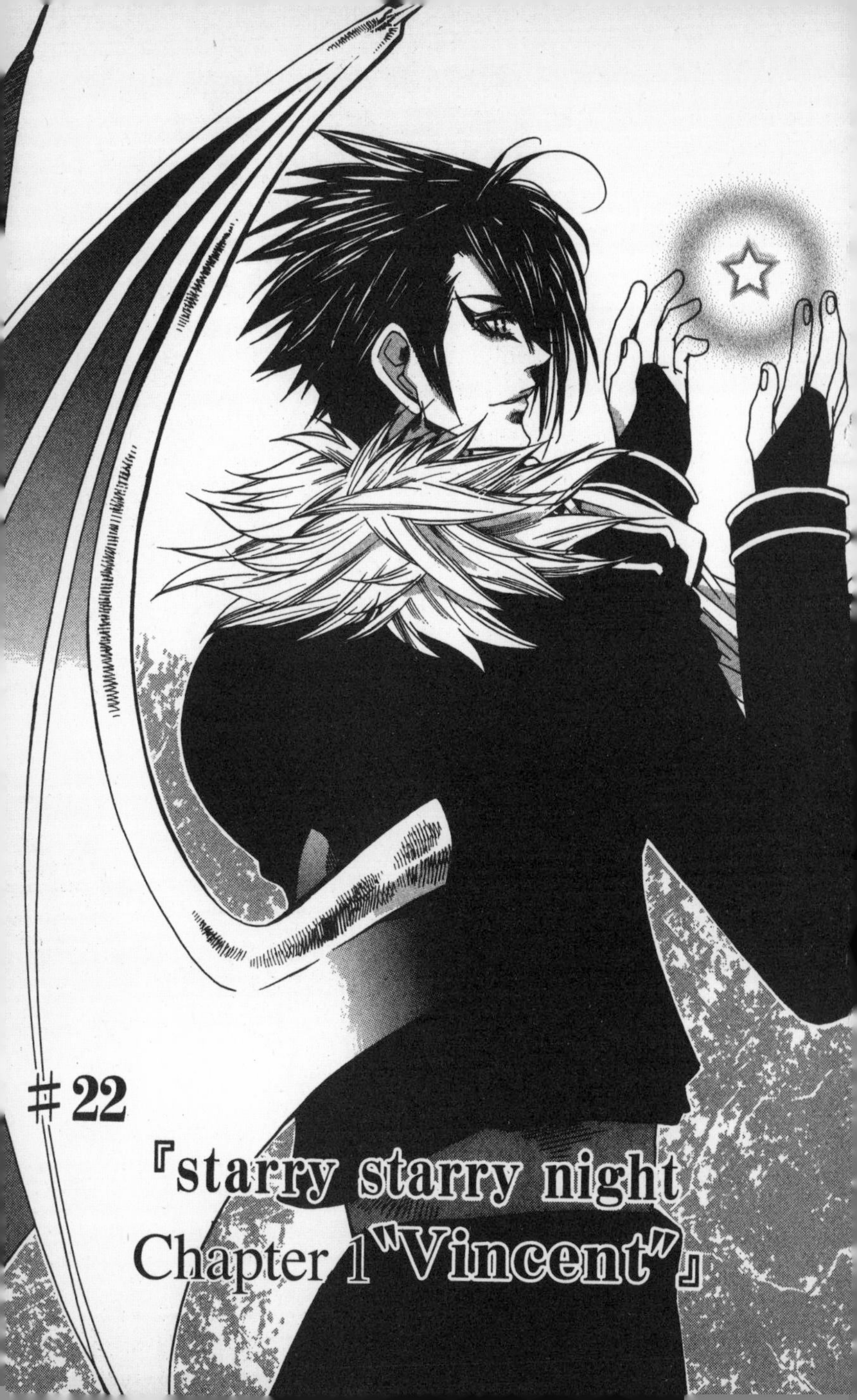
#22
『starry starry night
Chapter 1"Vincent"』

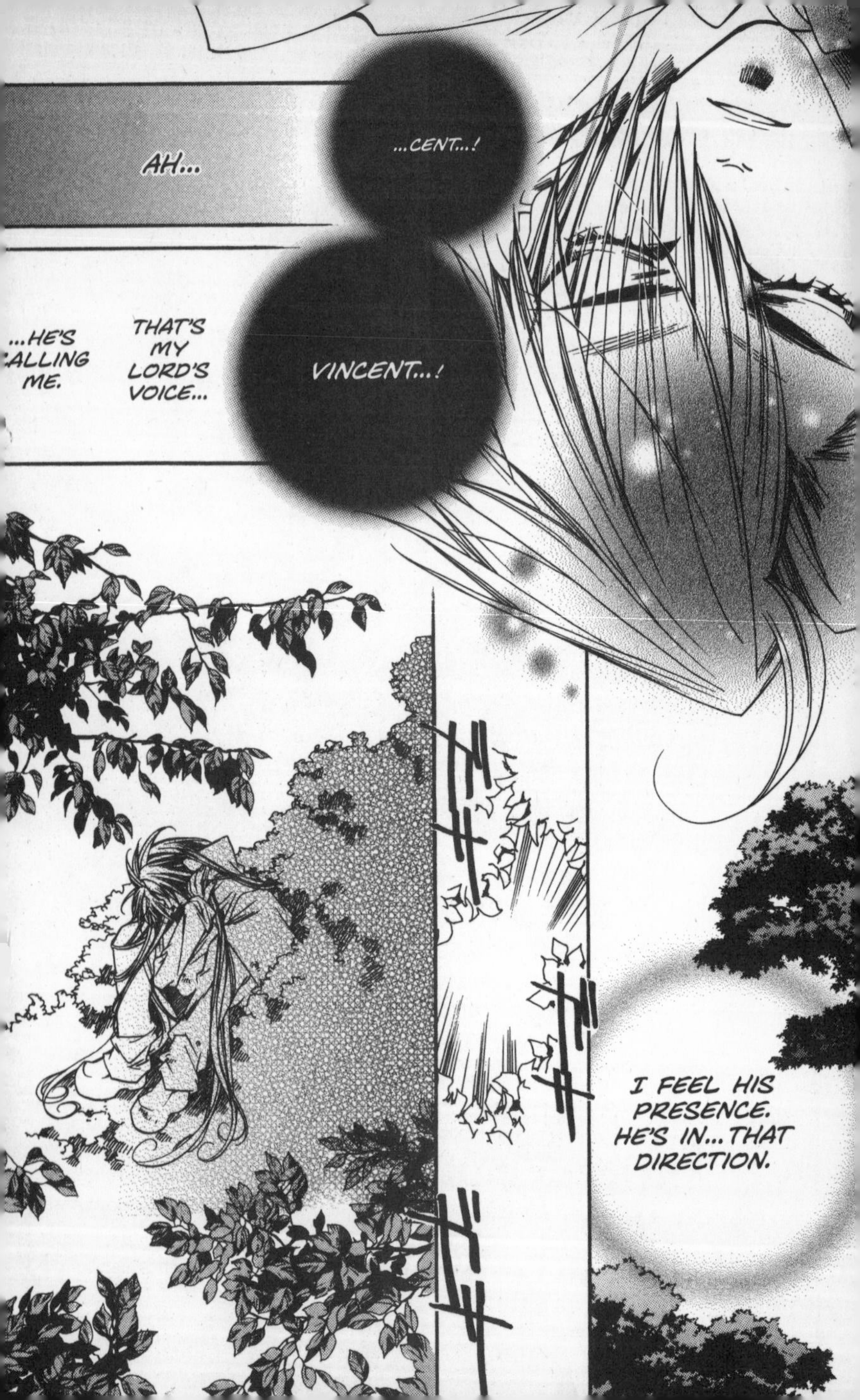
...CENT...!
AH...
VINCENT...!
THAT'S MY LORD'S VOICE...
...HE'S CALLING ME.
I FEEL HIS PRESENCE. HE'S IN...THAT DIRECTION.

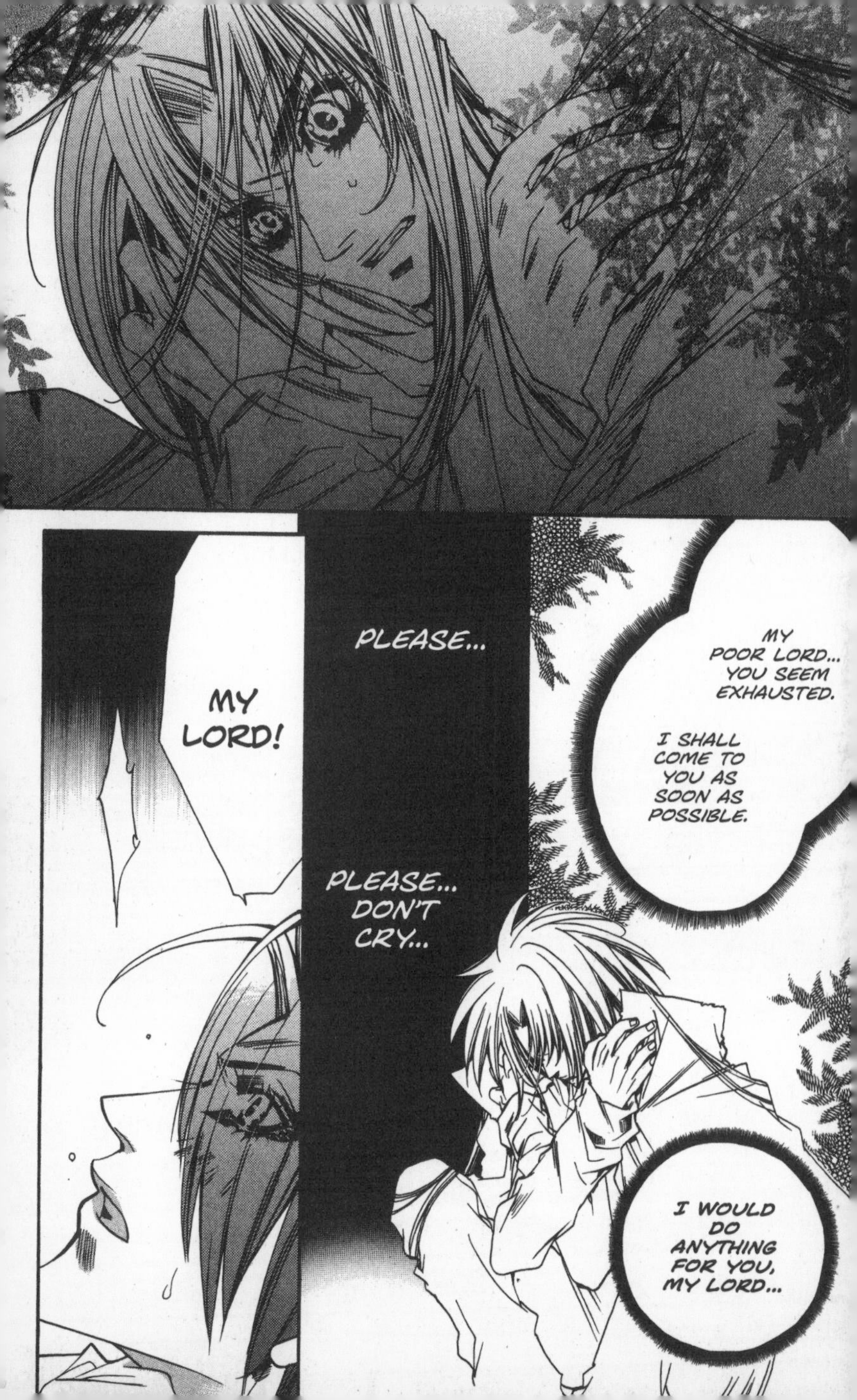
MY POOR LORD... YOU SEEM EXHAUSTED.
I SHALL COME TO YOU AS SOON AS POSSIBLE.
I WOULD DO ANYTHING FOR YOU, MY LORD...
PLEASE...
PLEASE... DON'T CRY...
MY LORD!

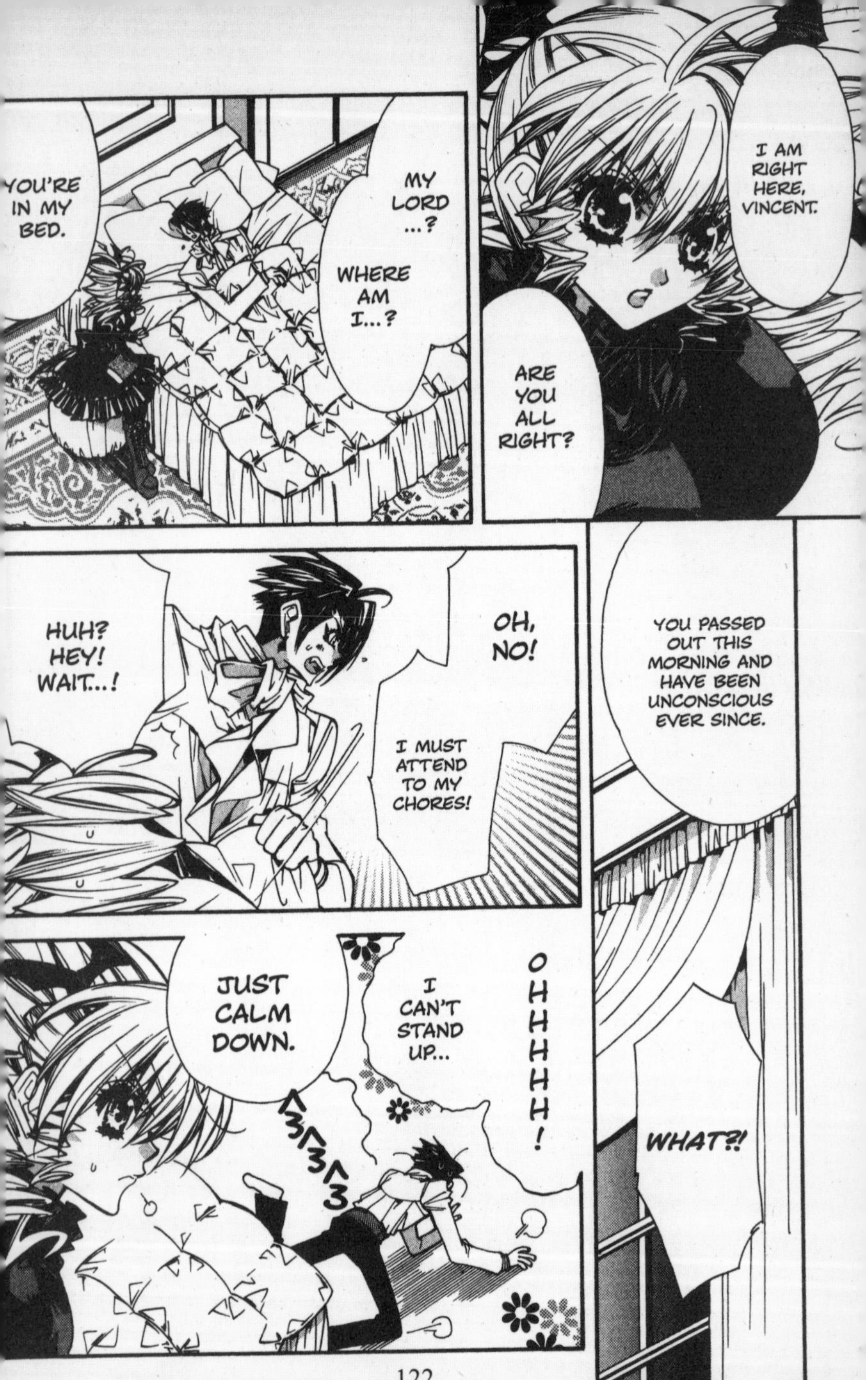
I AM RIGHT HERE, VINCENT.
ARE YOU ALL RIGHT?
MY LORD ...?
WHERE AM I...?
YOU'RE IN MY BED.
YOU PASSED OUT THIS MORNING AND HAVE BEEN UNCONSCIOUS EVER SINCE.
WHAT?!
OH, NO!
I MUST ATTEND TO MY CHORES!
HUH? HEY! WAIT...!
OHHHHHH!
I CAN'T STAND UP...
JUST CALM DOWN.
^3^3^3

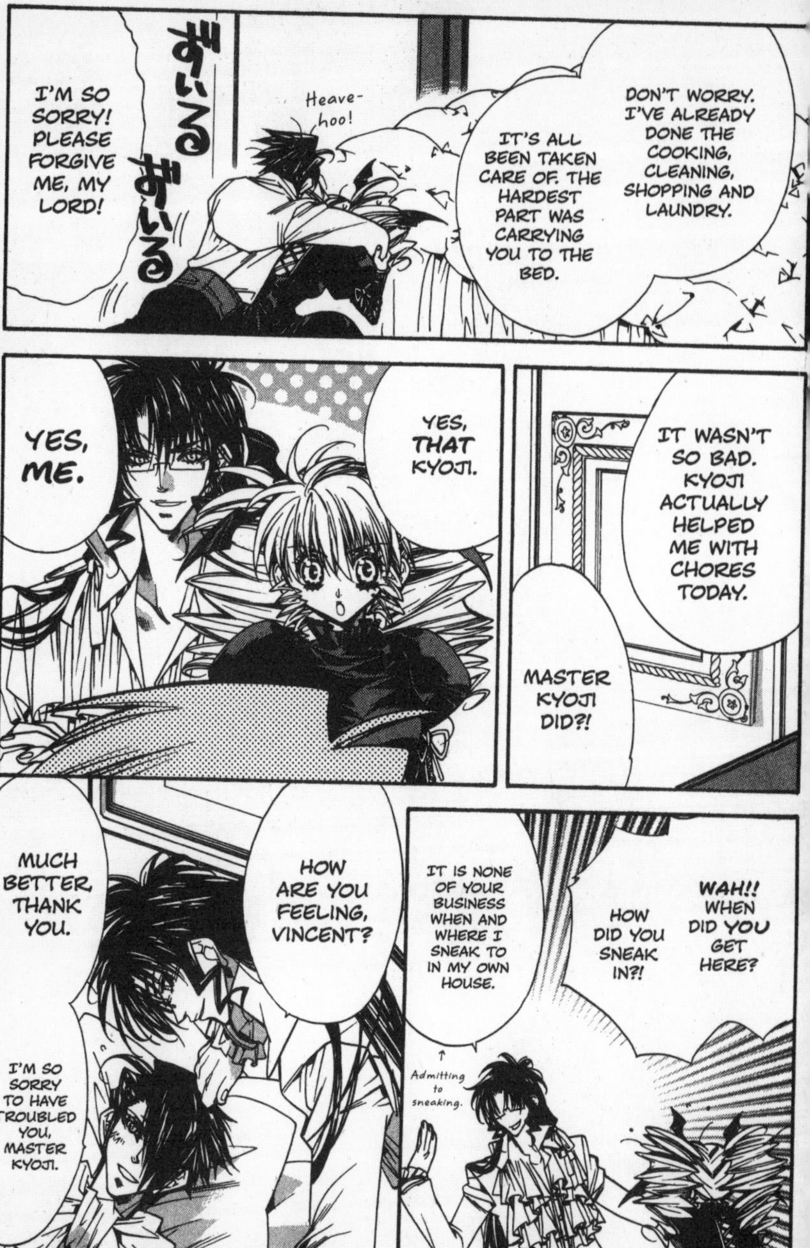
DON'T WORRY. I'VE ALREADY DONE THE COOKING, CLEANING, SHOPPING AND LAUNDRY.
IT'S ALL BEEN TAKEN CARE OF. THE HARDEST PART WAS CARRYING YOU TO THE BED.
Heave-hoo!
ずいる ずいる
I'M SO SORRY! PLEASE FORGIVE ME, MY LORD!
IT WASN'T SO BAD. KYOJI ACTUALLY HELPED ME WITH CHORES TODAY.
MASTER KYOJI DID?!
YES, THAT KYOJI.
YES, ME.
WAH!! WHEN DID YOU GET HERE?
HOW DID YOU SNEAK IN?!
IT IS NONE OF YOUR BUSINESS WHEN AND WHERE I SNEAK TO IN MY OWN HOUSE.
↑ Admitting to sneaking.
HOW ARE YOU FEELING, VINCENT?
MUCH BETTER THANK YOU.
I'M SO SORRY TO HAVE TROUBLED YOU, MASTER KYOJI.

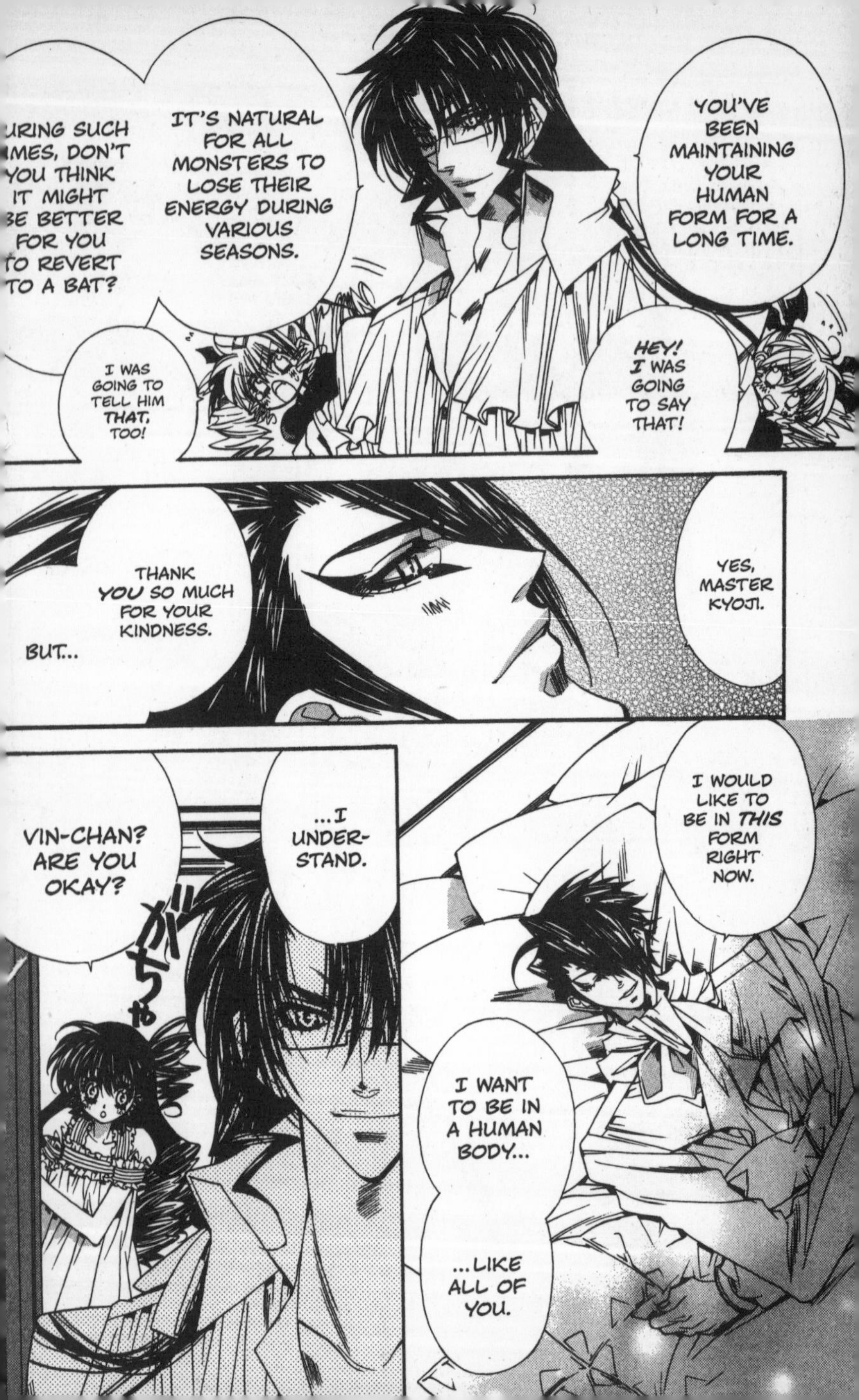
YOU'VE BEEN MAINTAINING YOUR HUMAN FORM FOR A LONG TIME.
IT'S NATURAL FOR ALL MONSTERS TO LOSE THEIR ENERGY DURING VARIOUS SEASONS.
URING SUCH IMES, DON'T YOU THINK IT MIGHT BE BETTER FOR YOU TO REVERT TO A BAT?
HEY! I WAS GOING TO SAY THAT!
I WAS GOING TO TELL HIM *THAT*, TOO!
YES, MASTER KYOJI.
THANK *YOU* SO MUCH FOR YOUR KINDNESS.
BUT...
I WOULD LIKE TO BE IN *THIS* FORM RIGHT NOW.
I WANT TO BE IN A HUMAN BODY...
...LIKE ALL OF YOU.
...I UNDER-STAND.
がちゃ
VIN-CHAN? ARE YOU OKAY?

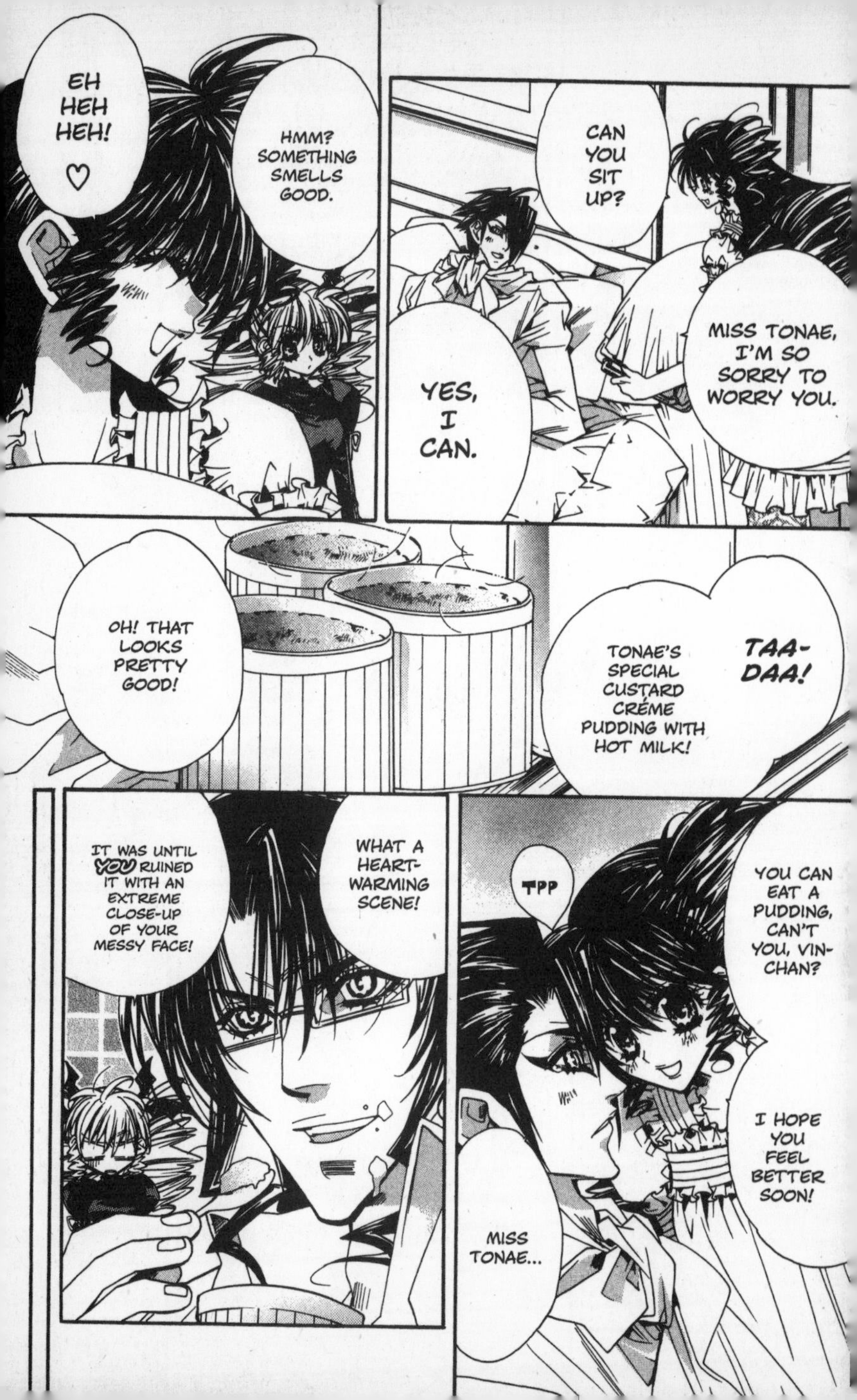
CAN YOU SIT UP?
MISS TONAE, I'M SO SORRY TO WORRY YOU.
YES, I CAN.
HMM? SOMETHING SMELLS GOOD.
EH HEH HEH! ♡
TAA-DAA!
TONAE'S SPECIAL CUSTARD CRÉME PUDDING WITH HOT MILK!
OH! THAT LOOKS PRETTY GOOD!
YOU CAN EAT A PUDDING, CAN'T YOU, VIN-CHAN?
TPP
I HOPE YOU FEEL BETTER SOON!
MISS TONAE...
WHAT A HEART-WARMING SCENE!
IT WAS UNTIL *YOU* RUINED IT WITH AN EXTREME CLOSE-UP OF YOUR MESSY FACE!

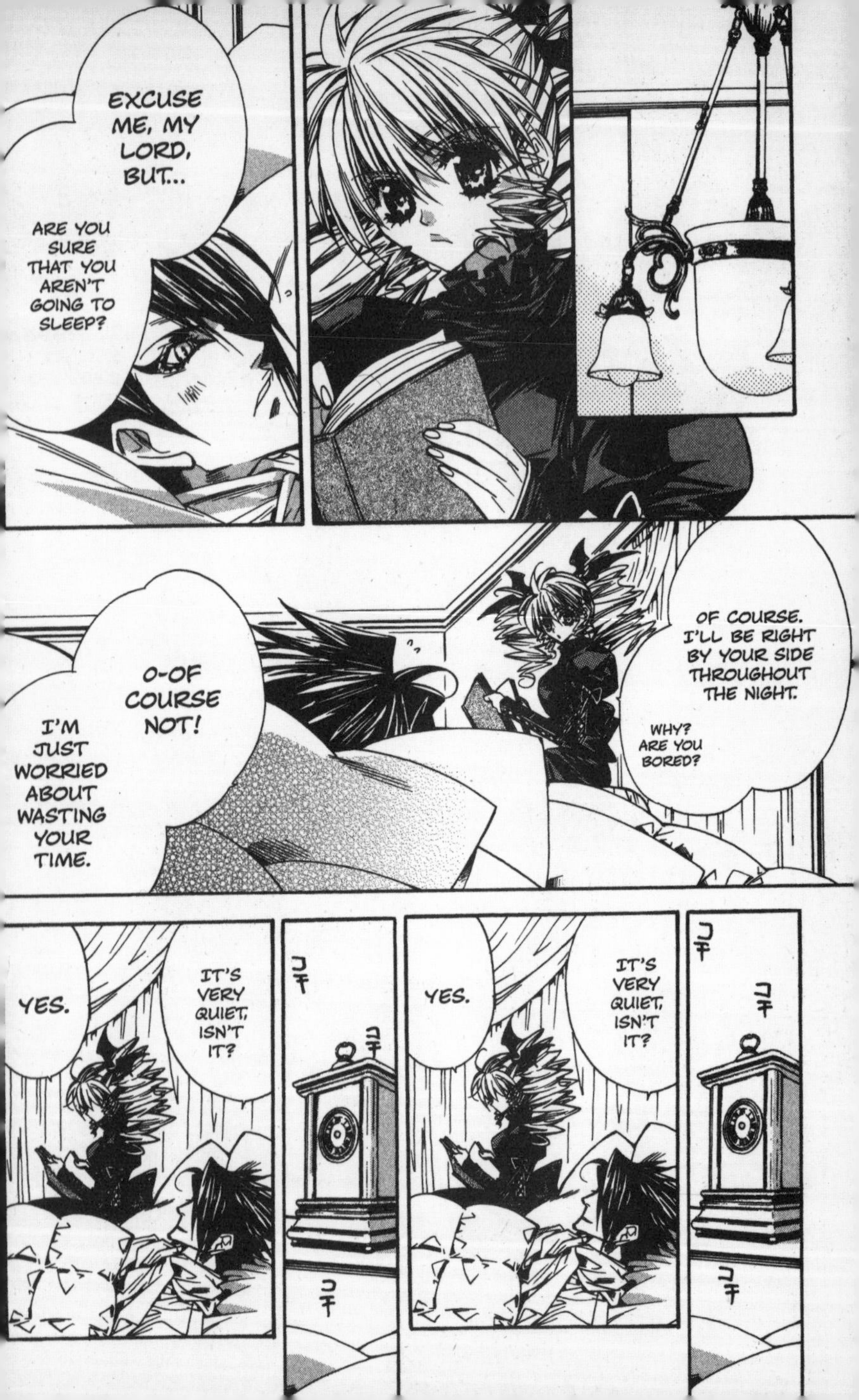
EXCUSE ME, MY LORD, BUT...
ARE YOU SURE THAT YOU AREN'T GOING TO SLEEP?
OF COURSE. I'LL BE RIGHT BY YOUR SIDE THROUGHOUT THE NIGHT.
WHY? ARE YOU BORED?
O-OF COURSE NOT!
I'M JUST WORRIED ABOUT WASTING YOUR TIME.
コチ
コチ
コチ
IT'S VERY QUIET, ISN'T IT?
YES.
コチ
コチ
コチ
IT'S VERY QUIET, ISN'T IT?
YES.

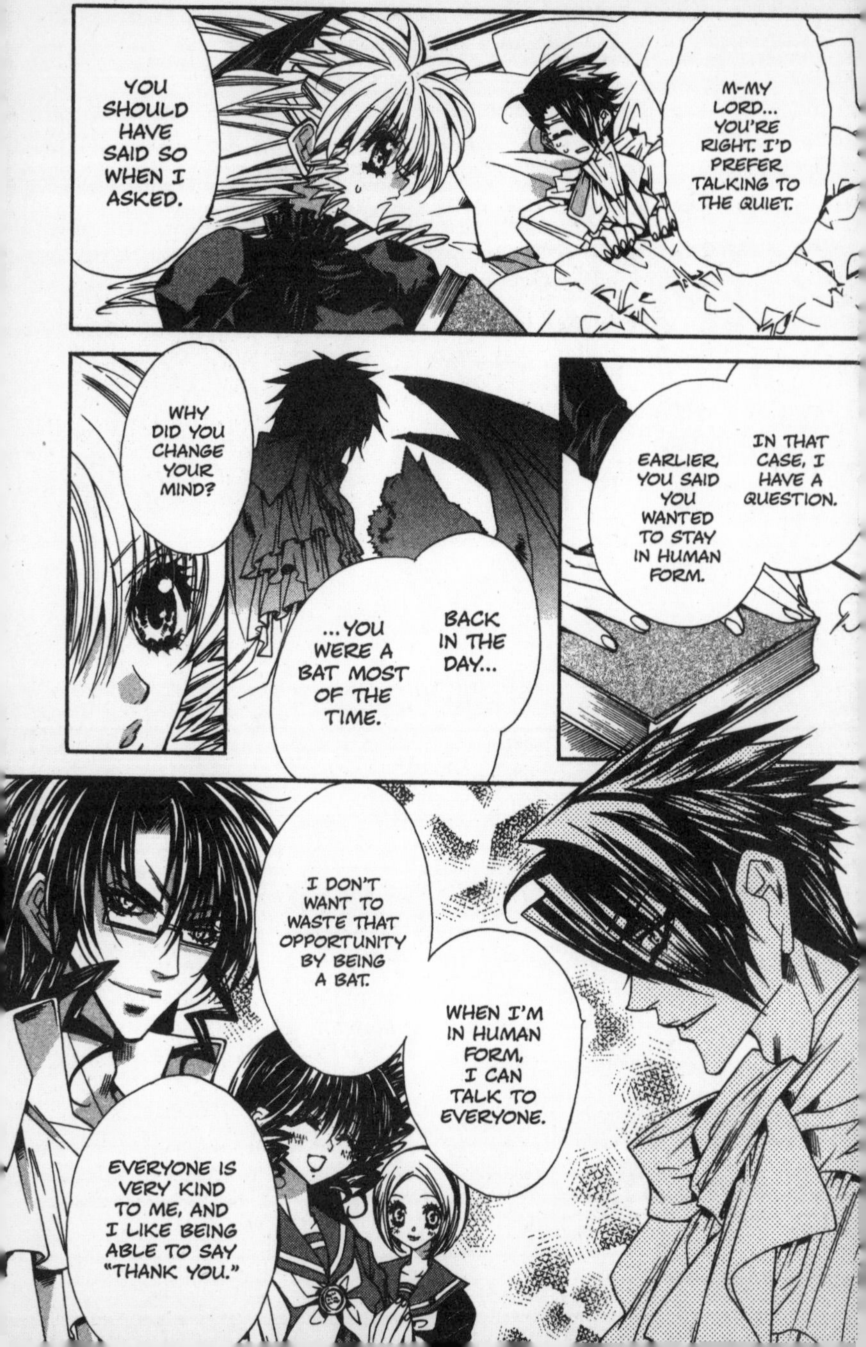
M-MY LORD... YOU'RE RIGHT. I'D PREFER TALKING TO THE QUIET.
YOU SHOULD HAVE SAID SO WHEN I ASKED.
IN THAT CASE, I HAVE A QUESTION.
EARLIER, YOU SAID YOU WANTED TO STAY IN HUMAN FORM.
BACK IN THE DAY...
...YOU WERE A BAT MOST OF THE TIME.
WHY DID YOU CHANGE YOUR MIND?
WHEN I'M IN HUMAN FORM, I CAN TALK TO EVERYONE.
I DON'T WANT TO WASTE THAT OPPORTUNITY BY BEING A BAT.
EVERYONE IS VERY KIND TO ME, AND I LIKE BEING ABLE TO SAY "THANK YOU."

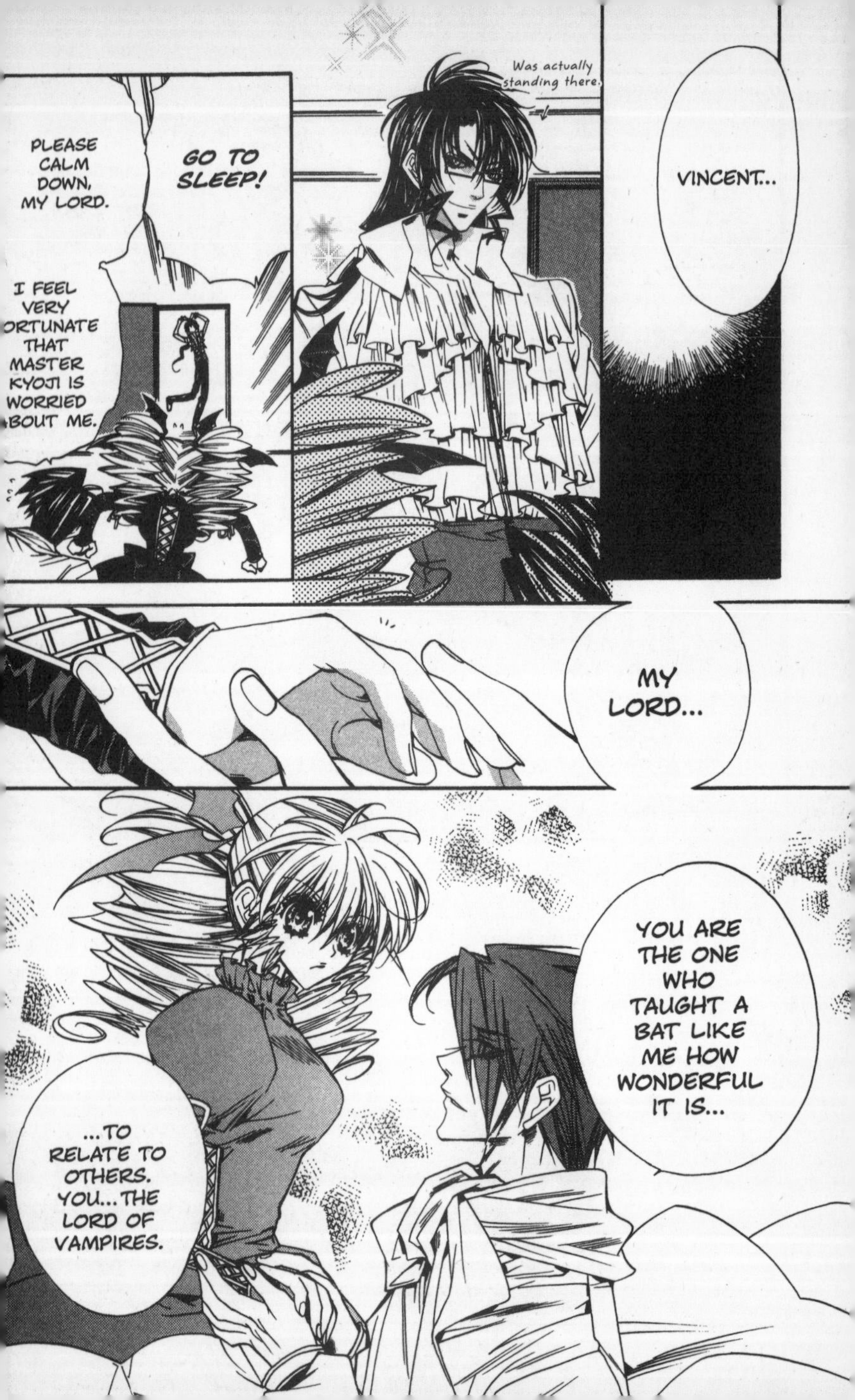
VINCENT...
Was actually standing there.
GO TO SLEEP!
PLEASE CALM DOWN, MY LORD.
I FEEL VERY ORTUNATE THAT MASTER KYOJI IS WORRIED BOUT ME.
MY LORD...
YOU ARE THE ONE WHO TAUGHT A BAT LIKE ME HOW WONDERFUL IT IS...
...TO RELATE TO OTHERS. YOU...THE LORD OF VAMPIRES.

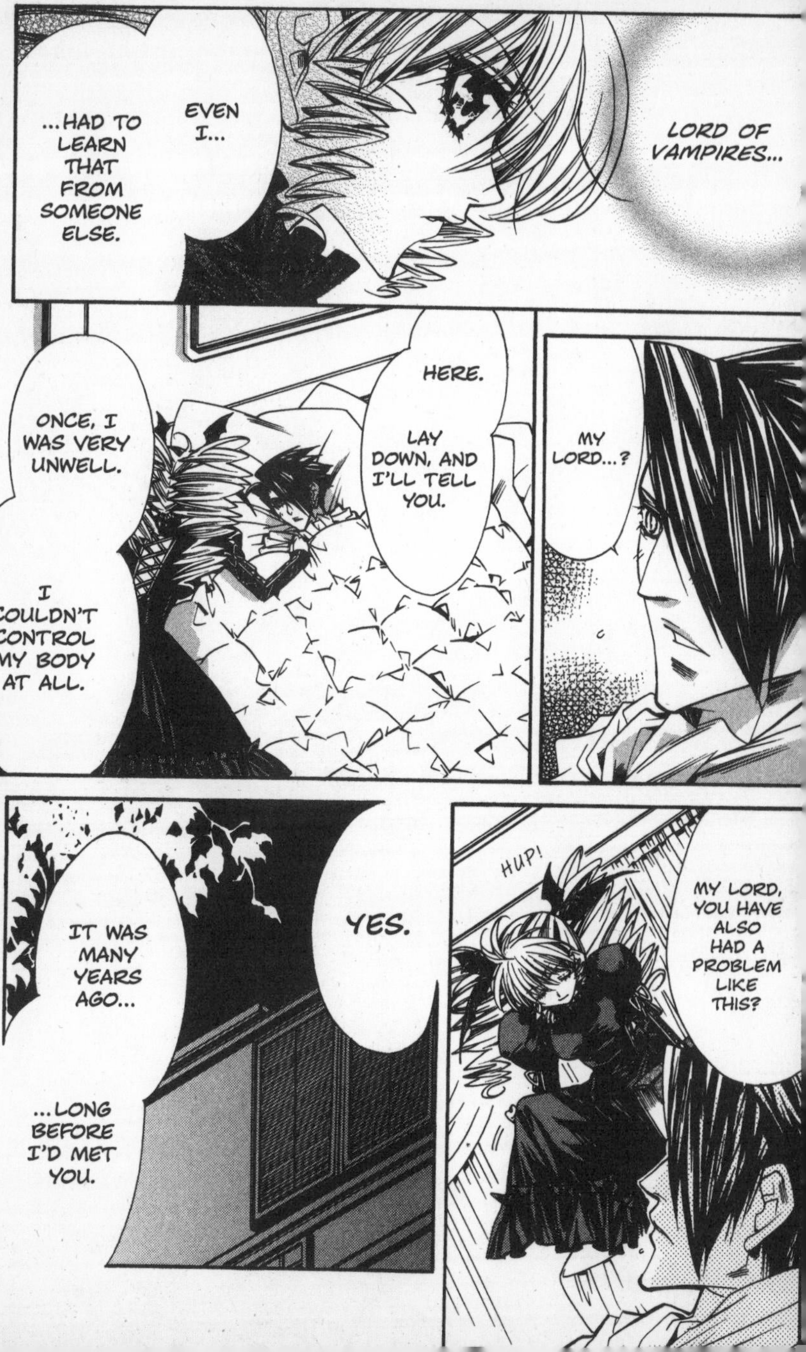
LORD OF VAMPIRES...
EVEN I...
...HAD TO LEARN THAT FROM SOMEONE ELSE.
MY LORD...?
HERE.
LAY DOWN, AND I'LL TELL YOU.
ONCE, I WAS VERY UNWELL.
I COULDN'T CONTROL MY BODY AT ALL.
MY LORD, YOU HAVE ALSO HAD A PROBLEM LIKE THIS?
HUP!
YES.
IT WAS MANY YEARS AGO...
...LONG BEFORE I'D MET YOU.

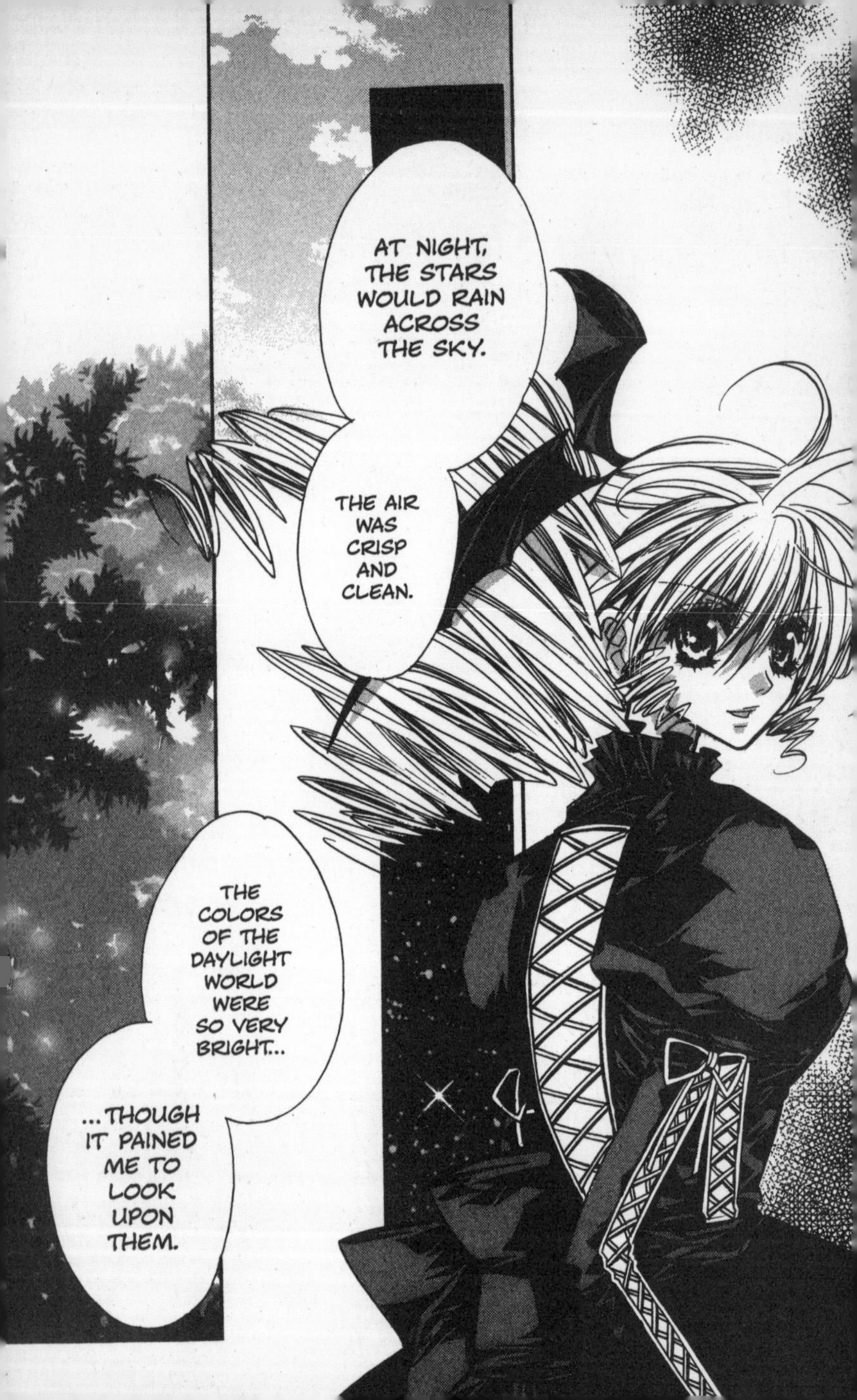
AT NIGHT, THE STARS WOULD RAIN ACROSS THE SKY.
THE AIR WAS CRISP AND CLEAN.
THE COLORS OF THE DAYLIGHT WORLD WERE SO VERY BRIGHT...
...THOUGH IT PAINED ME TO LOOK UPON THEM.

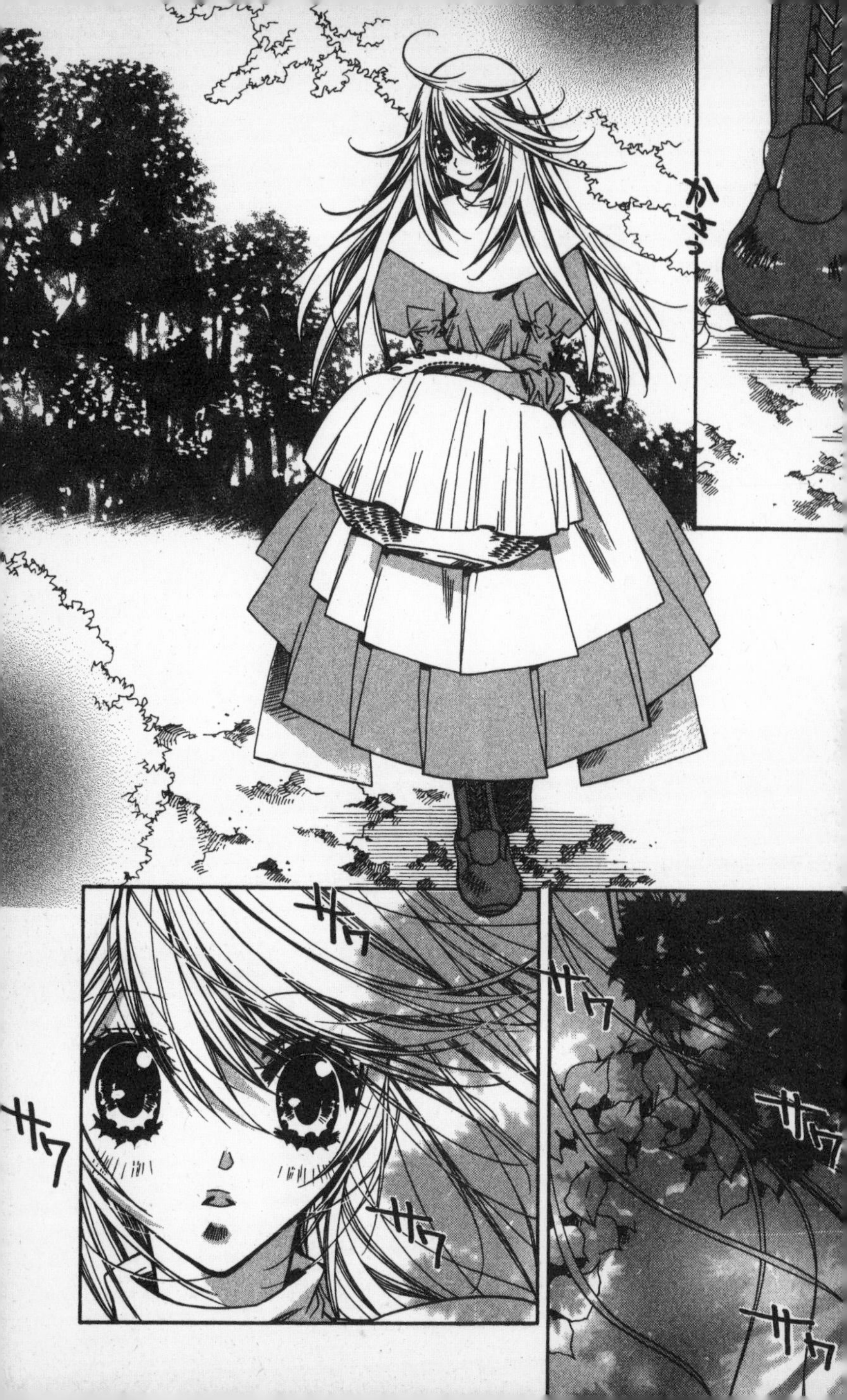
かさっ
サワ
サワ
サワ
サワ
サワ
サワ

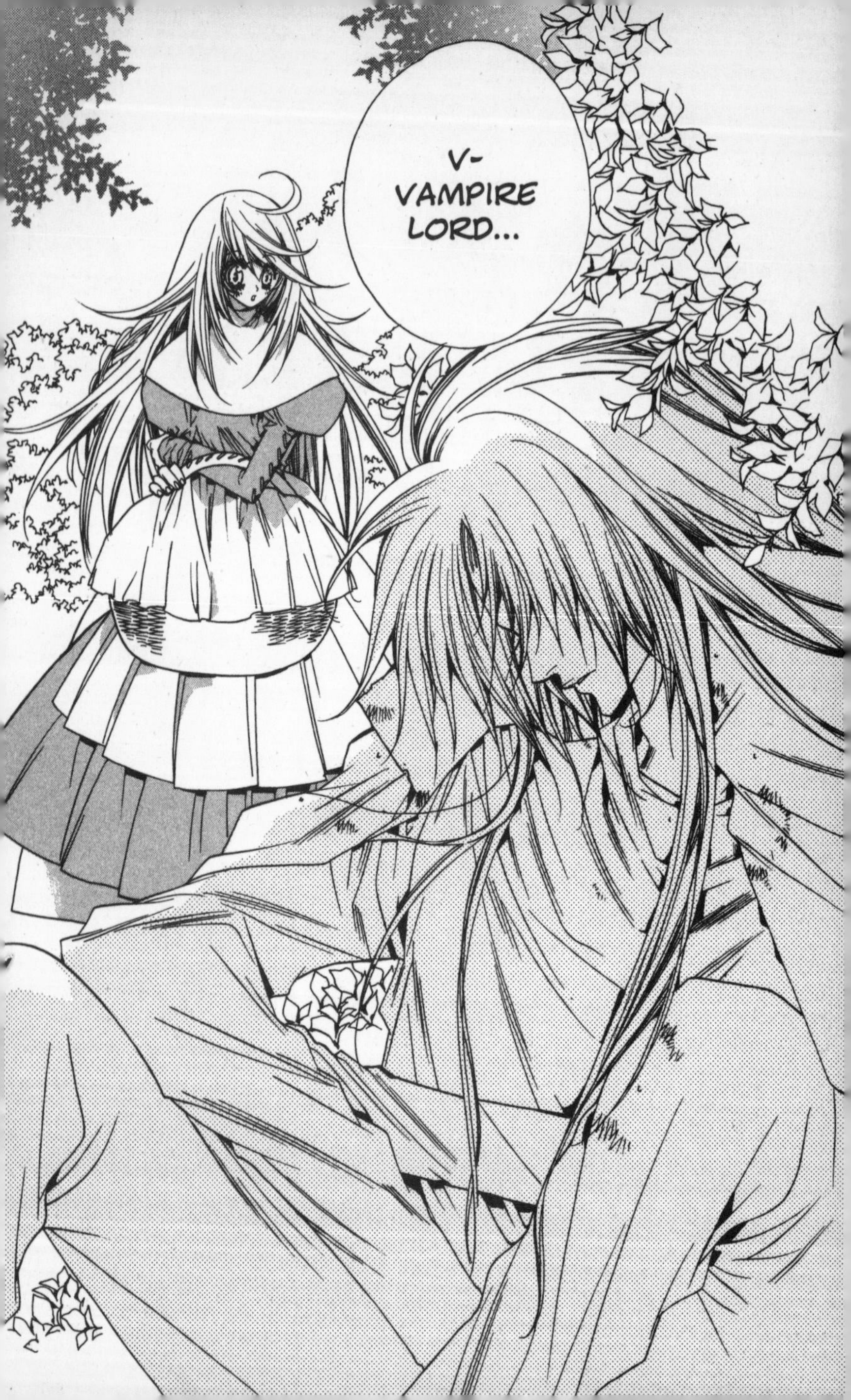
V-
VAMPIRE
LORD...

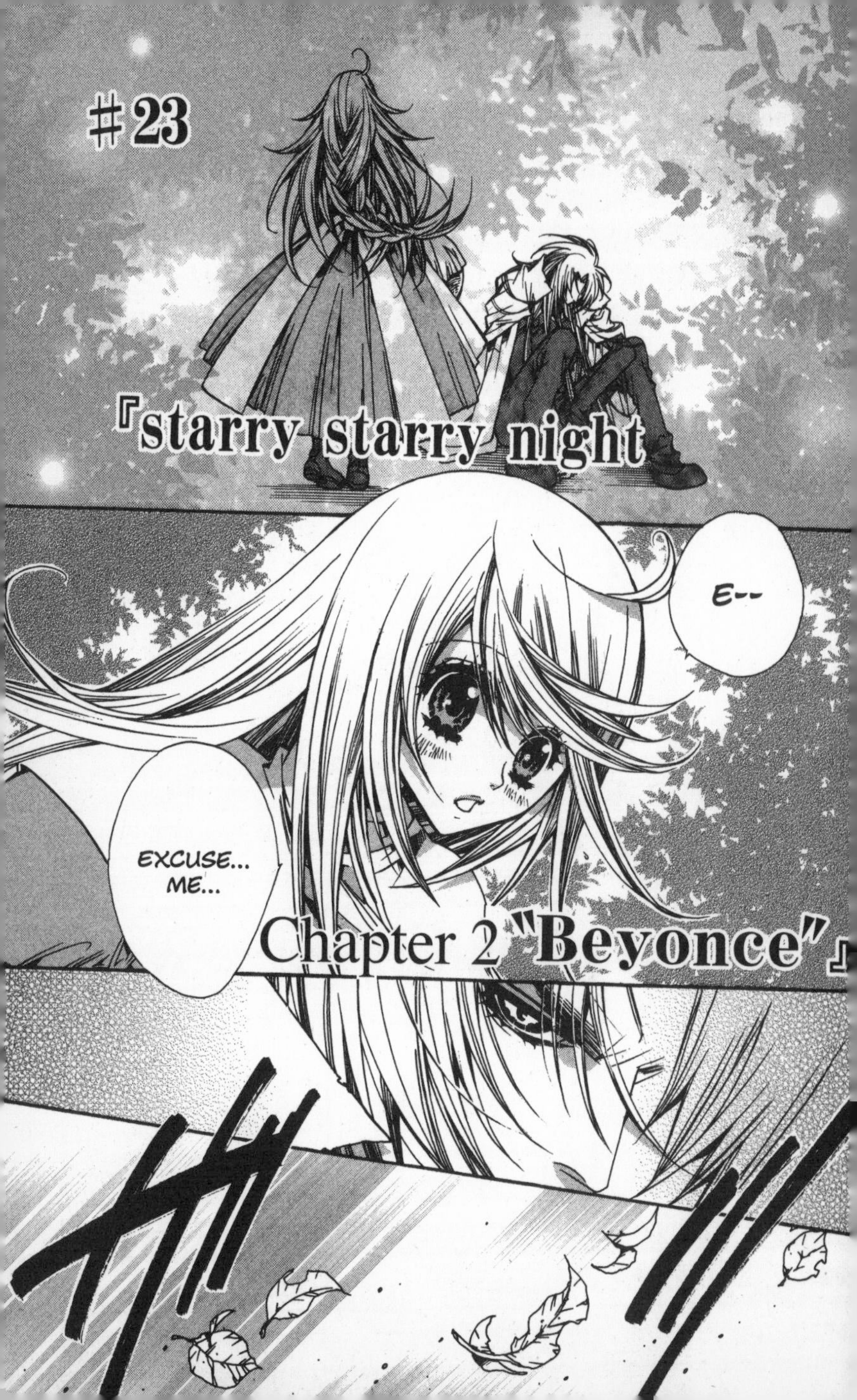
#23
『starry starry night
E--
EXCUSE... ME...
Chapter 2 "Beyonce"』

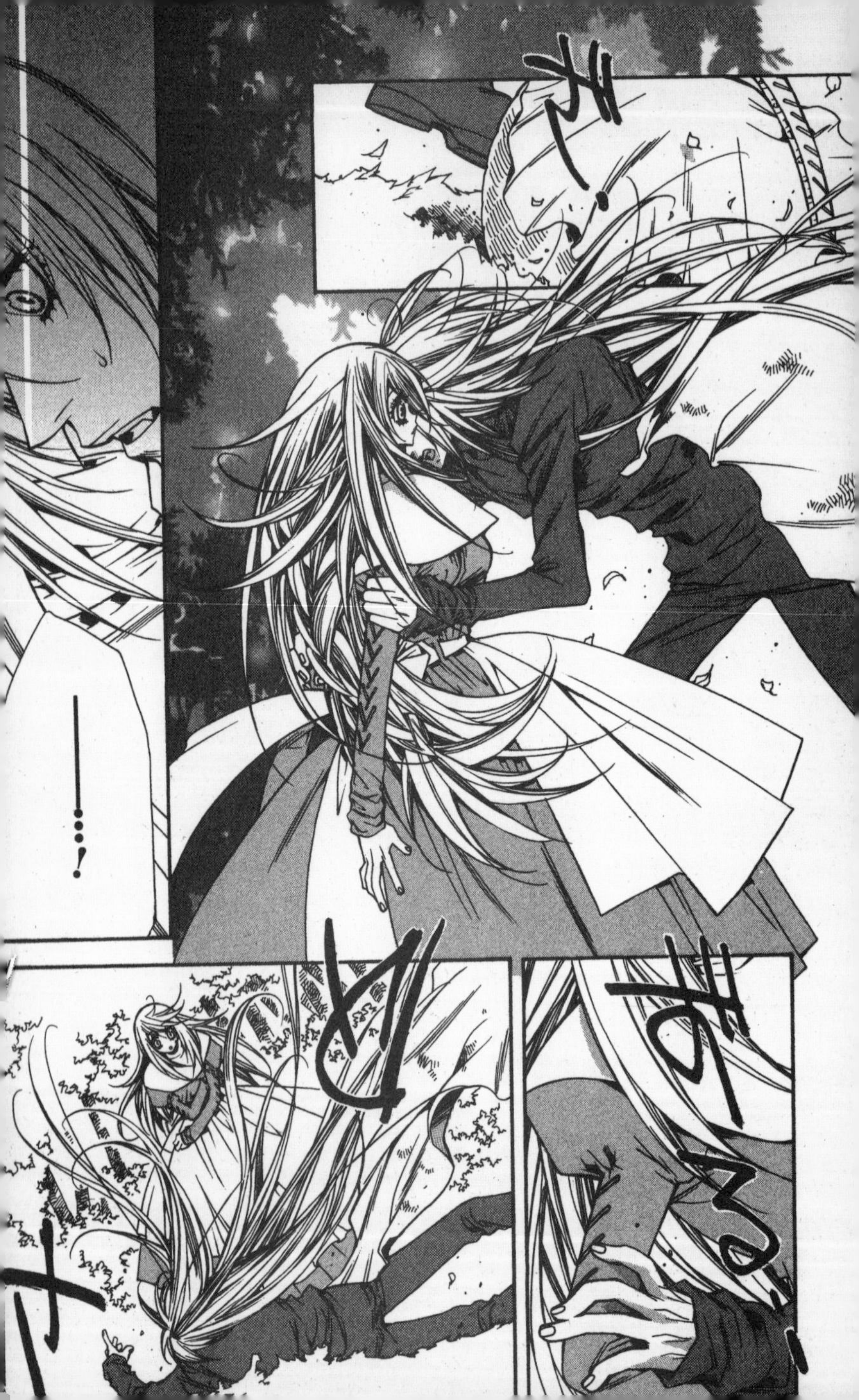
——...!

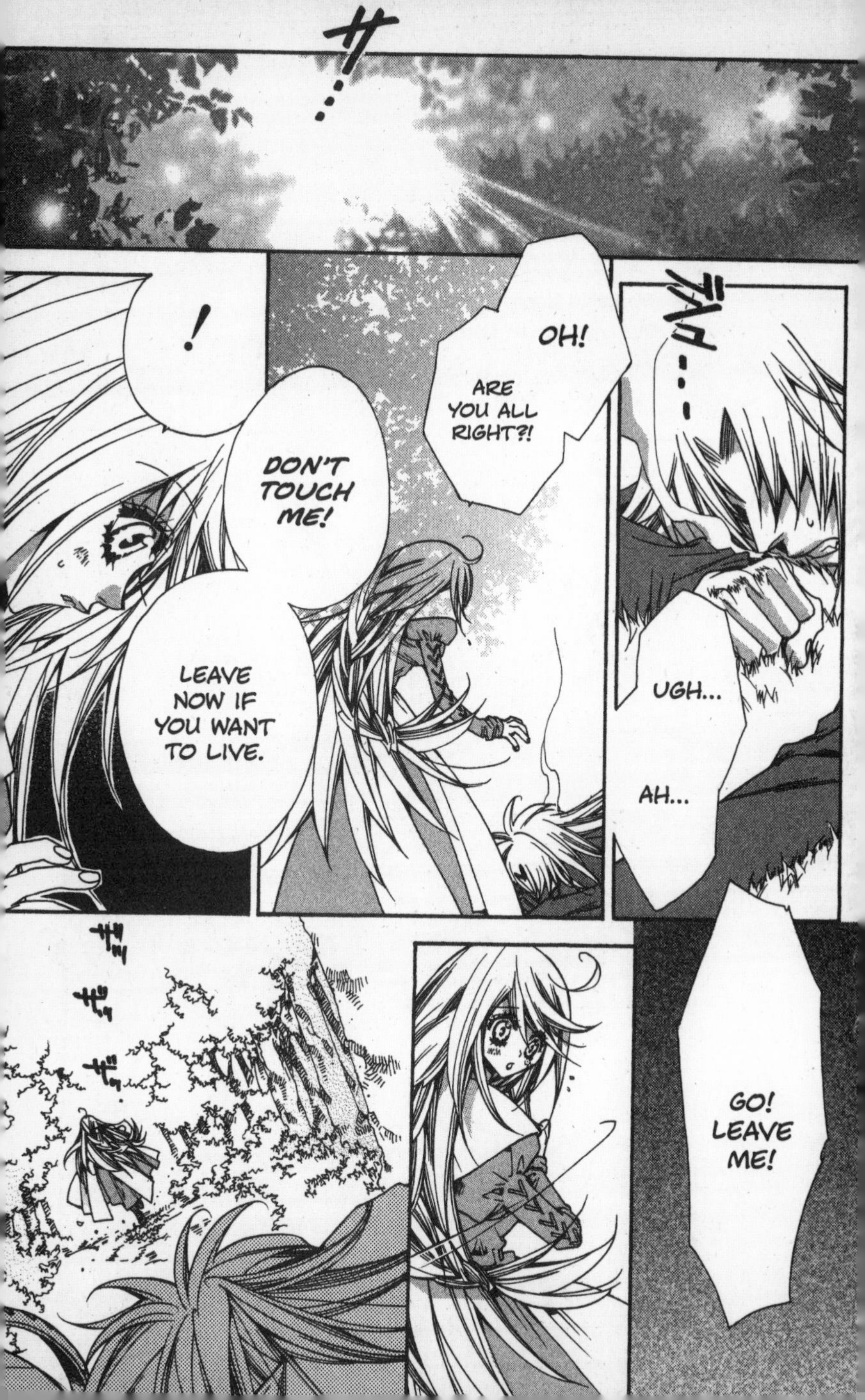
サ…
ズル…
UGH...
AH...
OH!
ARE YOU ALL RIGHT?!
!
DON'T TOUCH ME!
LEAVE NOW IF YOU WANT TO LIVE.
GO! LEAVE ME!
ザッ
ザッ
ザッ

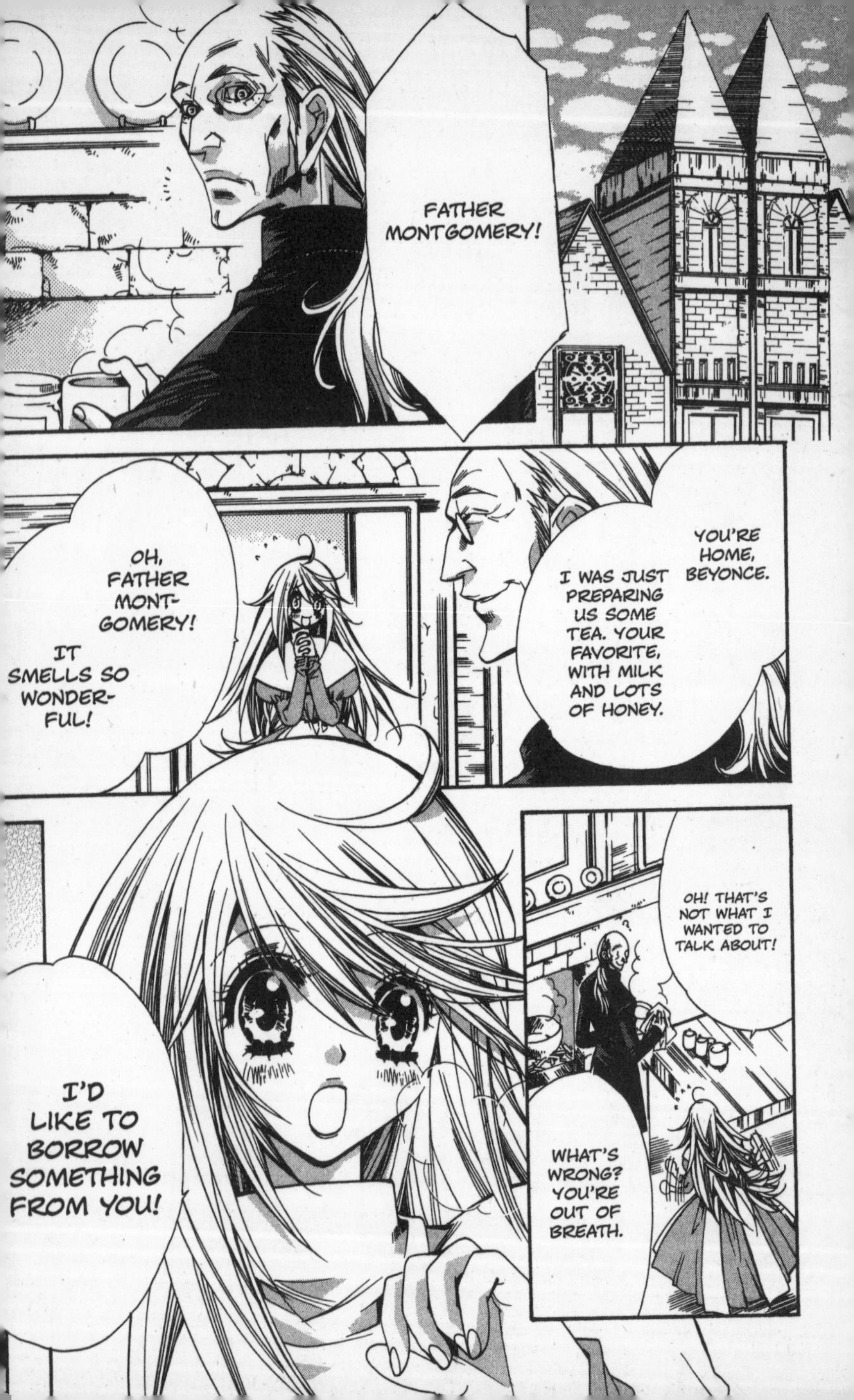
FATHER MONTGOMERY!
YOU'RE HOME, BEYONCE.
I WAS JUST PREPARING US SOME TEA. YOUR FAVORITE, WITH MILK AND LOTS OF HONEY.
OH, FATHER MONT-GOMERY!
IT SMELLS SO WONDER-FUL!
OH! THAT'S NOT WHAT I WANTED TO TALK ABOUT!
WHAT'S WRONG? YOU'RE OUT OF BREATH.
I'D LIKE TO BORROW SOMETHING FROM YOU!

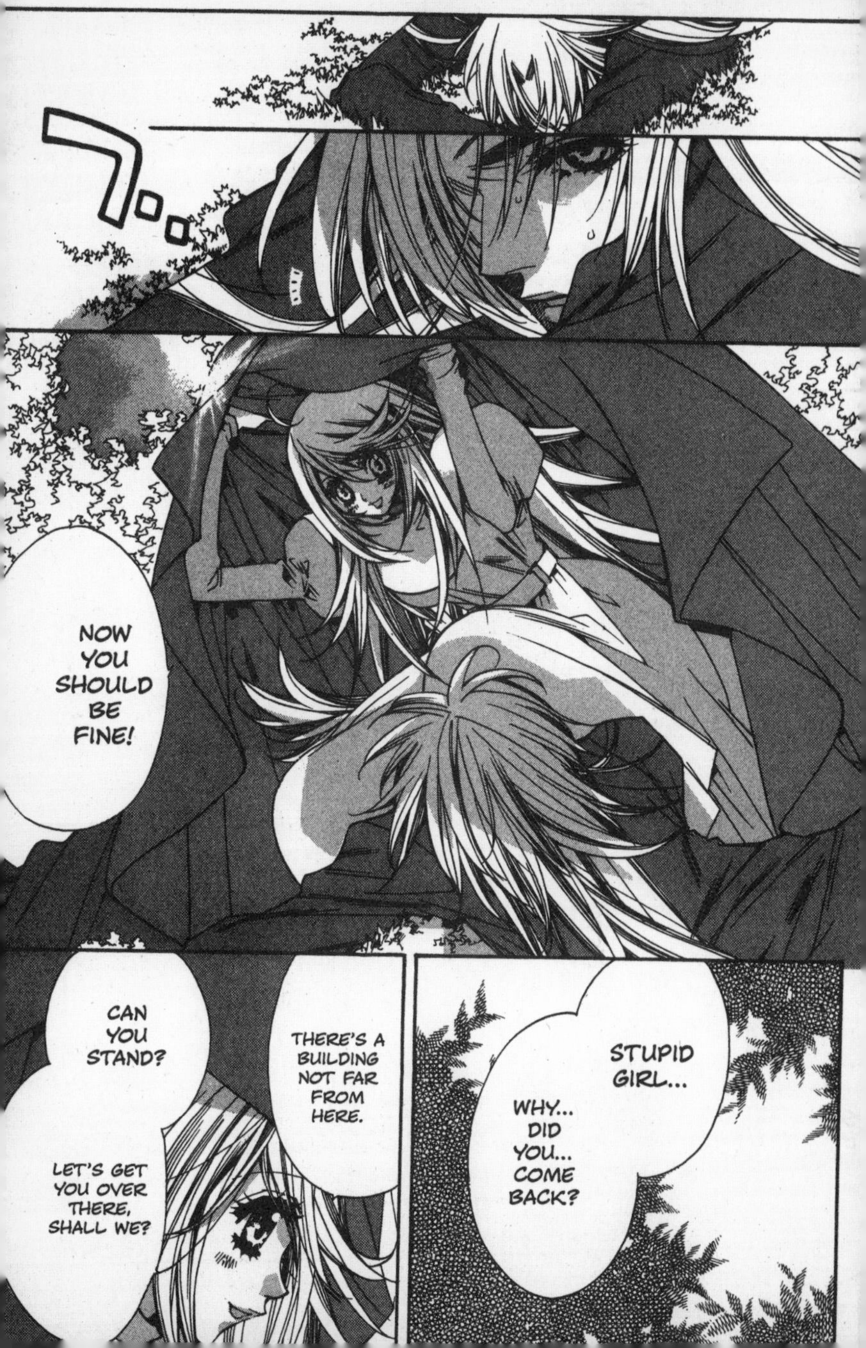
NOW YOU SHOULD BE FINE!
STUPID GIRL...
WHY... DID YOU... COME BACK?
THERE'S A BUILDING NOT FAR FROM HERE.
CAN YOU STAND?
LET'S GET YOU OVER THERE, SHALL WE?

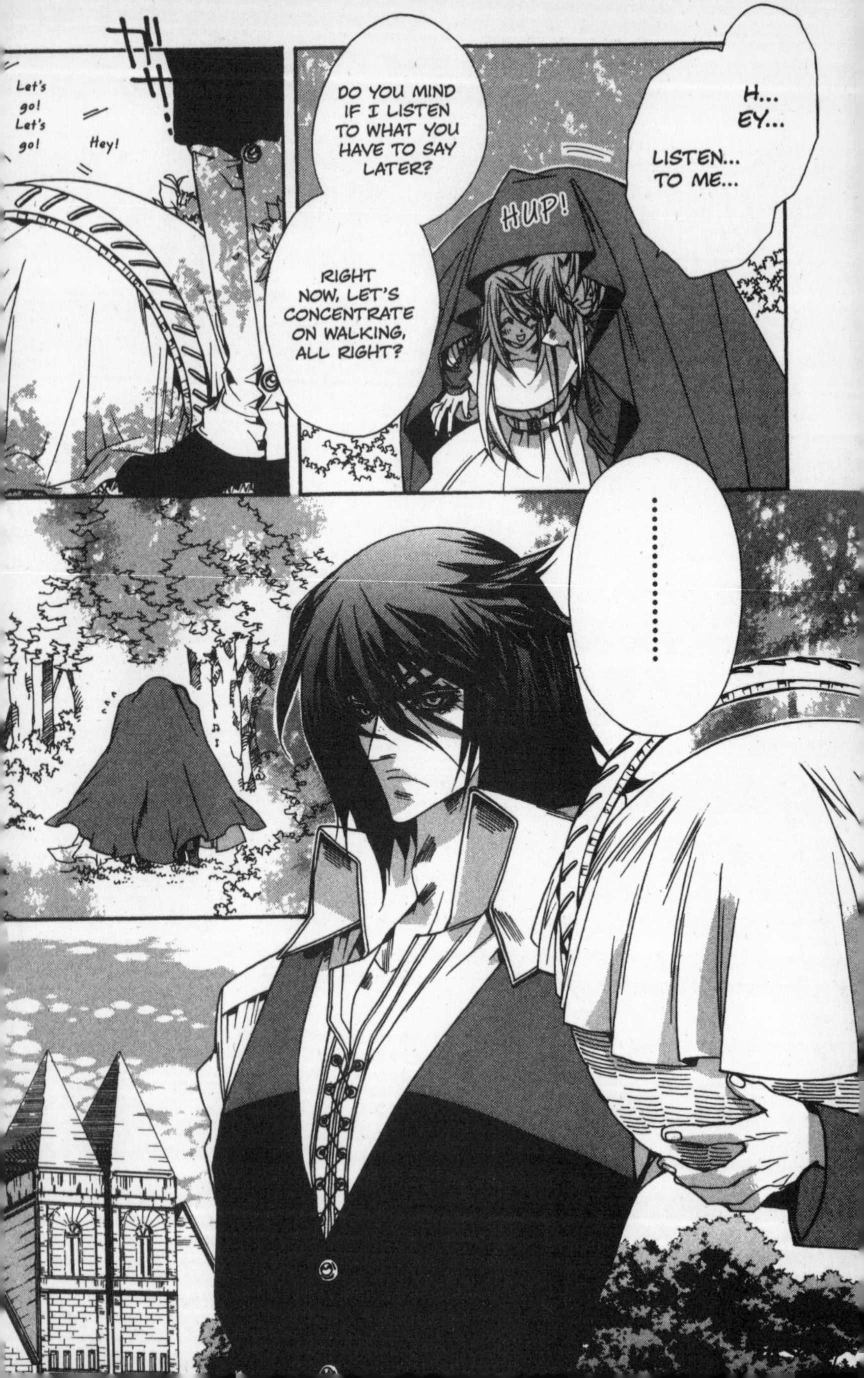
H... EY...
LISTEN... TO ME...
DO YOU MIND IF I LISTEN TO WHAT YOU HAVE TO SAY LATER?
HUP!
RIGHT NOW, LET'S CONCENTRATE ON WALKING, ALL RIGHT?
Hey!
Let's go! Let's go!
......

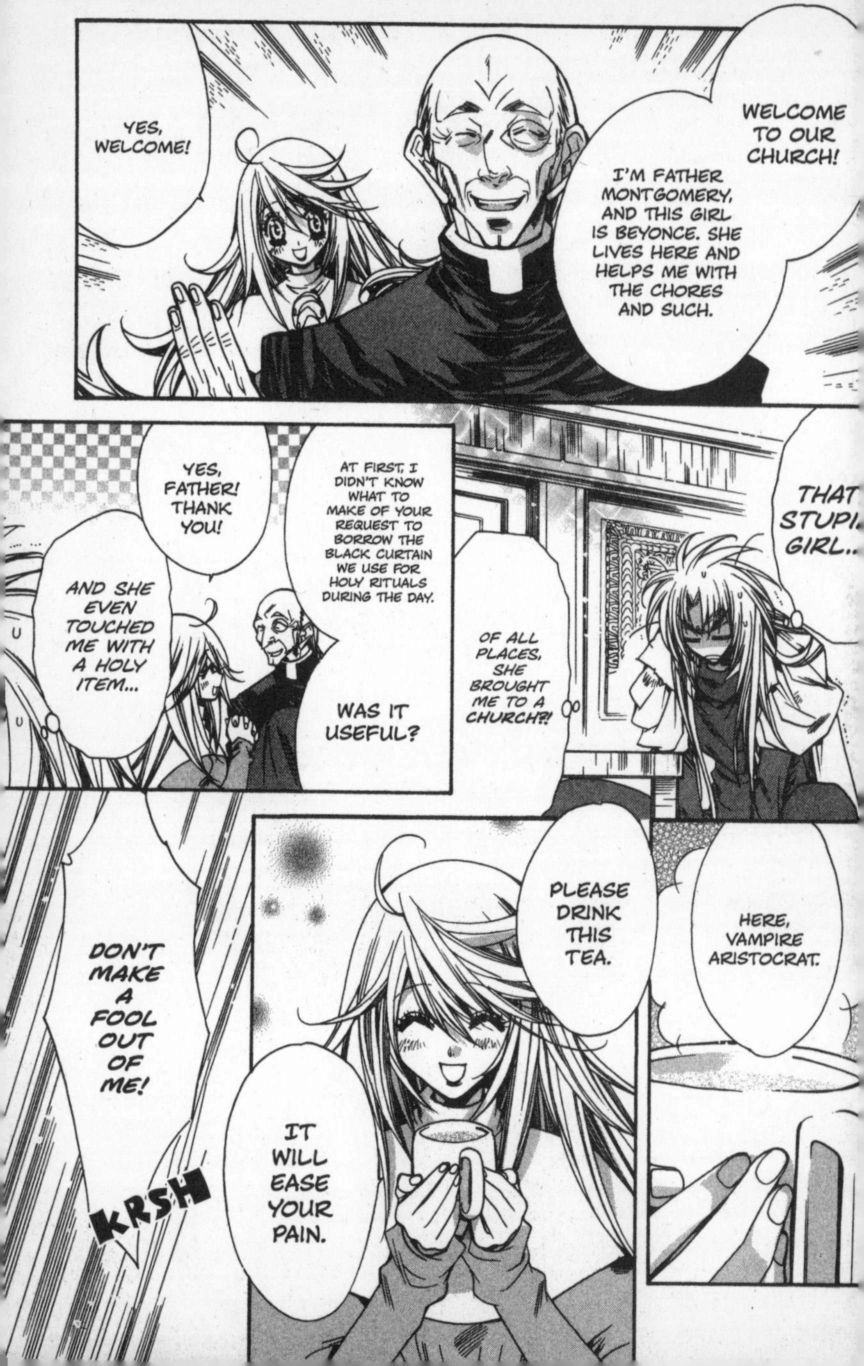
WELCOME TO OUR CHURCH!
I'M FATHER MONTGOMERY, AND THIS GIRL IS BEYONCE. SHE LIVES HERE AND HELPS ME WITH THE CHORES AND SUCH.
YES, WELCOME!
THAT STUPI GIRL...
OF ALL PLACES, SHE BROUGHT ME TO A CHURCH?!
AT FIRST, I DIDN'T KNOW WHAT TO MAKE OF YOUR REQUEST TO BORROW THE BLACK CURTAIN WE USE FOR HOLY RITUALS DURING THE DAY.
WAS IT USEFUL?
YES, FATHER! THANK YOU!
AND SHE EVEN TOUCHED ME WITH A HOLY ITEM...
HERE, VAMPIRE ARISTOCRAT.
PLEASE DRINK THIS TEA.
IT WILL EASE YOUR PAIN.
DON'T MAKE A FOOL OUT OF ME!
KRSH

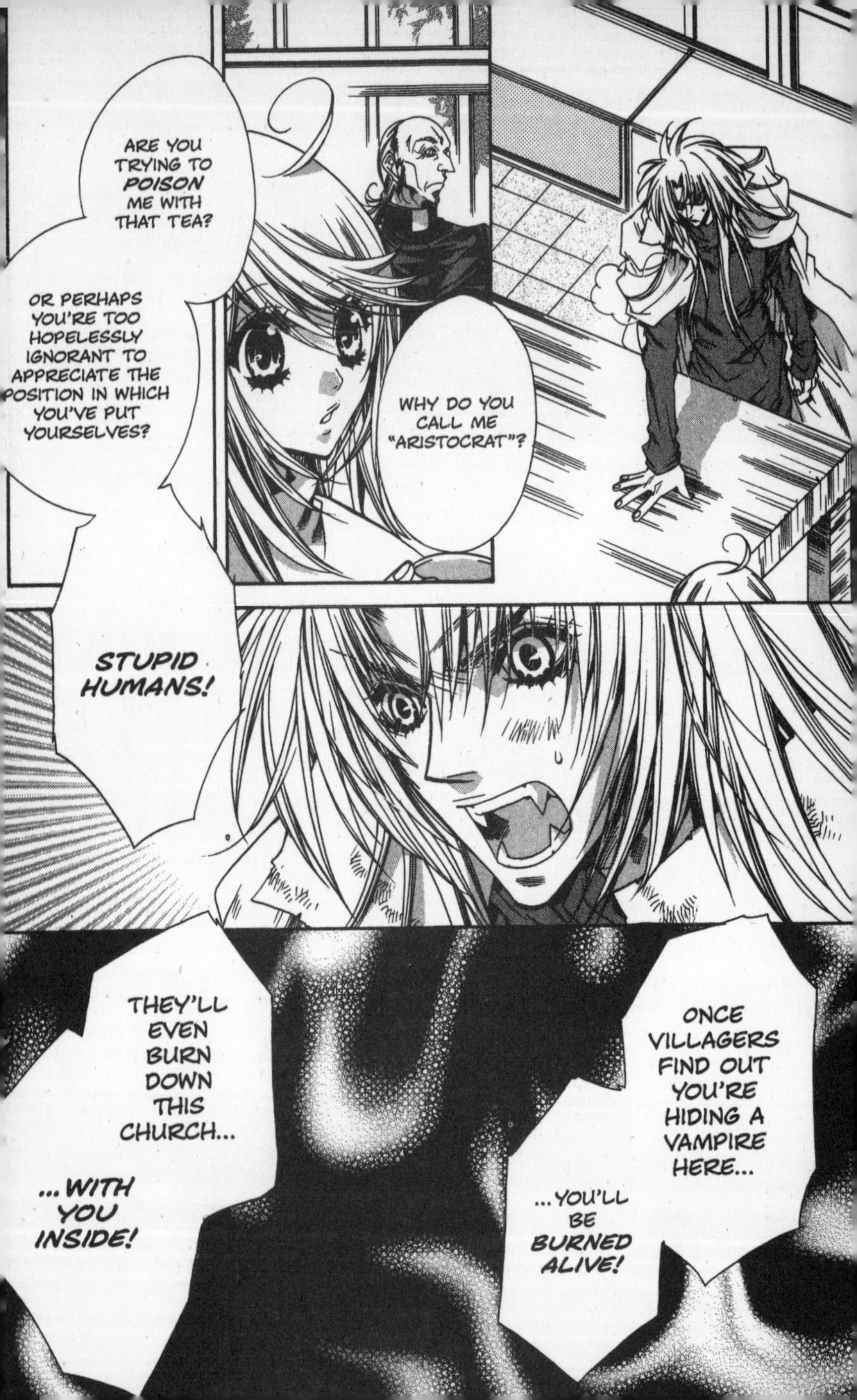
WHY DO YOU CALL ME "ARISTOCRAT"?
ARE YOU TRYING TO *POISON* ME WITH THAT TEA?
OR PERHAPS YOU'RE TOO HOPELESSLY IGNORANT TO APPRECIATE THE POSITION IN WHICH YOU'VE PUT YOURSELVES?
STUPID HUMANS!
ONCE VILLAGERS FIND OUT YOU'RE HIDING A VAMPIRE HERE...
...YOU'LL BE BURNED ALIVE!
THEY'LL EVEN BURN DOWN THIS CHURCH...
...WITH YOU INSIDE!

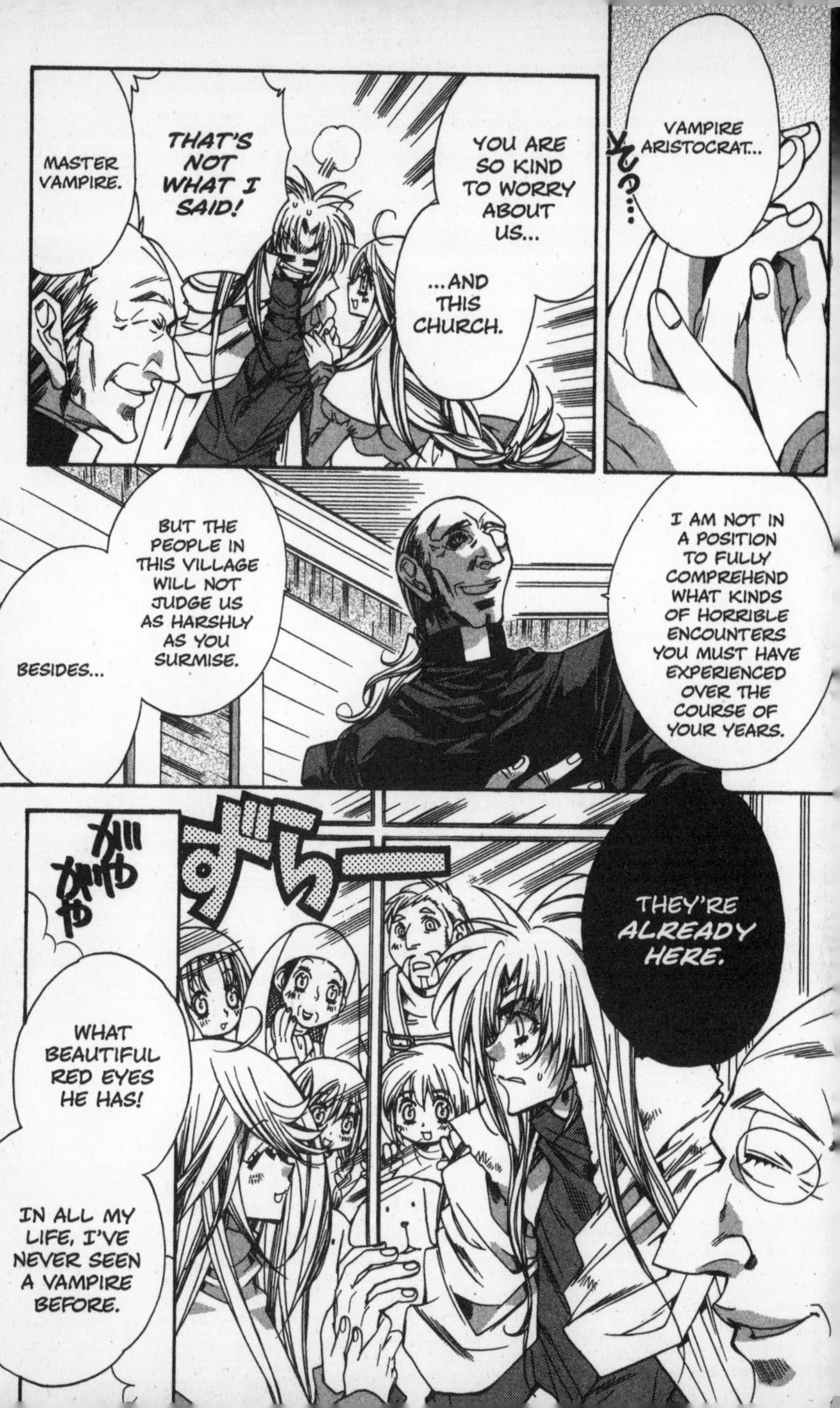
VAMPIRE ARISTOCRAT...
YOU ARE SO KIND TO WORRY ABOUT US...
...AND THIS CHURCH.
THAT'S NOT WHAT I SAID!
MASTER VAMPIRE.
I AM NOT IN A POSITION TO FULLY COMPREHEND WHAT KINDS OF HORRIBLE ENCOUNTERS YOU MUST HAVE EXPERIENCED OVER THE COURSE OF YOUR YEARS.
BUT THE PEOPLE IN THIS VILLAGE WILL NOT JUDGE US AS HARSHLY AS YOU SURMISE.
BESIDES...
THEY'RE ALREADY HERE.
ずらー
がやがや
WHAT BEAUTIFUL RED EYES HE HAS!
IN ALL MY LIFE, I'VE NEVER SEEN A VAMPIRE BEFORE.

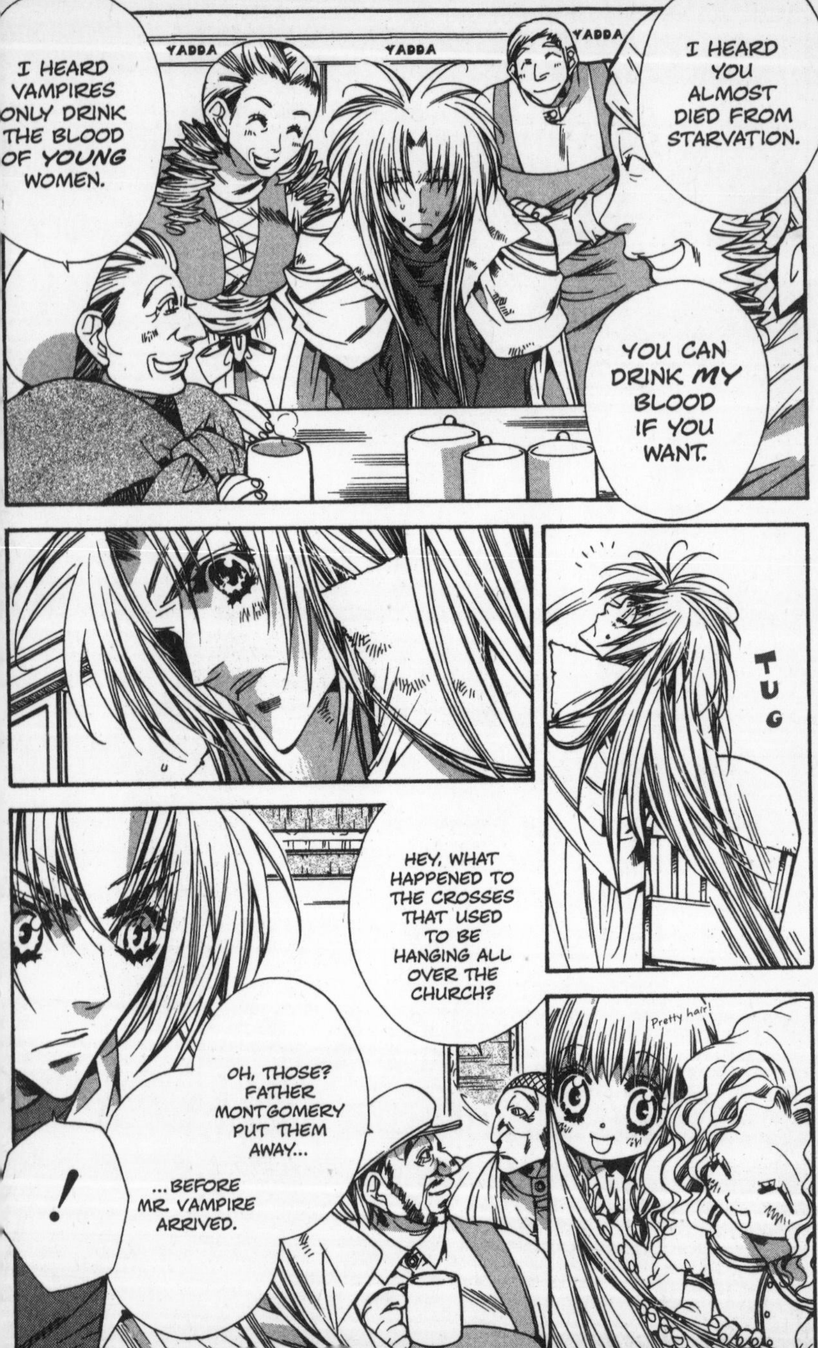
I HEARD YOU ALMOST DIED FROM STARVATION.
YADDA
YADDA
YADDA
I HEARD VAMPIRES ONLY DRINK THE BLOOD OF YOUNG WOMEN.
YOU CAN DRINK MY BLOOD IF YOU WANT.
TUG
HEY, WHAT HAPPENED TO THE CROSSES THAT USED TO BE HANGING ALL OVER THE CHURCH?
Pretty hair!
OH, THOSE? FATHER MONTGOMERY PUT THEM AWAY...
...BEFORE MR VAMPIRE ARRIVED.
!

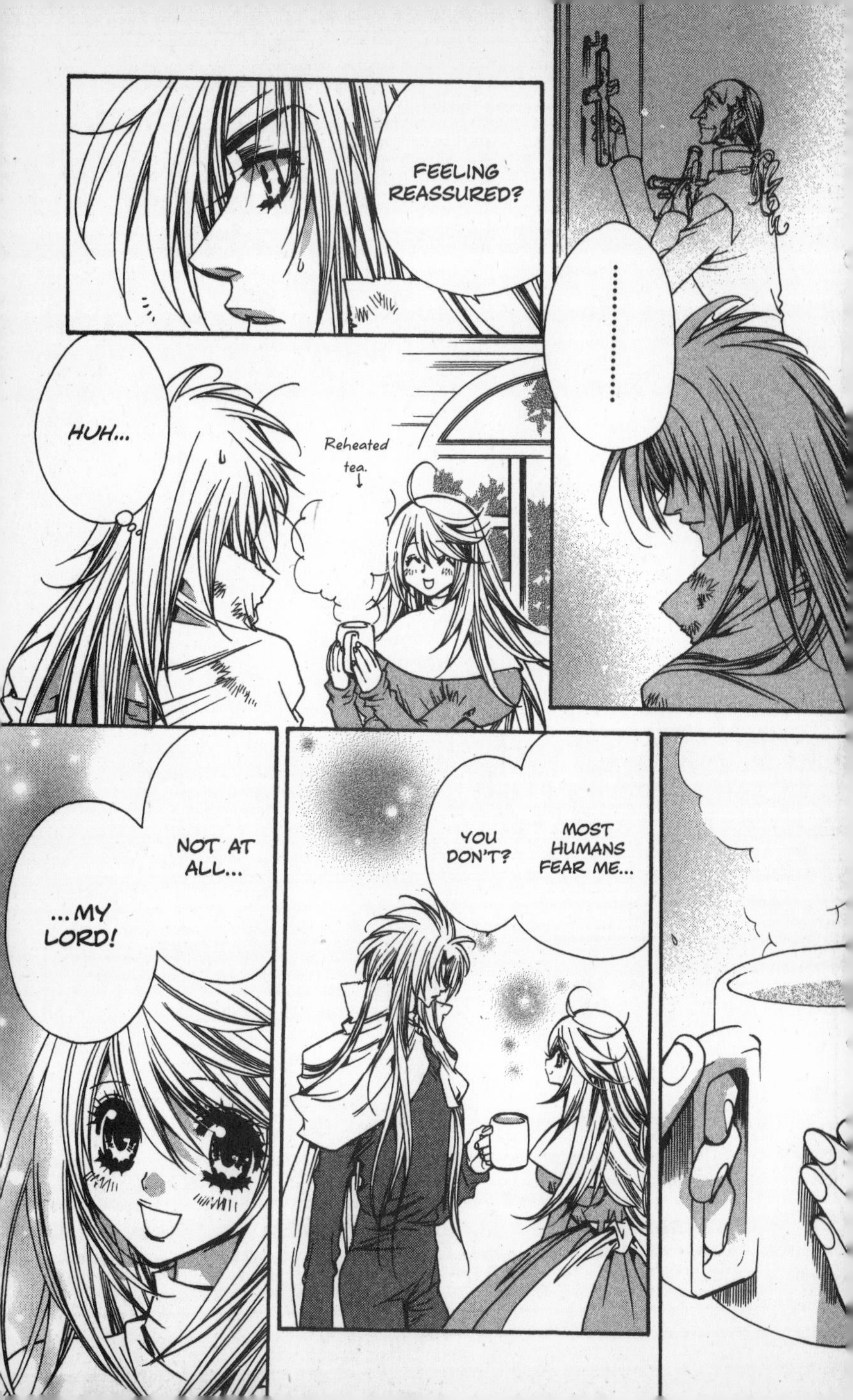
......
FEELING REASSURED?
HUH...
Reheated tea.
MOST HUMANS FEAR ME...
YOU DON'T?
NOT AT ALL...
...MY LORD!

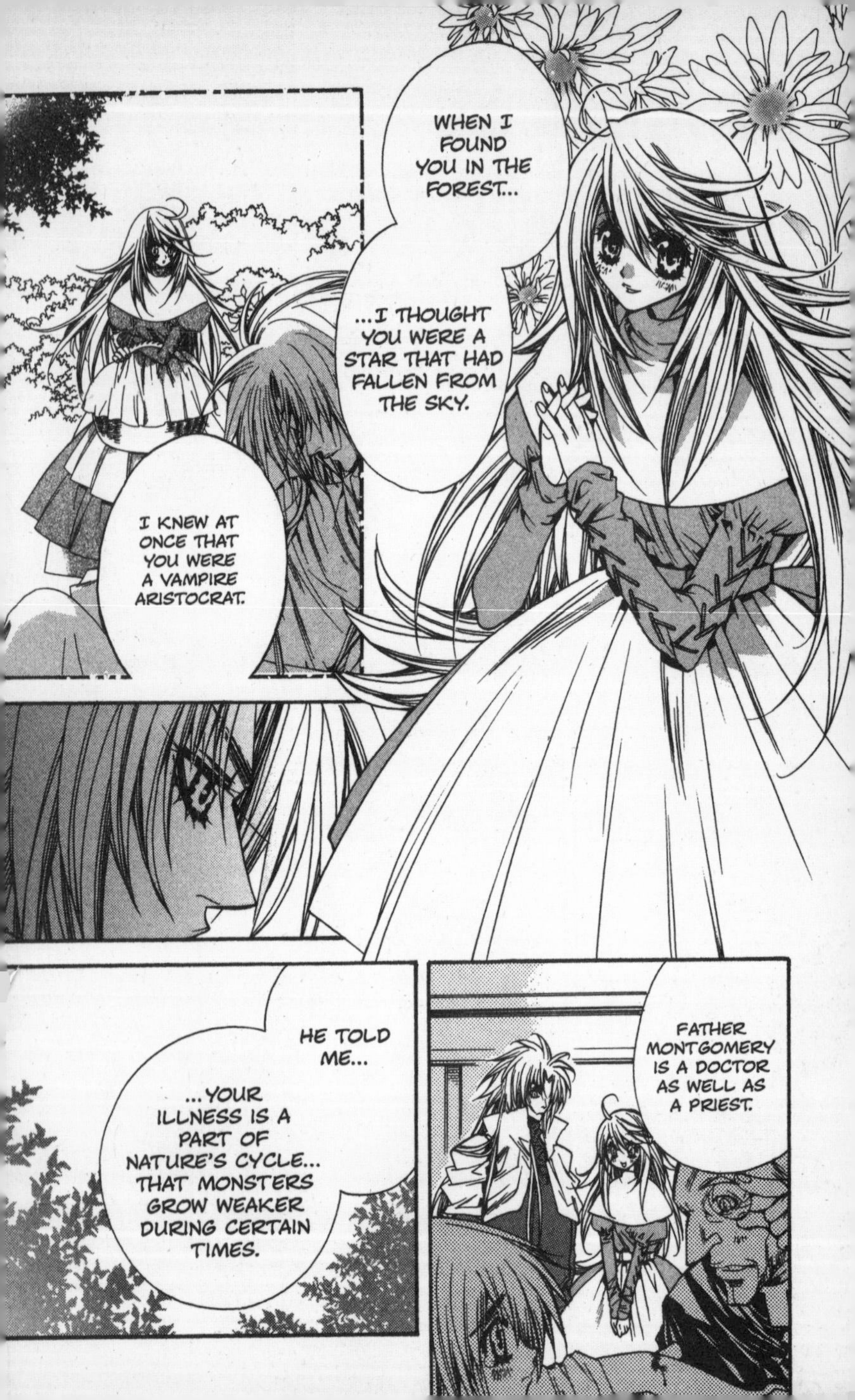
WHEN I FOUND YOU IN THE FOREST...
...I THOUGHT YOU WERE A STAR THAT HAD FALLEN FROM THE SKY.
I KNEW AT ONCE THAT YOU WERE A VAMPIRE ARISTOCRAT.
FATHER MONTGOMERY IS A DOCTOR AS WELL AS A PRIEST.
HE TOLD ME...
...YOUR ILLNESS IS A PART OF NATURE'S CYCLE... THAT MONSTERS GROW WEAKER DURING CERTAIN TIMES.

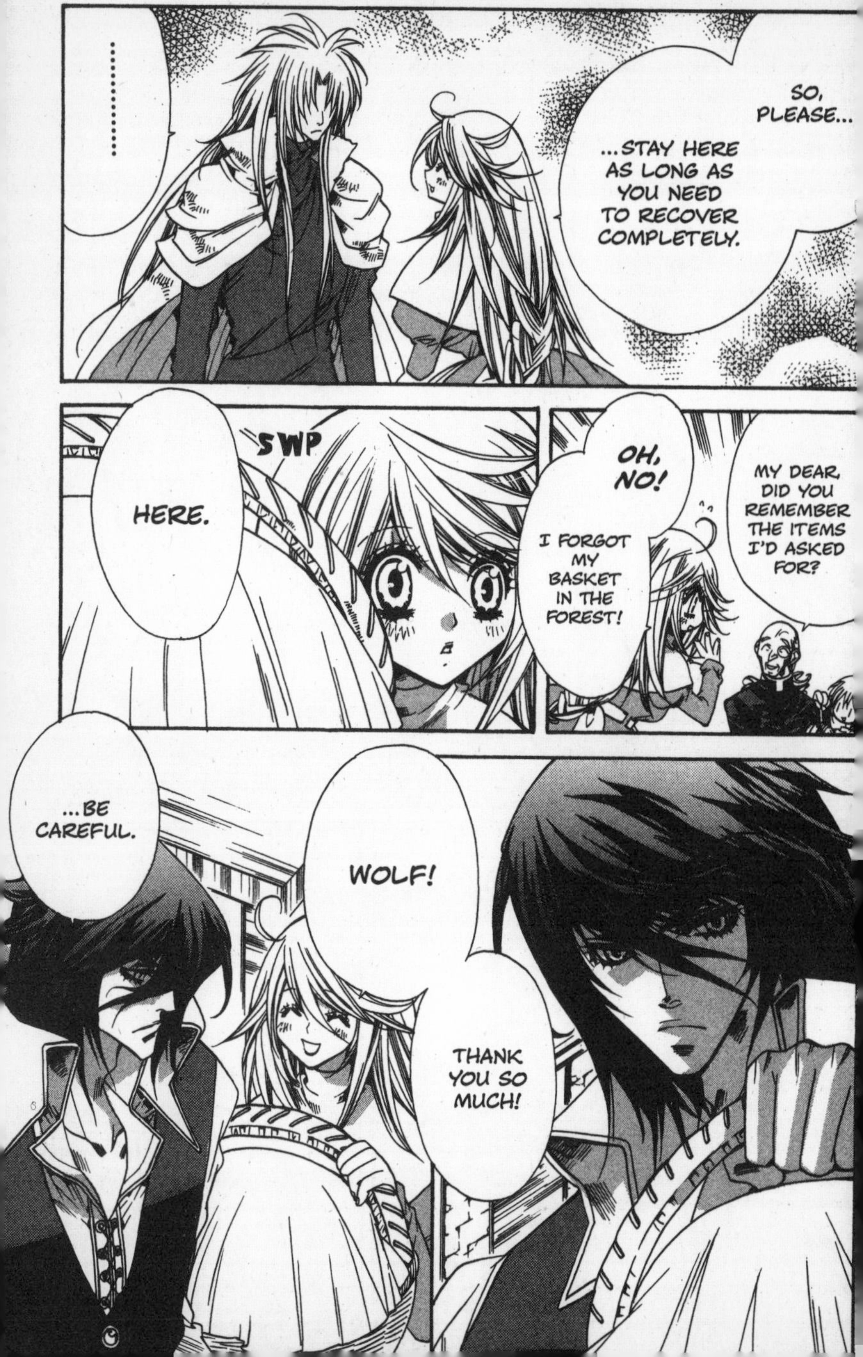
SO, PLEASE...
...STAY HERE AS LONG AS YOU NEED TO RECOVER COMPLETELY.
......
MY DEAR, DID YOU REMEMBER THE ITEMS I'D ASKED FOR?
OH, NO!
I FORGOT MY BASKET IN THE FOREST!
SWP
HERE.
WOLF!
THANK YOU SO MUCH!
...BE CAREFUL.

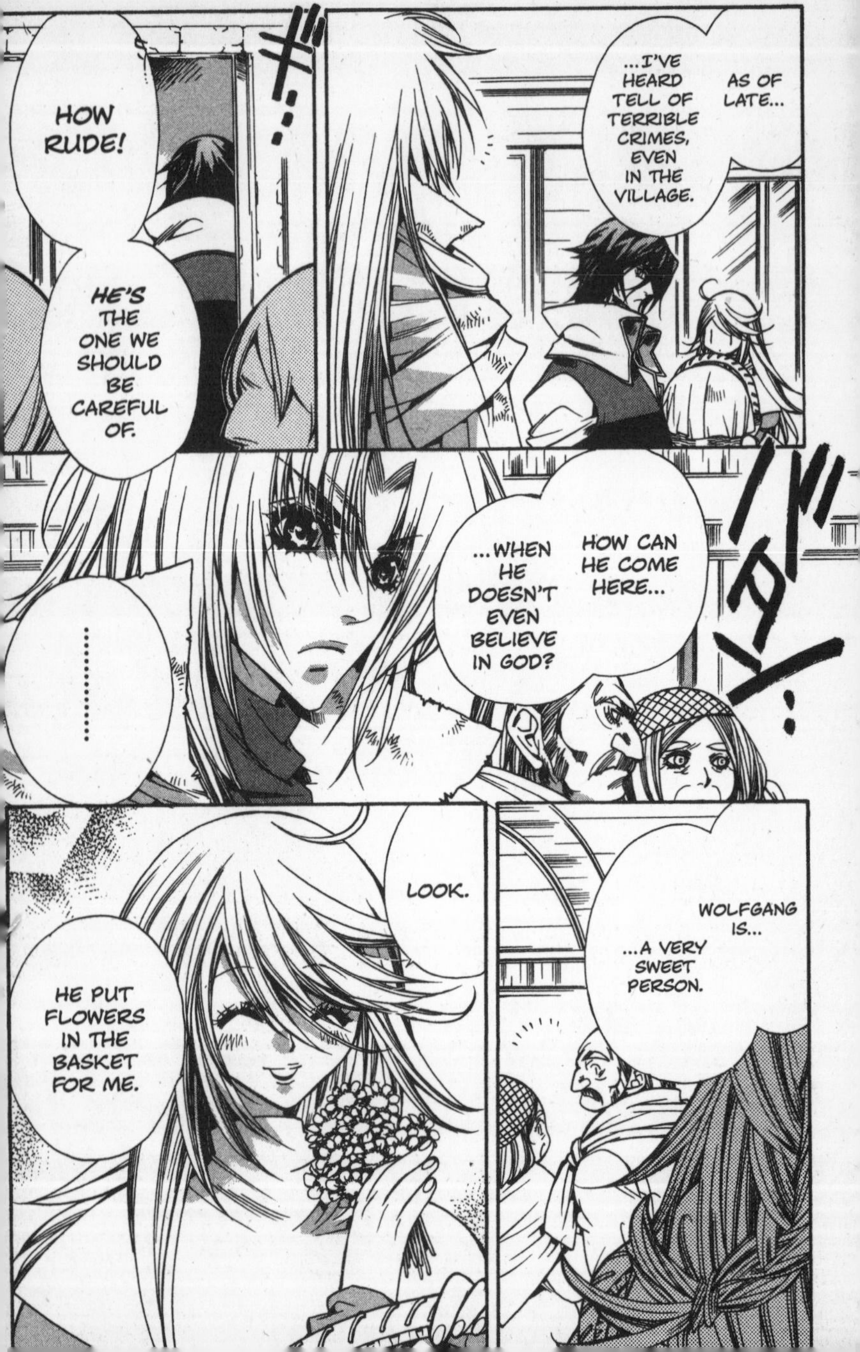
AS OF LATE...
...I'VE HEARD TELL OF TERRIBLE CRIMES, EVEN IN THE VILLAGE.
HOW RUDE!
HE'S THE ONE WE SHOULD BE CAREFUL OF.
HOW CAN HE COME HERE...
...WHEN HE DOESN'T EVEN BELIEVE IN GOD?
....
WOLFGANG IS...
...A VERY SWEET PERSON.
LOOK.
HE PUT FLOWERS IN THE BASKET FOR ME.

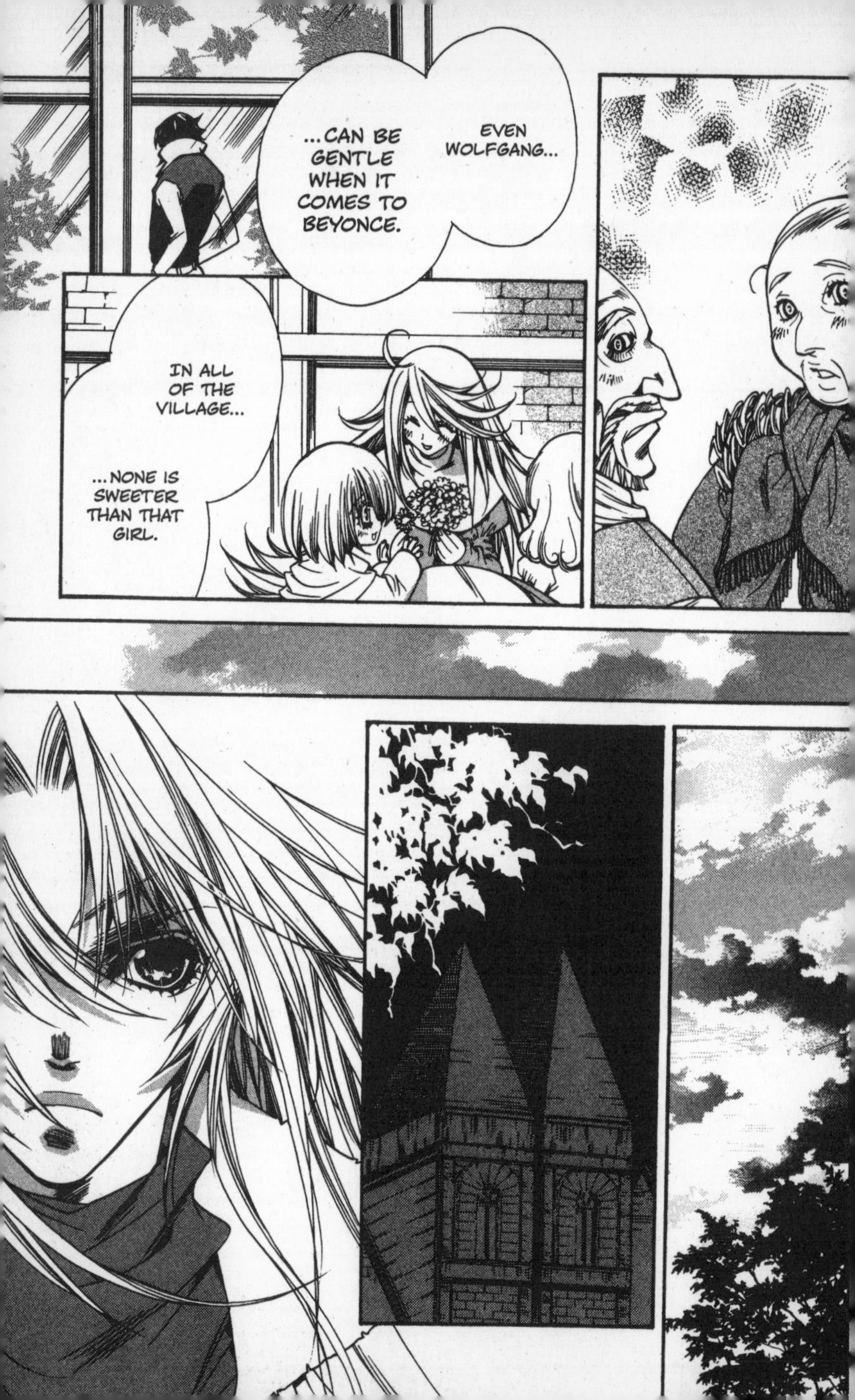
EVEN WOLFGANG...
...CAN BE GENTLE WHEN IT COMES TO BEYONCE.
IN ALL OF THE VILLAGE...
...NONE IS SWEETER THAN THAT GIRL.

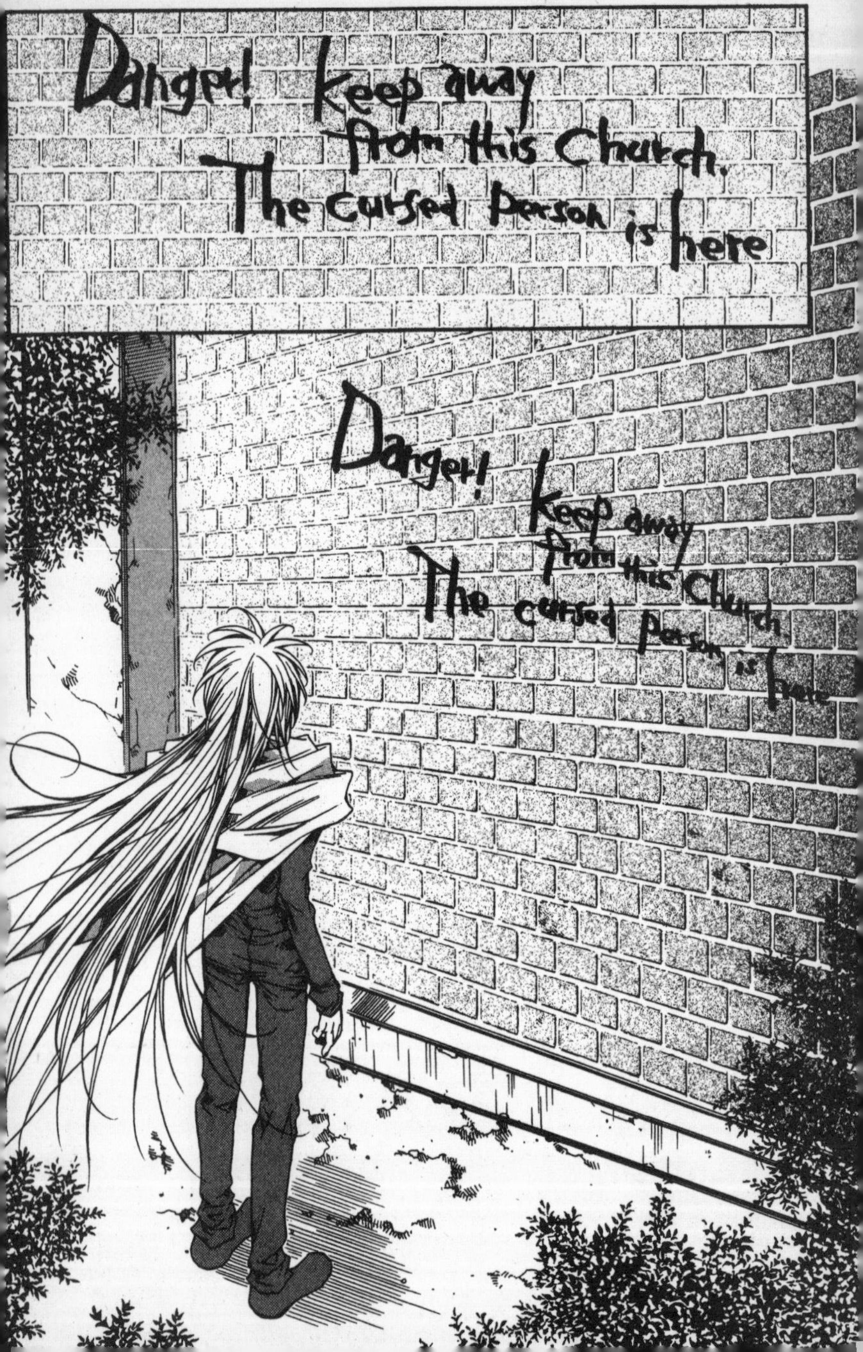

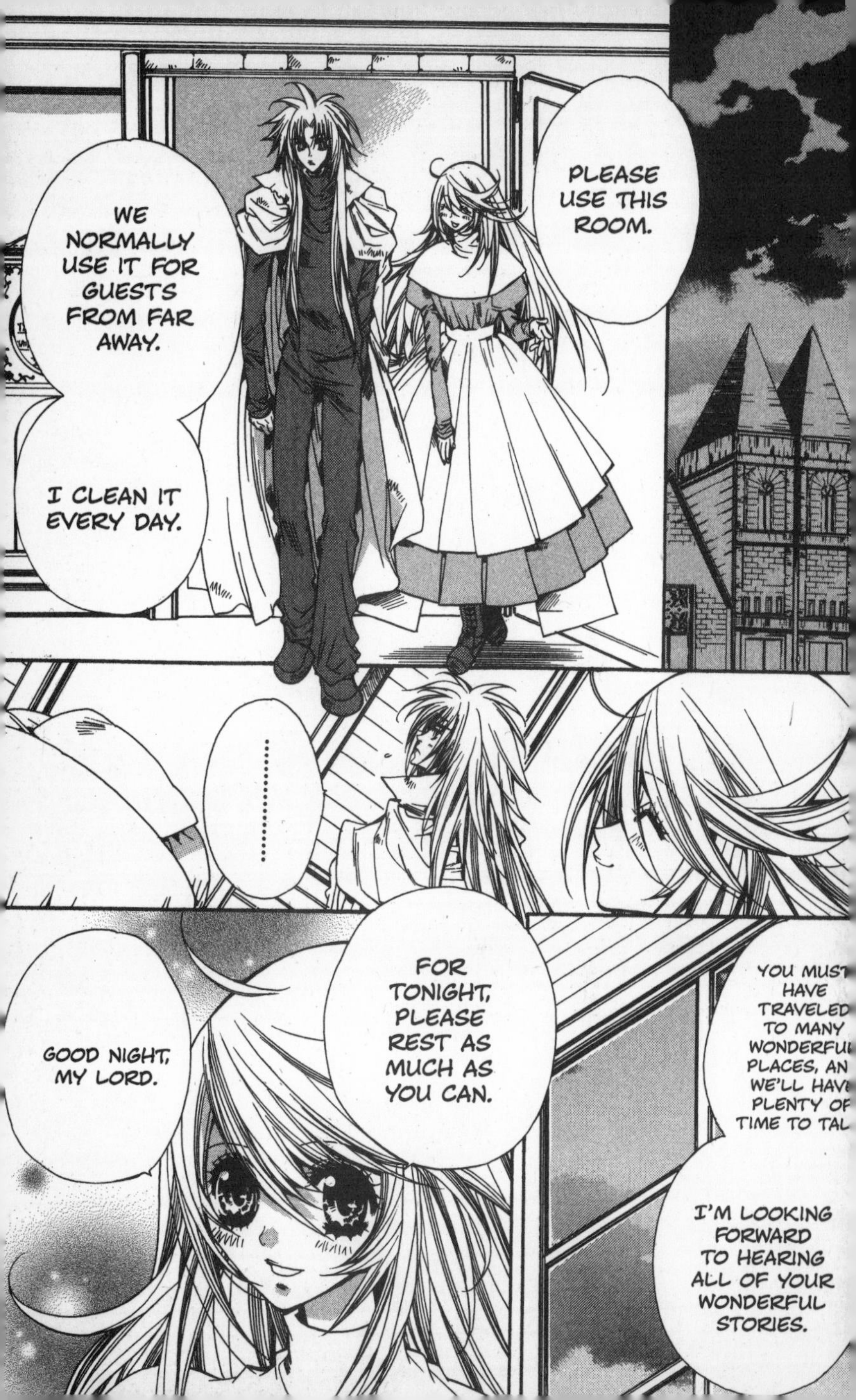
PLEASE USE THIS ROOM.
WE NORMALLY USE IT FOR GUESTS FROM FAR AWAY.
I CLEAN IT EVERY DAY.
......
YOU MUST HAVE TRAVELED TO MANY WONDERFU PLACES, AN WE'LL HAVE PLENTY OF TIME TO TAL
I'M LOOKING FORWARD TO HEARING ALL OF YOUR WONDERFUL STORIES.
FOR TONIGHT, PLEASE REST AS MUCH AS YOU CAN.
GOOD NIGHT, MY LORD.

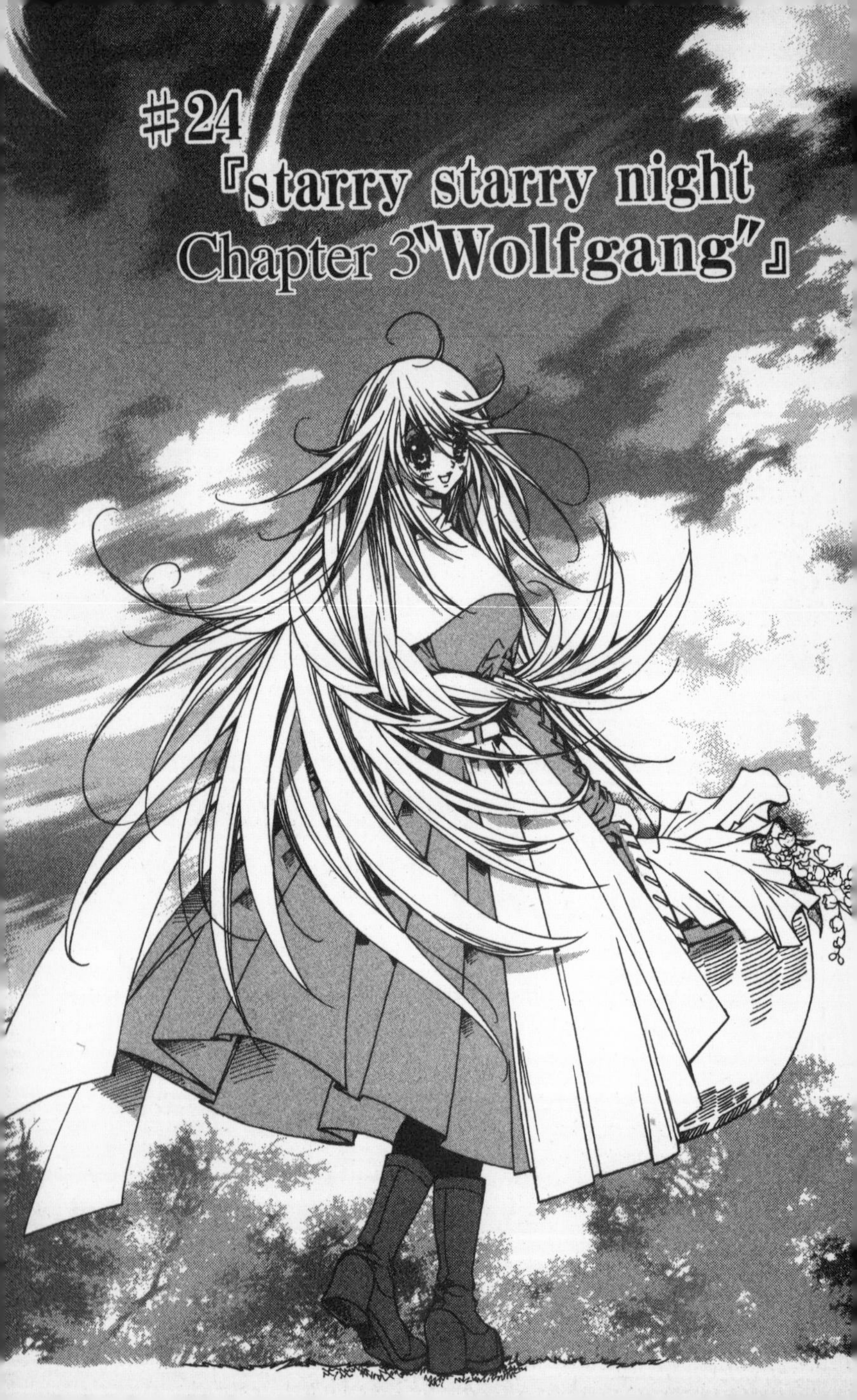
#24
『starry starry night
Chapter 3"Wolfgang"』

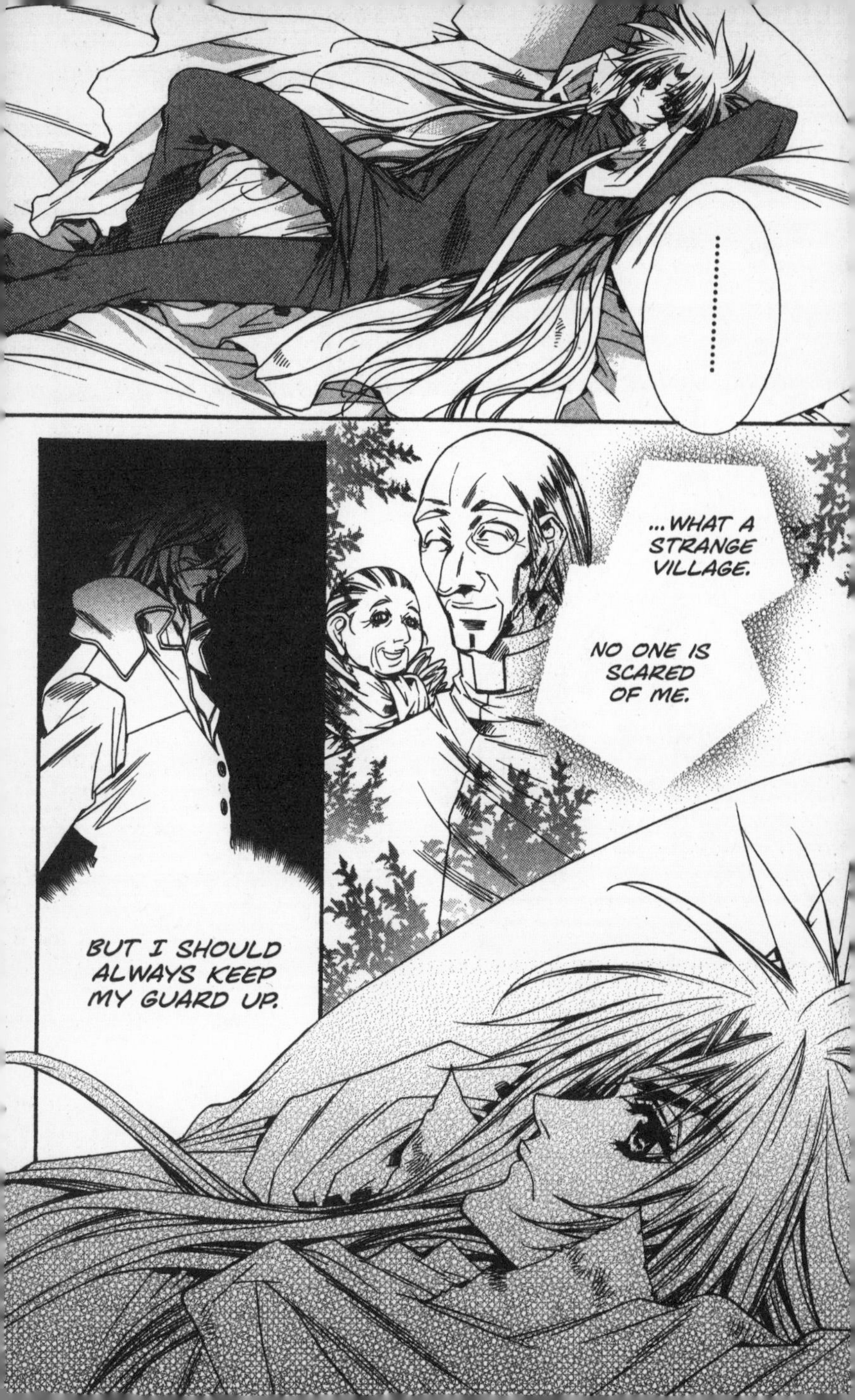
......
...WHAT A STRANGE VILLAGE.
NO ONE IS SCARED OF ME.
BUT I SHOULD ALWAYS KEEP MY GUARD UP.

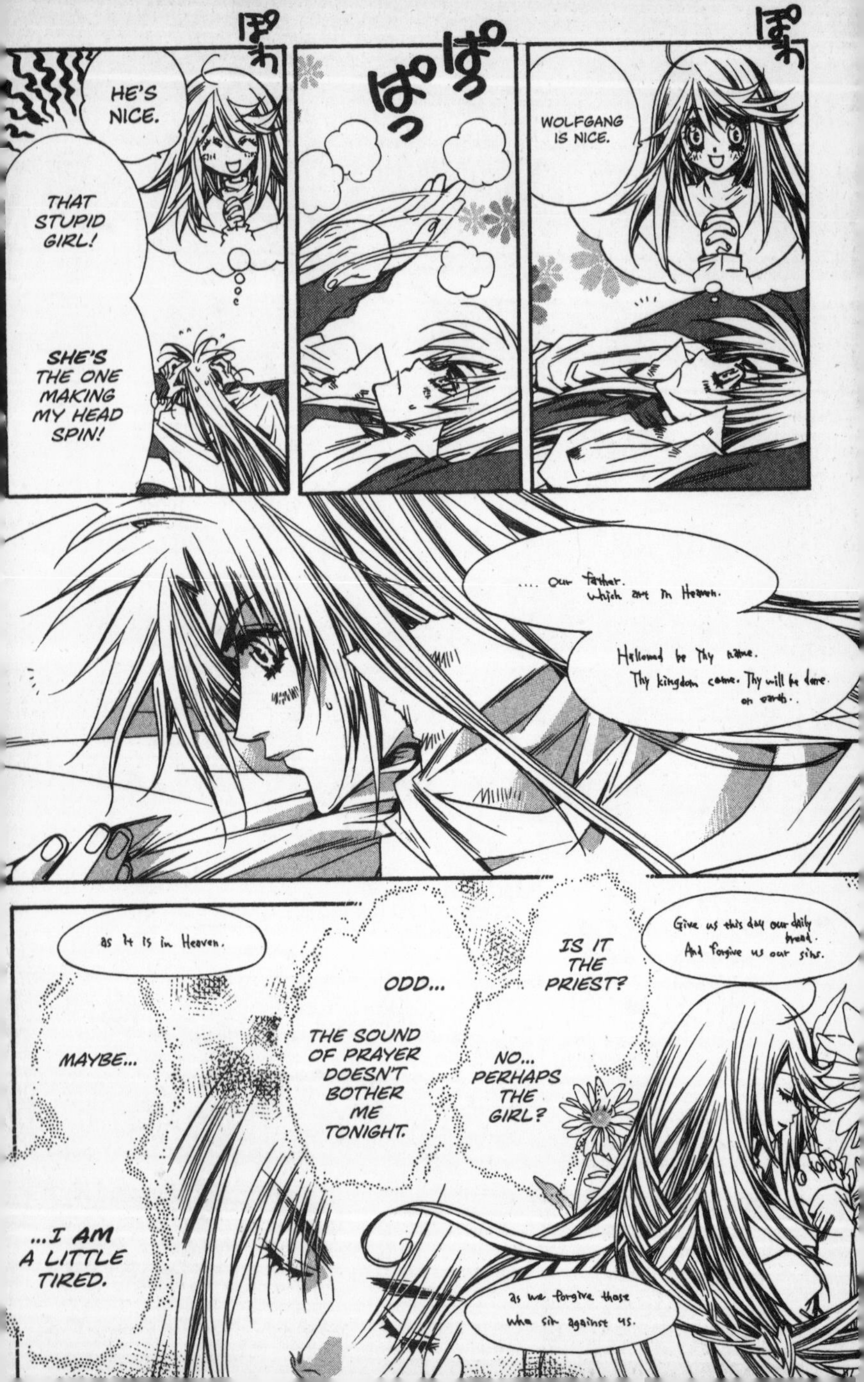
ぽわ
WOLFGANG IS NICE.
ぽっ ぽっ
ぽわ
HE'S NICE.
THAT STUPID GIRL!
SHE'S THE ONE MAKING MY HEAD SPIN!
... Our father, which art in Heaven.
Hallowed be Thy name. Thy kingdom come. Thy will be done on earth..
as it is in Heaven.
Give us this day our daily bread. And forgive us our sins.
IS IT THE PRIEST?
NO... PERHAPS THE GIRL?
ODD...
THE SOUND OF PRAYER DOESN'T BOTHER ME TONIGHT.
MAYBE...
...I AM A LITTLE TIRED.
as we forgive those who sin against us.

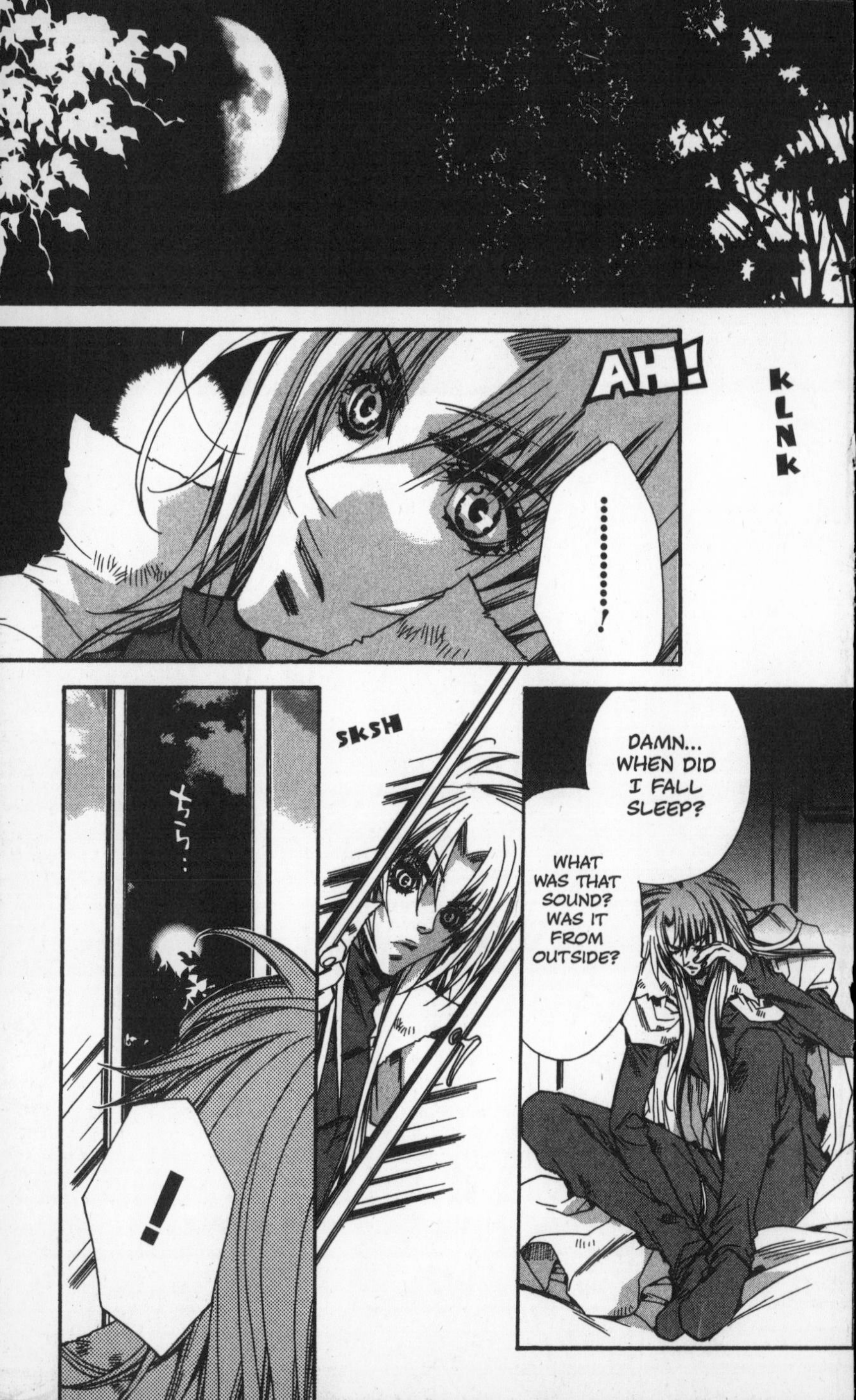
KLNK
AH!
..........!
DAMN... WHEN DID I FALL SLEEP?
WHAT WAS THAT SOUND? WAS IT FROM OUTSIDE?
SKSH
ちら..
!

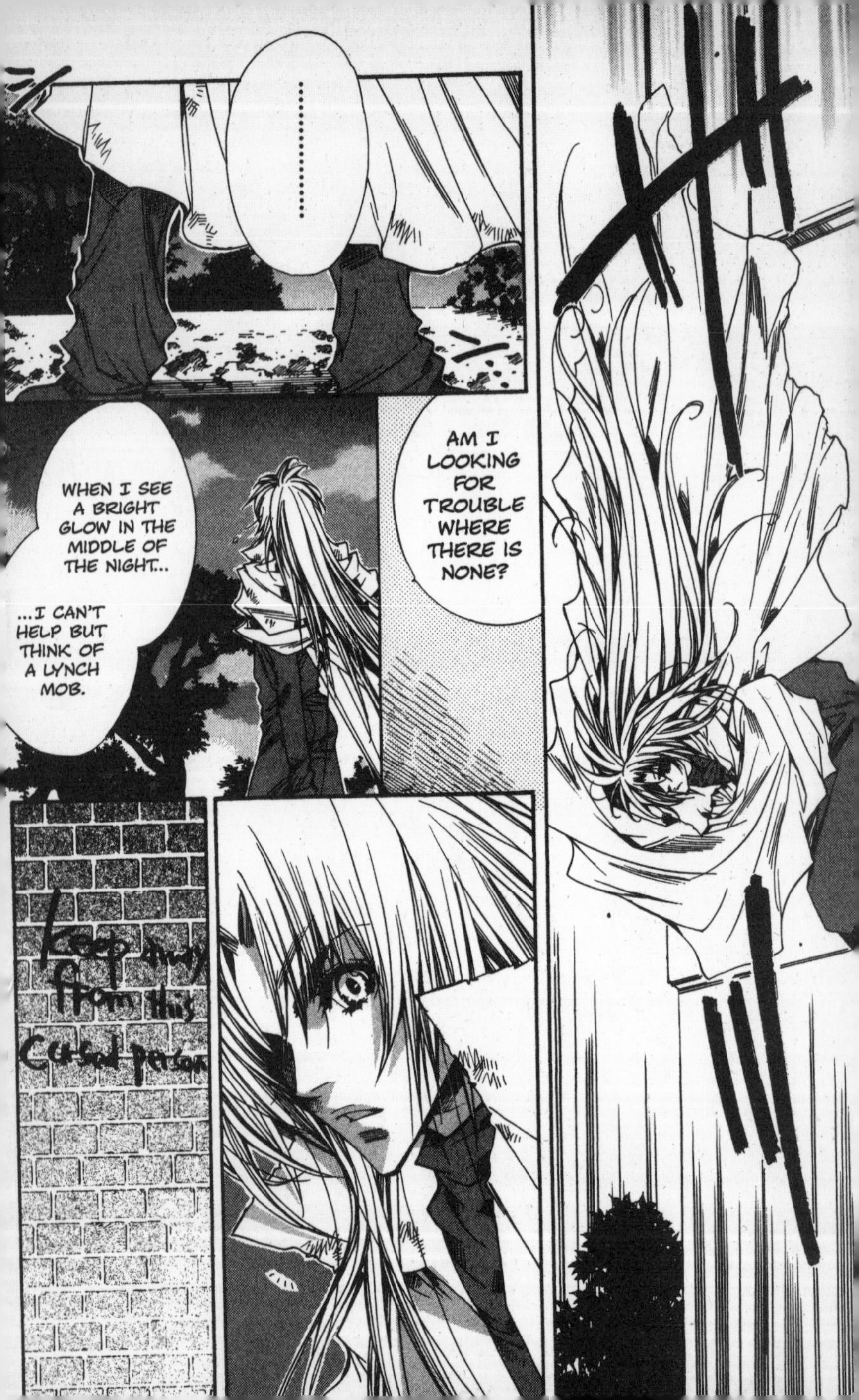
......
AM I LOOKING FOR TROUBLE WHERE THERE IS NONE?
WHEN I SEE A BRIGHT GLOW IN THE MIDDLE OF THE NIGHT...
...I CAN'T HELP BUT THINK OF A LYNCH MOB.
Keep away from this cursed person

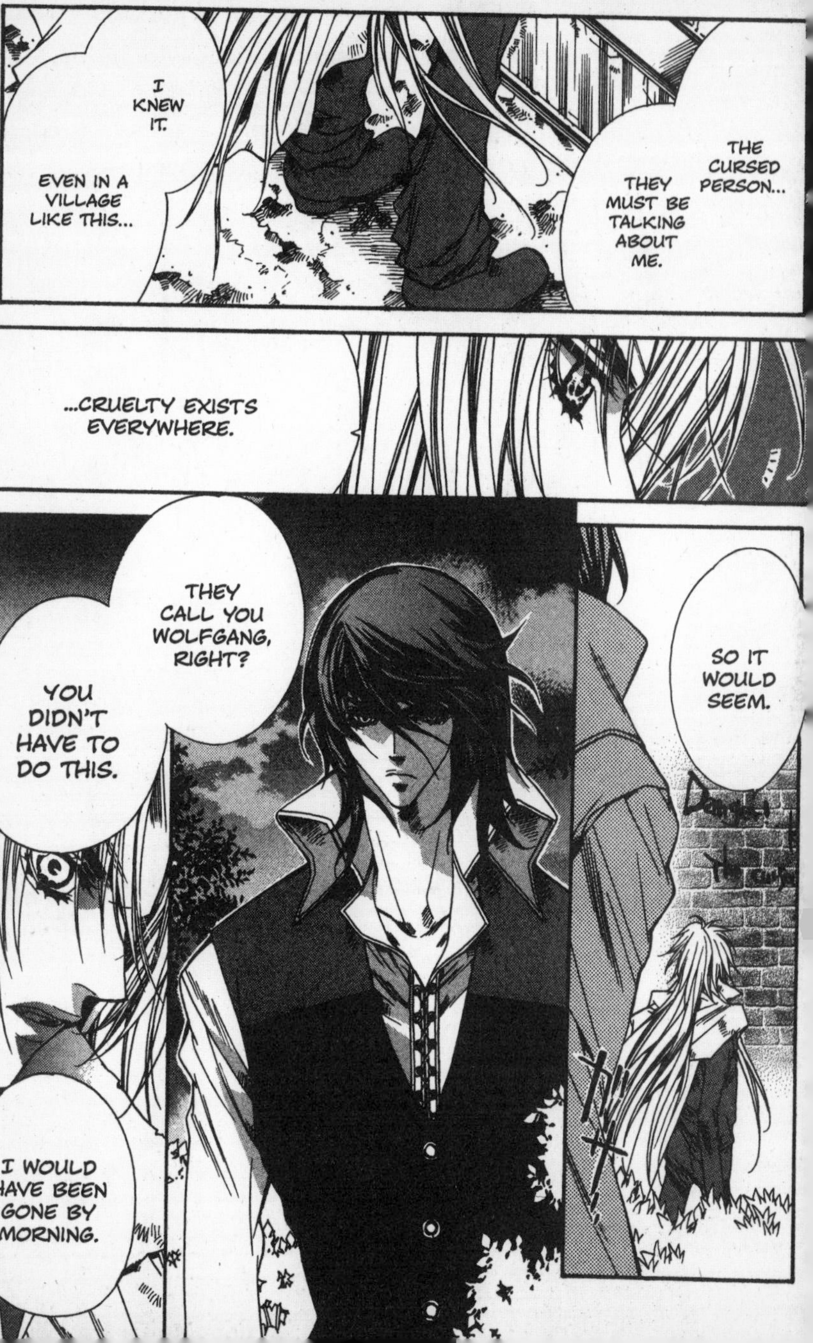
THE CURSED PERSON...
THEY MUST BE TALKING ABOUT ME.
I KNEW IT.
EVEN IN A VILLAGE LIKE THIS...
...CRUELTY EXISTS EVERYWHERE.
SO IT WOULD SEEM.
THEY CALL YOU WOLFGANG, RIGHT?
YOU DIDN'T HAVE TO DO THIS.
I WOULD HAVE BEEN GONE BY MORNING.

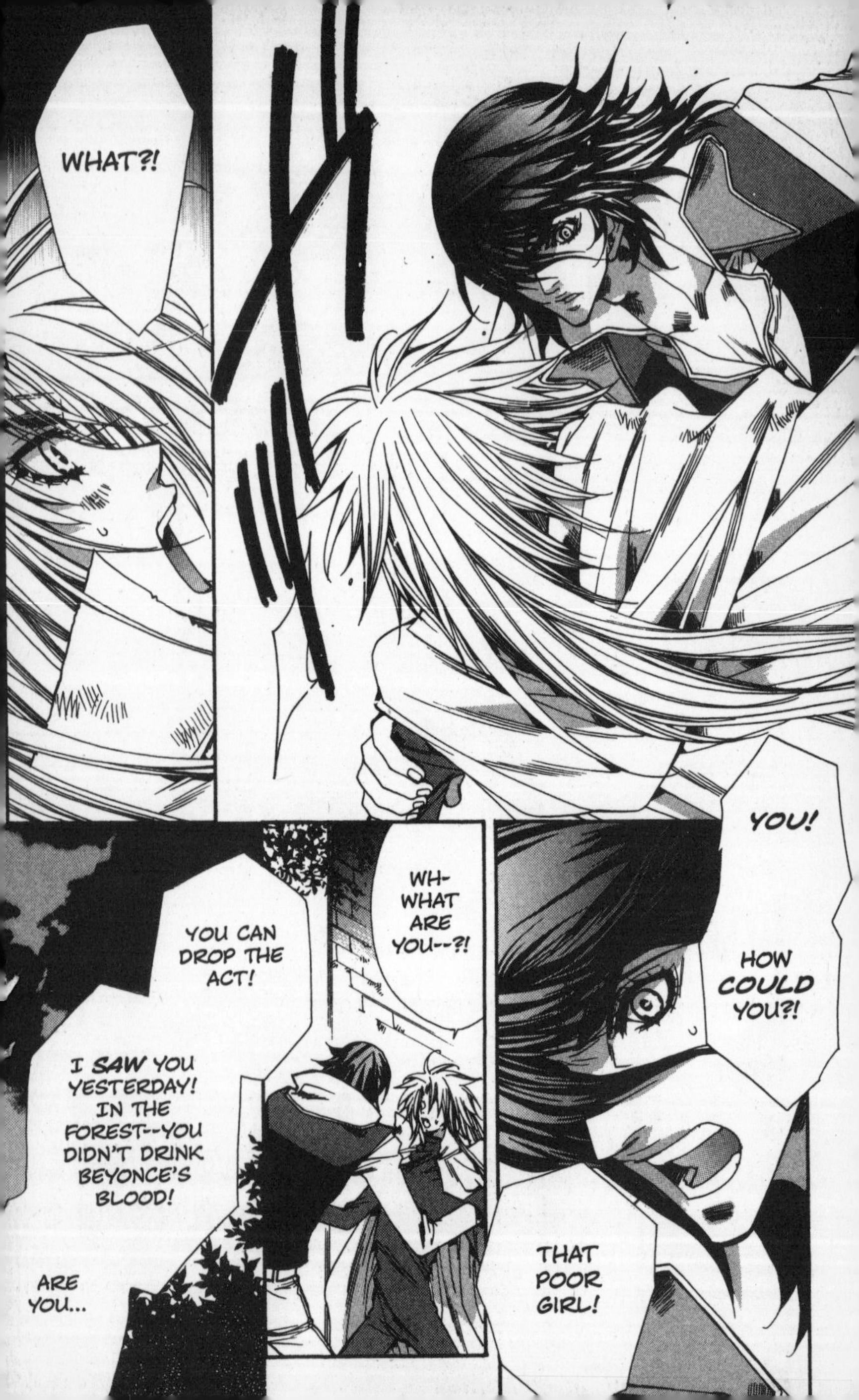
WHAT?!
YOU!
HOW COULD YOU?!
THAT POOR GIRL!
WH-WHAT ARE YOU--?!
YOU CAN DROP THE ACT!
I SAW YOU YESTERDAY! IN THE FOREST--YOU DIDN'T DRINK BEYONCE'S BLOOD!
ARE YOU...

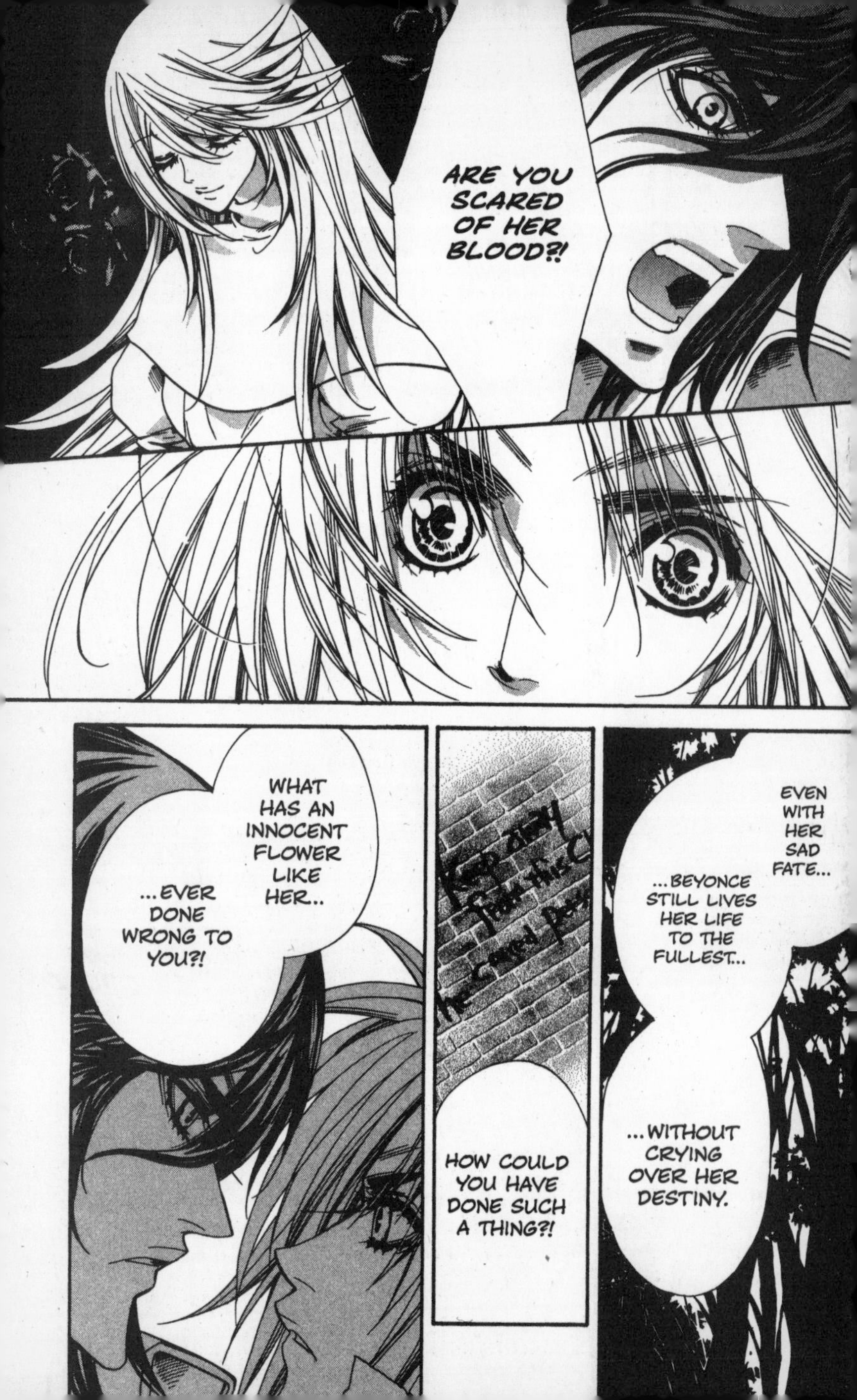
ARE YOU SCARED OF HER BLOOD?!
EVEN WITH HER SAD FATE...
...BEYONCE STILL LIVES HER LIFE TO THE FULLEST...
...WITHOUT CRYING OVER HER DESTINY.
HOW COULD YOU HAVE DONE SUCH A THING?!
WHAT HAS AN INNOCENT FLOWER LIKE HER..
...EVER DONE WRONG TO YOU?!

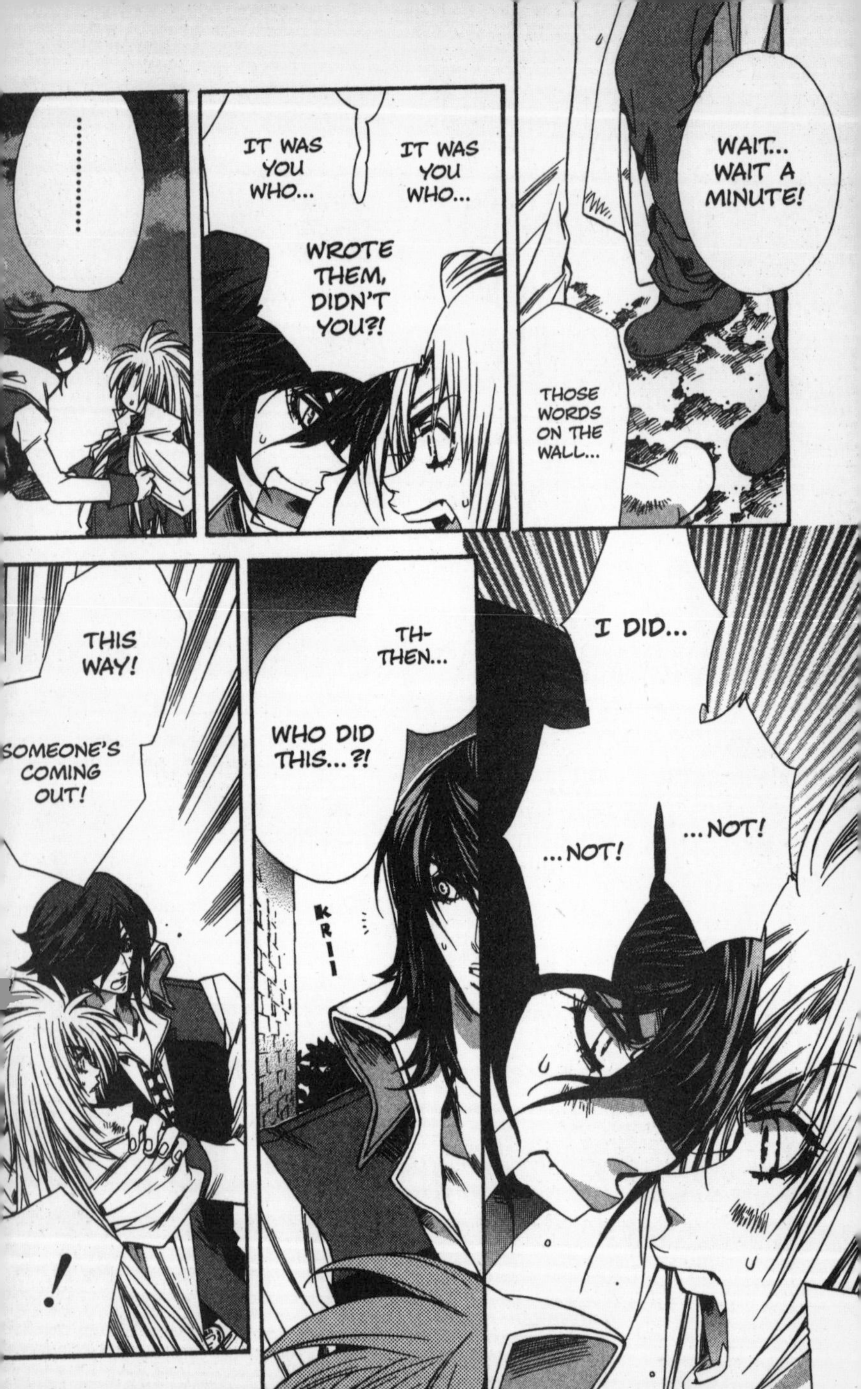
WAIT... WAIT A MINUTE!
THOSE WORDS ON THE WALL...
IT WAS YOU WHO...
IT WAS YOU WHO...
WROTE THEM, DIDN'T YOU?!
....
I DID...
...NOT!
...NOT!
TH- THEN...
WHO DID THIS...?!
KRII
THIS WAY!
SOMEONE'S COMING OUT!
!

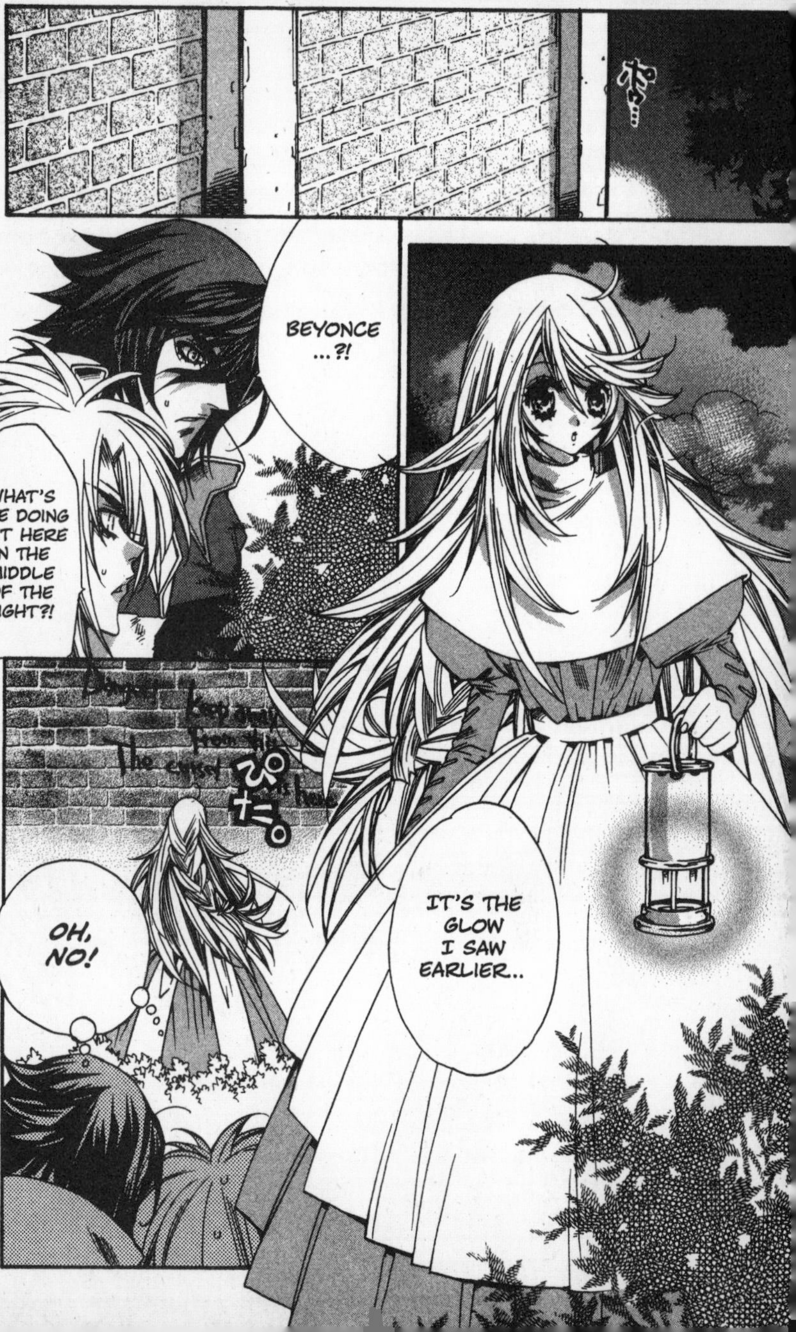
IT'S THE GLOW I SAW EARLIER..
BEYONCE ...?!
WHAT'S SHE DOING OUT HERE IN THE MIDDLE OF THE NIGHT?!
OH, NO!

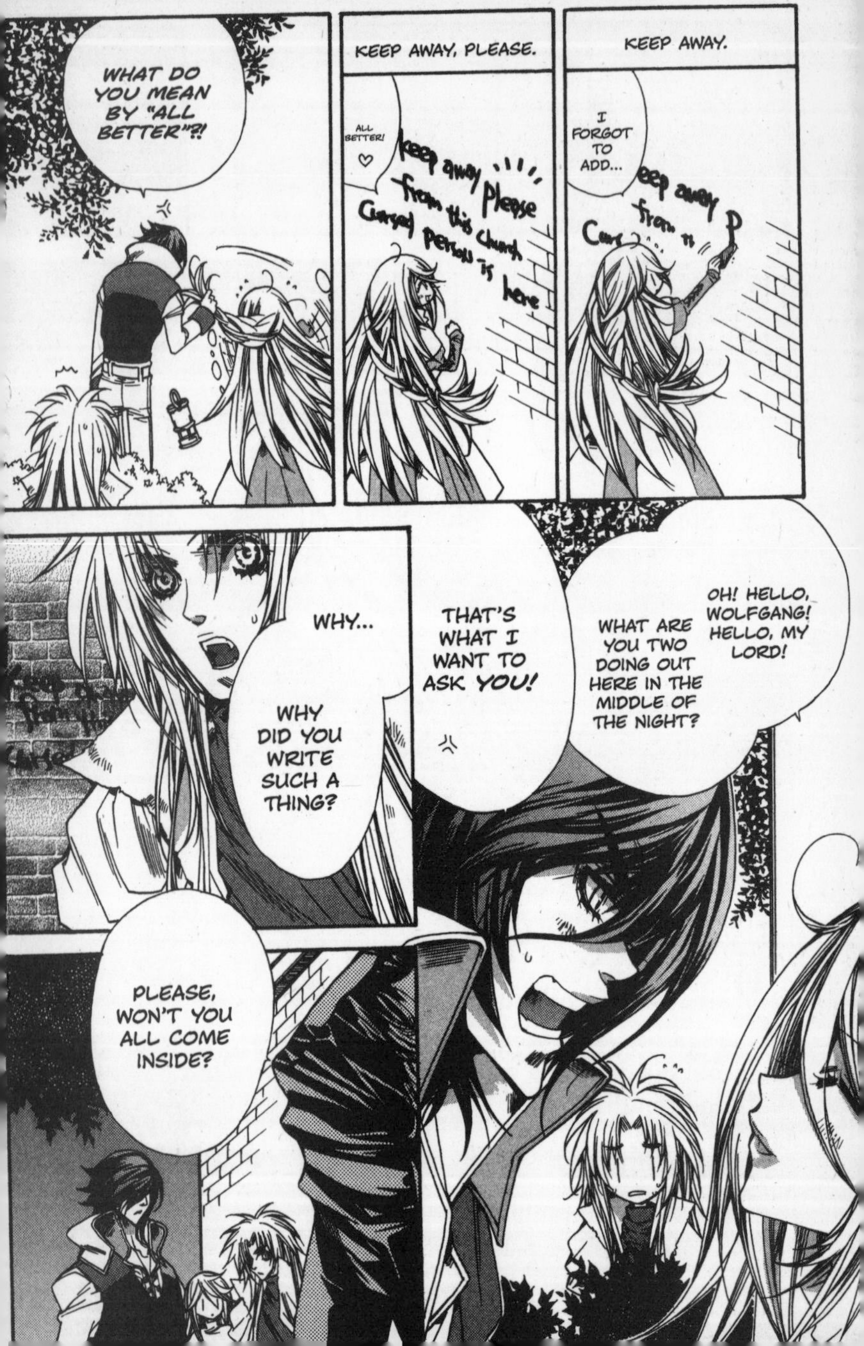
KEEP AWAY.
I FORGOT TO ADD...
KEEP AWAY, PLEASE.
ALL BETTER! ♡
keep away Please from this church Cursed person is here
WHAT DO YOU MEAN BY "ALL BETTER"?!
OH! HELLO, WOLFGANG! HELLO, MY LORD!
WHAT ARE YOU TWO DOING OUT HERE IN THE MIDDLE OF THE NIGHT?
THAT'S WHAT I WANT TO ASK YOU!
WHY...
WHY DID YOU WRITE SUCH A THING?
PLEASE, WON'T YOU ALL COME INSIDE?

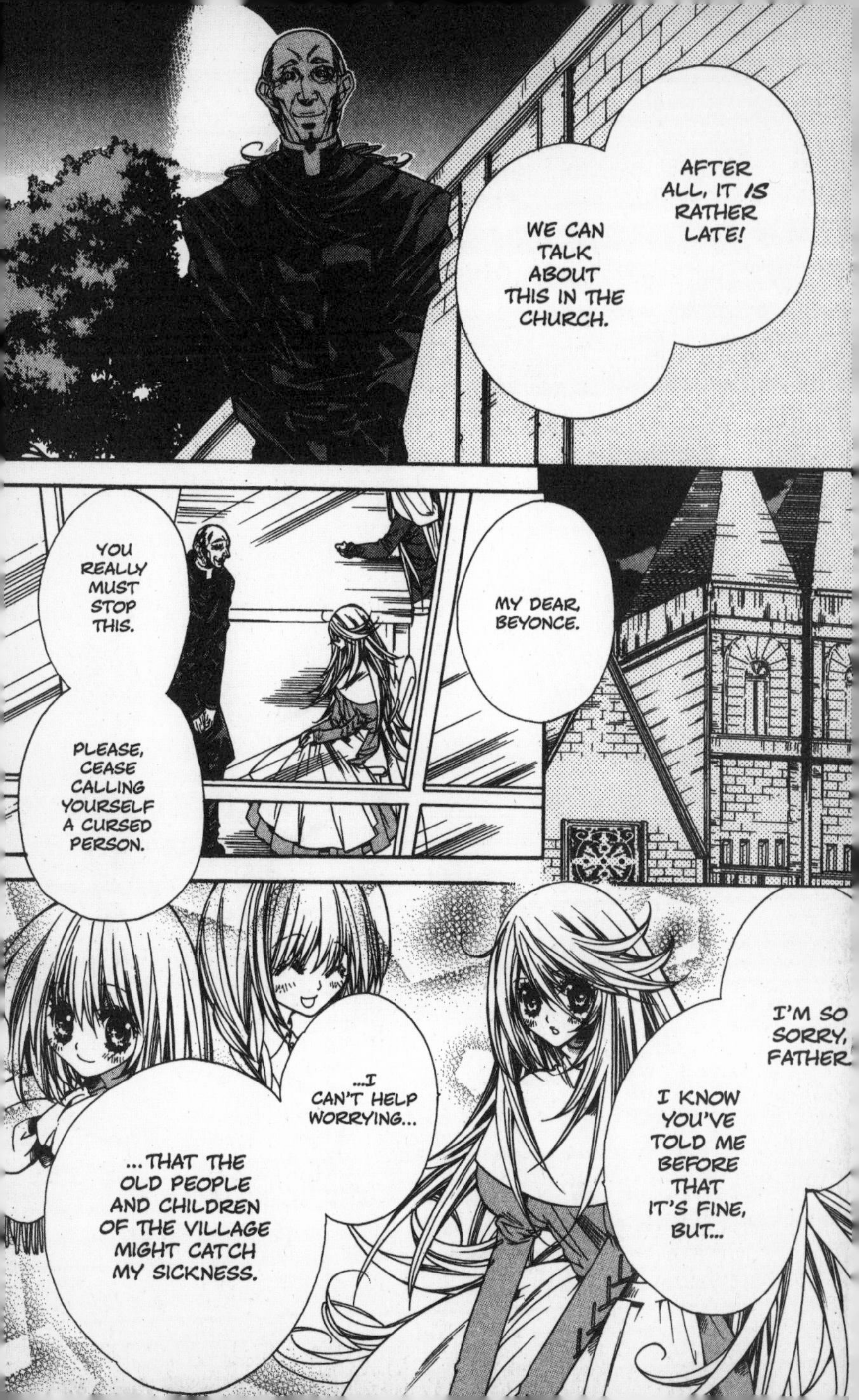
AFTER ALL, IT *IS* RATHER LATE!
WE CAN TALK ABOUT THIS IN THE CHURCH.
MY DEAR, BEYONCE.
YOU REALLY MUST STOP THIS.
PLEASE, CEASE CALLING YOURSELF A CURSED PERSON.
I'M SO SORRY, FATHER.
I KNOW YOU'VE TOLD ME BEFORE THAT IT'S FINE, BUT...
...I CAN'T HELP WORRYING...
...THAT THE OLD PEOPLE AND CHILDREN OF THE VILLAGE MIGHT CATCH MY SICKNESS.

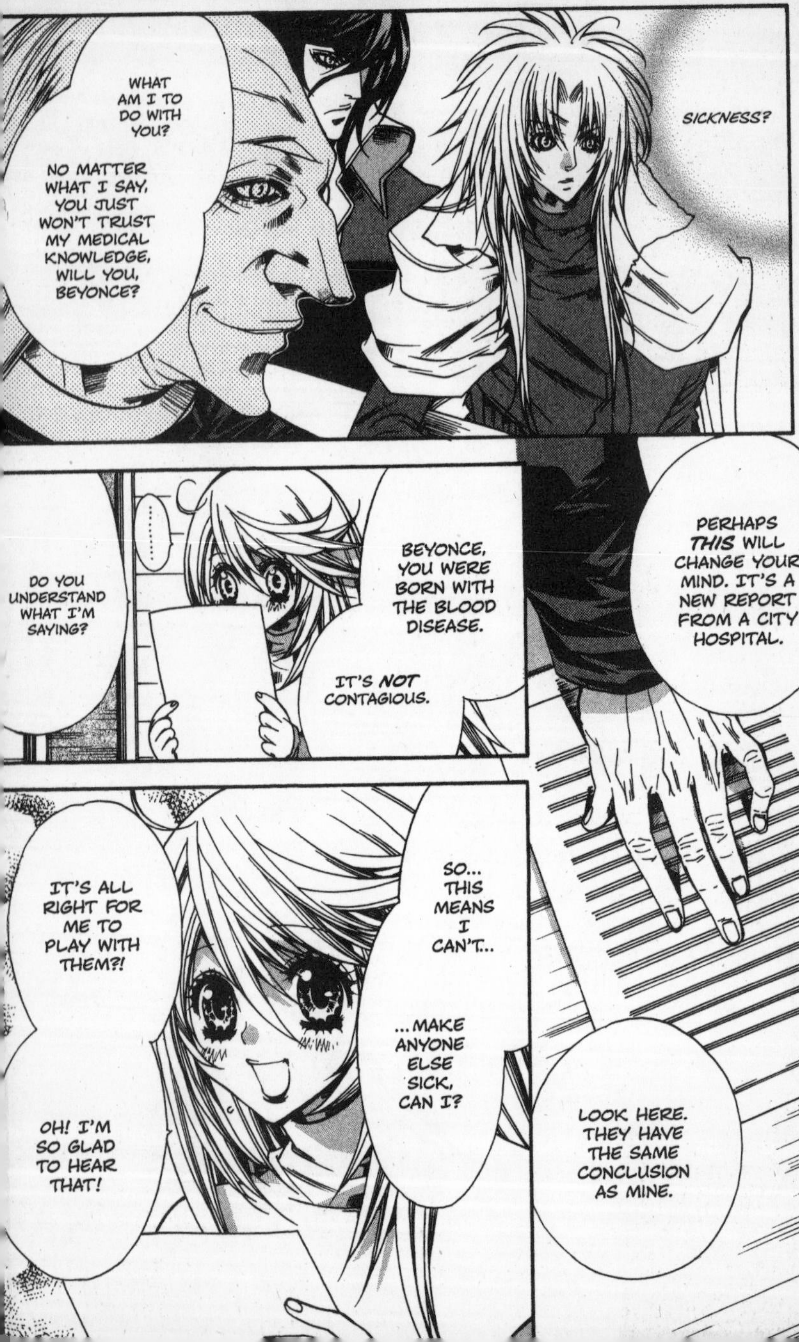
SICKNESS?
WHAT AM I TO DO WITH YOU?
NO MATTER WHAT I SAY, YOU JUST WON'T TRUST MY MEDICAL KNOWLEDGE, WILL YOU, BEYONCE?
PERHAPS *THIS* WILL CHANGE YOUR MIND. IT'S A NEW REPORT FROM A CITY HOSPITAL.
LOOK HERE. THEY HAVE THE SAME CONCLUSION AS MINE.
BEYONCE, YOU WERE BORN WITH THE BLOOD DISEASE.
IT'S *NOT* CONTAGIOUS.
......
DO YOU UNDERSTAND WHAT I'M SAYING?
SO... THIS MEANS I CAN'T...
...MAKE ANYONE ELSE SICK, CAN I?
IT'S ALL RIGHT FOR ME TO PLAY WITH THEM?!
OH! I'M SO GLAD TO HEAR THAT!

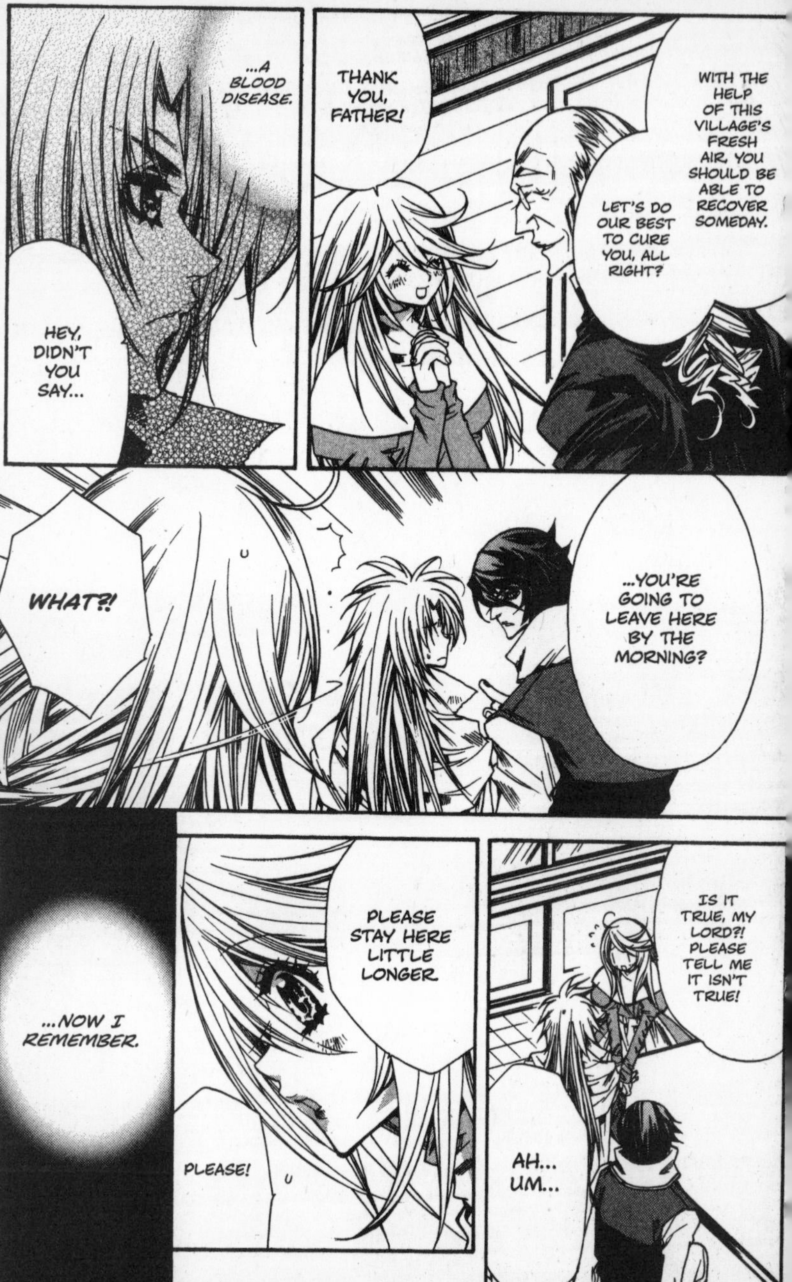
WITH THE HELP OF THIS VILLAGE'S FRESH AIR, YOU SHOULD BE ABLE TO RECOVER SOMEDAY.
LET'S DO OUR BEST TO CURE YOU, ALL RIGHT?
THANK YOU, FATHER!
...A BLOOD DISEASE.
HEY, DIDN'T YOU SAY...
...YOU'RE GOING TO LEAVE HERE BY THE MORNING?
WHAT?!
IS IT TRUE, MY LORD?! PLEASE TELL ME IT ISN'T TRUE!
AH... UM...
PLEASE STAY HERE LITTLE LONGER
PLEASE!
...NOW I REMEMBER.

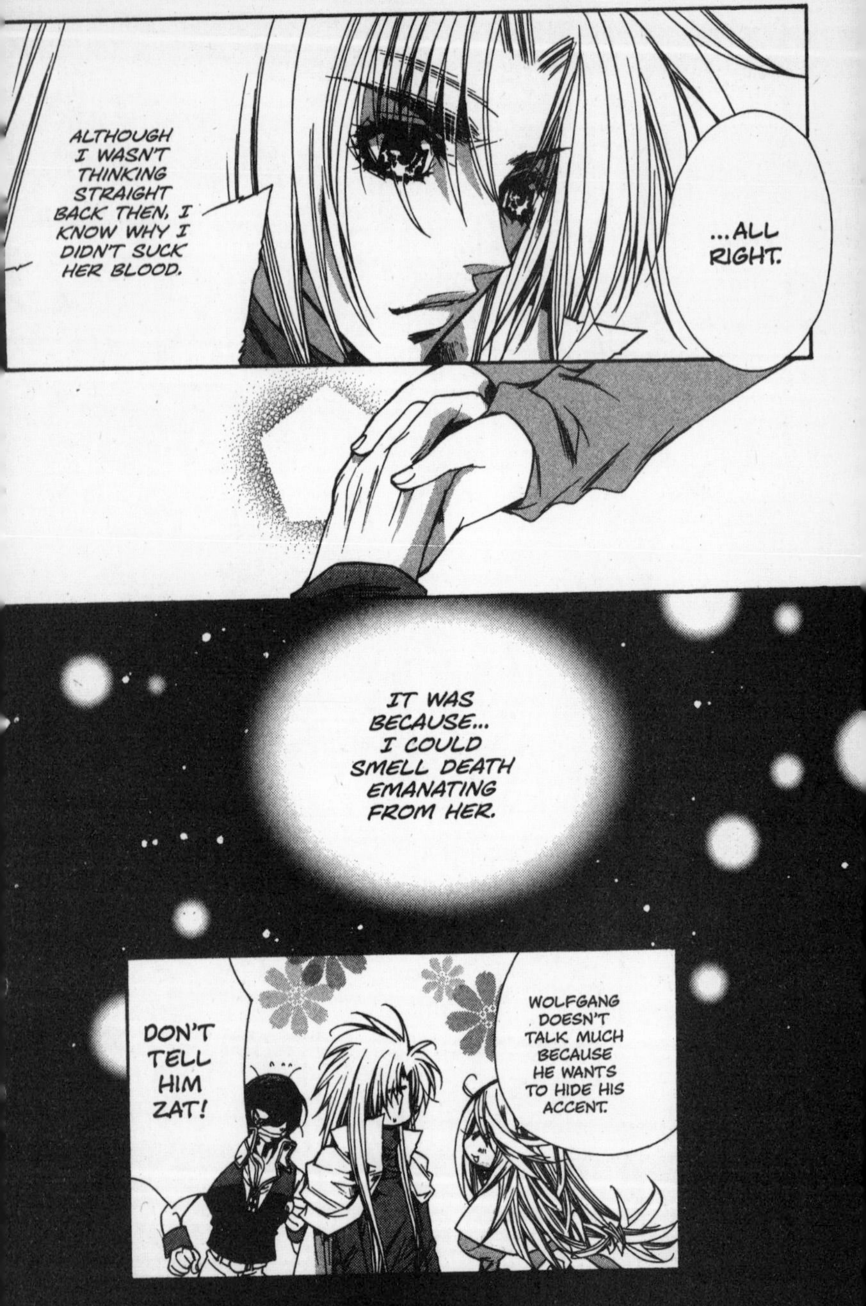
...ALL RIGHT.
ALTHOUGH I WASN'T THINKING STRAIGHT BACK THEN, I KNOW WHY I DIDN'T SUCK HER BLOOD.
IT WAS BECAUSE... I COULD SMELL DEATH EMANATING FROM HER.
WOLFGANG DOESN'T TALK MUCH BECAUSE HE WANTS TO HIDE HIS ACCENT.
DON'T TELL HIM ZAT!

BONUS COMIC STRIP

VAMPIRE DOLL REFLECTIONS

Starry Starry Night

WHAT'S YOUR NAME?
~THE PAST~
MY LORD, WHAT IS YOUR NAME?
I DON'T HAVE ANY FRIENDS, SO I DON'T NEED A NAME.
"VAMPIRE" SHOULD DO FOR A HUMAN LIKE YOU.
BUT IF YOU DON'T PICK A NAME, THE OLD PEOPLE WILL PICK ONE FOR YOU.
TARO.
GO-SAKU.
WAH!!
HEI-HACHI.

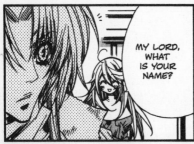

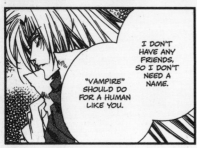

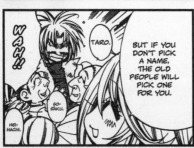

BONUS COMIC STRIP

R·P Guilt-na-Zan Part3

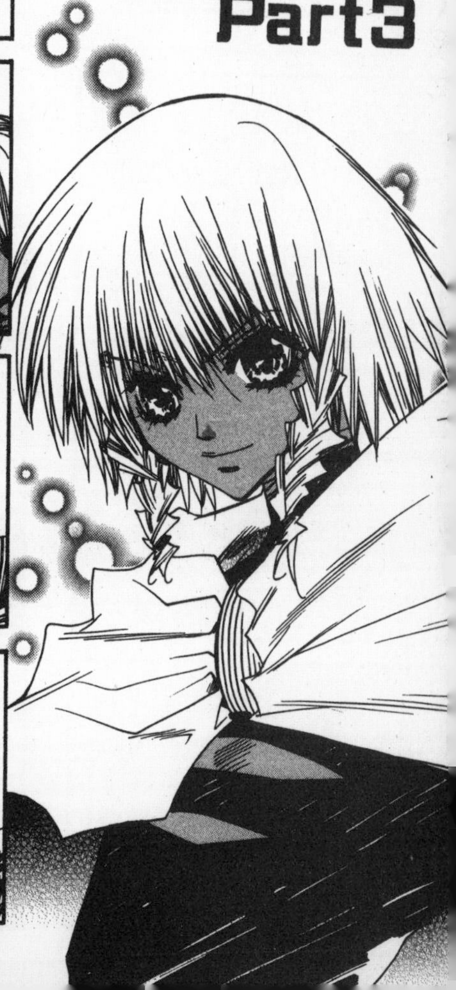

Comedy Short?

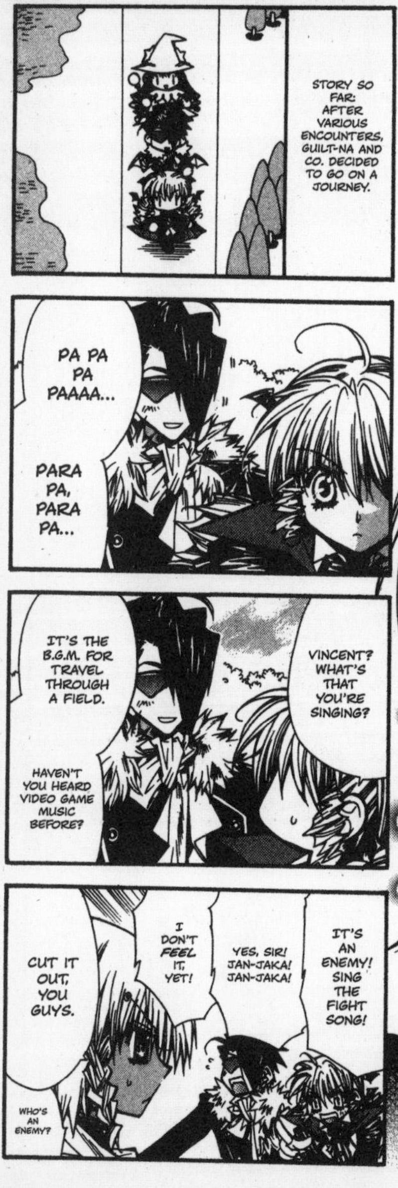
STORY SO FAR: AFTER VARIOUS ENCOUNTERS, GUILT-NA AND CO. DECIDED TO GO ON A JOURNEY.
PA PA PA PAAAA...
PARA PA, PARA PA...
VINCENT? WHAT'S THAT YOU'RE SINGING?
IT'S THE B.G.M. FOR TRAVEL THROUGH A FIELD.
HAVEN'T YOU HEARD VIDEO GAME MUSIC BEFORE?
IT'S AN ENEMY! SING THE FIGHT SONG!
YES, SIR! JAN-JAKA! JAN-JAKA!
I DON'T FEEL IT, YET!
CUT IT OUT, YOU GUYS.
WHO'S AN ENEMY?

Tower

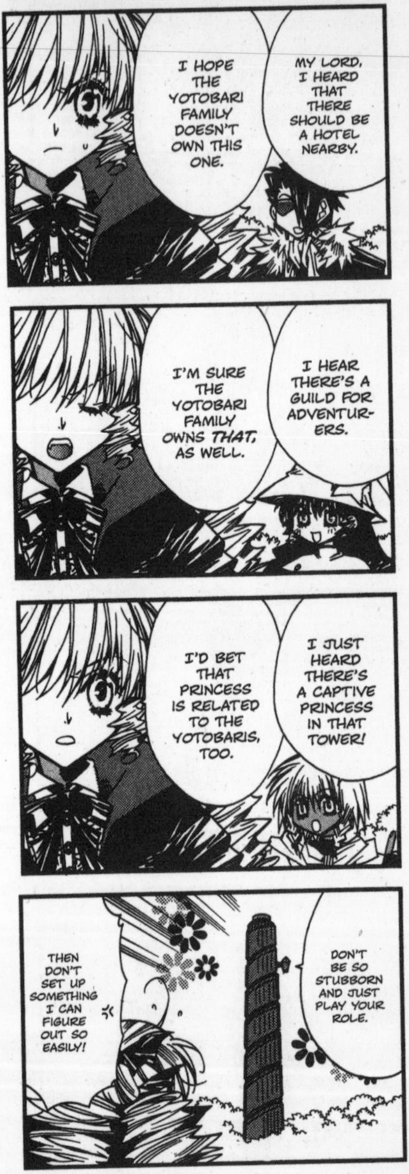
MY LORD, I HEARD THAT THERE SHOULD BE A HOTEL NEARBY.
I HOPE THE YOTOBARI FAMILY DOESN'T OWN THIS ONE.
I HEAR THERE'S A GUILD FOR ADVENTUR-ERS.
I'M SURE THE YOTOBARI FAMILY OWNS *THAT*, AS WELL.
I JUST HEARD THERE'S A CAPTIVE PRINCESS IN THAT TOWER!
I'D BET THAT PRINCESS IS RELATED TO THE YOTOBARIS, TOO.
DON'T BE SO STUBBORN AND JUST PLAY YOUR ROLE.
THEN DON'T SET UP SOMETHING I CAN FIGURE OUT SO EASILY!

Box

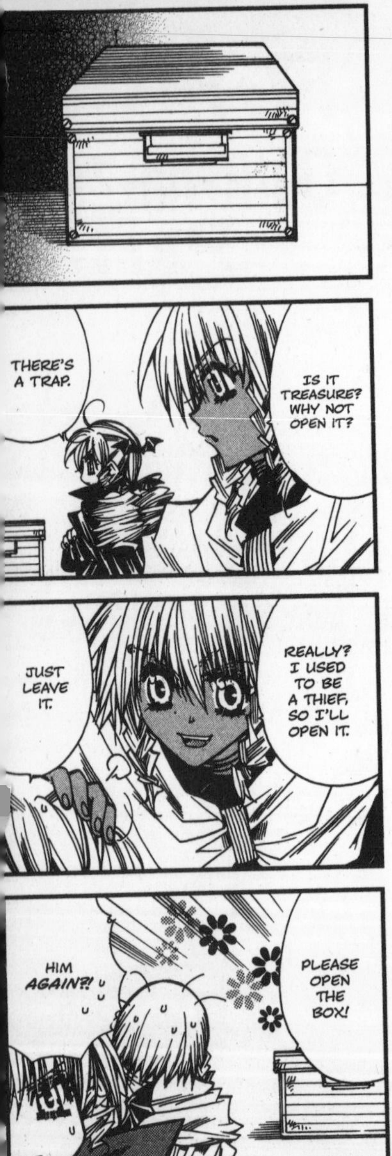
IS IT TREASURE? WHY NOT OPEN IT?
THERE'S A TRAP.
REALLY? I USED TO BE A THIEF, SO I'LL OPEN IT.
JUST LEAVE IT.
PLEASE OPEN THE BOX!
HIM *AGAIN?!*

GUILT-NA-ZAN BONUS COMIC STRIPS!

142cm

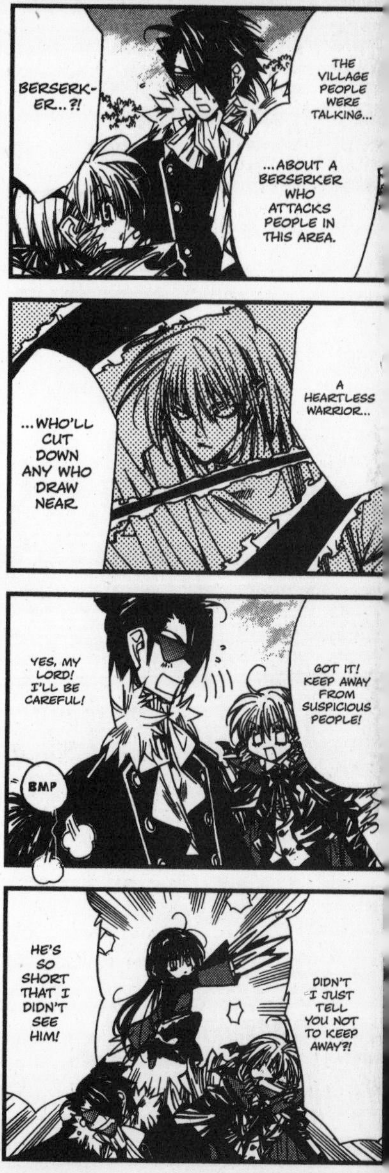
THE VILLAGE PEOPLE WERE TALKING...
...ABOUT A BERSERKER WHO ATTACKS PEOPLE IN THIS AREA.
BERSERK-ER...?!
A HEARTLESS WARRIOR...
...WHO'LL CUT DOWN ANY WHO DRAW NEAR
GOT IT! KEEP AWAY FROM SUSPICIOUS PEOPLE!
YES, MY LORD! I'LL BE CAREFUL!
BMP
DIDN'T I JUST TELL YOU NOT TO KEEP AWAY?!
HE'S SO SHORT THAT I DIDN'T SEE HIM!

Wiseman

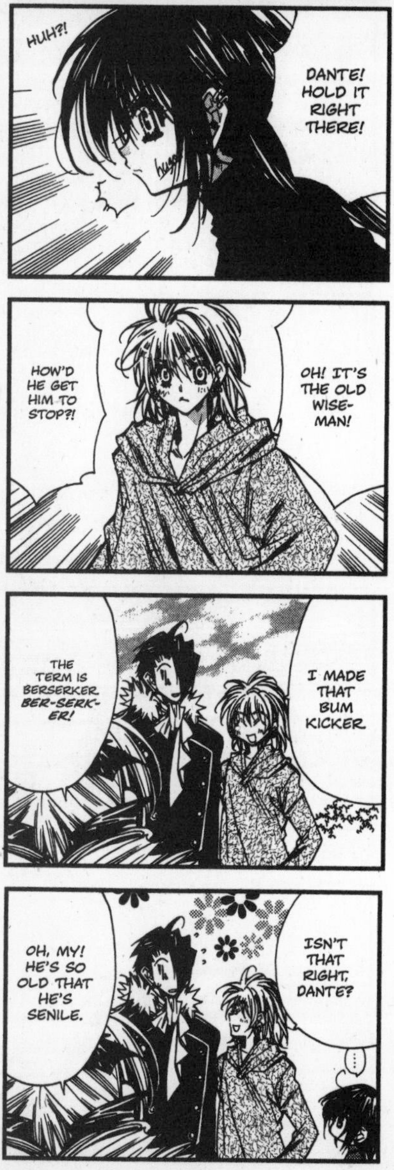
DANTE! HOLD IT RIGHT THERE!
HUH?!
OH! IT'S THE OLD WISE-MAN!
HOW'D HE GET HIM TO STOP?!
I MADE THAT BUM KICKER
THE TERM IS BERSERKER BER-SERK-ER!
ISN'T THAT RIGHT, DANTE?
OH, MY! HE'S SO OLD THAT HE'S SENILE.
....

Introduction

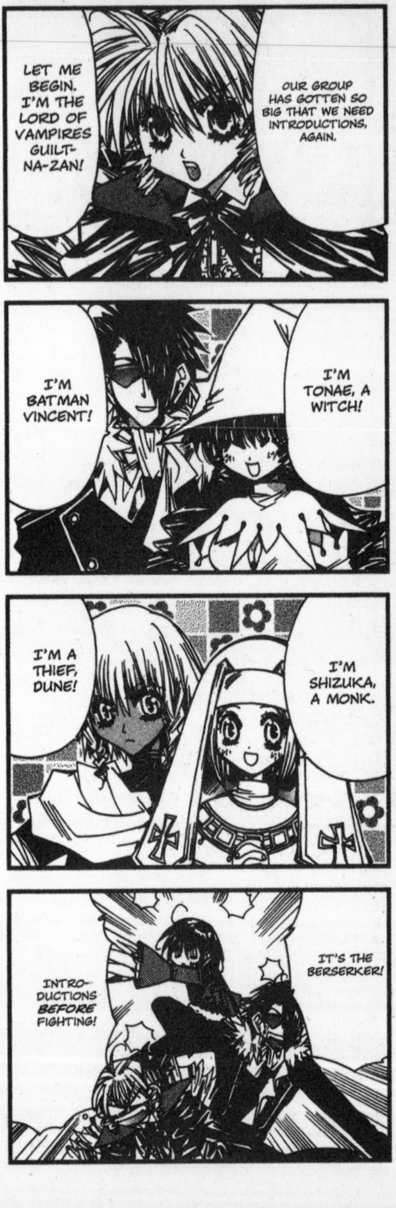
OUR GROUP HAS GOTTEN SO BIG THAT WE NEED INTRODUCTIONS, AGAIN.
LET ME BEGIN. I'M THE LORD OF VAMPIRES GUILT-NA-ZAN!
I'M TONAE, A WITCH!
I'M BATMAN VINCENT!
I'M SHIZUKA, A MONK.
I'M A THIEF, DUNE!
IT'S THE BERSERKER!
INTRO-DUCTIONS *BEFORE* FIGHTING!

Count

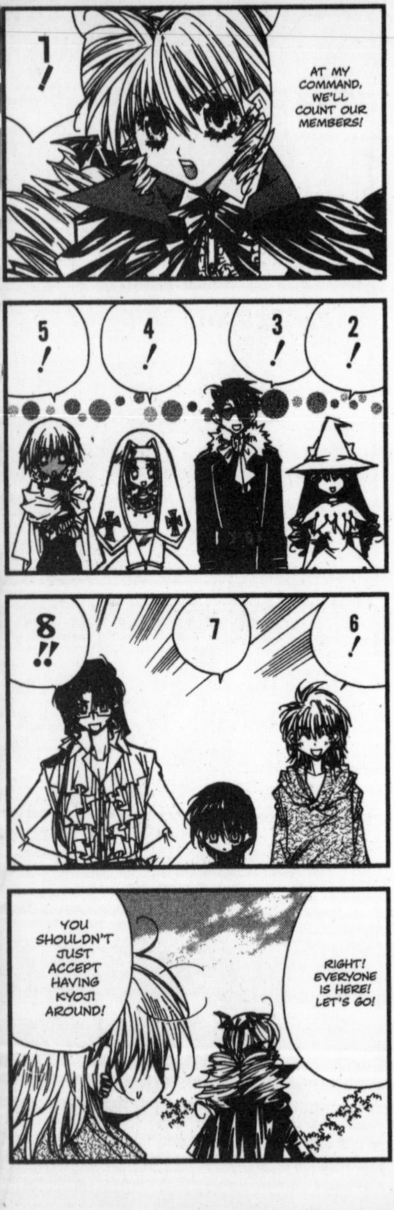
AT MY COMMAND, WE'LL COUNT OUR MEMBERS!
1!
2!
3!
4!
5!
6!
7
8!!
RIGHT! EVERYONE IS HERE! LET'S GO!
YOU SHOULDN'T JUST ACCEPT HAVING KYOJI AROUND!

BONUS COMIC STRIP

R·P
Guilt-na-Zan Part4

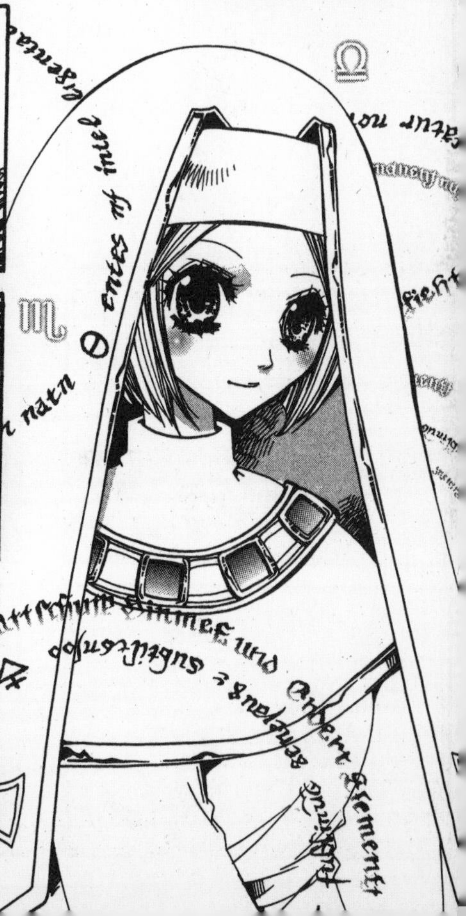

Maniac

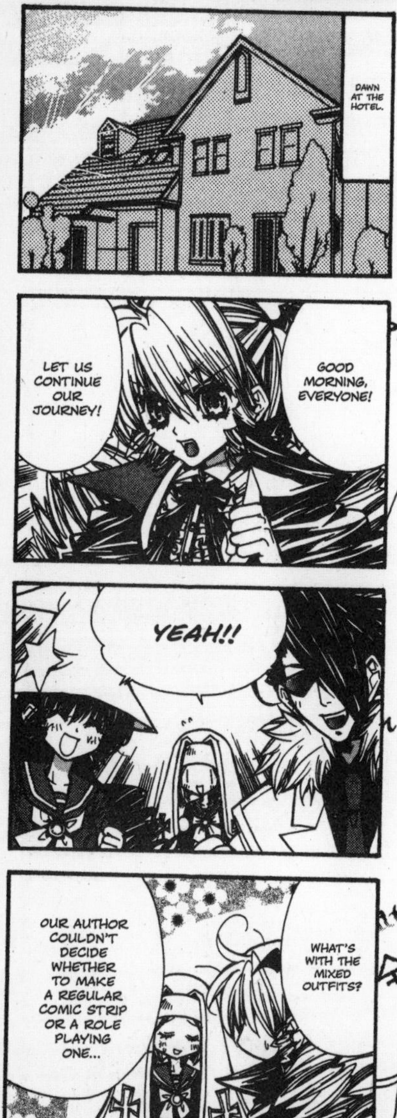
DAWN AT THE HOTEL.
GOOD MORNING, EVERYONE!
LET US CONTINUE OUR JOURNEY!
YEAH!!
WHAT'S WITH THE MIXED OUTFITS?
OUR AUTHOR COULDN'T DECIDE WHETHER TO MAKE A REGULAR COMIC STRIP OR A ROLE PLAYING ONE...

Finally

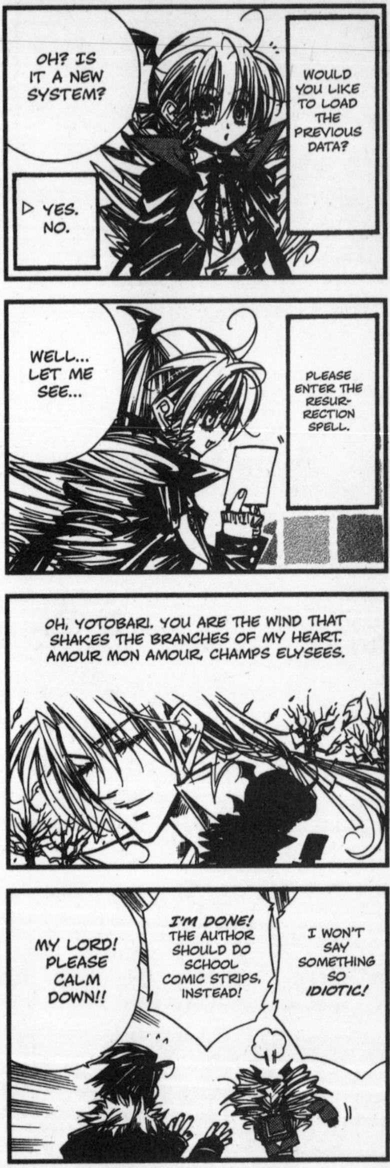
WOULD YOU LIKE TO LOAD THE PREVIOUS DATA?
OH? IS IT A NEW SYSTEM?
▷ YES.
NO.
PLEASE ENTER THE RESURRECTION SPELL.
WELL... LET ME SEE...
OH, YOTOBARI. YOU ARE THE WIND THAT SHAKES THE BRANCHES OF MY HEART. AMOUR MON AMOUR, CHAMPS ELYSEES.
I WON'T SAY SOMETHING SO *IDIOTIC!*
I'M DONE! THE AUTHOR SHOULD DO SCHOOL COMIC STRIPS, INSTEAD!
MY LORD! PLEASE CALM DOWN!!

Evenly Across

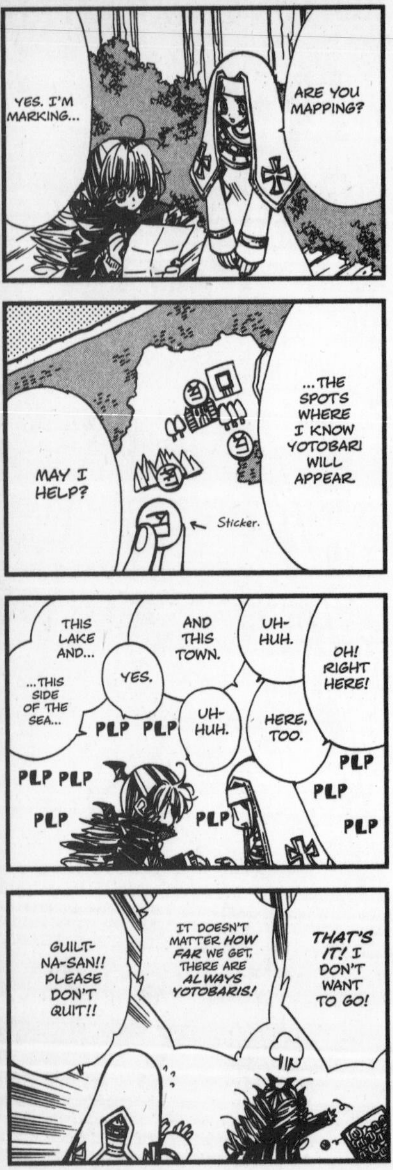
ARE YOU MAPPING?
YES. I'M MARKING...
...THE SPOTS WHERE I KNOW YOTOBARI WILL APPEAR
MAY I HELP?
Sticker.
OH! RIGHT HERE!
UH-HUH.
AND THIS TOWN.
THIS LAKE AND...
HERE, TOO.
UH-HUH.
YES.
...THIS SIDE OF THE SEA...
PLP PLP PLP PLP PLP PLP PLP PLP PLP
THAT'S IT! I DON'T WANT TO GO!
IT DOESN'T MATTER *HOW FAR* WE GET, THERE ARE *ALWAYS YOTOBARIS!*
GUILT-NA-SAN!! PLEASE DON'T QUIT!!

GUILT-NA-ZAN BONUS COMIC STRIPS!

Wish

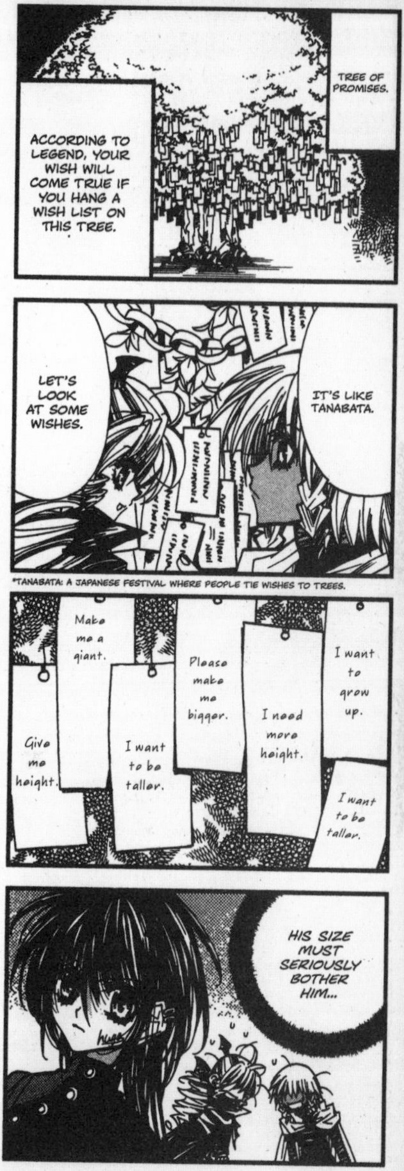
TREE OF PROMISES.
ACCORDING TO LEGEND, YOUR WISH WILL COME TRUE IF YOU HANG A WISH LIST ON THIS TREE.
IT'S LIKE TANABATA.
LET'S LOOK AT SOME WISHES.
I want to grow up.
I want to be taller.
I need more height.
Please make me bigger.
I want to be taller.
Make me a giant.
Give me height.
HIS SIZE MUST SERIOUSLY BOTHER HIM...

*TANABATA: A JAPANESE FESTIVAL WHERE PEOPLE TIE WISHES TO TREES.

Dream

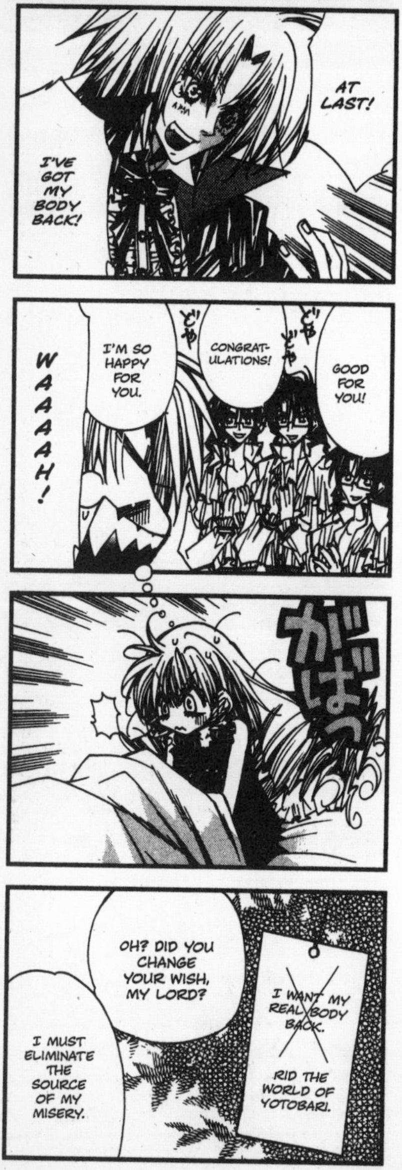
AT LAST!
I'VE GOT MY BODY BACK!
GOOD FOR YOU!
CONGRAT-ULATIONS!
I'M SO HAPPY FOR YOU.
WAAAAAH!
がばっ
I WANT MY REAL BODY BACK.
RID THE WORLD OF YOTOBARI.
OH? DID YOU CHANGE YOUR WISH, MY LORD?
I MUST ELIMINATE THE SOURCE OF MY MISERY.

Volunteer

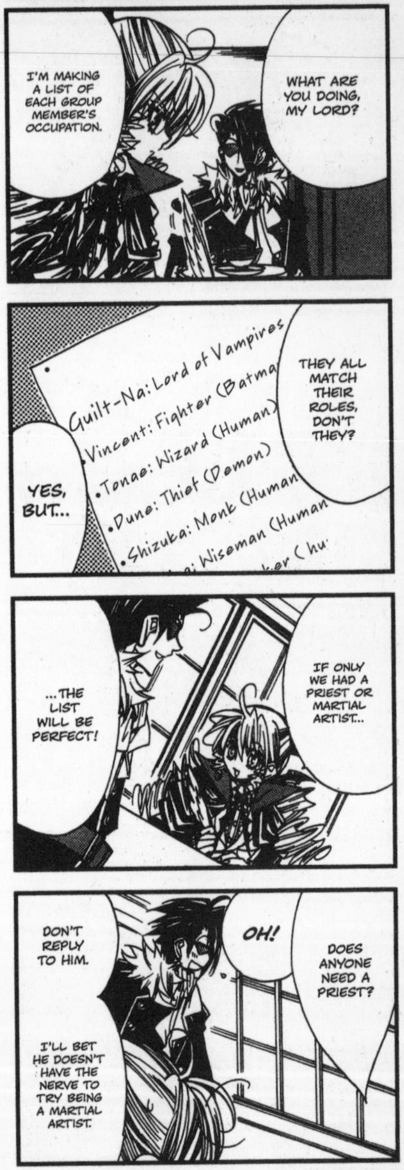
WHAT ARE YOU DOING, MY LORD?
I'M MAKING A LIST OF EACH GROUP MEMBER'S OCCUPATION.
THEY ALL MATCH THEIR ROLES, DON'T THEY?
• Guilt-Na: Lord of Vampires
• Vincent: Fighter (Batma
• Tonae: Wizard (Human)
• Dune: Thief (Demon)
• Shizuka: Monk (Human
Wiseman (Human
YES, BUT...
IF ONLY WE HAD A PRIEST OR MARTIAL ARTIST...
...THE LIST WILL BE PERFECT!
DOES ANYONE NEED A PRIEST?
OH!
DON'T REPLY TO HIM.
I'LL BET HE DOESN'T HAVE THE NERVE TO TRY BEING A MARTIAL ARTIST.

Bottom Line

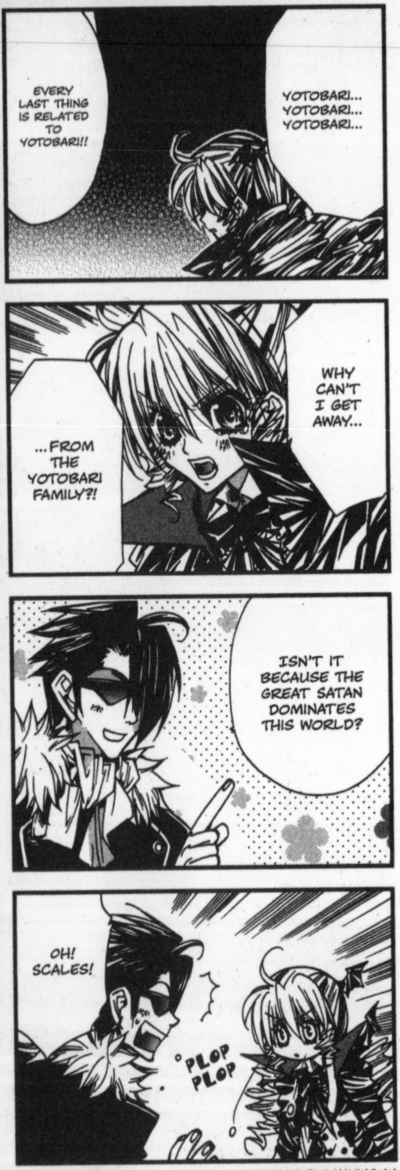
YOTOBARI... YOTOBARI... YOTOBARI...
EVERY LAST THING IS RELATED TO YOTOBARI!!
WHY CAN'T I GET AWAY...
...FROM THE YOTOBARI FAMILY?!
ISN'T IT BECAUSE THE GREAT SATAN DOMINATES THIS WORLD?
PLOP PLOP
OH! SCALES!

* SCALES FALLING FROM EYES IS A METAPHOR FOR HAVING AN EPIPHANY.

GUILT-NA-ZAN BONUS COMIC STRIPS!

Flying Unit

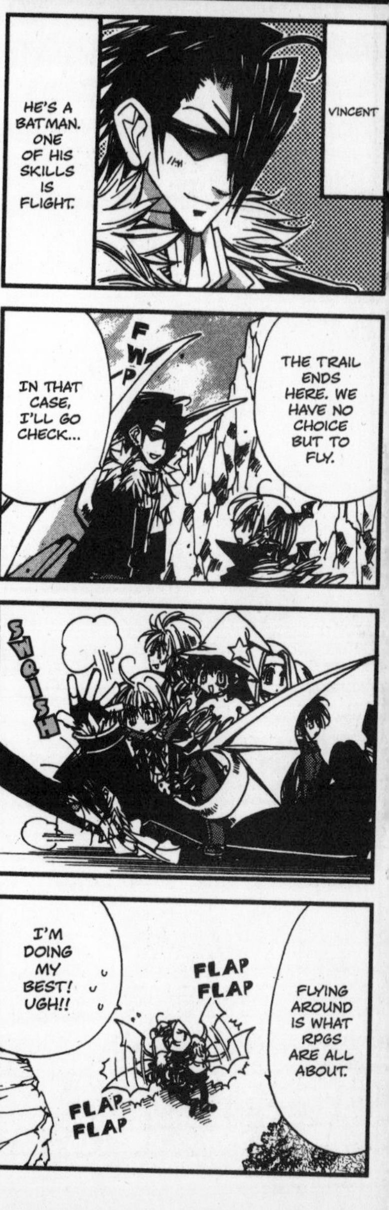
VINCENT
HE'S A BATMAN. ONE OF HIS SKILLS IS FLIGHT.
THE TRAIL ENDS HERE. WE HAVE NO CHOICE BUT TO FLY.
FWP
IN THAT CASE, I'LL GO CHECK...
SWQISH
FLYING AROUND IS WHAT RPGS ARE ALL ABOUT.
FLAP FLAP
I'M DOING MY BEST! UGH!!
FLAP FLAP

Futile Fight

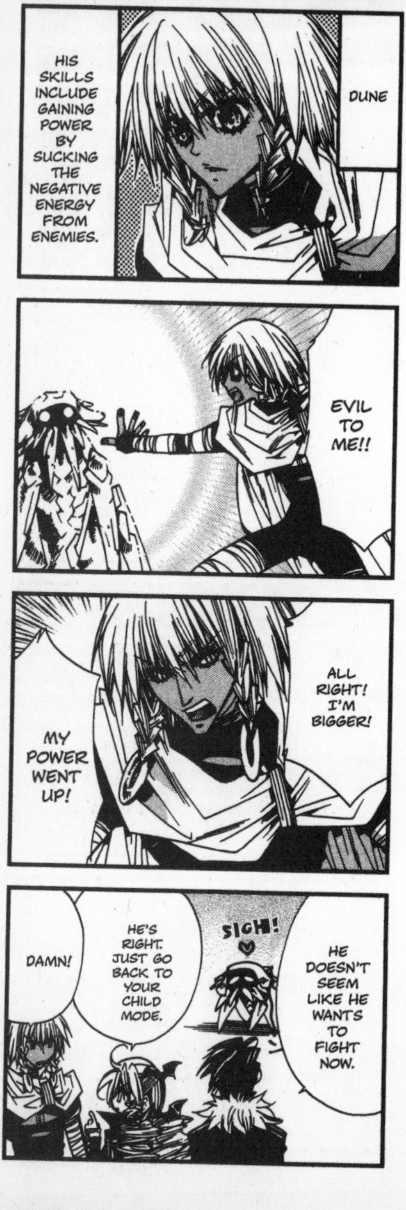
DUNE
HIS SKILLS INCLUDE GAINING POWER BY SUCKING THE NEGATIVE ENERGY FROM ENEMIES.
EVIL TO ME!!
ALL RIGHT! I'M BIGGER!
MY POWER WENT UP!
HE DOESN'T SEEM LIKE HE WANTS TO FIGHT NOW.
SIGH!
HE'S RIGHT. JUST GO BACK TO YOUR CHILD MODE.
DAMN!

Deal With It

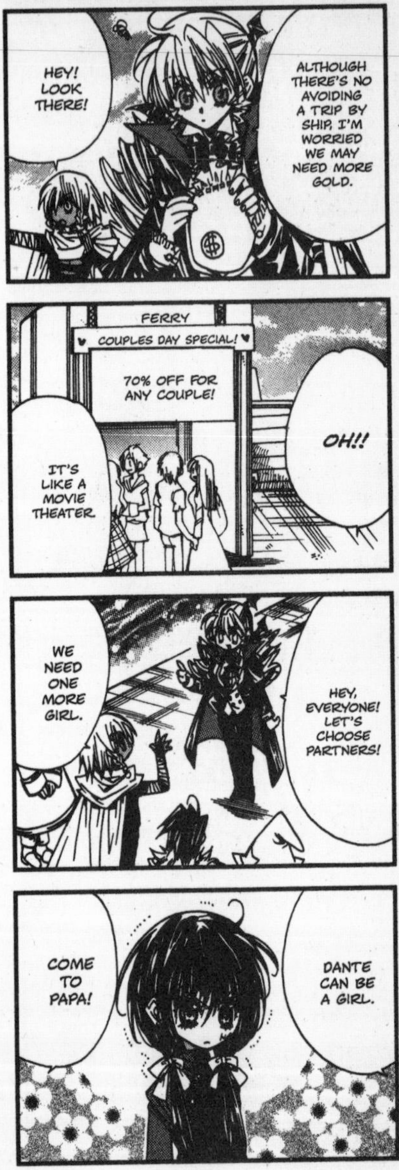
ALTHOUGH THERE'S NO AVOIDING A TRIP BY SHIP, I'M WORRIED WE MAY NEED MORE GOLD.
HEY! LOOK THERE!
FERRY
COUPLES DAY SPECIAL!
70% OFF FOR ANY COUPLE!
OH!!
IT'S LIKE A MOVIE THEATER.
HEY, EVERYONE! LET'S CHOOSE PARTNERS!
WE NEED ONE MORE GIRL.
DANTE CAN BE A GIRL.
COME TO PAPA!

Darling Honey

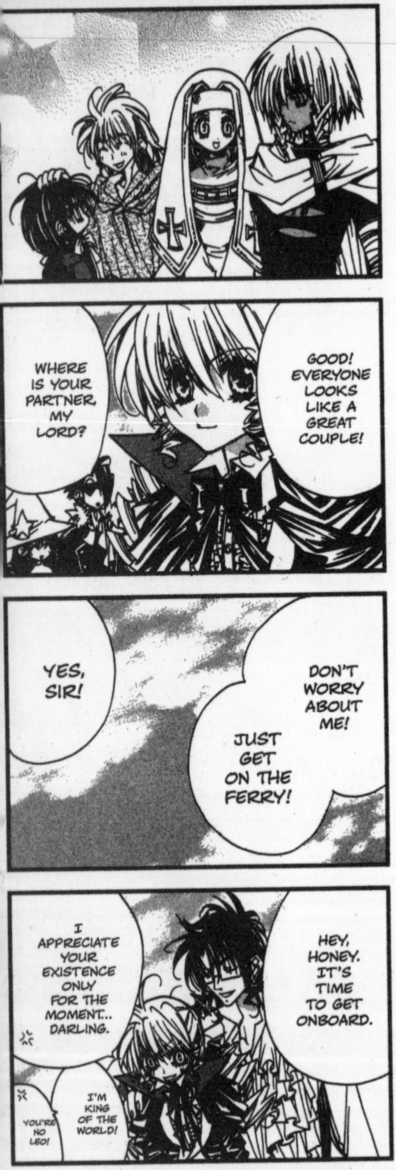
GOOD! EVERYONE LOOKS LIKE A GREAT COUPLE!
WHERE IS YOUR PARTNER, MY LORD?
DON'T WORRY ABOUT ME!
JUST GET ON THE FERRY!
YES, SIR!
HEY, HONEY. IT'S TIME TO GET ONBOARD.
I APPRECIATE YOUR EXISTENCE ONLY FOR THE MOMENT... DARLING.
I'M KING OF THE WORLD!
YOU'RE NO LEO!

BONUS COMIC STRIP

R·P
Guilt-na-Zan Part5

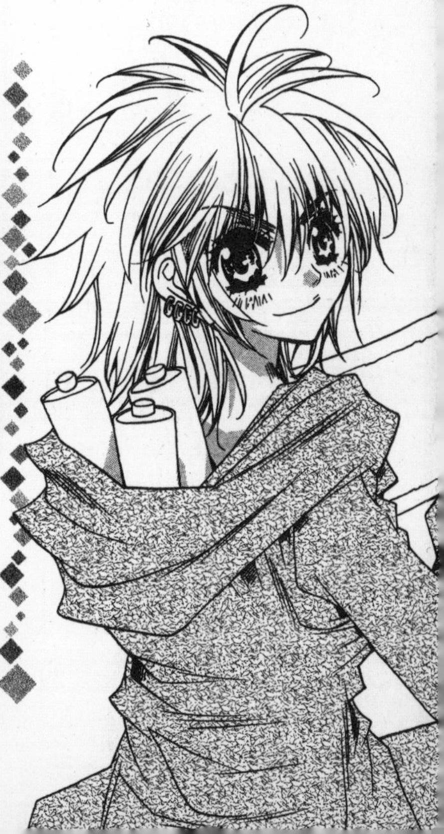

Weakness

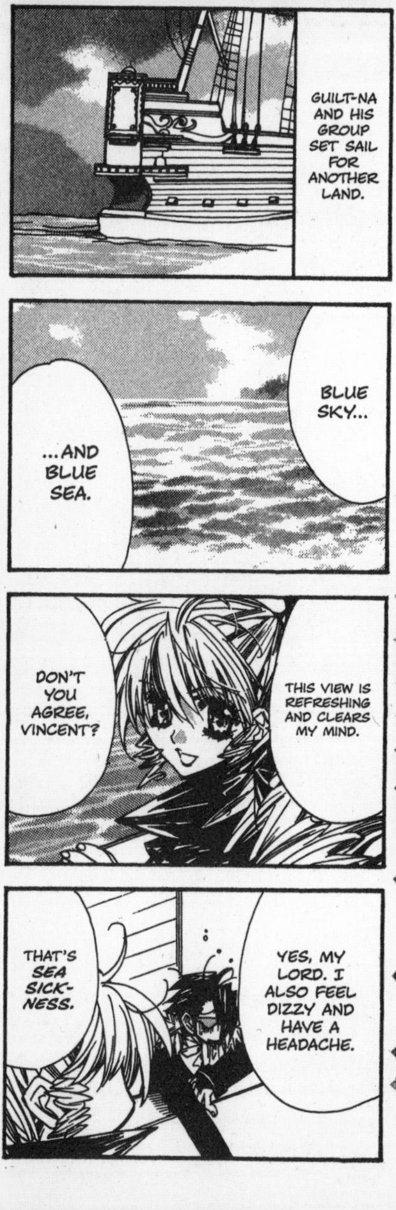
GUILT-NA AND HIS GROUP SET SAIL FOR ANOTHER LAND.
BLUE SKY...
...AND BLUE SEA.
THIS VIEW IS REFRESHING AND CLEARS MY MIND.
DON'T YOU AGREE, VINCENT?
YES, MY LORD. I ALSO FEEL DIZZY AND HAVE A HEADACHE.
THAT'S *SEA SICK-NESS*.

Danger

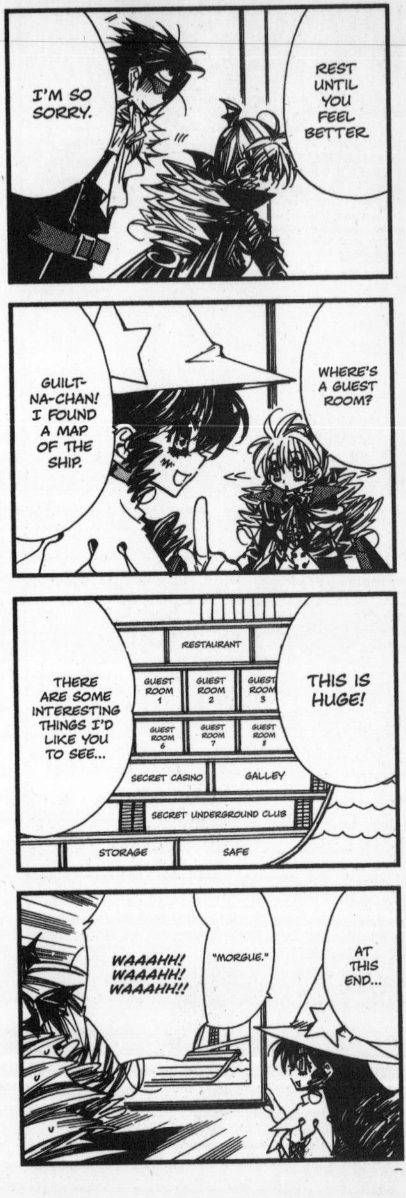
REST UNTIL YOU FEEL BETTER
I'M SO SORRY.
WHERE'S A GUEST ROOM?
GUILT-NA-CHAN! I FOUND A MAP OF THE SHIP.
THIS IS HUGE!
THERE ARE SOME INTERESTING THINGS I'D LIKE YOU TO SEE...
RESTAURANT
GUEST ROOM 1
GUEST ROOM 2
GUEST ROOM 3
GUEST ROOM 6
GUEST ROOM 7
GUEST ROOM 8
SECRET CASINO
GALLEY
SECRET UNDERGROUND CLUB
STORAGE
SAFE
AT THIS END...
"MORGUE."
WAAAHH! WAAAHH! WAAAHH!!

More Danger

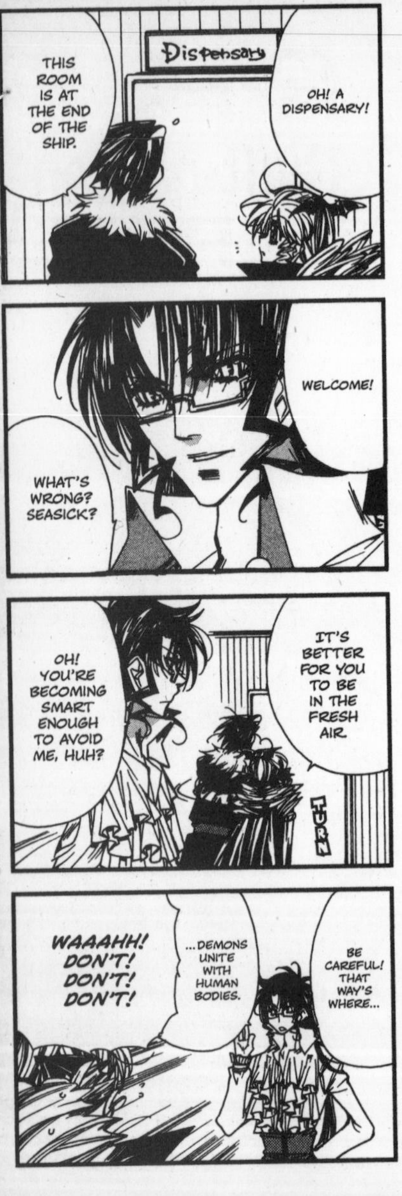
Dispensary
OH! A DISPENSARY!
THIS ROOM IS AT THE END OF THE SHIP.
WELCOME!
WHAT'S WRONG? SEASICK?
IT'S BETTER FOR YOU TO BE IN THE FRESH AIR
OH! YOU'RE BECOMING SMART ENOUGH TO AVOID ME, HUH?
TURN
BE CAREFUL! THAT WAY'S WHERE...
...DEMONS UNITE WITH HUMAN BODIES.
WAAAHH! DON'T! DON'T! DON'T!

GUILT-NA-ZAN BONUS COMIC STRIPS!

Couples Day

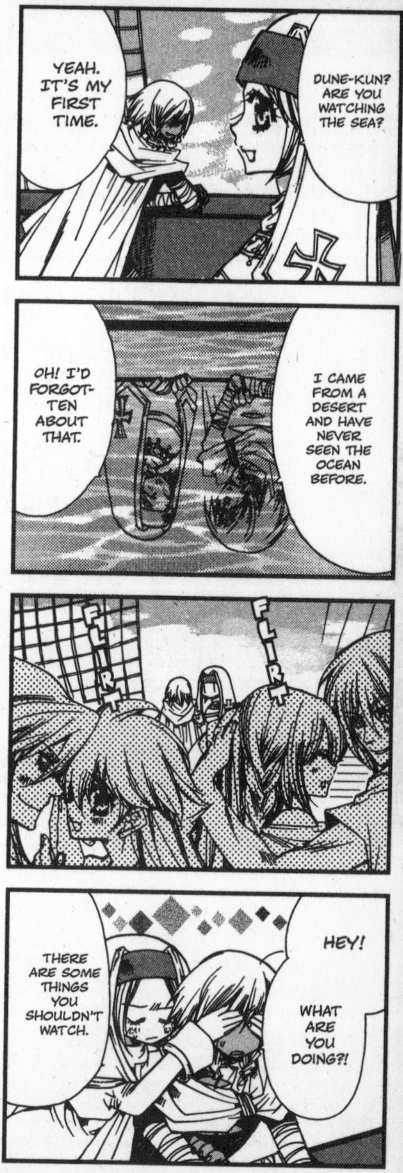
DUNE-KUN? ARE YOU WATCHING THE SEA?
YEAH. IT'S MY FIRST TIME.
I CAME FROM A DESERT AND HAVE NEVER SEEN THE OCEAN BEFORE.
OH! I'D FORGOT-TEN ABOUT THAT.
FLIRT
FLIRT
HEY! WHAT ARE YOU DOING?!
THERE ARE SOME THINGS YOU SHOULDN'T WATCH.

Eyes

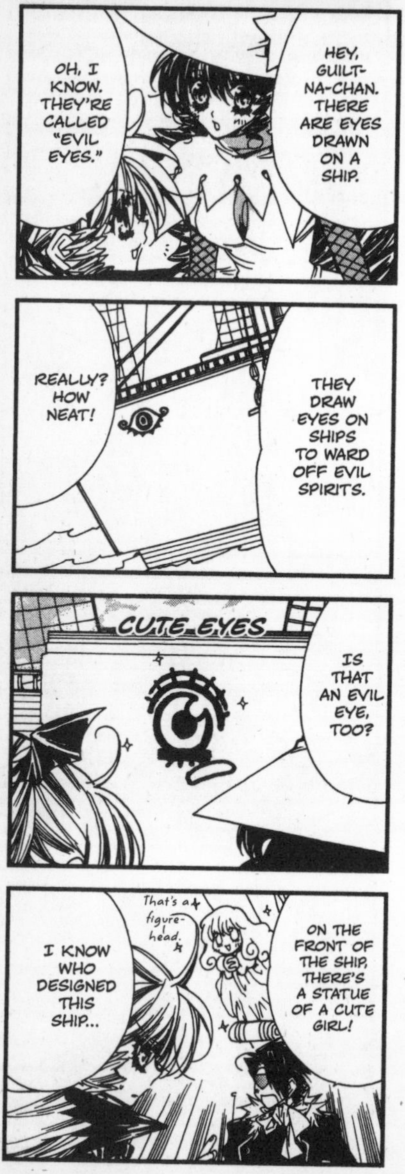
HEY, GUILT-NA-CHAN. THERE ARE EYES DRAWN ON A SHIP.
OH, I KNOW. THEY'RE CALLED "EVIL EYES."
THEY DRAW EYES ON SHIPS TO WARD OFF EVIL SPIRITS.
REALLY? HOW NEAT!
IS THAT AN EVIL EYE, TOO?
CUTE EYES
ON THE FRONT OF THE SHIP, THERE'S A STATUE OF A CUTE GIRL!
That's a figure-head.
I KNOW WHO DESIGNED THIS SHIP...

Eight Legs

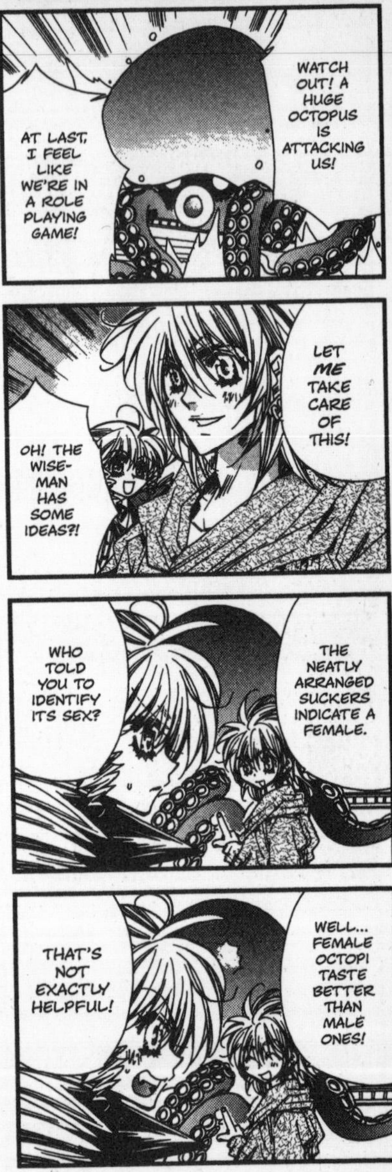
WATCH OUT! A HUGE OCTOPUS IS ATTACKING US!
AT LAST, I FEEL LIKE WE'RE IN A ROLE PLAYING GAME!
LET *ME* TAKE CARE OF THIS!
OH! THE WISE-MAN HAS SOME IDEAS?!
THE NEATLY ARRANGED SUCKERS INDICATE A FEMALE.
WHO TOLD YOU TO IDENTIFY ITS SEX?
WELL... FEMALE OCTOPI TASTE BETTER THAN MALE ONES!
THAT'S NOT EXACTLY HELPFUL!

Ten Legs

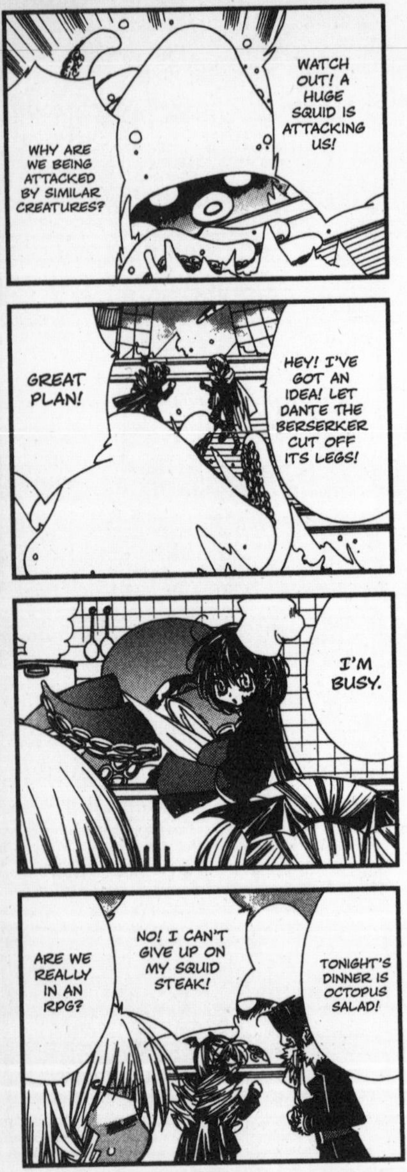
WATCH OUT! A HUGE SQUID IS ATTACKING US!
WHY ARE WE BEING ATTACKED BY SIMILAR CREATURES?
HEY! I'VE GOT AN IDEA! LET DANTE THE BERSERKER CUT OFF ITS LEGS!
GREAT PLAN!
I'M BUSY.
TONIGHT'S DINNER IS OCTOPUS SALAD!
NO! I CAN'T GIVE UP ON MY SQUID STEAK!
ARE WE REALLY IN AN RPG?

GUILT-NA-ZAN BONUS COMIC STRIPS!

Grim Reaper

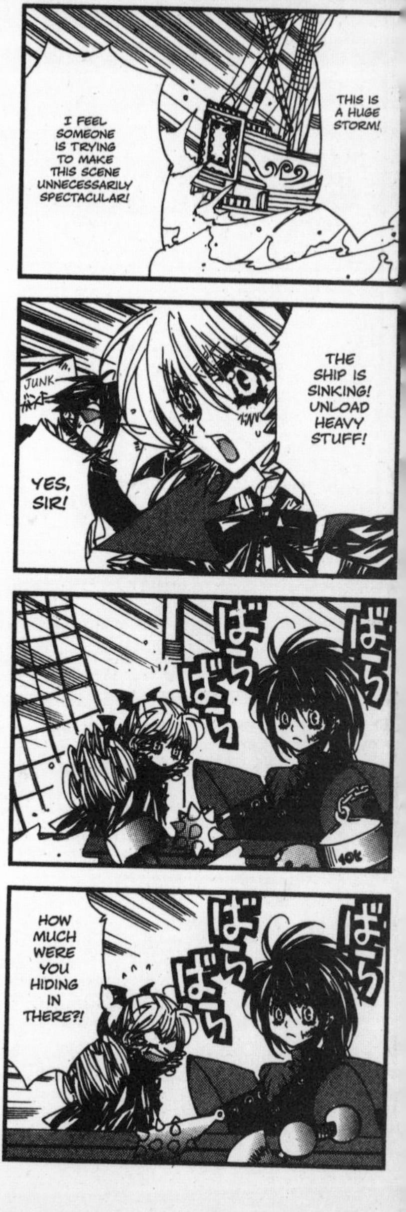
THIS IS A HUGE STORM!
I FEEL SOMEONE IS TRYING TO MAKE THIS SCENE UNNECESSARILY SPECTACULAR!
THE SHIP IS SINKING! UNLOAD HEAVY STUFF!
JUNK
YES, SIR!
ばら
ばら
ばら
ばら
ばら
ばら
HOW MUCH WERE YOU HIDING IN THERE?!

Retreat

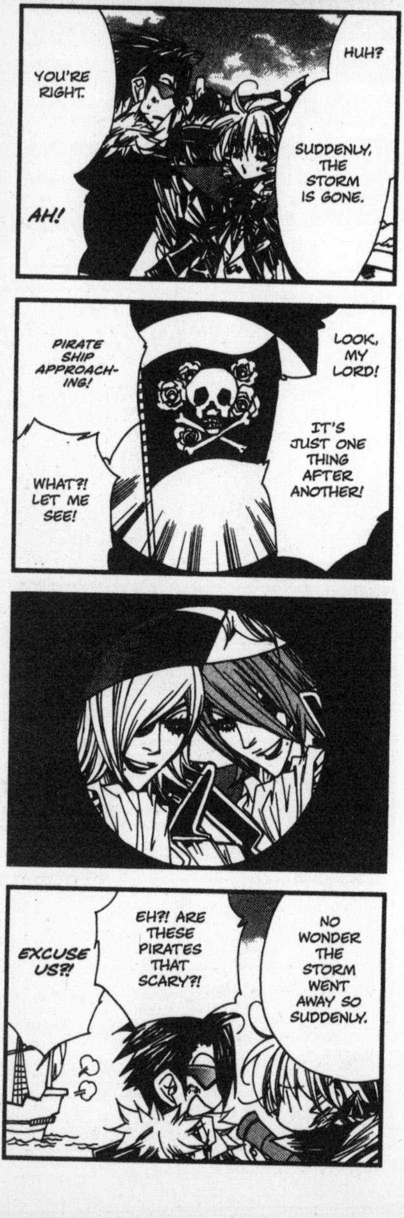
HUH?
SUDDENLY, THE STORM IS GONE.
YOU'RE RIGHT.
AH!
LOOK, MY LORD!
IT'S JUST ONE THING AFTER ANOTHER!
PIRATE SHIP APPROACHING!
WHAT?! LET ME SEE!
NO WONDER THE STORM WENT AWAY SO SUDDENLY.
EH?! ARE THESE PIRATES THAT SCARY?!
EXCUSE US?!

Punishment

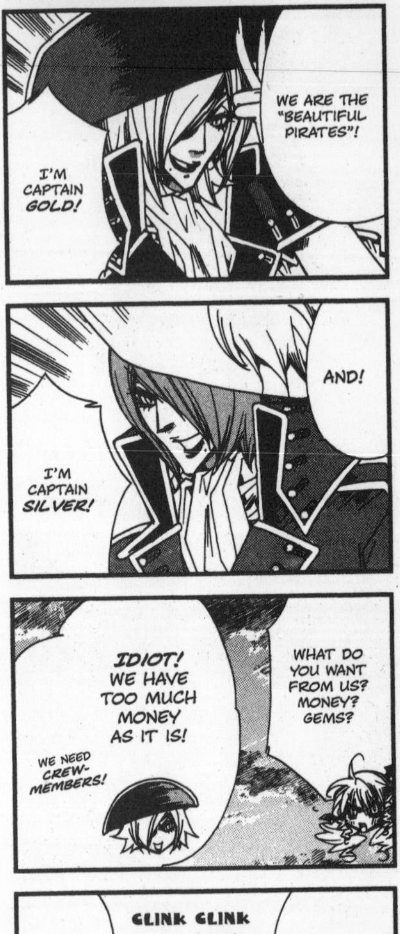
WE ARE THE "BEAUTIFUL PIRATES"!
I'M CAPTAIN GOLD!
AND!
I'M CAPTAIN SILVER!
WHAT DO YOU WANT FROM US? MONEY? GEMS?
IDIOT! WE HAVE TOO MUCH MONEY AS IT IS!
WE NEED CREW-MEMBERS!
CLINK CLINK
AS THE ONLY TWO ONBOARD, WE CAN ONLY OPERATE OUR SHIP LIKE THIS!
LOOKS LIKE FUN!

Weather

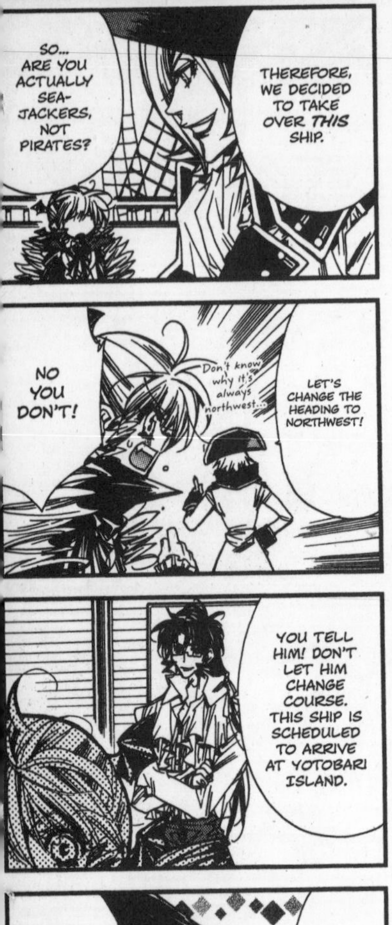
THEREFORE, WE DECIDED TO TAKE OVER THIS SHIP.
SO... ARE YOU ACTUALLY SEA-JACKERS, NOT PIRATES?
LET'S CHANGE THE HEADING TO NORTHWEST!
Don't know why it's always northwest...
NO YOU DON'T!
YOU TELL HIM! DON'T LET HIM CHANGE COURSE. THIS SHIP IS SCHEDULED TO ARRIVE AT YOTOBARI ISLAND.
WELL, THEN, I'M IN! LET'S GO NORTH-WEST.
YOU JUST CAN'T STOP GETTING NEW PARTY MEMBERS.

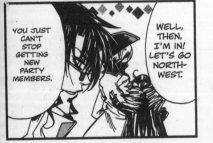

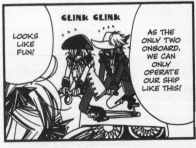

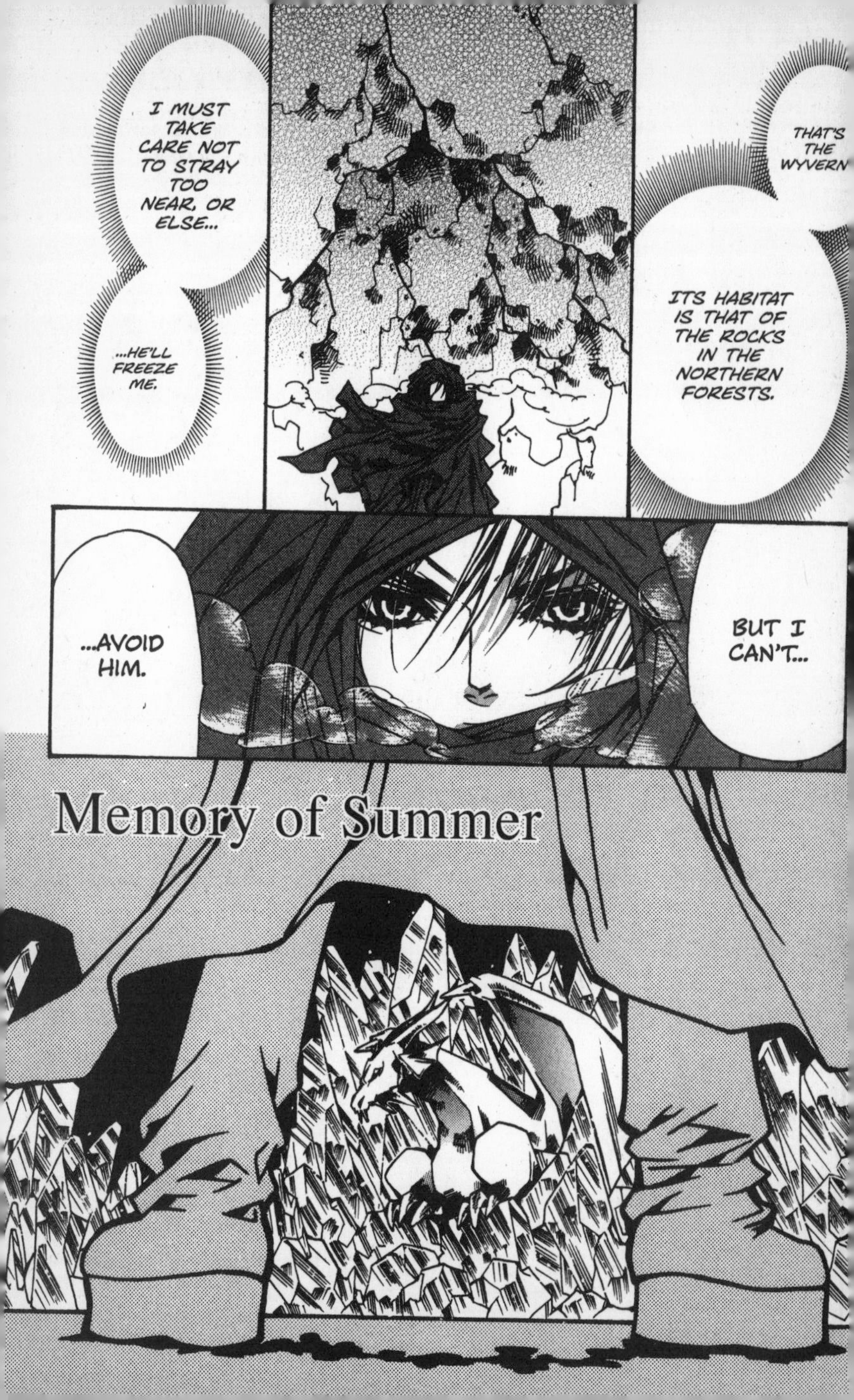
THAT'S THE WYVERN
ITS HABITAT IS THAT OF THE ROCKS IN THE NORTHERN FORESTS.
I MUST TAKE CARE NOT TO STRAY TOO NEAR, OR ELSE...
...HE'LL FREEZE ME.
BUT I CAN'T...
...AVOID HIM.
Memory of Summer

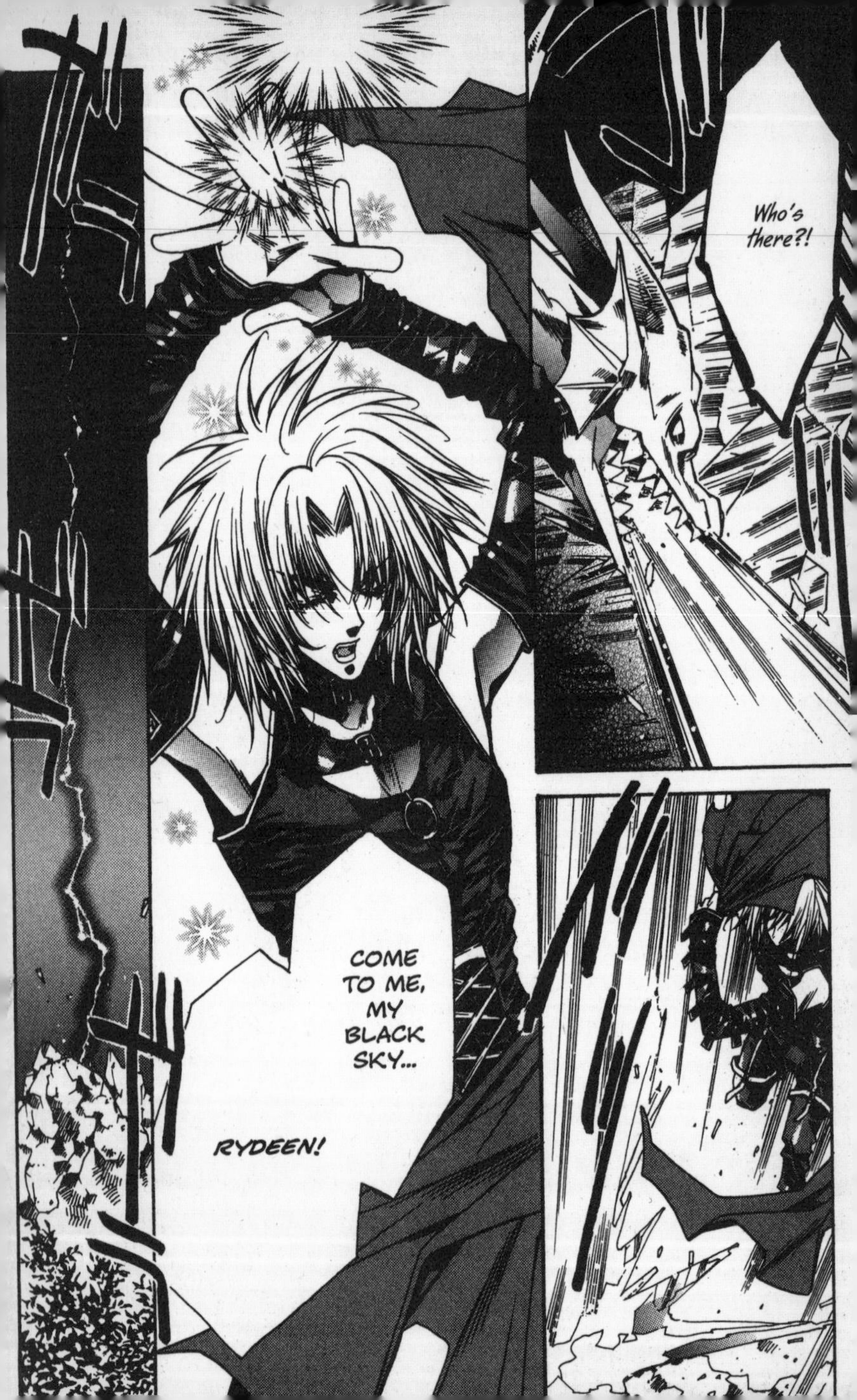
Who's there?!
COME TO ME, MY BLACK SKY...
RYDEEN!

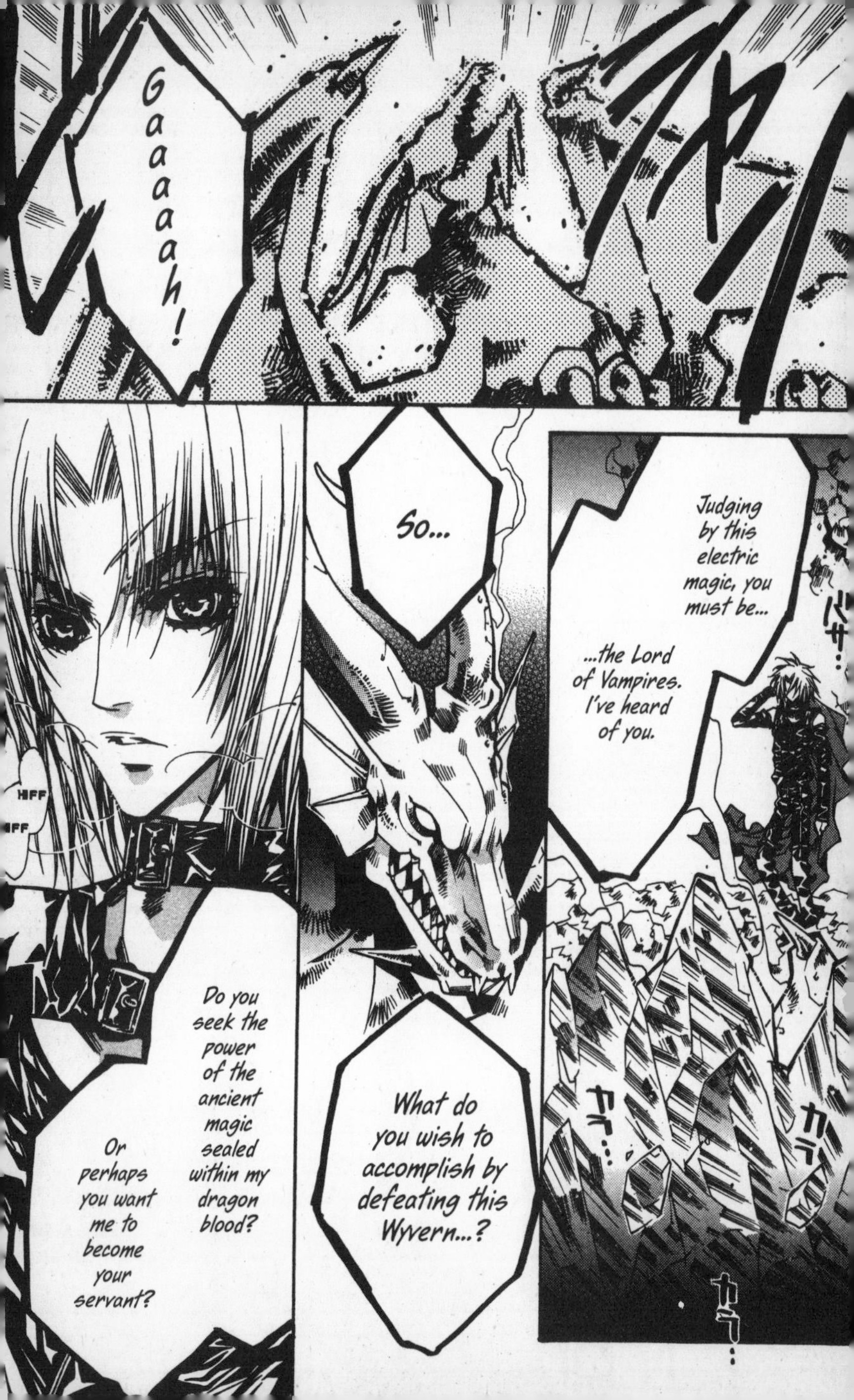
Gaaaaah!
Judging by this electric magic, you must be...
...the Lord of Vampires. I've heard of you.
カラ…
カラ…
So...
What do you wish to accomplish by defeating this Wyvern...?
HFF
HFF
Do you seek the power of the ancient magic sealed within my dragon blood?
Or perhaps you want me to become your servant?

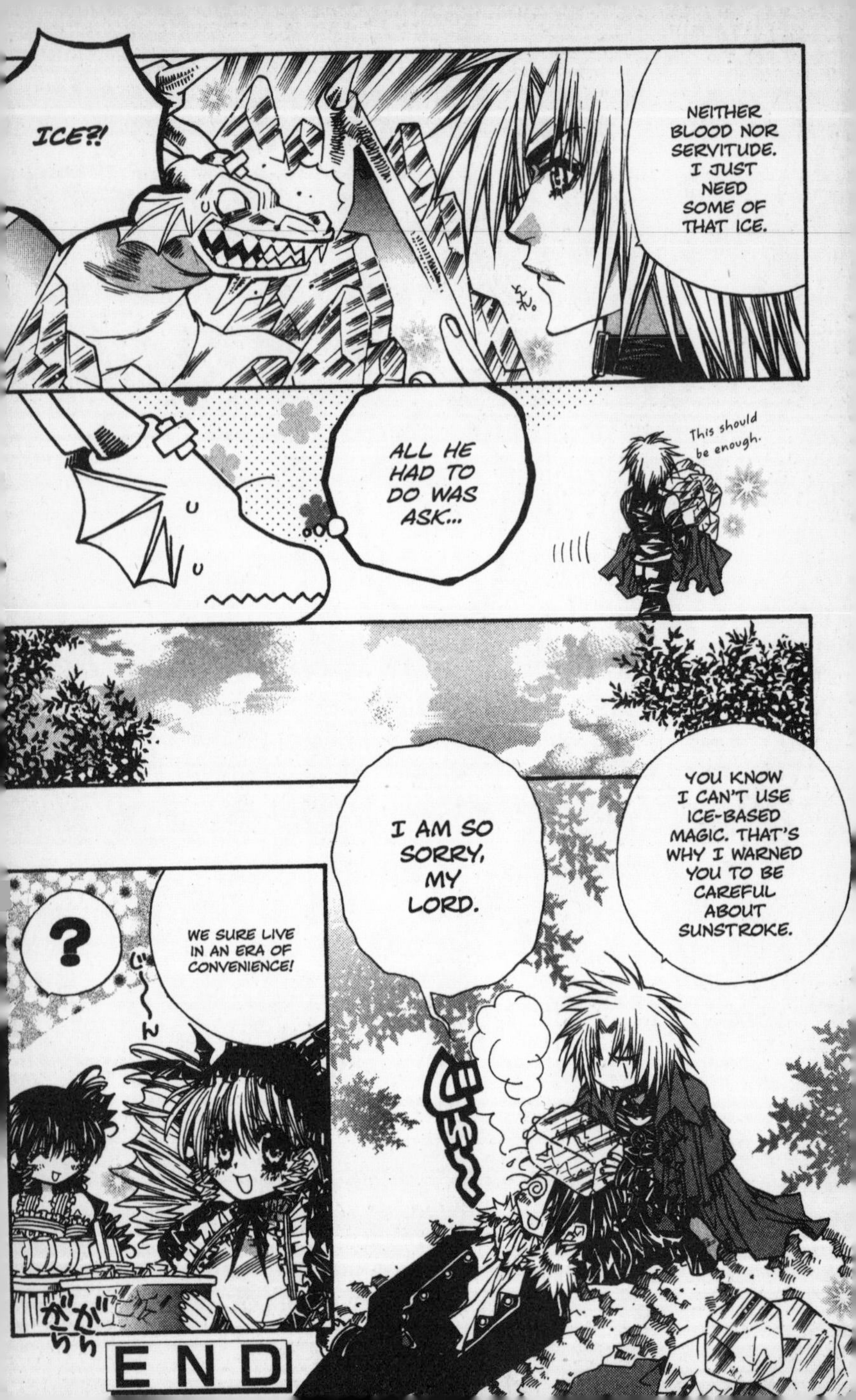

NEITHER BLOOD NOR SERVITUDE. I JUST NEED SOME OF THAT ICE.
ICE?!
This should be enough.
ALL HE HAD TO DO WAS ASK...
YOU KNOW I CAN'T USE ICE-BASED MAGIC. THAT'S WHY I WARNED YOU TO BE CAREFUL ABOUT SUNSTROKE.
I AM SO SORRY, MY LORD.
WE SURE LIVE IN AN ERA OF CONVENIENCE!
?
END

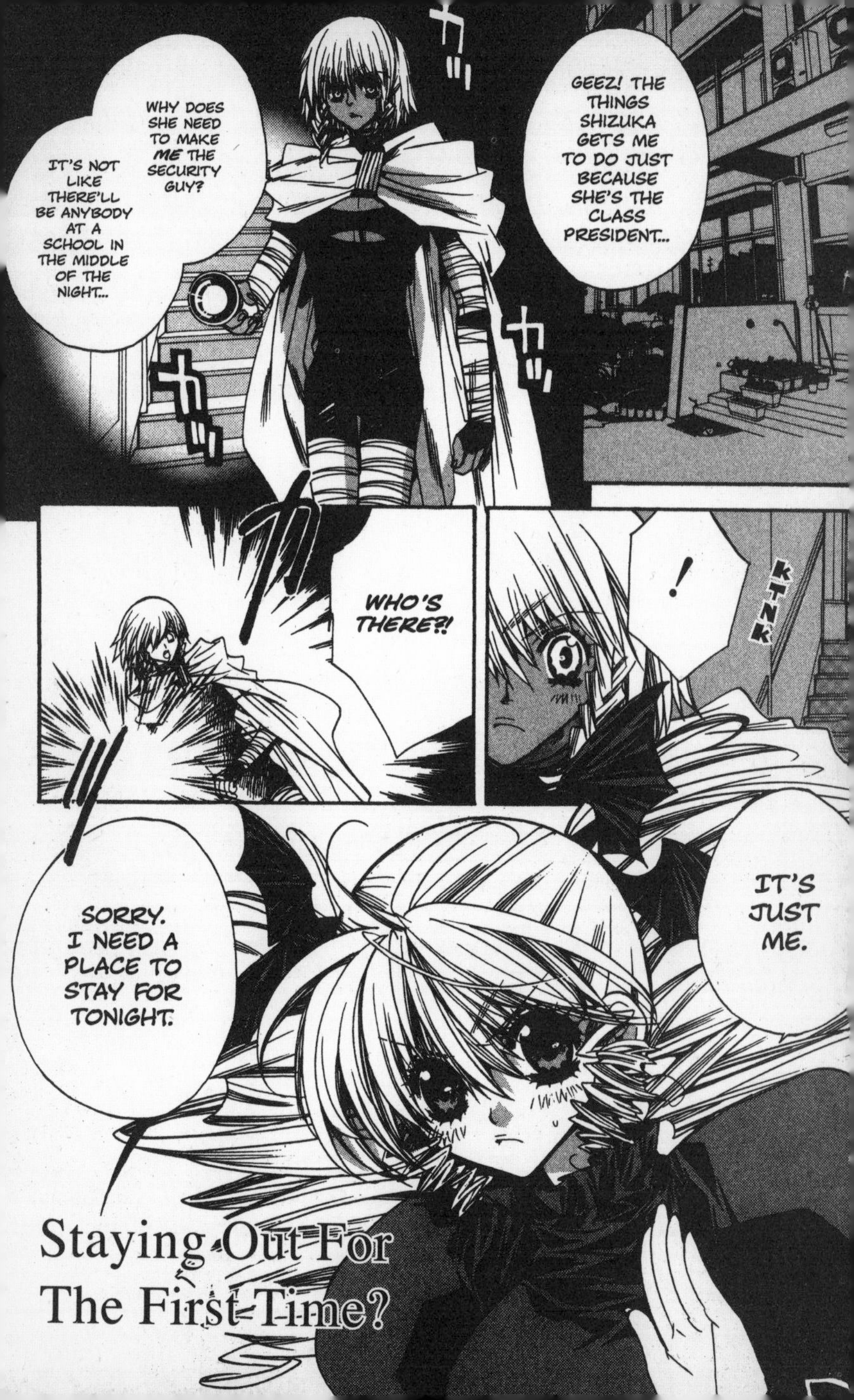
GEEZ! THE THINGS SHIZUKA GETS ME TO DO JUST BECAUSE SHE'S THE CLASS PRESIDENT...
WHY DOES SHE NEED TO MAKE *ME* THE SECURITY GUY?
IT'S NOT LIKE THERE'LL BE ANYBODY AT A SCHOOL IN THE MIDDLE OF THE NIGHT...
!
KTNK
WHO'S THERE?!
IT'S JUST ME.
SORRY. I NEED A PLACE TO STAY FOR TONIGHT.
Staying Out For The First Time?

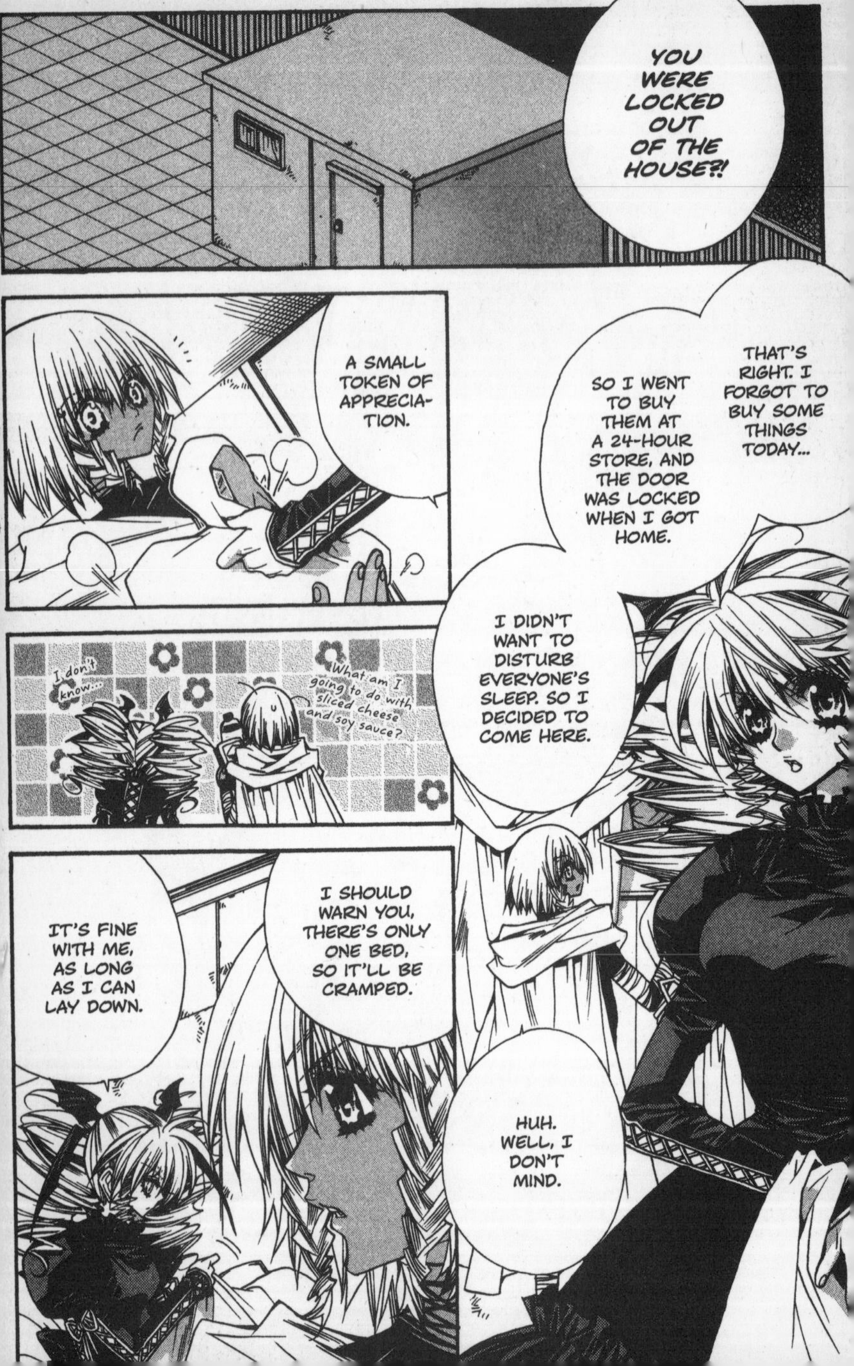
YOU WERE LOCKED OUT OF THE HOUSE?!
THAT'S RIGHT. I FORGOT TO BUY SOME THINGS TODAY...
SO I WENT TO BUY THEM AT A 24-HOUR STORE, AND THE DOOR WAS LOCKED WHEN I GOT HOME.
I DIDN'T WANT TO DISTURB EVERYONE'S SLEEP. SO I DECIDED TO COME HERE.
HUH. WELL, I DON'T MIND.
A SMALL TOKEN OF APPRECIATION.
What am I going to do with sliced cheese and soy sauce?
I don't know...
I SHOULD WARN YOU, THERE'S ONLY ONE BED, SO IT'LL BE CRAMPED.
IT'S FINE WITH ME, AS LONG AS I CAN LAY DOWN.

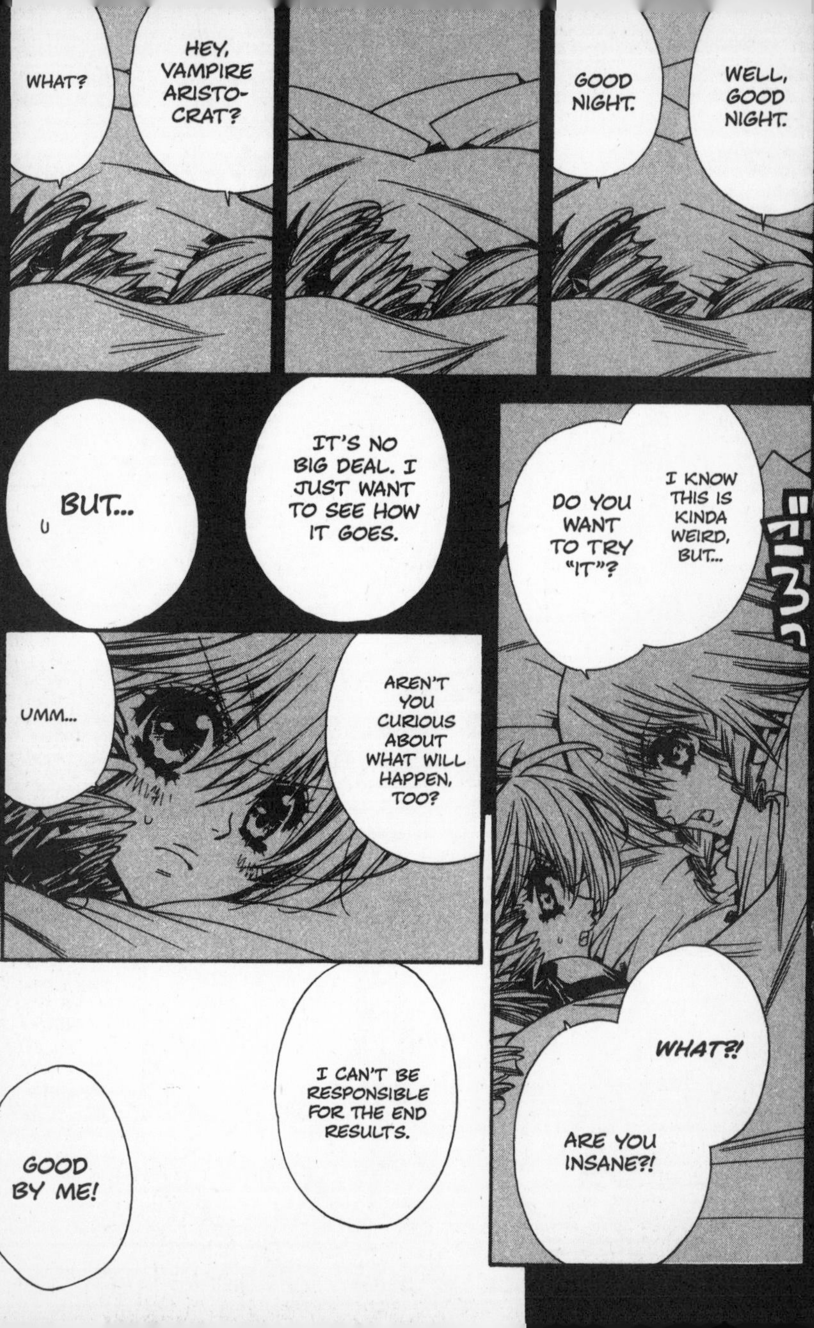
WELL, GOOD NIGHT.
GOOD NIGHT.
HEY, VAMPIRE ARISTO-CRAT?
WHAT?
I KNOW THIS IS KINDA WEIRD, BUT...
DO YOU WANT TO TRY "IT"?
WHAT?!
ARE YOU INSANE?!
IT'S NO BIG DEAL. I JUST WANT TO SEE HOW IT GOES.
BUT...
AREN'T YOU CURIOUS ABOUT WHAT WILL HAPPEN, TOO?
UMM...
I CAN'T BE RESPONSIBLE FOR THE END RESULTS.
GOOD BY ME!

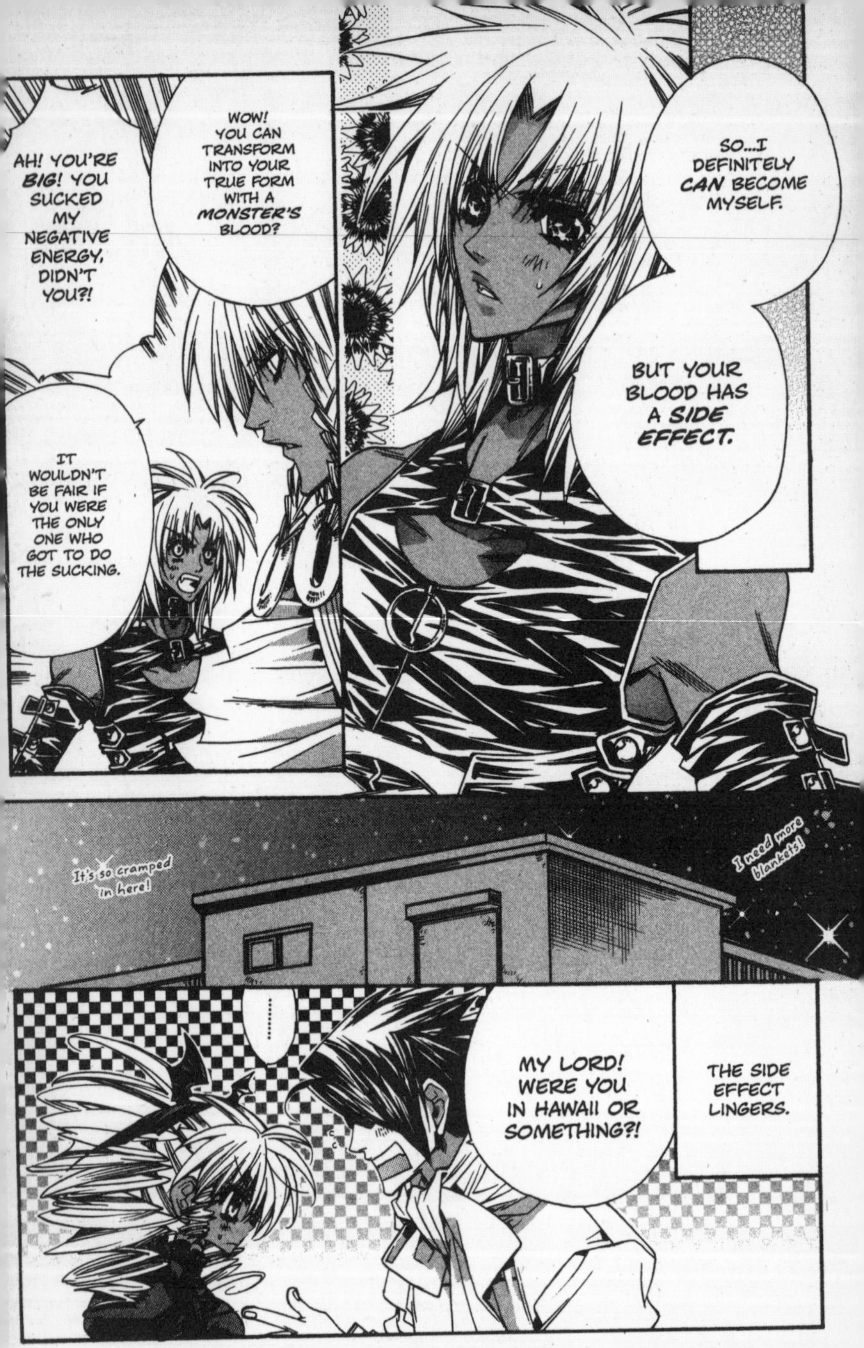
SO...I DEFINITELY *CAN* BECOME MYSELF.
BUT YOUR BLOOD HAS A *SIDE EFFECT.*
WOW! YOU CAN TRANSFORM INTO YOUR TRUE FORM WITH A *MONSTER'S* BLOOD?
AH! YOU'RE *BIG*! YOU SUCKED MY NEGATIVE ENERGY, DIDN'T YOU?!
IT WOULDN'T BE FAIR IF YOU WERE THE ONLY ONE WHO GOT TO DO THE SUCKING.
I need more blankets!
It's so cramped in here!
THE SIDE EFFECT LINGERS.
MY LORD! WERE YOU IN HAWAII OR SOMETHING?!
......

VAMPIRE DOLL GUILT-NA-ZAN VOLUME 3/END

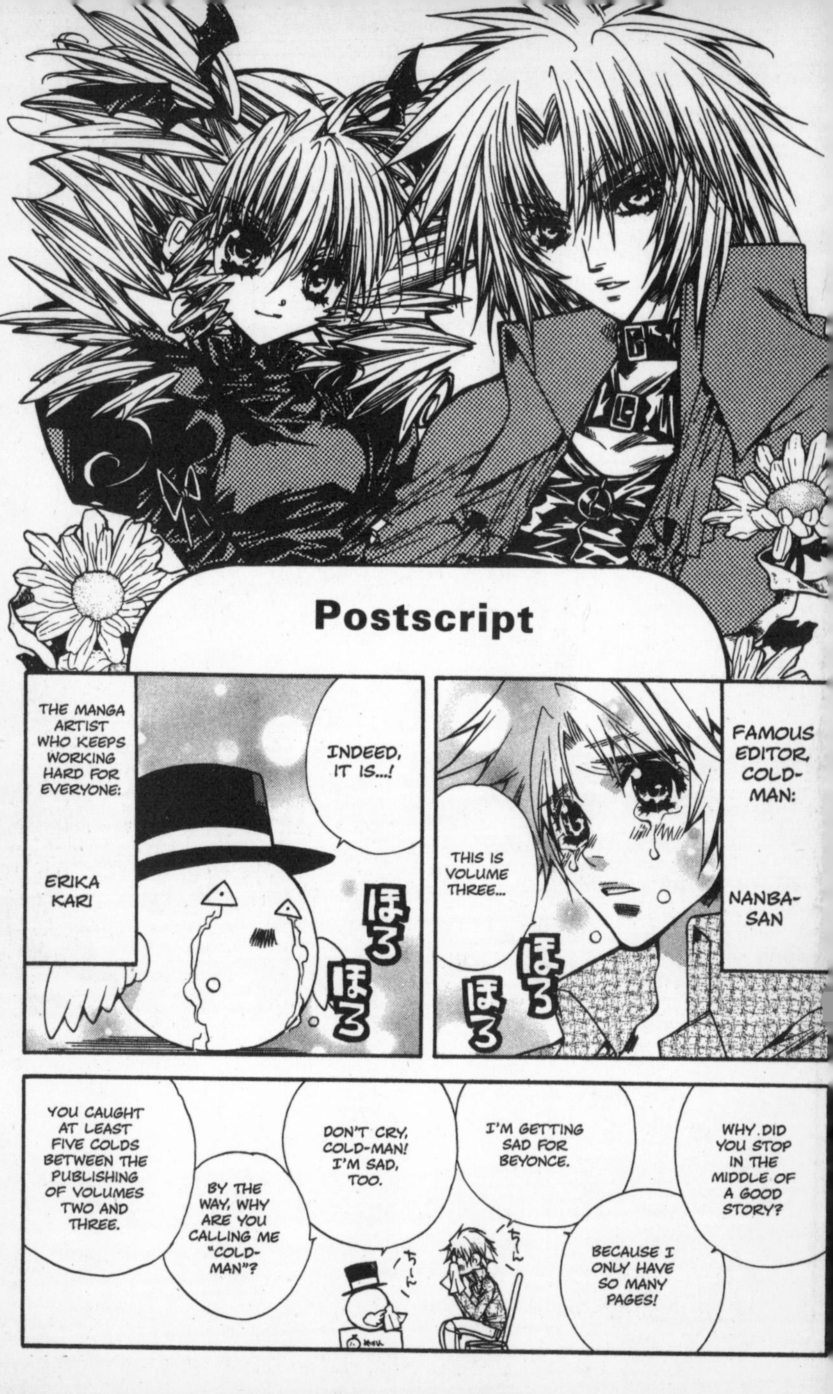
Postscript
FAMOUS EDITOR, COLD-MAN:
NANBA-SAN
THIS IS VOLUME THREE...
ほろほろ
THE MANGA ARTIST WHO KEEPS WORKING HARD FOR EVERYONE:
ERIKA KARI
INDEED, IT IS...!
ほろほろ
WHY DID YOU STOP IN THE MIDDLE OF A GOOD STORY?
BECAUSE I ONLY HAVE SO MANY PAGES!
I'M GETTING SAD FOR BEYONCE.
DON'T CRY, COLD-MAN! I'M SAD, TOO.
BY THE WAY, WHY ARE YOU CALLING ME "COLD-MAN"?
YOU CAUGHT AT LEAST FIVE COLDS BETWEEN THE PUBLISHING OF VOLUMES TWO AND THREE.

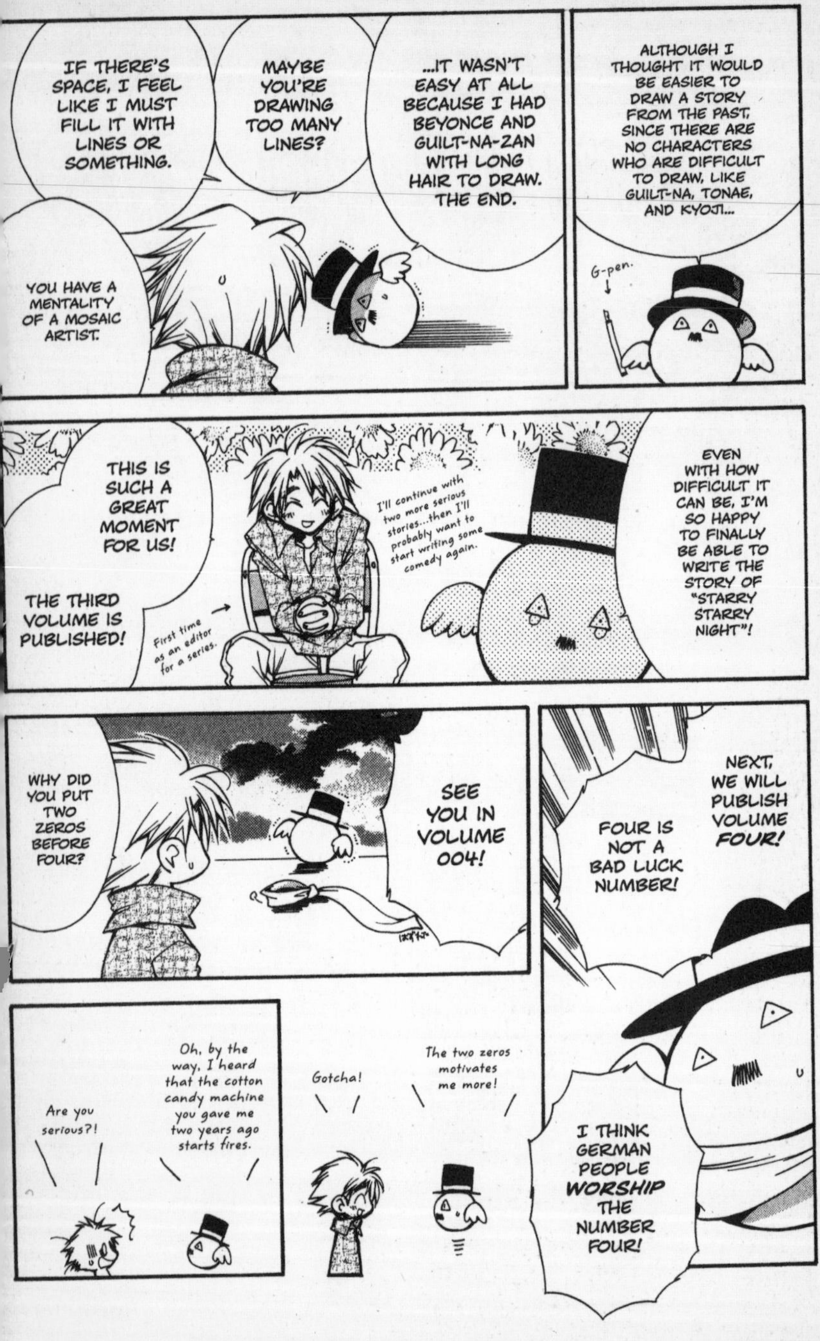
ALTHOUGH I THOUGHT IT WOULD BE EASIER TO DRAW A STORY FROM THE PAST, SINCE THERE ARE NO CHARACTERS WHO ARE DIFFICULT TO DRAW, LIKE GUILT-NA, TONAE, AND KYOJI...
G-pen.
...IT WASN'T EASY AT ALL BECAUSE I HAD BEYONCE AND GUILT-NA-ZAN WITH LONG HAIR TO DRAW. THE END.
MAYBE YOU'RE DRAWING TOO MANY LINES?
IF THERE'S SPACE, I FEEL LIKE I MUST FILL IT WITH LINES OR SOMETHING.
YOU HAVE A MENTALITY OF A MOSAIC ARTIST.
EVEN WITH HOW DIFFICULT IT CAN BE, I'M SO HAPPY TO FINALLY BE ABLE TO WRITE THE STORY OF "STARRY STARRY NIGHT"!
I'll continue with two more serious stories...then I'll probably want to start writing some comedy again.
THIS IS SUCH A GREAT MOMENT FOR US!
First time as an editor for a series.
THE THIRD VOLUME IS PUBLISHED!
NEXT, WE WILL PUBLISH VOLUME FOUR!
FOUR IS NOT A BAD LUCK NUMBER!
I THINK GERMAN PEOPLE WORSHIP THE NUMBER FOUR!
SEE YOU IN VOLUME 004!
WHY DID YOU PUT TWO ZEROS BEFORE FOUR?
The two zeros motivates me more!
Gotcha!
Oh, by the way, I heard that the cotton candy machine you gave me two years ago starts fires.
Are you serious?!

LET ME INTRODUCE MYSELF, AGAIN. THIS IS ERIKA KARI. THIS IS VOLUME THREE! WAAAAAHHHH! WHO AM I TO HAVE THREE BOOKS?! THANK YOU! THANK YOU! THANK YOU SO MUCH!

KYOICHI IS THE EASIEST CHARACTER TO DRAW. I'D LIKE HIM TO APPEAR MORE IN THE NEXT VOLUME.

AT FIRST, I WAS SAD THAT THE TV DRAMA "NOBUTA" WAS FINISHED. BUT "KUITAN" IS SO FUNNY, AND IT MADE ME HAPPY AGAIN. I CREATED THIS VOLUME DURING THAT PERIOD.

THERE ARE SOME NAMES OF GUILT-NA CHARACTERS HIDDEN INSIDE THE CLOTHES IN THE FIRST COLOR ILLUSTRATION PAGE. PLEASE LOOK FOR THEM AND WRITE YOUR ANSWER IN YOUR LETTERS, IF YOU HAPPEN TO FIND ANY!

THANK YOU SO MUCH FOR READING MY BOOK! XIE XIE! DANKE! MERCI BEAUCOUP! I HOPE YOU KEEP READING MY BOOKS! HASTA LA VISTA!

■ HOMEPAGE ■
http://www2.
tokai.or.jp/erieri/

ERIKA KARI
FEBRUARY 2006

DON'T SHOW YOUR CLAWS TO OUR READERS!

SORRY.

FROM PAGE 3.

Vampire Doll
Guilt-na-Zan

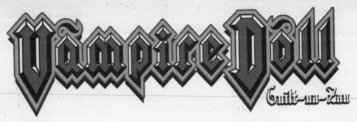

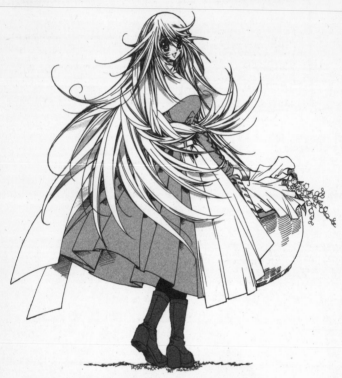

IN THE NEXT VOLUME!

WHAT IS THE DARK SHADOW OF DEATH THAT HANGS OVER POOR BEYONCE? CAN GUILT-NA-ZAN SAVE HER FROM THE SAD FATE SHE MUST ENDURE? THE SECRET PAST OF OUR FAVORITE VAMPIRE-ARISTOCRAT-TURNED-WAX-DOLL IS FINALLY REVEALED! ALL THIS AND MUCH MORE IN THE NEXT VOLUME OF *VAMPIRE DOLL: GUILT-NA-ZAN.*

TO BE CONTINUED IN *VAMPIRE DOLL GUILT-NA-ZAN* VOL.4

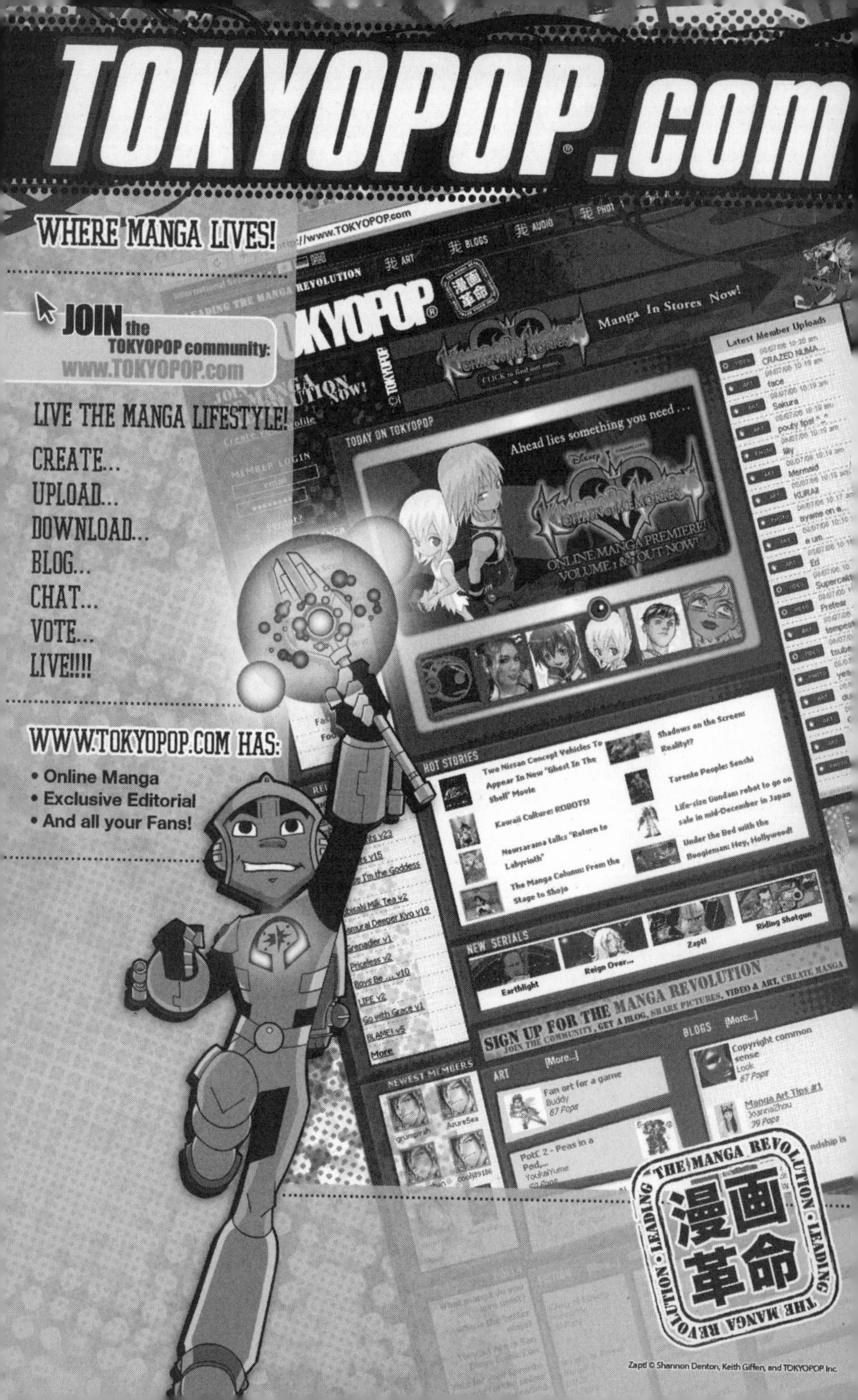
TOKYOPOP.com
WHERE MANGA LIVES!
JOIN the TOKYOPOP community: www.TOKYOPOP.com
LIVE THE MANGA LIFESTYLE!
CREATE...
UPLOAD...
DOWNLOAD...
BLOG...
CHAT...
VOTE...
LIVE!!!!
WWW.TOKYOPOP.COM HAS:
• Online Manga
• Exclusive Editorial
• And all your Fans!
THE MANGA REVOLUTION • LEADING • 漫画革命
Zap! © Shannon Denton, Keith Giffen, and TOKYOPOP Inc.

WARNING
Virus outbreak

Kasumi and he
sister, Shizuku
are infected with
the fatal Medusa
virus. There is no
cure, but Kasumi
is selected to go
into a cryogenic
freezer until a
cure is found.
But when
Kasumi awakens,
she must struggle
to survive in a
treacherous
world if she
hopes to
discover what
happened to
her sister.

From Yuji Iwahara,
the creator of
the popular
Chikyu Misaki
and *Koudelka*.

© YUJI IWAHARA

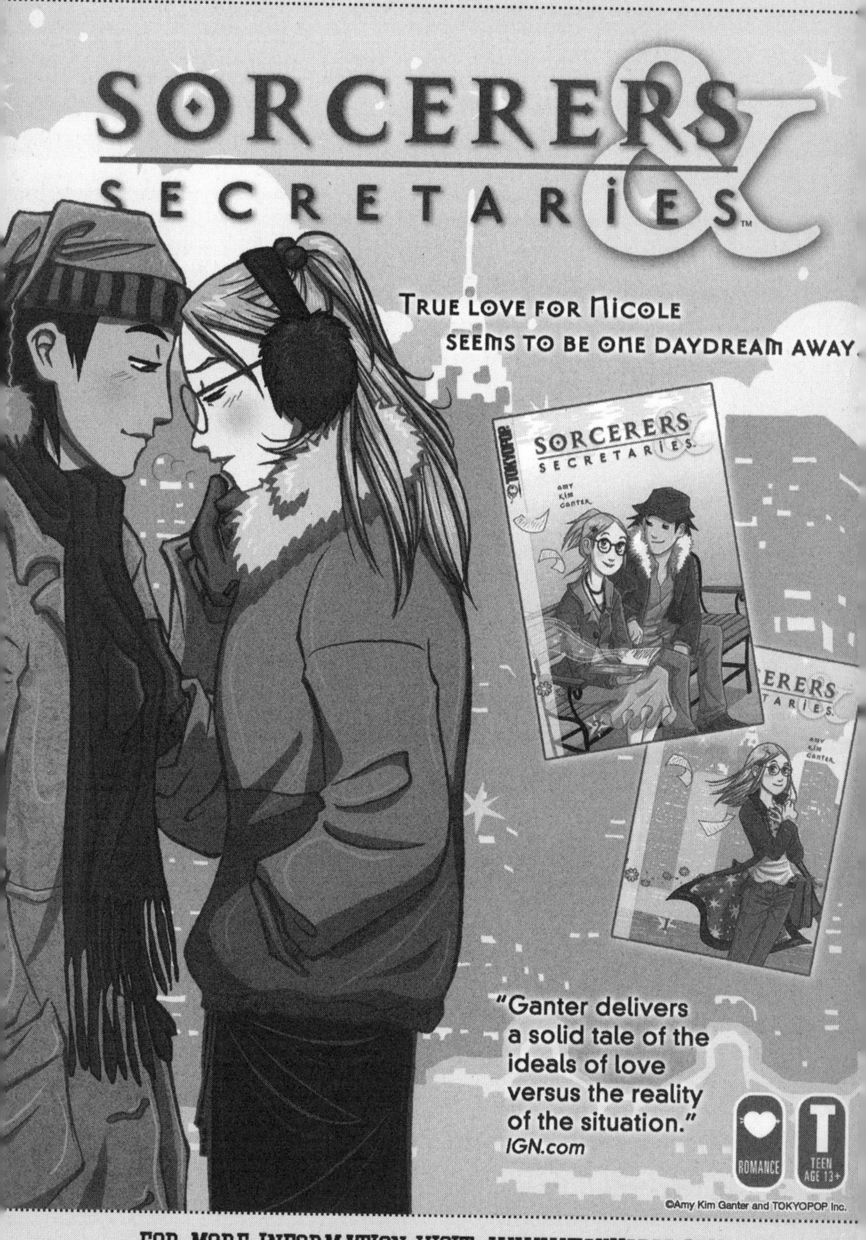
SORCERERS & SECRETARIES™
TRUE LOVE FOR NICOLE
SEEMS TO BE ONE DAYDREAM AWAY.
SORCERERS & SECRETARIES
TOKYOPOP
AMY KIM GANTER
"Ganter delivers a solid tale of the ideals of love versus the reality of the situation."
IGN.com
ROMANCE
T
TEEN AGE 13+
©Amy Kim Ganter and TOKYOPOP Inc.

EDITORS' PICKS TOKYOPOP MANGA SUPPLEMENT

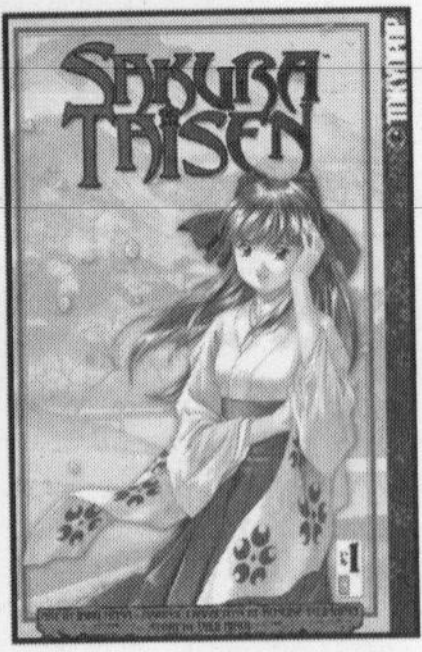
SAKURA TAISEN
TOKYOPOP
1

ACTION

T
TEEN AGE 13+

SAKURA TAISEN

BY OHJI HIROI, IKKU MASA AND KOSUKE FUJISHIMA

I really, really like this series. I'm a sucker for steampunk-type stories, and 1920s Japanese fashion, and throw in demon invaders, robot battles and references to Japanese popular theater? Sold! There's lots of fun tidbits for the clever reader to pick up in this series (all the characters have flower names, for one, and the fact that all the Floral Assault divisions are named after branches of the Takarazuka Review, Japan's sensational all-female theater troupe!), but the consistently stylish and clean art will appeal even to the most casual fan.

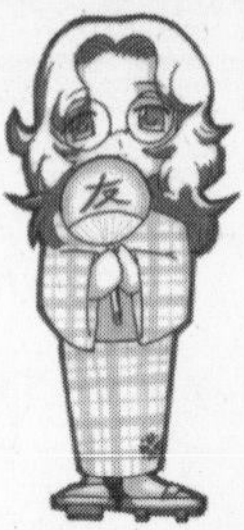

~Lillian Diaz-Przybyl, Editor

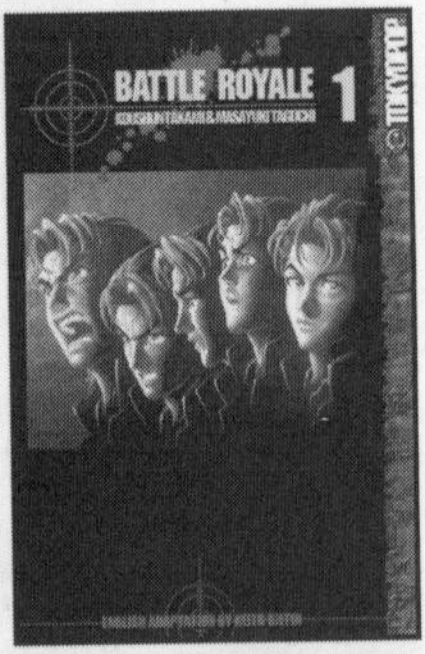
BATTLE ROYALE 1
KOUSHUN TAKAMI & MASAYUKI TAGUCHI
TOKYOPOP

ACTION

M
MATURE AGES 18+

BATTLE ROYALE

BY KOUSHUN TAKAMI AND MASAYUKI TAGUCHI

As far as cautionary tales go, you couldn't get any timelier than *Battle Royale*. Telling the bleak story of a class of middle school students who are forced to fight each other to the death on national television, Koushun Takami and Masayuki Taguchi have created a dark satire that's sickening, yet undeniably exciting as well. And if we have that reaction reading it, it becomes alarmingly clear how the students could so easily be swayed into doing it.

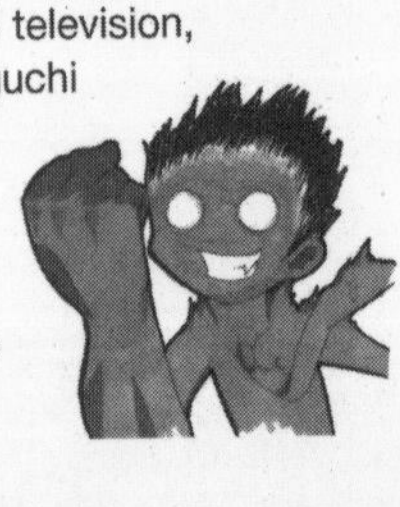

~Tim Beedle, Editor

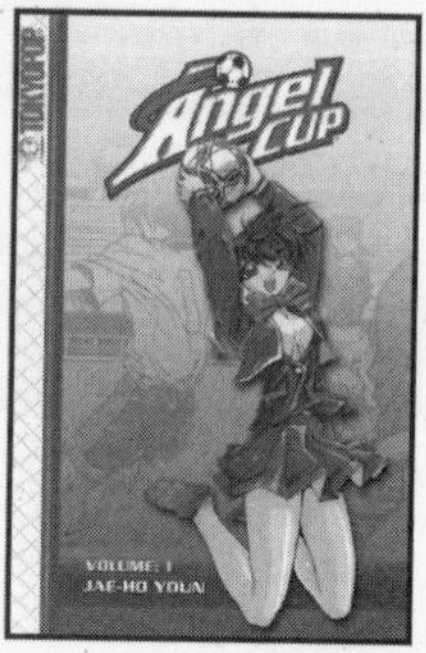
Angel Cup
VOLUME 1
JAE-HO YOUN
TOKYOPOP

ACTION

T TEEN AGE 13+

ANGEL CUP

BY JAE-HO YOUN

Who's the newest bouncing broad that bends it like Beckam better than Braz—er, you get the idea? So-jin of the hit Korean manhwa, *Angel Cup!* She and her misfit team of athletic amazoness tear up the soccer field, whether it's to face up against the boys' team, or wear their ribbons with pride against a rival high school. While the feminist in me cheers for So-jin and the gang, the more perverted side of me drools buckets over the sexy bust-shots and scandalous camera angles... But from any and every angle, *Angel Cup* will be sure to tantalize the soccer fan in you... or perv. Whichever!

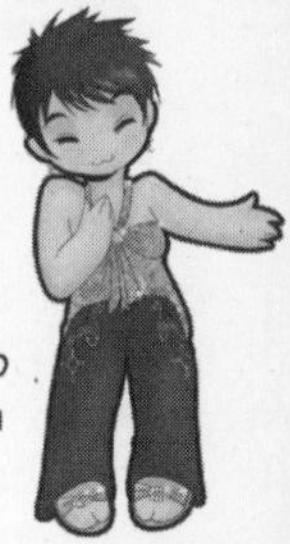

~Katherine Schilling, Jr. Editor

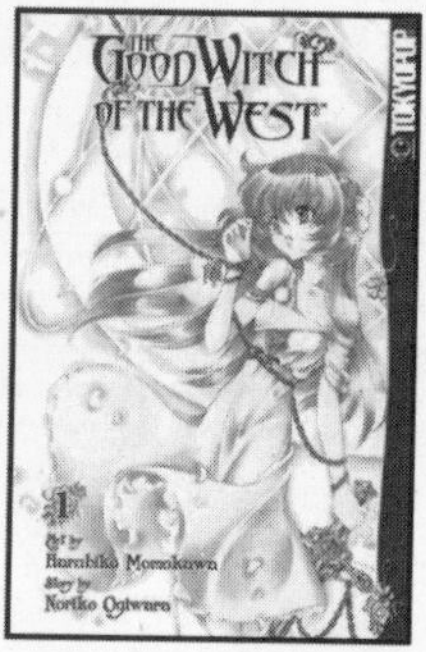
The Good Witch of the West
TOKYOPOP
1
Art by Haruhiko Momokawa
Story by Noriko Ogiwara

FANTASY

T TEEN AGE 13+

GOOD WITCH OF THE WEST

BY NORIKO OGIWARA AND HARUHIKO MOMOKAWA

For any dreamers who ever wanted more out of a fairytale, indulge yourself with *Good Witch*. Although there's lots of familiar territory fairytale-wise—peasant girl learns she's a princess—you'll be surprised as Firiel Dee's enemies turn out to be as diverse as religious fanaticism, evil finishing school student councils and dinosaurs. This touching, sophisticated tale will pull at your heartstrings while astounding you with breathtaking art. *Good Witch* has big shoes to fill, and it takes off running.

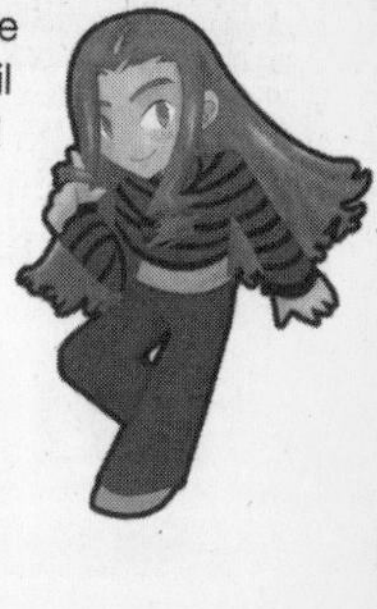

~Hope Donovan, Jr. Editor

STOP!

This is the back of the book.
You wouldn't want to spoil a great ending

This book is printed "manga-style," in the authentic Japanese right-to-left format. Since none of the artwork has been flipped or altered, readers get to experience the story just as the creator intended. You've been asking for it, so TOKYOPOP® delivered: authentic, hot-off-the-press, and far more fun!

DIRECTIONS

If this is your first time reading manga-style, here's a quick guide to help you understand how it works.

It's easy... just start in the top right panel and follow the numbers. Have fun, and look for more 100% authentic manga from TOKYOPOP®!